GREAT STORIES FROM THE MOUNTAIN

8 EXPANSIVE SHORT STORIES

STEVEN M. WEBB

This is a work of fiction. All of the characters, organizations and events portrayed in these short stories are either products of the author's imagination or are used fictitiously.

STORIES

THE IRISHMAN CIAN MACGERRITY

In 1805, tyranny, eviction and murder drive
an Irish tenant farmer to vengeance. Surely,
his deed will deliver him to the gallows—
and to the end of his troubles, or so he thinks.

THE IRISHMAN
CIAN MACGERRITY

This was the time after the rebellion had failed, when Michael Dwyer was brought down out of the Wicklow Mountains to surrender with his men. Tens of thousands in Ireland had died by musket ball, bayonet and cutlass, hung and starved, desperate for independence in the summer of 1798, achieving nothing. General Joseph Holt, gone. The leaders in Dublin, betrayed, arrested, dragged and hung. But Michael Dwyer had fought on in the mountains for five years, calling across the counties for survivors of the battles and the mass executions to come, to rally high in the Wicklows for Ireland. The patriots came up from blackened Wexford and down from the north, strong men out of Ulster. Mourners said the fighting in the Wicklows was hopeless and the cause was long lost. Most others said nothing that could be reported to the Redcoats.

In the green, wooded foothills of the Wicklows, south of Dublin, English and loyalist reprisals had been unforgiving for Gaelic speakers suspected of providing food or shelter for the rebels. Even Old Norman-English Catholics who thought themselves County Wicklow Irish were subject to Protestant denunciations for disloyalty to the Crown. Harshness, vengeance and avarice ruled the lowlands. In the mountains Dwyer's rebels stalked the Redcoat patrols and when they could, they shot them down and took their muskets.

Across Ireland many pointed to great grievances behind the

3

rebellion, including the assumption by the English elite that Ireland had been a Crown possession since the year 1171. The beneficiaries of the colonial assumption were the resident Protestant landlords who owned the farmland of a rural nation of eight million Catholics. The landlords made the laws, owned the guns and leased subsistence fields to millions of tenant farmers. These landlords saw advantage in converting some or all of their tenant fields to sheep pasture, when and if they pleased. They did so with impunity, evicting without notice or appeal, backed by laws written by the Protestant parliament in Dublin to which they had been elected.

It was in the northern foothills of the Wicklows that a tenant farmer, Hugh MacGerrity, with two cows, a few hens and two acres of potatoes had seen such evictions come to his neighbors near Curtlestown in 1798. He was a piper, a dancer, a fine singer, a bare-knuckle fighter and a quick man with a pike and sword. He was not the type to hold any love for callous landlords. In the summer of 1798 Hugh MacGerrity warned his capable sixteen-year-old son, Cian (*Kee*-ahn), to bring the harvest in on time and then went away with other Wicklow fighting men to rally to General Joseph Holt in Wexford, in the south-east of Ireland. There, in County Wexford, at a place known as Vinegar Hill, the strong men of Ireland, fighting for their freedom, faced 15,000 British regulars and squadrons of cavalry. Hugh MacGerrity never came back.

Hugh's wife, Maggie, went south into Wexford to look for him before Christmas of 1798. In January of the new year word came back to the son Cian that she had died in Wexford and been buried there. The place where she had fallen ill was near the battlefield at Vinegar Hill. Dazed and staring with disbelief, Cian was directed to move in with his mother's nearby relatives. Then, the cold early months of 1799 were spent in mourning for Hugh and Maggie MacGerrity and the freedom that continued to elude Ireland.

Those months of quiet staring into the distance changed the boy. He saw no hope to live for. There were no graves to kneel by. He was lifted from gloom only by his aunt's readings from a Bible in English, each evening after supper. Back and forth Aunt

Rose would go over the story of Abraham, asking questions about why he had left his homeland. Why would the old man have even considered the sacrifice of his youngest son Isaac? Why did he not offer his eldest son, Ishmael? How was Abraham aware of God, a presence he couldn't see? No one else in the house, even Dan, Rose's husband, could read English, so Rose usually had to answer her own questions.

In the summer, while Cian and his cousins were harvesting potatoes in the field outside his family's two-room wooden house, word came that the English parliament in London had taken up its power and done away with the corrupt Anglo-Irish parliament in Dublin. But it would not be official until the end of the year. Everyone who leased land in the Wicklow hills around Curtlestown began to gather on the muddy village green to discuss the effect this might have on the landlords. No one knew what new laws might come out of London. Would they come in time to restrain the landlords, before the landlords evicted everyone in their way? There were loud calls to bring some of Michael Dwyer's men down in secret from the mountains if the landlords sent eviction gangs to Curtlestown. Others countered that Dwyer's men would only attract more Redcoats to the county. And then there were cynics who called for the clergy to intervene and this caused the only laughter of the day.

It was because of this uncertainty about when, how and if the new laws would appear, that the milling crowd of several hundred tenant farmers and their families remained in debate for hours on the rough green in Curtlestown. And it was in that crowd that Cian locked eyes with a brown-haired girl his age. Apparently, like him, she was suddenly no longer aware of the high stakes accompanying the consideration of another rebellion. Then she moved out of his sight for no obvious reason. Looking between tall and short, Cian searched the crowd until he spotted her again. Curiously she moved away from him once more, blending into the crowd. Why wouldn't she stand her ground and let him get a closer look, he wondered.

Cian circled through the crowd, hearing deep concern in the voices of the tenants, their wives and clinging children, but he had the more pressing problem. Where was the girl? Who was she? He thought he knew everyone around Curtlestown, but he'd never seen her before. Where had she come from? He turned this way and that until suddenly she appeared from nowhere, a few feet away, looking directly into his eyes, bold, comely and bright.

"Are ye Cian MacGerrity?" she asked, swaying slightly on her bare feet.

"I am," he answered, startled.

"I was sorry to hear about ye father and ye ma'm."

"I thank ye for your thoughts, true now. I'd not be believing they're gone, some days. 'Tis Ireland, so it's not over yet," he answered, looking into her eyes. "Life, it goes on. I've not seen ye in Curtlestown. Where are ye from?"

"Glencree. We've had evictions. I'm here with the uncle."

"Then what's been done to stop it in Glencree?"

"Nothing. Nothing at all."

"Where would people go when the gangs come?"

"To family, until they come for them too."

"It's me would be thinking such things are only likely around Curtlestown."

"All over Ireland, I'd be hearing, and it's nothing new."

"'Tis not to be over yet either, being free o' the landlords," Cian said, observing every detail of her beautiful eyes, her high forehead and long hair, pulled back behind her neck. She swayed, ever so slightly in front of him, as if ready to dance, in spite of the gravity of the conversation.

"You'd not be going to Michael Dwyer would ye?" she asked.

"Dwyer? Naught that Dwyer can do up there. The Redcoats, building their road into the Wicklows already. A matter of time it is afore the safe havens are gone."

"Those there are who say it. 'Tis over soon."

Cian could tell by the way she stopped swaying that the portents of hopelessness deeply troubled her. She glanced toward the hills.

"And then, there's nothing left to say. Me uncle says we've been abandoned, by all."

"That too, by all," he answered quietly, before realizing something important. "Seeing ye here though in Curtlestown, your name, ye've not told me."

"Megan. Megan Armagh, I am," she said with a wry smile and a slight bow. "And I'm pleased to meet ye. A fine day on the green for all, even for me. There's the sun now."

Cian took his eyes off her for a moment and realized she was right. The sun was out, the clouds clearing and his pulse was pounding in a way he never thought possible. He could barely think. She was all of a spirit of joy, enveloping him in such a sense of wonder he had difficulty knowing what to say. That this beauty from God had approached him, known his name and taken time to speak to him was beyond his life's experience.

"'Tis a moment, I'm thinking," he stammered, "to ask if ye'd be willing to meet me Aunt Rose, over there, standing back behind in the blue dress. She can read. She'd be asking if ye can read, so ye know it aforetime. Not that ye must, if ye're not for meeting some more."

"I'd be reading a little, these days," Megan said. "We can meet with your aunt."

So it began. Megan and her uncle stayed that night in cots in Aunt Rose and Uncle Dan's house after a long evening of Bible readings around a peat-burning hearth. The room had been crowded all evening and candles had been lit. Dishes of salted potatoes and leeks and carrots had come in through the front door with half a dozen visitors. Cian kept his eyes on Megan far more often than on his aunt, whose Bible questions made her the center of attention for everyone else. Then Aunt Rose lead Dan into a ballad about some lost Gaelic hero, to clearly illustrate a point from the Bible, and everyone joined in, getting louder, crying and clapping.

Cian could tell Megan was aware he was looking at her, from the way she glanced back at him, just now and then. In between it all his thoughts returned to Megan's comment on the green that they, the people, had been abandoned by all. Here it was, he realized, that the people gained comfort from each other, that this feeling in the crowded hearth-lit room, with candles flickering in the windows, made life worth living.

Aunt Rose's husband, Dan, came up to the house the next day as Cian was bagging potatoes for the landlord's cut. Dan leaned against an unpainted fence post and looked at him loading the wheelbarrow.

"Ye've come to offer your opinion on something then," Cian said, by way of greeting.

"Dwyer would be dying up in the mountains soon enough. Redcoat road's going up. They'd be living like foxes running from the dogs. Don't be going up there."

"No plans to," Cian answered.

"Fine it is, it is," Dan said, looking at him carefully. "Now, the landlords, being without their Dublin parliament, so ye be hearing, have no plans or concerns about new laws coming out of London."

"How know ye that?"

"They live there in Dublin and would have the same magistrates under their thumbs still. New laws or naught. And the magistrates make things up as they go along, to get along then. Not easy finding new ones to work in those pits they'd be calling courts."

"Now what would Dublin magistrates do with us up here, Dan?"

"'Tis this I'm saying. Nothing's going to be changing. The years they'll go by and there'll be another rebellion. Ye'll be at the age when your blood will boil and ye'll go off like your father, thinking your sparring skills are for war. Ye fight Redcoats, ye don't come home."

"Oh, I'd be seeking another rebellion, the same, ye say?"

"There'd be no good change out of this 'new laws' business. Young men, they see that. They fight, they die, they go to be buried. For what, boy?"

"What would ye have me do, afore I go to be buried?"

"Ye make a pledge with the Lord," Dan said, lowering his voice in the overgrown lane where they were alone. "Ye've got a perfectly good young woman there, that Megan from Glencree. Marry her, in the presence of the Lord and pledge ye'll not leave your children orphans and your wife a widow. In return, ye enter the laity, I say."

"In return? You'd be saying make a pledge to the devil. That's what they'd be, Dan. 'Tis why we'd have no laity or priest in Curtlestown. The priests are beholden to the landlords."

"Cian, I'd be trying to save your life, boy," Dan replied. "If we'd not have young laity here 'tis a sign we rebel. The Church in Dublin thinks we resist order and we'd be with Dwyer. The landlords tell the Bishop to send us one o' the pudgy fools they pass off as priests, to keep an eye on us. All of us would be watched, year in, year out."

"Dan," Cian said, stopping work. "Ye think they'd leave us be, because I started reading verses? They'd not trust me any more than they'd trust me father at their pulpit."

"And what did they do to your father?"

"Ye can't stop the next rebellion, Dan. 'Tis coming. Just not me father's way."

"There is no way, Cian! Ye can't take on tens of thousands o' Redcoats!"

"True. But ye can cut off the heads that lead them."

"Can ye now? Is that the way o' the Lord? If ye can't see the trap o' pride the devil sets for this and every generation, all is lost, boy!"

"This is Ireland then, Dan. Always will be."

"Then don't be marrying that girl. A nation of widows and orphans and blind young men we have. Enough it is."

When the wheelbarrow was full Dan walked next to Cian along the lane but had little further to say. The suggestion of marriage, coming from Dan and probably Rose, seemed to give permission to an idea Cian had not yet admitted to himself. The next rebellion held no interest for him on that day, but taking a walk, to visit

9

folks in the direction of Glencree seemed like a fine notion.

And it was. That summer Cian would often walk the ten miles to Glencree and Megan would walk with him to Curtlestown. Then both would walk back through the hills and lanes to Glencree. All who saw them nodded to their faces then talked among themselves about the MacGerrity boy with no parents and no fear of notoriety.

In time, later that year, Cian and Megan were married by a pudgy priest who came all the way to Curtlestown from the south side of Dublin. All the village turned out for the ceremony on the green, for many were saying this fearless couple would lead those parts of County Wicklow in their maturity. There were hopes that Cian might change his mind about entering the laity, for Curtlestown's sake. There were hopes that Megan would take up the suggestions being offered, that she teach reading to the children who could be spared from the farms. Of course, Megan's parents and half of Glencree were there. Many looked in admiration on the couple, as if all their hopes were in them. When Rose got up to sing she wept and lifted her arms to heaven saying, "God, oh God. They are beautiful."

Cian and Megan were eighteen when they began married life in the small two-room house on leased farmland not far from Curtlestown. Then, when they were both twenty-one, with a two-year-old boy, Breen, and a year-old baby girl, Holly, in 1803, Michael Dwyer and his men were brought down in chains from the Wicklow Mountains. Many in Curtlestown watched in silence from a distance as the grim parade of prisoners and Redcoats wound down through the hills. Dan left the grassy rise next to Rose, Megan and the babies and drew Cian away, out of earshot. They stood still for a moment watching the far-off Redcoats.

"They'd be hanging Michael Dwyer in Dublin crossroads, leaving the carcass up high for everyone to look at," Dan whispered. "All that's left to know is how many of the others will hang. Heed it now."

Cian said nothing, though he admitted to himself that Dwyer

10

and his men had fought the good fight for Ireland for more than five years. There was something that concerned him more than Dwyer but he was not about to speak of it. He had been watching Megan's complexion changing over the past week. She had said she was fine but he sensed it wasn't so. Both pregnancies had made her glow. Now she seemed flushed in the face and slower to move. Yet there Megan was, next to Rose and Rose wouldn't see it.

Rose, it turned out, had seen it and came to the house that evening to put Megan to bed. The babies being fed, Cian was asked to take them down the lane to Rose and Dan's place for the night. It was unusual for Rose to intervene in such a way and Cian got no sleep that night in a strange cot, uneasy over Rose's attitude.

In the morning Rose was frowning when she drew Cian out of the house into the lane.

"I'm not knowing what to tell ye," she said. "I'd be straight with ye. I'm thinking it's the typhus."

"How do ye know?" Cian asked in alarm.

"There's a fever now. On her back and chest, the first signs."

"Is there a doctor for the thing?"

"This is the typhus that kills doctors, Cian," Rose said, holding his shirt front tight in both her hands. "There's no money for doctors here. None of them would come this far anyway now."

"No," Cian said. "Ye can't be right. Ye see something else and mistake it for the typhus. No one else here has it."

"I'd said the same thing to meself," Rose answered. "I sat up with her last night and called to the Lord. I called to the Lord, Cian and I'd never heard such a silence. Nothing. Just the girl murmuring for the babies and the Lord listening."

"You don't know the pledge we made, Rose. The Lord heard us."

"He hears us all. He hears us, every word. He sees all."

Then Rose stood silent in front of him while the wind whipped through the tall grass on either side of the lane. Cian's eyes widened in exasperation.

"Rose, what's to be done? Ye can't be right."

"Ye take," Rose began, stifling her sob, "the sign, the heart of the Virgin Mother, the sword through her heart. 'Tis hers now. No escape from the crucifixion. It's come for us. Naught given to understand."

"No, Rose, ye say too much. Ye can't speak of such things. Ye'll see it come right."

"Oh, me boy, now me boy," Rose cried, holding him for a moment. "Go see."

Rose was right. Megan's back and chest were dotted with lesions, her face flushed. Cian leaned over her in disbelief. Finally she opened her eyes and stared at him.

"Ye saw Rose then," she began. "I don't say I understand, not at all."

"We have a pledge with God. Family, afore all. So, he'll see us through."

"The babies?" she murmured.

"At Rose and Dan's."

"Cian, Rose and I, last night, she said she'd heard of this typhus, what it is. Came a time we had naught more to say. We both heard the silence. He was listening to us. He wasn't angry with us. 'Tis just that we don't understand his way."

Cian lowered his head in confusion at her acceptance. Across her neck and chest he could see the red welts staring at him in the candlelight.

"I'd ask for you to stay with me," she said. "Just here. You."

For a week Cian stayed by Megan's cot, bathing her, feeding her, if she would take any of the broth Rose sent each day. He went up the lane to be with the babies when Rose came to the house. During that week he came to see and hear Megan's body and speech weakening. He was thinking one night that the condition might soon come to him and to Rose and Dan when Megan interrupted his thoughts, moaning, speaking strangely.

"Come now and see, I told ye," she said, without looking at him, "See, there's naught to be done when it's been righted."

It took a moment for Cian to realize she was not aware he was leaning over her. He had no idea who she was talking to. She was delirious or dreaming but how was it possible, he wondered, she was losing a battle that only fell on the weak or elderly.

Over the next few days Cian heard her say again and again, "it's been righted," as her delirium deepened and nothing was right. He looked down on her in silence, not daring to pray, in case those pleas were not answered and his mind might fall to a place beyond that of the disillusioned or the betrayed.

Rose drew him aside one afternoon while the children were napping. Her eyes were brimming, deep lines marked her face.

"Time, Cian," she whispered. "Time for a priest. Oh, 'tis so. Ye cannot wait a moment longer. Cian."

"No. There be none such to stand over Megan," Cian answered with finality. "She deserves holiness. Ye be the one Rose. If there be last rites, ye be the holiest I know."

Megan died a day later. Cian was alone with her at the time and Rose found him in the dark, standing in a trance over her cot. She pulled a blanket over Megan, said a prayer and walked Cian up the lane. Dan came out of the front door with a lantern, took in Cian's dazed expression at a glance and guided him inside to rest on a stool next to the hearth. Vaguely, Cian was aware he was now with Dan and away from Megan and home, before his thoughts returned to the wedding pledge he made to God and Megan. The pledge had meant he would never lend himself to a cause that might leave Megan a widow or the children fatherless. Had it ever meant anything to God?

When Megan was buried at noon on the edge of the field he understood why so few people came. The clouds were low and gray and it was cold. He had forbidden any priest to attend. There was a sense of bewilderment in the village that such exuberance and confidence that had been on display at their courtship and marriage, the hopes they would be leaders in the valley, were, by the evidence, not acceptable offerings to God.

In the year that followed, Cian's cynicism grew, with the realization that not only had he not caught the typhus but no one else around Curtlestown had. The Lord had come in silence to take her, with no explanation. But the boy, Breen, was now three and the girl, Holly, two and it never ceased to surprise Cian how the two of them looked to him and tugged on him for answers he was supposed to know. They had an unending stream of questions, as if he now were some authority they ought to rely on. He played the part, looking at them, thinking at any moment they would call him out for not knowing anything at all.

Then on a drizzly afternoon in spring, while the two children were napping in their cots in the house, Cian heard strange shouting noises coming from up the lane near Curtlestown. There were harsh yells so he wiped the dirt from his hands and walked across the field to look to the village. Four men wearing tall hats and holding billy clubs could be seen on the rise in the lane outside Rose and Dan's house. Cian watched from the field as the men pushed through the rickety wooden gate. A moment later Dan was dragged out of the house by his coat collar and thrown face-first into the lane. Rose ran out behind him, chased by another man. The first two men kicked at Dan on the ground and pulled him to his feet. Dan could be heard shouting at them while Rose screamed at them. Then the billy clubs came down on their shoulders and they were pursued over the rise and out of sight.

Cian's first instinct was to run toward them but when he saw smoke and then fire in the windows of Dan's house he paused by the potato shed. Three of the men appeared back over the rise seconds later. They crossed a field and went into old Brach's house and did the same thing. Brach and his wife came right out with their idiot adult son, meekly took to the lane with their heads down and shuffled toward Curtlestown. Their house too was alight.

In an instant it was obvious to Cian what was happening. Although he had never seen the four men before they were unmistakably an eviction gang. Their commission could only have come from the local landlord's Dublin agent, Jasper O'Hanlon. O'Hanlon was a name no one in the county would pronounce above a whisper. It was associated with dread and with the law. Estate manager O'Hanlon counted many of the former Irish

Protestant parliament members among his landlord clientele. The parliament had been defunct for four years and the laws issued from London now restricted the landlords, who were seen by London as a root cause of the 1798 rebellion. But local magistrates, preferring to keep their comfortable homes in Dublin, found no difficulty placating the English minders when they came knocking. "The rule of law prevails," the magistrates would tell them, "and only the rule of law."

The four men with billy clubs, moving up the lane toward Cian, were representatives of a legal system that no longer existed, yet on they came to enforce it. His farm was next, with the children sleeping in their cots. In a sporting sense Cian might have relished the test of skills in a four-on-one contest, even when the four carried hardwood clubs. But this was different and the stakes brought a cool evenness to his feelings. Instead of brashly challenging them and enjoying the exhilaration of a brawl he probably wouldn't win Cian waited quietly for them, leaning against a post by the side of the lane.

"Ye be MacGerrity," the leader announced. "Get on up the lane."

The four of them were in their mid-twenties, Protestant bullies from Dublin, probably out of the Liberty Boys gang or the Ormonde Boys. They were unsmiling and cocky, wearing the kind of tall hats and broad-buckle belts that Redcoat regulars wore. Now they were recognized graduates of the alleys, paid to enforce non-existing laws. Cian had heard rumors that murder was common during gang fights in Dublin and by their cold, wolf eyes they looked as though they had seen some of that. There would be no reasoning with them, no quarter. The neighbors' houses were fully alight behind them.

Cian didn't respond to the directive to get on up the lane. He looked at them, as if unable to understand. Then, knowing they were not Gaelic speakers, Cian spoke to them calmly in Gaelic, explaining he had two sleeping children in the house. His odd behavior had the desired effect. They came closer, perhaps thinking

15

to prod the barefoot illiterate with their clubs, perhaps thinking their work that day would be rewarded with a little extra bother.

They leaned toward him, incredulous at his bumpkin speech. In a flash Cian stabbed one bare foot up into the groin of the leader. His right fist swung quick and hard against the side of the man's head while his left hand wrenched the billy club free. An instant later a wrist-slam of the club registered against the ear of the man to the right. The return swing connected against the head of the one to the left. The three injured men staggered on their feet. The fourth realized they had underestimated Cian and backed away, preparing to defend himself. But it was too late for the leader. Cian swung the heavy end of the club hard against both sides of his head, his gut and chin. Two more quick strikes felled the other two to their knees.

Cian and the fourth, untouched man, circled each other in the lane. A calm, unflinching resolve came to Cian, knowing as he did, all his father's best moves with a pike. A feint, a parry, a jab to the gut and a vertical strike up under the thug's chin sent him reeling. Then a final snapping crack to the head sent the last alley man into a puddle in the center of the lane. Two of the wounded groaned as they began to get up but collapsed senseless under strikes from the heavy club, blood trickling from their ears.

There was nothing Cian could do to stop his neighbor's houses from burning to the ground in the fields up the lane. But he could speak to the Dublin agent, O'Hanlon, in a way the man would understand. He stripped the boots, belts, dungarees and underwear from the four unconscious men, carried the bundle of clothing and boots across a field and tossed them into the flames inside Brach's house. Leaving the tall hats on the Dublin thugs' heads he dragged each by the coat collar through the muck in the lane until their bare buttocks and legs were caked and dripping with black mud. Then he tied them tight, with long wet strips of potato sack to the rails of Brach's fence. He left them stretched on the fence, immobilized, unconscious and in a shameful state, bleeding under their Redcoat hats and went back into the house to wash his hands.

Breen and Holly woke as Cian was drying his hands by the washbowl. He sat with them for a moment then got them broth from the cauldron on the hearth. Outside he heard voices. Keeping one of the four billy clubs by his side he looked out the open window. People had come from Curtlestown to see the fires but most were gathered in the lane, staring at the semi-naked thugs.

Quiet Dal from a farm nearby came to Cian's door and shook his hand.

"I see ye father standing in front of me," Dal said. "Now, boy, ye leave it to us. There be a cart then, going into Dublin today, filled with rubbish. Nobody knows where it came from. Nobody knows where it would end up."

And so, in a way not looked for, Cian's reputation as a man became aligned with that of his father, the feisty patriot, until people in County Wicklow were speaking of him in the same sentence as Michael Dwyer, as the next Michael Dwyer. Dwyer, it was now known, had not been hung in Dublin crossroads, probably because the London authorities wanted to avoid giving him the status of martyr. Dwyer had then bargained for passage to the United States, offering to take voluntary exile there with his family. The Americans were not interested in any Irish "politicals" and so Dwyer was kept out of sight indefinitely in a Dublin penitentiary.

Cian, though, was unimpressed with vain talk from the village and kept to his field and his children. He knew O'Hanlon had been ridiculed in Dublin as a clumsy incompetent, an embarrassment to his clients. The event, he was told, had been reported in the scandal rags that passed for newspapers. What was coming as O'Hanlon's response would be swift and by night. It was obvious O'Hanlon would get the contiguous sheep pastures his client wanted, by whatever means necessary. It would involve murder, the unseen kind, and Cian would not expose the children or his neighbors to mortal risk. For the likes of O'Hanlon, Dublin eviction gangs could be moved hither and yon, anywhere in Ireland. So Cian, one rainy morning, put his two children and their belongings in a wheelbarrow and pushed it down a lane toward Glencree, abandoning the lease on his farm.

Cian had hope that there would be an out-of-sight and welcoming refuge in Glencree, among Megan's relatives. But it was on the way to Glencree, when he sheltered with farmers who knew the Armaghs, he was told a posse from Dublin had taken the Armagh family away to a magistrate for questioning. The authorities were expecting Cian in Glencree that day. Men and horses would be in the lanes, waiting behind trees.

"Ye done a wonder," the farmer, Robert Carney, said to Cian, walking in his field. "Dwyer, killing Redcoats for five years, gets cake in gaol. Ye, you're saving your babes from burning and they're for hanging ye for treason. Sedition against the Crown, they say! Such a wonder, I'd be saying. And the wife in the house, she's for bringing ye inside, staying here, babes and all."

Carney's wife, Ren, took them into the farmhouse with the best of intentions, but that very day a posse of horsemen were on the road from Glencree to Curtlestown. They rode up to the house, straight across the potato field. Robert Carney went out the front door to meet them in his shirtsleeves. Ren Carney hustled Cian, Breen and Holly out the back door, past the outhouse to a series of sheds.

"They'd be coming back here, for sure," Ren whispered, holding her finger to her mouth in front of the children. "So quiet, we are, no sound, no crying. Shhh, now."

Ren pointed to a brook not far from the sheds and waved Cian toward the cover of the trees along its banks. The horsemen, in rough, wet coats and tall hats walked through the mud around the house and tapped on the sheds with their canes. By a gift of Providence neither Breen nor Holly made a sound, lying hidden on the bank on either side of Cian. He lay with his bare feet in the cold water, a finger to his lips.

Not all the horsemen left Carney's farm that day. Two set up a tent and a fireplace at the side of the lane, apparently with orders to keep watch, day and night. Carney came out to the brook at dusk and gave Cian directions to the nearest farmhouse, two miles to the west.

All Cian could find that night in the dark was an abandoned shed, part stacked with straw bales for sheep. The children were cold and crying. He couldn't remember the last time he'd fed them. Snugging them tight against him, between bales placed against the wind, he told himself they would continue to the west at daylight. But as he lay back, imagining a farmhouse where kind ones would take them in he felt Holly shivering uncontrollably. She made no sound, no complaint, simply accepting her condition. He sat up, frightened and pressed her against his chest, singing softly to her. Still she shivered, without complaint. He pulled Breen closer, stared into the dark and whispered a rhyme for them, over and over.

"God, oh, God, find a home for these children, these your children on Earth. Find a home for the children, a home. A warm hearth, good broth and soft bed. Hide them now, hide them from the devil, because he can't ever, ever have them."

The next overcast day, as Cian walked across fen and field, looking for a farmhouse, Breen began to let him know how hungry, angry, wet, cold and uncomfortable he was. The boy cried and screamed, not able to understand the circumstances. Breen would walk a short distance across rough, marshy ground then sit down and want to be carried. Then he would wriggle off Cian's back, slump in the dirt and cry and kick. But Breen was not Cian's main concern. Holly would not cry, only shiver and stare at nothing.

Desperate by mid-morning, Cian hoisted Breen onto his back, held Holly tight to his chest and regardless of risk took to the nearest lane, running in the direction it took him, in search of a farmhouse. Perhaps an hour later he knocked at the door of a run-down house and an old farmer let him in. The man was feeble, alone and seemed to accept Cian as if they'd just been talking at the gate earlier in the day.

It was more of a shack than a house. There was a stack of peat outside but no fire in the hearth. Without asking, Cian brought in peat and fanned a smoky fire, placing Holly and Breen in front of it. The old man came in and marveled.

"Sure now, that looks like a good idea. We used to have a fire going here. Peat, see."

Cian ignored him and rummaged through the man's cellar, looking for food, until he froze in place over an empty potato crate. The old man was slowly starving to death. He had little more than they did. Cian tightened his fists to prevent himself from panicking.

"What do you have to eat here?" he asked the old man.

"Oh, not much now. See in the cupboard, we used to have jars but I can't open them."

"How far away are your neighbors?"

"I don't talk to them anymore."

"Where are they? How far?"

"Oh, the lane," the old man said, pointing vaguely to the north.

Cian scooped up Breen and Holly and rushed out to the lane, finding the next farmhouse ten minutes later.

"A poorly child," Cian said to the woman of the house, indicating Holly, laying against his arm.

The middle-aged woman's eyes widened as she looked at Holly. She took her from Cian and nodded for them to come inside. The woman's husband came in from the backyard and she yelled at him.

"Get that fire going! Heat stew in the pan, right now! For God's sake, man!"

The husband fanned the fire then brought a small jug of whiskey from the mantel to Cian and shook his hand.

"Jack Onslow, Deb Onslow," the man said, indicating his wife. "Ye be he."

Over the next two days Breen ate and slept. Cian kept watch on the lane from the front window and Deb Onslow paced with Holly, white-faced, in the short hallway. Deb barked orders to her husband, cooked and fed Holly warm broth every hour. On the second day Deb began weeping. Cian left Breen by the hearth and came to her.

"My God, my God, what can we do?" Deb Onslow cried and kept biting her lip. "There's naught anyone in these parts could know. There's no heat in her. God help us to know what to do."

Jack tugged the whiskey jug off the mantelpiece and approached Holly in Deb's arms.

"There now, little one," Jack said, softly, "infant or no, ye test the Lord's will. Now, Deb, ye baulked before but not now. Here we go."

Drops of whiskey were applied to Jack's finger and pressed into Holly's mouth, again and again. Cian could see that though Deb had a habit of barking at the man, by the light in his eyes he was no fool. His eyes were focused on Holly's face and shallow breathing. As more and more drops of whiskey touched Holly's lips, without response, Jack drew back, saying nothing. Deb held Holly and wept.

That night Cian found Deb in her rocking chair, staring down at Holly in her arms. By her unmoving expression Cian knew Holly had passed on to join her mother in a far place. He stood where he was and thought of Rose's picture of the Virgin Mother, her sacred heart pierced by the sword, her face serene. What was it with saints, he grieved, that they see what we can't see and don't even flinch? He slid to his knees, placed his head against the rough planks and listened to Deb crying. Sometime later he realized the keening sounds were his own.

During the night Cian began thinking he was in a dream, that it was not possible for anything to have happened to Holly. He wondered why he was in someone else's house and not at home with Megan. He would have grieved for days, avoiding the horror he dreaded, of burying his youngest child. But early the next morning Jack rushed into the house, stamping his boots.

"Horsemen," he said, indicating the direction of the feeble old man's house. "I saw them go into Donny Sligh's now. Did Donny see ye passing by afore?"

Cian pulled Breen up from the blanket by the hearth, tossed

21

him onto his back and headed out the back door into a fog. Although Breen murmured about the inconvenience and strangeness of the fog Cian felt reassured they would remain unseen in the fields until the horsemen left the Onslows. He hoisted Breen up higher on his back and tramped toward a line of trees and shrubs at the top of a hill, shapes barely visible in the fog. Closer to the top he paused to make out a shape, wider than a tree. The shape whinnied and turned and a horse was spurred toward him. Another came from the left.

One hand behind him, holding Breen to his back, Cian leapt across the field into a fog so thick he couldn't see ten feet in front of him. Neither could the horsemen, but it was likely they were well paid and under orders to restore O'Hanlon's reputation. Cian knew from Dublin's recent history one sign of such a restoration was a head on a pike, displayed in a public place. An alternative was a crowded show trial, public hanging and weeks of display, the offender rotting in the wind.

Cian had no idea where the horsemen were. He hurried on into the fog, knowing they couldn't see him either, yet amazingly they began firing pistols into the mist behind him. Breathless, Cian kept going, thinking they were berserk. What insanity, other than the devil's, would drive O'Hanlon to pay openly for murder? It meant O'Hanlon in his disgrace had chosen the pike, swift execution, over the drawn-out smugness of a hanging judge.

Then Cian heard a horseman behind him, following him downhill, a wild shot now and then until Cian stepped knee deep into a bog. He waded on into the surreal gray, knowing he and Breen would be safer there, as long as the fog held. One forceful step at a time he slogged on, straining over the noise of his breathing to hear horses splashing in water.

When the horsemen's shouts became distant he slowed his pace in the dark water, wondering if they were waiting for him on the other side of the bog. Breathing heavily, he stood still, listening for hoofbeats coming from any direction. Breen was heavy on his back and when Cian swung the boy down he lost his grip.

Breen fell backwards, limp, into the murky water, blood running from his head.

Eyes wide, turning side to side in the water, Cian held his son's bleeding head against his own. He could hear his voice grunting and gasping, as if he was out of his mind, observing an insane stranger.

Some time that afternoon when the fog began to lift Jack Onslow came looking for Cian and found him on his back on a damp hillside. Breen was draped bloody and lifeless on his chest. Deb came out and knelt with Jack in the field next to Breen's body. Cian thought he heard her praying but her voice came softly from far off in the distance.

By dusk, Jack had carried Breen's body to the house and come back to walk Cian in. Jack's face was grave, motioning Deb aside. Perhaps there was something comforting, profound or wise Jack started to say but then he remained silent. Cian watched Jack watching him in the lantern light, somewhere near the hearth. Cian stood motionless for a moment then reached for the jug on top of the mantelpiece, swung it over his shoulder and paused.

"'Tis O'Hanlon," Cian heard himself say, as he saw his body from above, walking out the front door.

"No, Cian," Jack said slowly to him, as Cian felt himself floating out into the moonless dark, hearing the tone in every word. "They'd be waiting for ye on the road to Dublin! Good Lord in heaven, man! They mean to hang ye and worse! Go up to the Wicklows, up high!"

That night Cian fell drunk into a ditch and woke up in a gray mist, cold and aching. In the gloom he crawled out of the ditch and lay under a tree, remembering Jack Onslow's last words to him. Running away from O'Hanlon, into the Wicklows was not his purpose. But the part of Jack's warning that resonated was that he not make it easy for O'Hanlon to murder him and display the remains for shame. Instead, he would stalk O'Hanlon in Dublin, for Breen. The pledge to God was void. The gallows, when O'Hanlon was done, would be a welcome end to the foolishness of living in an Ireland abandoned by God.

All that day as Cian walked across country, northeast toward Dublin, he avoided the lanes whenever possible. He stole a cloth cap and a heavy coat from a farm shed he passed by and bending forward transformed his appearance to that of an older farmer. By late in the afternoon he had attached himself to a line of farmers' wagons making their plodding way through the outer townships and on into the squalid city markets of Dublin.

At the grain market Cian stole bread and carrots from farmers' stalls and made his way toward the wealthier part of Dublin, wondering how he might discover O'Hanlon's place of business or residence. It would be a tricky thing, asking questions without arousing suspicion. He didn't know Dublin and soon discovered there were dangerous neighborhoods he wanted to avoid, as well as those unlikely to harbor Jasper O'Hanlon. Then, after an hour of searching, he realized he was not only lost in Dublin but tiring rapidly.

Night had fallen and he needed a place to rest. Cian sagged against a weathered stone wall and looked around. He was on a cobblestone broadway, lamp-lit, both sides fully curbed and lined with large brownstone buildings. It was the type of street where he might expect to find Jasper O'Hanlon's offices. Suddenly, haunting, melancholy choral music caught his attention, the sound of a multitude of angelic voices, coming from another large building on the street. He listened, transfixed for a long moment, then stepped off the curb and looked up at massive, dark spires. It was a cathedral. He was in the center of Dublin. Protestant or Catholic, he didn't care what the building was, only that the mood of the music matched how he felt.

Entranced by the sweeping, harmonious sound of braided voices, surging beyond anything he could imagine, Cian made his way into an off-street garden alcove on one side of the cathedral, crouching among manicured shrubs and lawn. He looked up at several open, diamond-paned windows, just above his head, where the candles were brightest and the music easiest to hear. Exposed only to Irish ballads and jigs, sung, in his experience by one or a few rollicking performers, this new sound, Cian realized, was English. It was majestic. There could easily have been forty voices singing at the same time, but not all the same melody. He could discern various groups, each weaving a complementary melody above and below other groups in a rich, swirling lament, as if all the voices were mourning for someone. When they stopped and started he gathered they were practicing for an event and not performing for him, on his knees outside under a dark, trimmed bush.

Out of sight of the choir, Cian moved closer still to the source of the music. He leaned against the mossy stones of the cathedral, hung his head and wept silently, for Hugh and Maggie, Megan, Holly, Breen, Rose, Dan and for all of Ireland, now alone. For an hour he listened in the dark, caught up in the lament, as if only he and the choristers understood what it meant when God turned away. Not only had God turned away from him, his wife, son and daughter, but from all of Ireland. Nothing mattered now, except O'Hanlon. That event would come by careful, casual inquiry, the deed done within a week. After O'Hanlon his duty to Ireland was over. There would be peace waiting at the gallows. It would mean the end of being evicted, the end of being hunted, the end of suffering loss.

Inside the cathedral a new piece of choral work began, much softer and more delicate than those before it. He strained to hear the strands of melody, gradually growing in strength. But as he looked up toward the candlelit windows, anticipating the precision and harmony of each chord, a brilliant flash of light blinded him. At the same instant glass shards cut into the side of his head and something metallic and hefty slammed his head against the damp, cold stonework.

"Scum! I see you!" a voice yelled at him from inches away. "Setting here for the night! The worst, you scum of the earth! Going to teach . . . the likes of you . . . to steal!"

Cian was stunned and temporarily blinded by whoever had

25

attacked him. He didn't see the second or third swings of the lantern as they cut into his head at about the same point as the first blow. He staggered away from the wall, raising his hands against the next strike and tripped over a shrub in the garden. The fall saved him from a fourth strike as the attacker had to adjust his position. Cian caught a glimpse of a large man in a coat holding a sizable broken lantern. As the man moved toward him again he tried to speak up, but his mind couldn't form thoughts, let alone an explanation of his presence there. He parried the next blow from the lantern but the man kept coming, fuming that Cian was a thief, no, far worse, a church thief, stealing from God, proof of the decadence of the pit of hell that Dublin had fallen into. Cian kept backing away, trying to buy time to get his mind engaged, until he found himself cornered.

"Stop, ye fool, go back," Cian said, gesturing to the man.

"No, you are going back, you filthy thief! Back to gaol, this night!"

When the man swung again Cian had had enough. He ducked and as the lantern clipped his hair he launched a right at the man's jaw, a straight left under his chin and another hard right to the side of his head. The man fell backwards into the shrubs, unconscious. There were gasps and murmurs directly above Cian. He turned and saw more than a few members of the choir whispering and looking down at him from candlelit windows.

Hesitation at the curb, not knowing whether to run right or left on a dark, unfamiliar street cost Cian valuable time. At the end of the cathedral block he heard whistles, saw men running toward him and as he turned he realized he was trapped. Worse, he was on O'Hanlon's turf.

The gaol for night offenders in Dublin was proof of the decadence that the city had fallen into. The decay of souls, evident in the demented howling, stink of urine, vomit and body odors in the corridors seemed to come from the sides of the pit of hell. A heavy, barred door creaked open and Cian felt himself shoved forward. He found the end of a bench in a corner of an awful, darkened cell, crowded with a dozen seedy men, some pacing and muttering, others bragging or arguing. He kept his head lowered, avoided breathing deeply and tried to make himself inconspicuous. One smoky lantern lit a wall in the corridor. There was nowhere to lie down, even if someone wanted to sleep on the wads of phlegm and acrid urine pooling on the cracked, uneven floor.

Around midnight gaol guards began shouting. The tramping of many men's boots echoed in the grim corridors. There were more shouts and a flurry of smartly-dressed men entered the enclosure near Cian's cell. A short man stepped forward from the group and pointed a finger at Cian, through the bars. A taller man, carrying a swagger stick and lantern, studied Cian. Cian guessed it was O'Hanlon.

"That?" the well-dressed man said, as he squinted, pointing his swagger stick at Cian.

The short man nodded. O'Hanlon then turned and left with his entourage. Moments later Cian was dragged from the crowded cell and locked up further down the corridor in pitch black confinement. The cell reeked of mold and mildew. No one answered when he asked if anyone else was in there with him.

Escape, thoughts of how to escape, how to avoid giving O'Hanlon an easy triumph, ran in circles through Cian's thoughts in the dark. To hang publicly, for fighting the good fight in Curtlestown was one thing, but to fall into O'Hanlon's hands without getting near him exasperated Cian. His humiliation deepened as he listened in the dark to the hellish screams, shouting and wailing echoing down the corridor from other reaches of the gaol. Cian tilted his head back against the cold, smelly wall and waited for morning.

Gaol guards came for him early. The Dublin County Gaol, Cian saw and heard as he was shoved along the corridors, was more than overcrowded. Some of the teeming inmates seemed resigned to it. Others, in their boredom and fury, looked for any distraction. They reached out at him and yelled as he was hurried past them. Something about the hurrying may have indicated things were different for Cian than for them.

"They be hanging ye today! Today it is! Your last day, ye bastard!" one man yelled, followed by another. "Fifty feet up in the air, and they can see your eyes bugging out!"

The hooting laughter accompanying the macabre commentary was that of the insane. Cian was chained and handcuffed in a hallway, dragged out into bright daylight, placed in a barred wagon and taken to another dark stone building. At every step Cian thought of O'Hanlon, unrepentant, free to burn, evict and murder at will and under law.

Cian had never had cause to see a Dublin courtroom before. The dim chamber he was brought into shocked him. There were only a few lanterns, scarred wooden benches, dirty, smudged walls, a foul odor like an unclean church and a sense of dread permeating the still air. Over the decades untold numbers of defendants had apparently left living records of terror and despair embedded in the atmosphere of the place. It appeared to be one of the levels of hell, Cian thought, a judgment room where the devil presided, looking out through the eyes of gray legal authorities. This day the authorities were in a hurry. Wigged barristers whispered among themselves on benches at the center of the room. At a glance, Cian could feel the personalities of the courtroom had prepared a dry, rule-bound ritual where legality would be served as a formality before a public hanging. O'Hanlon was not visible.

Five barristers in powdered wigs ceased murmuring and stood up next to their benches, as if waiting for someone. One barrister separated from the group and moved across the room to another bench by himself. Then eight more men with shorter wigs came in and stood behind the first group. Bailiffs allowed members of the public into the bench rows at the back of the room. At the front of the court a chief bailiff shouted out something about an honor. A hunched-over, gray-faced man in a long wig and black gown came out of a paneled door and sat down carefully at a high seat facing all. Cian's heart dropped. The master of the ritual had the kind of grim, unemotional features that matched O'Hanlon.

28

The judge began slowly and deliberately, informing Cian he had been formally charged by the Crown with attempted murder of a senior Church official, a capital offence. Cian pleaded not guilty, and the judge instructed one of the prosecutors for the Crown, a Mr. Alistair Carray, to proceed. The charge had nothing to do with O'Hanlon, but everything to do with the lantern swinger at the cathedral. The victim of the attempted murder was the head vicar of the diocese, First Assistant to the Anglican Bishop of Dublin. The pastor was unable to present witness in court as he was fighting for his life in an infirmary.

As the trial proceeded, Cian discerned several subtexts occurring in the room, reflected in the delivery of legal vocabulary. First, all the wigged men knew each other, and their dry tones and sarcasm indicated they knew what each would say next. Second, the judge seemed part of an oft-rehearsed act, but his laconic manner suggested he was finding no amusement in his lines. It was possible he was inconvenienced by the early hour. Third, from time to time the judge pointed at the lone wigged barrister at a table off by himself. When the barrister shook his head, the judge would return his attention to Mr. Alistair Carray. Carray consulted with the other wigged men next to him and received notes brought in by couriers. But what Cian noticed most was the judge's expression as he looked over his spectacles at the lone barrister on the far side of the room.

"Mr. Amhurst?" the judge asked.

When Mr. Amhurst shook his head again, Cian realized Amhurst was the court-appointed barrister assigned to defend him against the Crown. After the visual exchange there was a poignant silence in the court for a few moments while the judge composed his notes. The judge then instructed a bailiff to bring Cian forward to the high bench. The bailiff had him turn in place so the judge could examine the lacerations from the lantern. From his rotating perspective Cian could see members of the public gallery through the tobacco smoke at the back of the room. Many of the benches were occupied, but none in the gallery were people he knew. To one side, directly behind the barrister for Cian's defense, was a priest, possibly assigned to the court in case of an expedient need for last rites after sentencing.

When Cian was sent back to his chair, one of the prosecutors, Mr. Carray, began to speak about the dangers of attacks on the Church by mutinous and divisive elements within Ireland, exemplified by the attempted murder of a senior minister in the center of Dublin. Such an act was sedition. It set precedent for similar crimes across Ireland. There was a need to illustrate the consequences of such capital crimes to the inhabitants of Ireland by publicly hanging the culprit. The distinguished victim, as well as the offended public, deserved swift and reasonable justice. The judge tapped the gavel and interrupted him.

"Mr. Carray, the evidence."

"Your honor, the evidence is in the very absence of the victim, who lies at this moment on the threshold of death."

"His physicians, Mr. Carray? The court will hear from his physicians now."

"They are fully occupied, your honor. The senior vicar's life must be saved."

"Yes, indeed. Is there a choirmaster, Mr. Carray? One who overheard."

"If that should be necessary, your honor, the Crown will offer the choirmaster."

"Will offer? It is indeed necessary the Crown offer the choirmaster now, Mr. Carray. The prosecution will present evidence, according to procedure, having had time to prepare."

"Well, yes, of course, your honor. However, the Crown, in sympathy with the public had assumed, rightly so, that violent crime against the Church is the same as an assault on the Crown. His Majesty King George III, at court in London, as the head of the Church would most certainly expect the protection of his justices."

"Mr. Carray, this court does not entertain assumptions, however widely they are held."

The prosecutors seemed to resent the break from the

prescribed ritual and Mr. Carray's tone became more insistent. The judge looked over his spectacles and studied him. At last Mr. Carray yielded to another barrister for the Crown, who stood with gravity and gathered himself.

"Your honor," a more experienced barrister, Mr. Harmon Mably, said, his voice as cutting as a knife. "We have seen in another place the matter of rebellion and sedition against the Crown, as adjudicated in the case of the traitor, Michael Dwyer. The Crown, in accordance with His Majesty's most gracious discretion, thought not to inflame rebellion and did proceed to exercise extraordinary accommodations in the matter of a man known to be responsible for the deaths of numerous subjects of the Crown. It was fully expected the public would respond favorably to His Majesty's grace by foreswearing any further sentiments of mutiny, shunning the rebel Michael Dwyer entirely, in order to preserve the peace in Ireland. We see here, in this room, that the Crown has been betrayed. Not only has there been no cessation in the rumors of mutiny in Ireland, but we have five more victims, four in County Wicklow and one in the center of Dublin. And here, we see the one responsible for those crimes. Michael Dwyer has been offered clemency in vain. The stench of the next rebellion, emanates from the next Michael Dwyer, the one seated in that chair. You asked for evidence, your honor. It is at hand. The brutal attempted murders of four officers of the peace in County Wicklow this summer, by this man, MacGerrity, and by the evidence, your honor, of the brutal attempted murder of a highly respected leader of the Church of Ireland. This man, MacGerrity, has influenced public opinion toward the next rebellion and that is fact! It is evidenced! He is without doubt unrepentant, malignant and murderous in the extreme. He is, by the evidence of his bloody hands, the next Michael Dwyer, and the Crown will not countenance, in any manner, any repetition of the disasters of 1798! This is, your honor, no matter merely for the representatives of the Crown in this court. The matter goes to the attention of His Majesty's Cabinet in London. They are charged by His Majesty to avoid the expense and tragedy of further insurrection in Ireland. To that end, your honor, the Crown seeks, and will have, the prevention of further disturbance by indicating to all Ireland that this man will hang, this day!"

"Mr. Amhurst?" the judge asked, barely pausing for the shake of the head. "Indeed. The court awaits counsel. Mr. Mably, Mr. Amhurst, the prosecution and the defense will approach the bench."

What followed was difficult for Cian to understand. Some rift seemed to have occurred in the pact between the wigged men. The hushed tones of the judge at the bench shifted from deliberate to firm. The off-handed sarcasm was long gone.

"In the matter of evidence, as required in this case," the judge began when the barristers were dismissed, "it is such that the prosecution appears either unwilling or unable to present documents or witnesses supportive to claims. The defense appears either unwilling or unable to present capable statement, for and on behalf of the defendant. Such is the record of this proceeding. Haste, it is most evident, has root and branch in this."

A surge of voices welled up from the back of the room. Some men rushed out of the gallery, others tried to squeeze in against the weight of the bailiffs' backs. The judge hit the gavel repeatedly until some semblance of order returned.

"In the matter of evidence," the judge continued, pausing to glare at Mably, Carray and the others, "the defendant, MacGerrity, was, by sworn deposition of witnesses, now possessed by this court, seen to trespass on property of the Church of Ireland, the night of last evening. No opinions, polemics or hearsay represented by the Crown, other than that fact of trespass, are admissible as evidence. Assumptions of procedure or precedent held by the prosecution have no standing in this jurisdiction."

The prosecutors were outraged and stood up, protesting. The court pact, whatever its initial form, was now broken. The judge looked over his spectacles again at them and called for bailiffs. He threatened the barristers with contempt of court and they were forced to sit down. But the prosecutors and some in the gallery would not be silent and openly threatened the judge with political sanctions in the King's name. Determination seemed to enter the judge's expression, as if he were through with them and had decided to end the matter. Unintimidated by the ruckus, he held his gaze directly on Mably. After a moment the judge motioned to a bailiff, who called for all to rise. Cian heard someone behind him whisper "mistrial." Someone else countered, saying, "another judge." The judge took his time and then spoke.

"The defendant, Cian MacGerrity, farmer of County Wicklow, is found guilty of trespass and sentenced to transportation for seven years to New South Wales, effective on this day, 1805. Bailiff."

Tumult filled the dark room. Men rushed in and out of the now open doors. The barristers shouted at the judge, who was escorted to his chambers by bailiffs. Law clerks milled in confusion. Cian sat in chains on a hard wooden chair and wondered what it meant to be guilty of trespassing. He had heard only part of the sentence over the noise and wondered why he would be sent to Wales. As the bailiffs lifted him to his feet, Cian noticed that the priest at the back of the room was still watching him. No last rites, Cian thought, imagining that the priest, like the prosecution, felt cheated. It then occurred to him that the outrage in the courtroom meant O'Hanlon and his landlord clients would not let the matter rest. If they couldn't have their way in court, they might settle for an incident in a gaol cell.

Haste had its way in the next few minutes. Cian was taken by bailiffs to a six-horse black wagon with iron bars on the rear window. Pressed against others chained next to him, Cian was driven out of Dublin on the high road, then southward along the coast, heading to Cork, someone said.

Stops were made for fresh horse teams every twenty miles or so, and then the driver turned the heavy wagon without delay back onto the coast road. Sometime that night the horses were slowed and the bitter tang of salty sea air wafted into the wagon.

It began to rain as a bailiff told Cian to get out. They were on the docks in Cork. The chains were unlocked and dropped onto wet brick paving stones. Bailiffs carrying lanterns lit the way across a dock of uneven wooden beams. In front and above Cian a gang-plank stretched up to a ship's deck, and he was herded toward it. At the bow of the merchant vessel, he noticed the ship's name on a plaque in gold script and tried to spell it as he waited in line. Letter by letter he tried, as Megan had shown him, to pronounce it, *Tellicherry*.

The enclosures below deck were cramped, shared cells, but less filthy than the dungeons in Dublin. Cian's hammock was at-tached to two bulkheads directly below the main deck. Inches from his head a hinged, black steel plate, in lieu of a window, was left half-open for ventilation. He glanced out through raindrops to a view of three lanterns hanging from posts on the dock. Some-one shouted from the rear of the ship and two sailors strode down the gangplank. They waited for a cloaked man to get down from a coach then carried his bags aboard the ship. As soon as he disap-peared from view the sailors loosed the gangplank and hauled it aboard the *Tellicherry*.

Cian said almost nothing and listened quietly to conversations in the semi-darkness below deck. It was not a happy place, but no one said anything suggesting O'Hanlon had a part in the haste to Cork. The crew were active before dawn and the ship was moving in the harbor by sunrise. Wardens holding lanterns crouched for head clearance as they made their way along each deck, reading instructions for guests of the Crown. Certain times of the day would be allotted by roster for time above deck, weather permitting. Heavy labor, assisting the crew, would be required in foul weather. There were strict rules for seasickness.

By mid-morning, the *Tellicherry* was at sea and Cian was sent up a narrow ladder to the rear of the main deck. He had never been to sea before and assumed they were heading east toward Cardiff, in the south of Wales. The tangle of rigging seemed complicated and unwieldy as he watched the crew at work. But as he watched them toil, he froze in place. Standing just ten feet away, against the ship's rail, was the priest he'd noticed watching him in Dublin Court the day before. He nodded uneasily at the priest and wondered how he could turn away without words and return below deck. The priest held his gaze on Cian.

"Father," Cian said, warily.

"Mr. MacGerrity," the priest replied.

"Ye'd be traveling with us to Wales," Cian said, being polite.

"New South Wales. The other side of the Earth," the priest said, glancing at the whitecaps. "Terra Australis."

Cian stood stunned, thinking the priest had spoken to him in Latin, or a language that made no sense. The priest moved away and began speaking to someone else. Cian thought to find someone in authority, the warden below deck, and explain that a mistake had been made. The judge had ordered him to somewhere in Wales. This was the wrong ship. Let me off, he thought, let me off, take me back to land.

But there was no returning to land, only more surprises. That morning below deck Cian heard more talk, just as difficult to believe. Michael Dwyer was aboard the *Tellicherry*. He had with him his wife, his children and four men who had fought with him against the Redcoats in the Wicklows. Even stranger, Dwyer had received a grant from the Crown, a land grant of a hundred acres, by a freshwater stream in the land they were traveling to. And there was more. Joseph Holt was alive and imprisoned in the same land. Some there had accused Holt of raising another Irish insurrection against the Crown. Cian lay in his hammock and spoke to no one, fearing either O'Hanlon or the Crown had placed agents on board the *Tellicherry*.

The next day Cian spent his time above deck alone, gazing out at the rolling gray-white swells, trying not to be seasick. No land was visible. The priest appeared nearby at the rail.

"If ye walk a little more, the feeling will subside," the priest said.

"Father," Cian responded, not moving.

"Father Clare. Samuel Clare. Will ye walk?"

The walking helped as Cian crossed the quarterdeck unsteadily with the priest and noticed the man was not as frightening as he'd first thought. The priest, clean-shaven, straight-backed and apparently in his fifties, didn't behave formally or use platitudes and verse the way priests were supposed to. He wore the clothing of a modest gentleman, topped with a blue tri-corner hat. He showed Cian how to adjust the roll in his walk with the movement of the ship. There was a discipline in the man, a calm harmony in his voice and an awareness in his blue eyes that matched no priest Cian had seen.

"Are ye from Dublin?" Cian asked, attempting politeness as he walked.

"No."

"Do ye know anyone here on board?"

"I do."

"Did ye know the man Michael Dwyer, he's on board?"

"That's true."

"Is he safe here? Are there enemies on this ship?"

"Michael Dwyer is under the care of the Lord."

"Father, if I may ask, how can the Crown give him land, a hundred acres, with Redcoat blood on his hands?"

"Not your concern."

"Have ye heard of General Joseph Holt then, Father?"

"He's no longer a general."

"I could see that. But would ye mind telling me then, where it is we're going and how far?"

"We go to labor and to wait."

The cryptic, enigmatic answers caught Cian off guard every time he spoke to Father Clare above deck. He would ask the simplest question of the man, something anyone could answer, and receive words in return he would mull over for days. The conversations were usually short because Cian would be stumped for a way to draw the priest out into saying things he could understand. Father Clare would tip his hat, join someone else on the deck and begin another conversation. He seemed to know everyone on board, including the captain, and apparently kept track of a hundred different conversations about the sea and the weather every day.

Then a week later something changed when Cian found the priest near the ship's wheel, talking to the helmsman. Father Clare tipped his hat to the helmsman and motioned Cian away.

"Mr. MacGerrity, see there now, to port," Father Clare said. "Morocco. Over there, behind us, the Straits of Gibraltar and Spain. These waters, between here and Ireland, are contested."

"By who then?" Cian asked.

"Bonaparte, it is, and his navy, allied with the Spanish. They outnumber the English. For your consideration, Napoleon Bonaparte would be a name best not mentioned in the place we're going. 'Tis an English claim and they fear him. Are ye aware then of Bonaparte's efforts in Ireland during the rebellion?"

Cian had never heard of Napoleon Bonaparte or the three attempted landings in Ireland, including one involving fourteen thousand French regulars. One landing had been successful, and the French had joined with five thousand Irish militia. Fierce battles against British regulars had taken place in the west and center of Ireland.

"I wouldn't know of this Bonaparte," Cian said.

"Ye do well to know. 'Tis the Emperor of France and his will was to invade England from Ireland in the west and from France in the east. 'Tis still a deep fear of the English."

"So much, they would not hear his name spoken?"

"Most especially not among the Irish, if they be wise. Ye've heard then of Joseph Holt, of the rebellion?" Father Clare asked.

"I have," Cian answered, looking across the waves to Morocco on the horizon. "But he was imprisoned, maybe worse, in this land we go to."

"He is alive, where we're going, along with many others who escaped the slaughter. 'Politicals' they're called, by the Crown. Aligned with Bonaparte, they say. Out of the way they've been hidden, in New South Wales. Now, the news, still hidden from Ireland, is that the Irish rose up again in rebellion a year ago.

Not in Ireland indeed, but there now, in New South Wales. At a place called Castle Hill. More than two thousand were to rally and take the armories. But their signals for the main gathering were missed along the Hawkesbury River. Troops massed against them and they were cut down, just as in Ireland."

"A rebellion, as in Ireland?" Cian queried, wondering whether Father Clare's allegiance was with the next rebellion.

"Though you, yourself, may not have heard of Castle Hill and the hangings afterward, Bonaparte heard of it. His Grande Armée is strong on land. But at sea, he's at risk. In the waters around us here, the contest is not yet resolved. It may not always go his way. It may be his will to weaken the resolve of the Sea Lords in London with a grievous loss on the other side of the world. He may vex them with this choice: regain New South Wales from the French navy, far from home, or defend England, off its coasts."

"What are ye saying?"

"There be French frigates, French marines on the other side of the world too. There be some Irish in New South Wales who have Bonaparte's promise. The combination, ye understand, French and Irish, is feared by the Admiralty. The strength of the King's single infantry regiment in Sydney is known and could be overwhelmed.

"What would this have to do with me?"

"'Tis this. We'd be at sea here, in confined quarters, for some twenty-two weeks. People talk, make offers. Michael Dwyer's reputation will precede him. His arrival in Sydney will not go unnoticed, he will not be left untouched. He will be popular. He will be tempted. He may receive the vision of a New Ireland from some and recruit in secret for another rebellion. And it is you, who are not unknown, who may also be touched."

"No one knows who I am."

"If you receive a note, a whisper, an invitation, ye set it aside."

"So ye say," Cian replied, again wary. "Are ye with the Crown then?"

"No. I work for no man."

"So then, how would ye be knowing what's feared by the Admiralty and what's offered by Bonaparte? Do ye walk their halls?"

"Not your concern."

"But a New Ireland would be my concern, and a fine one. I'd take the note for Ireland."

"And do what?"

"Fight for Ireland, for a New Ireland. God abandoned the old Ireland."

"Oh? Ye set it aside," Father Clare said, carefully. "We do not reconstitute errors."

Silence followed as Cian considered the priest's meaning over the rhythm of steady clanking in the ship's rigging. When the idyll was broken by shouting from the watch aloft, Father Clare was no longer above deck. The watch reported a fast ship, a frigate, approaching under full sail, a mile further out to sea. Officers trained telescopes on the ship for several minutes before it was announced that the battle flag was French. Many gathered by the rail and in hushed tones watched it speed by with no apparent interest in the *Tellicherry*.

The weather became hotter as the *Tellicherry* sailed south along the coast of Africa. Cian heard they had crossed the equator and noticed the distant blur of land on the horizon slowly changing from green to brown. Something jagged, unseen and unhappy, seemed to proceed outward from a teeming confusion there, but as he couldn't explain the feeling he said nothing to others.

For reasons of trust concerning unspoken feelings Cian found himself anticipating another conversation, however brief, with Father Clare. He went looking for him one morning and encountered Father Clare on deck, between conversations with others. For want of a starting point Cian boldly decided to ask him what he'd be doing when the ship arrived in Sydney. The priest was noncommittal. Cian persisted.

"How is it now, if I may ask, that ye don't dress or speak like the priests in Dublin?"

"There were laws, Crown law then," Father Clare answered, looking out at the rolling gray Atlantic Ocean swells, "restricting the movements of the Catholic clergy. So, it was law. The King is Protestant, ye understand, and his oath to the realm when Ireland joined the Union was that Catholic Ireland be Protestant, like it or not. 'Tis an error, that's all. For me, a convenience it is to travel freely as laity. But now, Mr. MacGerrity, there's another thing ye'd best be ready to know."

Father Clare pointed to the brown smudge of land on the horizon and told Cian they would soon be passing the southern end of Africa at a place called the Cape of Good Hope. Then the pace of the voyage would change.

"Ye see, then, we'd be that far south on the Earth, the winds would come straight from the west at that time. Not a breeze as we see now, but a gale without ceasing. Fast passage 'twill be, propelled by a following gale for five thousand miles. High speeds we'd be making, with the roaring coming from behind us, pushing us on. And the seas be huge, coming over the decks, on and on. Ye bilge and sleep, bilge and sleep. In between, ye lay flat and with sincerity ye pray for the ship."

"Are ye saying ye've been this way before, that ye know this?"

"Indeed. When the times comes, ye stay below deck and ye work."

Father Clare was right. After the *Tellicherry* rounded the Cape of Good Hope, Cian didn't see the priest for weeks. All but the crew kept below decks, not daring to risk being swept overboard. The crew, when they appeared below were soaking wet, exhausted and wearing rope harnesses.

Cian was assigned to a bilge crew in the stern, passing buckets of water up from the keel to an upper deck where the water was tossed out a sluice door, back into the Southern Ocean. Three shifts ran day and night through all watches. When the water kept rising in the hold the captain ordered all able women to join bucket lines. When hands grew blistered and feet slipped on wet boards the work went on. Every hour a crewman in the standing water over the keel would call out the depth of seawater in the hold. The worst of it was, no one could tell when it would end. Tempers would fray, men would collapse and harsh shouting and arguing would be heard.

Cian grew sensitive in the dark to the creaking of the bulwarks next to his hammock. In his weary state he would imagine the caulked and joined beams were speaking to each other, groaning at the strain of staying together. He thought of the builders who had crafted the beams of the hull together in a safe, dry shipyard in Belfast. He imagined and hoped there had been dedication in the artisans' care, when every join was shaped to be perfect.

Then at one point in the endless nights of bilge service a strange absence of groaning between the bulwarks woke Cian in the dark after a ten-hour shift in the hold. He sat up and looked around. Others heard it too. On deck Cian looked out at a rough gray Southern Ocean, tipped with whitecaps, but there were no green-white surges pouring over the rails. The next thing he knew Father Clare was standing by the rail next to him.

"Ye endured," the priest said, calm but pleased.

"Where are we?"

"On our right, to the south, Van Diemen's Land. Over there, north of us, the continent."

There it was. Cian held his breath. It was not what he had expected. The distant green line on the horizon met his eyes with an emotional charge he had never experienced before. There was nothing about it that matched the political entanglements of Ireland. It had none of the jagged fears and confusion of dread Africa. In an instant he felt its presence. It was ancient, beyond words. It was a vast single spirit, lonely, waiting and anticipating an undefined something or someone who would eventually come. A saviour, a comforter, a protector, a redeemer. It had been waiting a very long time for joy.

Father Clare was silent for a while too, then held a pocket compass on the rail in front of Cian.

"Soon we turn to the north-east," the priest said. "We'd be

there in a week. It would be best if you came to terms with your purpose here."

"To terms? Father, are ye jesting? What would my terms be, if I had any?"

"It would not be for hanging on display for all, above County Dublin Gaol. Ye are bought. Ye have worth."

"Some seven years o' worth, I've been told," Cian said. "Not by me own will."

"Well, then. Look back at what ye've left behind. What was it driving O'Hanlon and the like across Ireland? I'd be speaking of principalities of darkness. Fear, worthlessness, anger, the unforgiving, the pride, envy, selfishness, cruelty and ignorance are principalities, Cian. Mere words until put into practice by men. They justify the error by a proud name and a cause. Would ye reconstitute darkness here?"

"'Tis behind me."

"Oh, it is? Ye have the anger, Cian," Father Clare said, in a matter-of-fact tone. "Ye have the anger. The others follow swiftly."

"And if I have it? Who would deny it? Those in their unmarked graves in Ireland?"

"Ye give it up, all of it, bit by bit, rooted out in favor of beauty, then freedom."

"Ye speak of things done that cannot be undone."

"Indeed they can, in ways ye cannot yet fathom. Your purpose here, high above the labor, is to be a steward of your own thoughts, as if ye'd be guarding the land, preparing it for the time when ye do understand."

"Now, how so? A steward, meself? An ordinary man I am and less than that."

"So ye think. Ye have a way to go, young man. In these seven years ye take advantage of the care of the Lord. Ye'll have no passivity, no brooding over grievances. Ye fill your days with work. Ye'll learn to read, and more than the Bible. Ye'll seek out those who can teach ye to read maps. In maps ye take some learning, to your advantage.

42

"Ye say it as if I had some choice. I'd do what I'm told, for the next seven years."

"But ye be alive. Alive enough to expect opportunity. Seek assignment in the furthest reaches."

"So, ye say, keep out of trouble. Set aside invitations, as if anyone would notice me."

"I advise, Cian, only advise. Free ye are to consent or not."

"And where would ye be then, in these seven years, if ye only advise?"

"I move freely."

"And if ye be gone, what happens to the care of the Lord for Michael Dwyer?"

"One step at a time, it is."

A week later, on a glaring, hot summer day in February 1806, the *Tellicherry* turned hard to port, leaving the Pacific Ocean for the glassy swells of Sydney Heads, passing massive, five hundred foot high cliffs on either side. From the quarterdeck the arms of a great harbor opened out in front of Cian. Near and far, forested heights in shimmering heat obscured the far reaches of the harbor to the north and west. He overheard one of the ship's officers saying the first governor of the colony saw it as safe anchor for a thousand ships-of-the-line.

An hour later the *Tellicherry* anchored in the center of Sydney Cove, a scattered settlement of low wooden buildings on either side of a stream. Cian's labor began in the unloading of passengers, goods and livestock down onto small barges. Once ashore though there was no lingering in the heat. He was assigned immediately to a portage gang and carried his load along a rocky trail through a green-gray, aromatic, open forest. It was on this trek that Cian began putting together the military elements described by Father Clare. There was an unspoken tension in the air among the overseers along the route. Prudence suggested Cian keep his observations to himself.

He could see Sydney Cove itself was fine as an anchorage but the vicinity apparently lacked enough fertile soil. After eighteen years of settlement there were few large farms there. Even without military experience Cian could see Sydney Cove was indefensible against a French attack. Father Clare had said the first governor wasted no time siting Government House, larger farms and military headquarters fourteen miles to the west at Parramatta. The Parramatta River was navigable for warships, Cian could see as he toted his load, but the banks were easily defensible. Pickets and sharpshooters of the King's 102nd Foot Regiment could be seen now and then, positioned by artillery under trees on high points above the forest. Cian assumed more pickets and artillery were in place, in an unbroken line-of-sight, all the way to Sydney Heads.

The tension along the route through the forest was not surprising. The military probably suspected many in their own labor force had been participants in the armed rebellion two years earlier. It was possible a few were keeping observations for the French. In the event of a French assault most of the military, especially the officers, would die. Most of the labor force, informants or not, would be freed by French officers. Free passage back to Ireland or free land in Bonaparte's New France would be their reward.

Cian anticipated a grim time when they reached Parramatta. He expected an adversarial setting involving harsh treatment and verbal abuse from overseers. But he had to smile to himself when by an odd coincidence, he was assigned to proceed without delay to join a road survey gang, forming that day on the outskirts of Parramatta. The new road crew would leave in the morning for the furthest northern reaches of the colony, a place known as Wiseman's Ferry.

Two days later, in the one-road wilderness near Wiseman's Ferry, thirty miles north of Parramatta, Cian met the leader of the survey crew, Rodney Cavanagh. The leading hands had talked freely about Cavanagh on the long walk north. Cavanagh was an Ulsterman, a former Royal Army engineer, who had been cashiered for insubordination and transported for property damage caused while drunk. The big man was a superior engineer, who read the land like no one else. He was capable of quick, accurate and sound engineering decisions. His problem was he suffered fools badly and pompous fools even worse.

Wiseman's Ferry was one of many locations along the Hawkesbury River where the colony had developed farms on highly fertile soil. Cavanagh's job, as overseer of both surveyors and labor, was to join those farms by passable roads and link them to Parramatta. In this he was frequently frustrated by insufficient allocation of resources. The military, the Governor and the bureaucrats wanted a network of roads built overnight, he claimed, but wouldn't give him the men and equipment to meet the timelines.

Cian performed whatever labor was required of him by the crew while taking in his new surroundings. He liked it. The sun was far brighter, the air clear and dry and the atmosphere held no sadness or pain compared to Ireland. The green-gray leaves on the eucalyptus trees in the forest had a clean, sharp and pure fragrance when broken open. Kangaroos and wallabies abounded in the forest and with potatoes and carrots their lean gamey meat was the mainstay of three generous meals a day. More important for Cian, everyone was busy with abundant, tangible work and all had the same vision of what had to be accomplished. There was no sense of threat in the still, open forest, no plotting landowners behind his back, no dread of something terrible about to occur.

A few inquiries over meals gave Cian perspective concerning this place on the other side of the world. Unlike Ireland's eight million, kept tightly in a class system, there were only five thousand or so in the colony after eighteen years of settlement. Everyone had an assignment and there was more work to be done than all five thousand could possibly accomplish. A tacit understanding of what it meant to survive on the other side of the world from the Old World seemed to have caused a lessening of the class system. Even the complainers realized the military's purpose in building roads to the farms and no one spoke, at least openly, of rebellion. Instead, Cian heard new words used, such as emancipists and squatters, terms that had positive, aspirational connotations among the men here, implying opportunity, freedom and the exchange of hard work for wealth.

After two weeks of these quiet observations, Cian found himself one day waiting for orders in the company of three leading hands when the big Ulsterman Rod Cavanagh came by. Cavanagh was impatient that no labor had arrived to begin a new spur road. Cian listened to the conversation. It seemed obvious that Cavanagh had failed to communicate his needs to the right bureaucrat but none of the leading hands caught it. To his utter amazement Cian heard the words come out of his own mouth, "I understand it." Cavanagh turned an eye on him.

"MacGerrity are ye? County Wicklow?" Cavanagh growled. "Ye understand this, ye say? Ye better. Ye come with me."

What ensued was another failure to communicate, by both Rod Cavanagh and Cian MacGerrity. Cavanagh assumed Cian could read and Cian decided not to say anything against the assumption. When Cian realized Cavanagh wished to take him into his confidence after Cian had clarified the labor allocation question, it was too late to turn back the clock even five minutes. So Cian, against his expectations, was thrown into a contest with his own sense of limitation, as to how quickly he could learn to read.

Stealthily, rapidly, feigning eye problems from dust, Cian sought out those in the survey and labor crew who could read. Using old labor orders and the memory of basic lessons from Megan, Cian went to select members of the crew. Determined to avoid disappointing Cavanagh, as well as himself, he quickly grasped the letters of the alphabet, the phonetics, vocabulary and syntax of bureaucratic writing in a week of heightened concentration and forced insight. Even more amazing, Cian realized, Cavanagh never seemed to notice the deficiency.

When Cavanagh received new orders to begin a road west, into the mountains, it began another round of confrontations with bureaucrats. Cian was present, listening to Cavanagh prepare for a meeting in Parramatta, when he realized the man needed help with his negotiating technique. He picked up the maps and road plans from the floor when Cavanagh threw them in the air.

"Bloody English!" Cavanagh bellowed. "Where are the people for this?"

Cian looked Cavanagh in the eye as he folded the plans and wondered how Father Clare might answer the question.

"It would be just a matter of saying then, 'if this, then that,'" Cian offered, "so they know the results they'd get with so many men, so many horses."

"If this, then that!" Cavanagh scowled. "You can tell 'em, Mac-Gerrity! You bloody tell 'em, this then that!"

So Cian became Cavanagh's assistant in negotiations and labor planning at the age of twenty-six. All the while his reading skills improved, certainly far beyond Cavanagh's when it came to bureaucratic English. Then one day in the wilderness, while nursing his secret in a planning shed near Penrith, Cian realized how far he'd come. He could read. He thought suddenly of his Aunt Rose, once of Curtlestown, from whom he should have learned to read. Rose, Rose, he thought, Rose and Dan, where did you go?

A year went by for Cian in productive labor facilitation, easing tensions between the wilderness and Parramatta. Cavanagh relaxed on the job and even became possessive of Cian's service, not wanting him to be transferred to a titled position in Parramatta near Government House. Cian let Cavanagh speak for him in that instance, as he had no wish to leave his post with the road crews and his sense of unhurried freedom in the bush.

Now and then Cian thought of Father Clare and decided the priest had most likely returned to Ireland for good, probably on the *Tellicherry* a year ago. Early in the summer of 1807, he was reading plans in a dusty shack with several leading hands when the door of the shack opened and there was Father Clare, beckoning him outside.

"Ye look well," the priest said. "Broader, taller, stronger. I hear ye're doing well. But I bring news and a warning."

Father Clare drew Cian away from the shed and cleared his throat.

"Michael Dwyer has been arrested and held without charge."

"Michael Dwyer? Of the land grant and the family? Why?"

"The authorities arrested him for conspiracy to mount an Irish insurrection against the Crown here, though there's no charge made public yet."

"What did he do? Would he throw everything away?"

"Not what he did, but what he said."

Cian stood in amazement, gesturing for the answer.

"'All Irish will be free in this new country' is what he said," Father Clare responded. "In the context of our times it was a sentiment to be felt rather than said in public. You don't know what has passed in Europe. The fear of Bonaparte is a reality, even here. The Governor has a list of suspected provocateurs. Irish, Scots, Cockneys."

"What has happened?"

"Bonaparte is unbeaten on land. Every power that has stood against him has been swept away by his Grande Armée. All of Europe is his now. All its wealth. He intended to invade Britain and Ireland a year ago but his navy was defeated at Trafalgar, off the coast of Spain. He'll try again. He's banned all trade between Europe and Britain. Russia is coerced to his side. Britain is the only state in Europe left to oppose him."

"He would invade Britain and Ireland, London itself? How would that be possible?"

"Weight of numbers, Cian. The Crown can afford no more than a hundred ships-of-the-line now, a great navy indeed. But Bonaparte has been plundering Europe for ten years and can afford a hundred and fifty ships-of-the-line, now under construction. He sees it as only a matter of time and numbers. Less than ten years. This place would become part of his Empire. New France, indeed."

"And Dwyer?"

"The Governor and the military here are under pressure from the Sea Lords. The call is for hanging provocateurs and informants. They won't risk losing the colony. Now the warning I bring ye is that your name, too, is known in London. If ye be unwitting,

48

there be those here who look for patterns and positioning, who say ye do work for Bonaparte, having knowledge of the roads."

"I've no umbrage here, or in London. Why me?"

"In the event ye receive a quiet word from one of Dwyer's supporters, set it aside. They want ye to speak in Parramatta, in his favor. Ye'd be watched and followed."

"If I set it aside, they'd come to me again. I could say I'd be biding me time, but for how long?"

"Someone is biding their time," the priest said. "We know that two years afore the 1804 rebellion one of Bonaparte's agents, a Francois Peron, was here in Sydney Cove. He came in with French naturalists. Did he treat with Irish the way the French did in Ireland in 1793 and 1798, afore the landings in that rebellion? The Governor's men think so."

"Was it Dwyer then, or his people?"

"It would not have been Dwyer, but be warned. The Governor's men it may be who encourage ye to speak in Parramatta. Set a thief to catch a thief."

"I'd have nothing to do with any of this. I'd not be anyone's next Michael Dwyer, or a governor's man. I like it fine out in the bush."

"So, keep it that way. There be some from the rebellion here who bide their time for recklessness, yet again. Governor King is a navy man, a fighter-at-sea by profession. He's not trained to handle something this delicate, this political. And the next governor will be, by error of the Sea Lords, a Captain William Bligh, late of *H.M.S. Bounty*."

"Bligh, no. A damaged man he is."

"A superb navigator he is and a devout man. But thin-skinned and a disciplinarian, unsuited to civil law or the high purpose of this place."

"If he be so flawed the Sea Lords would see it, I'd say."

"'Tis their preoccupation with Bonaparte. They expect more battles at sea, off the English coast. They guard England and this place with their own toughs, to preempt Bonaparte."

"Ye say all the governors be navy men?"

"The Admiralty sees this place as a fortress, a survival state designed for defense."

"And if not that, what is it then?"

"Far more than that. Ye see it yourself, already. When those mountains are pierced a large slice of Ireland and England will want to come here, if they can. The right man is needed to seed the expansion and carry it with a deft hand for the law and defense. It won't be a naval officer."

"But, ye speak afore of Governor's men and others fearing the Irish. If they do come to me, what is it I say? I'd have no love for Bonaparte."

"Ye labor and ye wait. Ye set all else aside."

"What would ye do about Dwyer?"

"Not your concern. But think on this. Do ye remember Joseph Holt of the battles in County Wexford and County Wicklow, the war of 1798?"

"Me father fought for him at Vinegar Hill."

"Cian, me boy, Joseph Holt, the general, was sent here as a 'political' in 1800. So dangerous he was to them, he was imprisoned after he arrived. Even so, he was privy to the French and knew of the rebellion before it began in 1804. It was he who went to the Governor and told him what would happen aforetime. If not for Joseph Holt the troops would not have been at Parramatta in time. Government House would have been overrun, the granaries burned. He saw it. Most of the five thousand souls here now would have starved. The rebels had no plans other than recklessness. And this place is for far more than that. Joseph Holt saw it. So it may be ye see it yourself."

Although Father Clare stayed for the evening meal of stew and tea, he tipped his hat and was gone before dark without elaborating on Joseph Holt or the purpose of the place. Cian didn't see him again for three years.

During those years Cian remained apolitical and remote in the bush, preoccupied in his job with the road crews, shielding

Cavanagh from Parramatta and seeing a new road wind between the farms in the Hawkesbury River valley. But one item of political news did reach Cian in the winter of 1807 and was a source of relief. Michael Dwyer, arrested but not charged with insurrection, was finally brought to trial. In court he denied plans to march on Parramatta. Due to insufficient evidence Dwyer was found not guilty of conspiracy to mount an Irish insurrection against the Crown. The news spread quickly across the colony. The verdict lifted a dread Cian had held that if Dwyer were to hang, his furious, hidden supporters might come knocking at the door of the next Michael Dwyer. Left alone in his anonymity, in the bush thirty miles north of Parramatta, Cian felt free to consider the mountain range Father Clare had said was meant to be pierced.

The mountains Father Clare had referred to were the Blue Mountains, sixty miles west of Sydney. This labyrinth of mountains had captured the imagination of the first settlers in 1788 and still baffled the five thousand who lived on the rolling hills between the impassable range and the coast. Several serious expeditions, military and civilian, skilled explorers and unknowns, had been defeated in each attempt to cross the Blue Mountains. No one in the colony had any idea what was on the other side. Rumors persisted that there was an inland sea to the west. But no one knew.

But then a few weeks later Cian's relief at Michael Dwyer's freedom returned to dread and uncertainty. Father Clare's predictions about the Sea Lords' error in appointing the next governor came true. Governor William Bligh, a capable and disciplined sea-going naval officer, succumbed to his suspicions of mutiny and without evidence nullified Michael Dwyer's not guilty verdict. By autocratic caprice, he publicly retried Dwyer for insurrection, stripped him of free-settler status and sentenced him to hard labor in Van Diemen's Land. The same ham-fisted manner of command that had mishandled the fickle Fletcher Christian on the *Bounty* was now on course to incite mutiny among the two thousand or more Irish around Sydney. Cockneys and Scots were in sympathy. When Cian mentioned the risk of another uprising to Cavanagh, in the

51

privacy of the drafting shed, the big man simply looked down and bit his lip.

"Ye say nothing, Mr. Cavanagh?" Cian asked. "Nothing at all to the men?"

"We say nothing," Cavanagh replied. "There be hangings coming, I feel it. The hangings, ye know, could go either way around Parramatta. I can see the rope on his neck."

But Governor Bligh had only just begun to exercise his suspicions. In addition to despising the character of Irish, Scots and Cockneys, Bligh found the increasingly wealthy and self-interested free settlers mutinous against his commands. Dissent against Bligh came from every quarter. In the following year, 1808, it was not the Irish who mounted an insurrection against Crown rule, it was the monopolistic English landowners and senior officers of the King's 102nd Foot Regiment, who now called themselves the New South Wales Corps. They denounced, arrested and imprisoned Governor Bligh. Bligh, the sole legal representative of the Crown, was himself effectively exiled to Van Diemen's Land. In that year, 1808, the wealthy took over the government of New South Wales.

Remote and uninvolved with politics, planning roads in the foothills of the Blue Mountains, Cian heard the news with dismay. It was the worst of Father Clare's predictions come true. Although others in the road crews joked about new liberties that would surely come from the wealthy landowners' connivance with senior military officers, Cian would not accept any of it. It rubbed too close to the bone, too close to memories of the real rulers of Dublin, above and below Jasper O'Hanlon. Now, these wealthy landowners of the New World had taken the rule of law to themselves and made it no different from the Old World.

Cian could not work when he heard Bligh had multiplied his errors with all sectors, mishandling the wealthy as well as the poor. The consequence of the errors was that the government had been usurped. What would happen if the cabal received offers from the highest bidder in Europe? Cian paced alone in the forest, wondering what to do, where to go.

News of the military insurrection against Bligh and the loss of order came at a time when Cian experienced something he should have long been hardened against. There is a white and brown medium-sized bird of the kingfisher family, known as the kookaburra, resident in the Blue Mountains and across most of the continent. It has a territorial call which sounds like hilarious laughter, coming from unseen heights in the forest. The emotional effect of such high-pitched hooting and hilarity on a man on the forest floor below depends on the balance of his mind at the time. To Cian the kookaburra's call was inescapable, directed solely at him. Its tone was so reminiscent of the laughter of the insane in County Dublin Goal that it dropped on him as a great weight of condemnation. He had endured, only to have the worst of the Old World find him just as unprepared for an O'Hanlon in the New World.

He ran away from the hideous, obsessive taunting until he was lost somewhere in the bush, far from the drafting shed. Exhausted, he slid down against a rock and wondered how it was that he was still so easily rattled. There was a poison in him from Ireland that had not come out. The anger was still there. Then, out of nowhere, a prompting came to him, something Father Clare had said when they were approaching the southern end of Africa, "Pray for the ship."

Months later, Cian received word from Cavanagh, of all people, that the wealthy private and military usurpers of government had been returned to London for courts martial and Crown trials. A new governor was on his way, an expert in civil law, commerce, administration and the military. He was a colonel, an experienced infantry officer, who had served in many capacities in America, India and Egypt and who happened to be Scottish.

On New Year's Day 1810, Cian was in his roadside map shed when one of the leading hands on the crew told him Governor Lachlan Macquarie had landed at Sydney Cove with his own infantry regiment, the 73rd. Also, Cian had a visitor.

"Is it an odd coincidence," Cian asked Father Clare as they

walked along a wooded trail next to a new road, "that ye arrived on the same ship as the new governor?"

"Ye may be pleased to know that the governor is a fine man."

"How so?"

"Macquarie would be given opportunity to be an instrument of the Father of all."

Cian listened to Father Clare's comments about the new governor's qualifications, as well as news of Bonaparte's wars and blockades in Europe. But they were distant causes, and if order was about to return he had other things on his mind.

"Father, a matter we spoke of last time," Cian began. "The mountains up there. No one's crossed them after twenty-two years. Something new is needed. I have an idea."

Cian's idea was to find a way to spend more time with the few Aboriginal men who were occasionally seen watching the process of road building from a safe distance. He suspected these men already knew more than one way over the Blue Mountains, but no one had seriously engaged them as guides. Cian's proposal included applying for a ticket of leave, an early release from road service for exemplary behavior.

"The idea's fine," Father Clare said, "but not for yourself. Here's why. Your ticket of leave would prohibit ye bearing arms. Ye'd not be free to travel around, let alone take to the mountains. Ye'd have to renew the ticket each year, on approval. Ye'd have to attend muster each day in Parramatta and church each Sunday, Anglican for sure."

"Even with the new governor?"

"Even so," the priest said. "I'd not be here to break your heart, but someone else has got to do it."

"When?"

"When it happens. After that, as I said, half of Ireland and England will go over those mountains, if they can."

"And I'd be turning pages in a road shack as they go by."

"'Tis a test," Father Clare said. "To labor and to wait. Even three more years."

Those three years became progressively more difficult for Cian. As an observer of all around him he noticed that Cavanagh had become less irritable, even comfortable with the bureaucrats in Parramatta. Many of the road crew he'd known had done their service and been granted land along the Hawkesbury. They were now landowners, free citizens, among those personally known and favored by the governor. In contrast, many of the former officers of the New South Wales Corps resented their sudden loss of influence and were locked in adversarial relationships with the government and each other. As an observer of himself, Cian realized that by the time his service expired he would be thirty-one years old. His life, he felt, was sliding by in a dusty portable shack, carrying reports on horseback back and forth from the wilderness to Parramatta each week, with nothing to show for it but another mile or so of road through the bush.

As if aware of Cian's trial of patience, Father Clare appeared at Cian's work camp in a remote location in the foothills of the Blue Mountains in the autumn of 1812 with news. Cian had four months service remaining and at first sight of Father Clare thought the news might be about an early release.

"'Tis happening," Father Clare told Cian as they walked in the dry eucalyptus forest. "Bad news for everyone. The drought now could be the worst we've seen."

"How would ye be so pleased about it?"

"The landowners are taking losses, livestock, grain. Fires in various places. But there be one who'd not take it any longer. And he has the means to do something about it."

"What would that be?"

"He's tried to cross these mountains above us once already. There has been a suggestion made that he try again, by different means."

"Father, I'd be done in four months! After all this time, I'd be done! I could go!"

"A better idea there is. Come to me in Parramatta, in February, when ye're done. Ye'd get a land grant around here, but it won't be worth much in a long drought. They'd not be giving away river frontage. Come to see me, when ye're done."

"What would ye be offering?"

"Work," the priest said. "There's a fine Anglican church, a cathedral of sorts, in Parramatta now. Ye've seen it. Nothing there for Catholics to speak of. 'Tis a chapel we need for a start. There'd be a new priest arriving in May. It would be fine to have a roof over and a place for him to say Mass."

"Parramatta? A chapel?" Cian asked, in disbelief. "What about these mountains?"

"One step at a time, me boy. Ye have no money. Ye don't even own the shirt on your back. Work for me."

"A new priest?" Cian asked, sensing another abandonment. "A new priest? Are ye leaving again?"

"Work for me."

"Stay, for me," Cian responded.

"The Lord has never left ye. Ye look to a man for strength and miss the Lord hidden in ye. 'Tis another test, me boy, how much and how often ye expect the knowing. 'Tis when the edge of the circle knows the center. Ye think on it."

Cian looked to the west over the forest, at the blue haze of impenetrable mountains and breathed out heavily. It could take the next four months or more, he thought, to mull over and decipher what it was that Father Clare had just said.

In those last four months of service Cian found the time, when not pressed by talk among the road crews, to think on the priest's words. But in the portable map shed and on the new roads there was no stinting the Crown, and Cian worked to the last minute of the last day. All he had grasped from thinking about the edge and the center was that the priest had left more than a few words unsaid. To draw out the unsaid words he would have to find Father Clare, wherever he was. For seven years Father Clare had always managed to find him.

Early in the morning of Cian's first day of freedom in the New World, he reported to a clerk in Parramatta who informed him officially that he had repaid the Crown in full for the cost of his transportation. A land grant was issued to Cian, and as Father Clare had predicted the plot was in an area Cian knew was dry ground, far from roads, worth almost nothing. Cian, with no money, had no means of traveling to see it or of doing anything with it. There was simply no alternative but to look for Father Clare. After numerous inquiries, Cian found the priest in a white-wall tent on the wooded outskirts of Parramatta.

"This is how ye live?" Cian asked as he entered the tent. "I thought ye came over with the governor, went over the heads of the Sea Lords to the Lord knows who."

"Wipe your boots. Funds have been carefully allocated for the work. These are the plans," Father Clare said, looking up from his simple desk, with no indication of surprise. "A fine new chapel. Modest, but adequate for now."

"Father," Cian acknowledged, glancing over the plans. "London, Paris, Berlin, Parramatta."

Father Clare leaned back in his chair and studied Cian.

"And this is a free man I see. Ye did well, Cian. All this time, ye did well. Ye were patient. Ye labored and ye waited."

Father Clare stood and rather than shaking hands embraced Cian and looked at him with sudden tears in his eyes.

"Oh, me boy, I can tell ye now. I go back more than seven years in me mind, to a courtroom in Dublin. He was there then, as I knew, even in hell with ye. He'd be there, wherever ye go."

Cian looked at Father Clare, surprised at the sudden emotion from a man he considered imperturbable. In a moment Father Clare recovered his composure and resumed his normally calm tone.

"I have to say I'm glad ye found me current address. I'd have need of your help here."

The plans for the chapel were indeed modest. But despite the appearance of the white-wall tent and the one near it for Cian, there seemed to be no shortage of funds for the very large site and good quality building materials staged nearby.

Cian discovered the next morning that the new chapel would be set on precisely square and level footings for the best possible foundation. It took all of burning hot February and into a dry March to install the foundation to the priest's satisfaction. Father Clare employed other workers on site, but in the evening he would sit in his tent with all the canvas doors and walls rolled up and make notes on the plans. Each evening Cian buried a canister of salted dough under the coals and cooked stew on an open fire nearby. Then, hoping for a breeze to ease the heat of the day, they conversed over supper.

"So what would ye do if a way was found over the mountains?" Father Clare asked Cian one hot evening.

"I'd be following the same way over. I'd be claiming a place where there's green grass, water all year. I'd go soon, soon as I could find a map, afore the rush."

"And how many would there be in your exploration party?"

"It would be me. I'd travel alone."

"Is that so? How long would it be afore ye found yourself on your back, in the dirt up there, with a spear through your chest? One man traveling alone."

"Ye say yourself I'd not be alone. I'd take the care of the Lord with me."

"The care of the Lord implies wisdom, me boy. It means thoughtful preparation, so ye'd not be wanting for the best horse, your muskets and a long list of things ye'd need. Such wisdom costs some money. More than ye think."

"Are ye saying now, after all this time, I'd not be free at all to go? I'd be stuck here for want of money? I'd be scrimping for years down here, while a road was built up there and the world passed me by?"

"No, not saying that," Father Clare said. "Ye see the plans here? Ye see the care taken to amend the work each day, correcting it to meet the plans?"

"I'd see the chapel done right, if that's what you're saying."

"'Tis more than that, boy. See beyond this labor and prepare for the next one. Your plans for travel must be as thorough as these for the chapel. Ye must imagine adversity and defeat it afore-time. These are the days for it."

So in the heat of a dead-drought autumn and the rigor of framing a chapel, which the priest insisted should be made with perfect joins, Cian began planning for travel. He drew on road planning procedures from memory and applied everything he had learned from Cavanagh. Father Clare read Cian's drafts of his journey's purpose and a list of proposed equipment. Then he suggested imagined adversities to indicate omissions in prepara-tion. The priest would then stand aside and allow Cian to make his amendments.

The roof of the chapel began to take shape in May. Cian was finishing a full day up on the roof trusses when Father Clare re-turned to the site with a wagonload of roof shingles. The priest waved Cian toward the main tent.

"It's been done, boy!" Father Clare said, clapping Cian heartily on the shoulder. "Blaxland and his men got over the Blue Moun-tains! It took them twenty-one days to climb up and over."

"How? How was it done? With guides?"

"No, no, Blaxland's too proud for that. But they did change the approach from the last twenty-five years. They followed the ridges, wherever they went, instead of following the creeks."

"How many people know?"

"Everyone in Parramatta, everyone in Sydney. They'll know in London and Dublin in twenty weeks."

"Well, now, what's up there? Is there an inland sea?"

"Not from their report. They looked out from the top of a high mountain. Only hundreds of miles of the finest grazing land these men had ever seen, to the north, south and west. Well-watered, open woodland on a grand scale."

"What would the Governor do, then?"

"He'd see the route properly surveyed and a road built be-tween the mountains within a year."

"A year? I'd not wait a year," Cian replied, then remembered what it would cost to travel well prepared.

"Why not wait a year? Ye know nothing of where ye go." Father Clare asked. "Ye could take employment, with your experience. Take a salary for a year and seek a land grant by road and river."

"No," Cian said. "No, I'd not be told by the Crown where I'd have me land. I'd find it for meself."

"I say again," Father Clare responded. "What they saw was on a grand scale. Ye'd be spoiled for choice, even a year from now. Ye'd take a squatter's risk if ye go alone now. And if ye did, what would make ye say then, this land here, right here?"

"I'd been thinking on that, these few days now. Something in me will know the place. 'Tis a sweet spot I'd know, where everything needed is there."

"What is it in ye that would be so sure?"

"It pulled me out of that courtroom in Dublin and through these seven years, for a reason."

"And it must be realized without delay?"

"It must. 'Tis ready now. For no one else."

"Then," Father Clare said, nodding thoughtfully, "that is what ye must do."

"Father, I wouldn't ask for me wages so soon, if not for this news."

"Well, when would ye gather the things ye'd need?"

"Tomorrow, if there be gold under me tent and if the roof can wait for other hands."

"It can."

"Father, I thank ye for your leave," Cian said, holding the equipment list up but lowering his head. "But even if ye'd be so kind as to pay me wages on the morrow, 'tis the main thing now to cut this to size. Me first adversity is the lack of money."

"Your wages? In this case there's no such limitation. I don't decide them."

"Who else have I been working for? Ye said, work for me."

"That I did, in a manner of speaking. 'Tis a watchful Father, Son and Holy Spirit who supply your needs. Such power in Heaven and on Earth takes the cost of every item on your list and matches it. More than enough ye'll be awarded."

"Father, the Trinity is in Heaven. What have I done on Earth to warrant any merit at all?"

"Ye built a house on Earth for the children of Heaven. Ye built with care and patience. The Lord sees everywhere, even the very balance of his light in ye. Ye'll have what ye need."

"Father, God bless ye. Ye can do that, through the Church?"

"No, no. I have no such authority in the Roman Catholic Church. Only wages come from the Church. 'Tis the care of the Lord it is. Ye'll have what ye need and more, this day."

"Thank ye, I'd be grateful," Cian said, still surprised, uncertain of how this could be accomplished. "I didn't think of ye, a priest, ye know, as having money at all."

"No, 'tis not meself. 'Tis unearned, a grace ye cannot fathom."

Cian smiled and bowed his head, thinking of the days a long time ago when he was convinced that he and most of Ireland had been abandoned by all.

The next day, work on the chapel roof continued without interruption as Father Clare supervised two other laborers. Meanwhile, Cian traveled around Parramatta, grateful for the cash in hand. He spent the next two days procuring a lead horse, a pack-horse, a saddle and gear, two border collies from separate owners, muskets, pistols, three hundred rounds of ball and powder, horseshoes, knives, a tent and cooking pans, rope, seeds, saws, nails, tools, mirrors, medical alcohol and bandages, blankets, a flute, a Bible, a telescope, oilcloths, water bags and everything else on the two-page list.

The evening before Cian was hoping to depart, Father Clare made his way to Cian's tent, patted the two staked dogs and talked to them. Dusk was falling as Cian came out of the tent with his equipment list, stoked the campfire and enquired about the chapel roof.

"All proceeding to the schedule we have," Father Clare said. "A few thoughts there are, to be taking with ye afore the morn."

61

"I'd be taking a few of me own."

"'Tis a long way ye've come from Curtlestown, indeed. And, ye'd leave us here, to go ahead of the surveyors and the builders, for fortune's sake. But what ye enter up there is something ancient, unchanging for tens of thousands of years. Ye enter far realms alone, where the Aborigines there have not heard of the Irish, nor the English. Ye and the horses present nothing they believe could exist, so different a manner ye bring."

"So ye warn," Cian replied.

"These, who would wonder when they see ye, are stewards of the land, Cian, God's children attuned to nature indeed, but in stasis as souls. Change for them can only come from the outside. 'Tis the nature of the Father to transcend himself through his creation. If the creation not change, he sends the change, and the free will to bring new expression. We, in our limitation, carry that change, for better or for worse. We bring that which is golden and that which is poison, for their choice, as well as ours."

"I'd be witness to that," Cian said. "So few of them now, around here. 'Tis the disease we bring."

"True it is. But they, like us, are souls. Some, loosed of their bodies will choose life again among us newcomers, born in these towns to Irish and English, because they trust to find the golden in the change. Others will choose to retain the stasis. Some will choose the poison and lament. They have free will, as we do. They have the right to be tested, as we do."

"They may not feel the need to be tested, Father. I'd be watching the Aboriginal men near the road crews and they seemed to think we'd be fools, laboring for no good reason."

"That which applies to them, as to us, is the Parable of the Talents. The Father gives the gifts and we perceive his return in a while to see what we've made of them."

"They hardly rush to our idea of God or parables, in the seven years I'd be seeing them."

"So it may be in the realms ye enter. Ye bring, by example, revelation to the unchanging. Ye keep your distance, for ye know not yet that which is golden and that which is poison in ye. Nor can the men tell from the sight of ye."

"I'd keep me distance."

"And for yourself, ye speak of a sweet spot ye'll know, when it appears. Let it not be of harm or disadvantage to them. Ye must be steward. Yet it may be that ye travel for years without finding this place."

"How so? I'd not be a wanderer the rest of me life."

"The anger ye bring from the Old World it is. When 'tis gone the sweet spot will appear."

"So now, how would I draw off this anger I no longer see?"

"Some is gone these seven years—a little, but far from all. The worst of it hides from sight. That which roots it out is joy, as the days become years. Ye sing, ye pray, ye look left and right, up and down, ye look for beauty and freedom. Gratitude it is, draws it off."

"Ye say that; I hear it. But I don't forget who I left, or why."

"Then, me boy, ye set yourself up as a law unto yourself. 'Tis the law of unforgiveness. By that law of yours ye carry O'Hanlon and the landlords of Ireland on your back. And ye think ye won't be a wanderer all your life?"

"So, forgive ye say. Forgive 'em all. Words ye can speak till the cows come home. But the feelings don't change. They don't listen to your words, at all."

"Then turn your law of unforgiveness on its head. Put those creatures of memory in a strong box. Shut them in. See yourself nailing the lid shut. Then hand the full box to the Lord. 'Tis his burden, which is light. Give it back to him. All of it. Without the weight of that box 'tis possible, even easier then, to follow the law of forgiveness. Much lighter it is, without the things in that box. And there's freedom there, giving that thing away."

Cian said nothing for a while as he contemplated the last seven years of service, the journey itself and the place in hell he'd come from.

"Ye know, Father," he said quietly, "I'd not be certain of what I go to, nor where."

"Ye go ahead of that which is known. There's one who'd hear your questions at any hour. But in time ye'll remember this world. When ye find that which ye seek, ye let me know. Find a way to let me know."

"How? Who knows how far I'd go and how far ye'll go."

"Find a way."

The next morning Cian bid Father Clare his best and set out from Parramatta on horseback, thinking he'd be alone on the journey up into the mountains. He was not. He fell in with a loose train of adventurers, equipped much the same as he was, each having some version of a diagram depicting the winding route along the ridges. Cian camped near where they camped and listened to their opinions and exaggerations but otherwise kept to himself.

The unmarked trail along forested ridges made for a dangerous climb on horseback. Cian initially let the two dogs run beside the lead horse, but when larger hunting dogs belonging to other horsemen harassed the sheepdogs it delayed and bothered Cian. Changes had to be made. He found little sense of courtesy among forceful men, essentially competing in an extended race to claim prime riverfront acreage before the Crown or anyone else could. Cian could tell by the tone of the other horsemen's voices that they were intoxicated with the stakes of the gamble they were engaged in. Their gamble was to prove staked possession of vast virgin acreage to be ten-tenths of Crown law and a speedy ticket to wealth, for the modest cost of getting there. It occurred to Cian that where their vast acreage claims overlapped there might be little peace among driven men.

Cian's solution to the risk of having his dogs killed was to hollow out a place between the equipment strapped to the pack horse. He then lifted one of the dogs, Win, up there for the ride. The other dog, Bonny, was placed between the saddlebags behind him on the lead horse. Both dogs seemed to adjust in a moment to the arrangement, as if they were entitled to the better view.

The proof of the exertions made by man and horse came

after two weeks of winding through labyrinthine forested heights. When each man in the expanding group of horsemen came to the place listed on their diagram as "Mount York Lookout," they saw what Blaxland, Wentworth and Lawson had seen. The vista hushed all the strained opinions and cocky bravado with sheer awe as each man pondered his fortune. There indeed, stretching to a far horizon, was a land of plenty. The rush was on.

Whooping and yelling, the ad hoc train of adventurers began to break up, some hurtling their horses pell-mell down the track-less mountain, pans and shovels clanging and rattling as if there was a finish line somewhere on the immense slopes below. Cian watched them in silence from a ledge on Mount York.

The mountains, Cian observed, were unlike anything he'd seen in Ireland. South of Dublin the Wicklows might be ten miles wide by thirty miles long, with the Irish Sea visible to the east. Here in the New World the mountains were higher, more forested and precipitous, stretching on and on in all directions. Even to the west there were more peaks on the horizon.

Cian followed the hoof-prints of the other horsemen, in no particular hurry. He stopped now and then to consider the majesty of the river drainages which angled and turned in every direction. His compass indicated the other horsemen were moving west, and eventually he noticed a good-sized river in a valley below, generally tending westward.

Over two days he descended from the heights and followed the north bank of the river. But as fine as the land looked for grazing it felt odd to Cian to be going into land probably already claimed. Who knew where claim posts would appear the next day? Who knew the endless wrangling bound to ensue when claims overlapped in the Promised Land? He would have no part in creating new memories of greedy men standing toe to toe over land.

Toward dusk on the second day Cian rode back up to a higher elevation and looked out over the westward expanse. It was a still, clear evening and there were perhaps twenty campfires indicated by thin columns of smoke far in the distance. What was once wilderness to Anglo horsemen and hunting land to Aborigines already felt crowded, and Cian wanted to be completely free of competitive conversation for a while.

The next morning Cian decided to turn due north, where he had seen no campfires the previous evening. He allowed Win and Bonny to run loose in the open woodland, calling them to keep pace with the lead horse. Heading away from other men felt like a relief and so he pressed on, northward.

Relief soon turned to caution the following day. Cian noticed he was being observed and then stalked, not by noisy Anglo-Irish horsemen but by twenty silent Aborigine men, whose hunting lands he had apparently entered. Father Clare's warning about finding himself on his back in the dirt with a spear through his chest came quickly to mind. Cian turned the lead horse straight uphill to gain elevation and to discern their intent. Fortunately, the dogs followed and the twenty Aborigines, for the moment, did not.

The forested heights made traveling difficult and slow. Water was harder to find. The loose rocks under the horses' hoofs were more treacherous than the lower grassy slopes, and Cian saw far fewer kangaroos or wallabies to hunt. By evening the Aborigines were no longer in sight. If this is what it took, Cian thought, to avoid confrontation, he would remain in the high country where the Aborigines seemed to have little or no hunting interests.

Now and then, over the following days, Cian used the telescope at various high vantage points to observe smoke plumes from Aborigine campsites and confirm what now seemed obvious. Both the Aborigines and their hunting quarry preferred lower elevations, wherever water, grass and flatter terrain made rapid movement easier. For Cian, remaining in the heights offered a buffer of safety, but it also required more thought about finding decent grass and water for the horses and meat for the dogs. He realized that without care he could burn through three hundred rounds of ball and powder within weeks. Every shot had to count. He began to take more time to ride from lookout to lookout, in order to scan the forest below for movement.

Planning a hunt where a single round at close range would reliably bring down a wallaby took patience. Cian experimented by positioning Win to lay and wait downwind from a mob of wallabies on a slope. Bonny would follow Cian to whatever hiding place could be found. A whistle brought Win at a run, toward the mob. Sometimes the startled wallabies scattered in the wrong direction. Sometimes they bounded close enough for a single, effective shot. It didn't work every time, and so Cian was forced to learn by heightened concentration the fastest way to adapt to the wind and terrain.

Hunger pains taught Cian to keep meat tightly wrapped in oilcloth for the days when hunting was not successful. He also noticed the dogs were prone to picking up ticks in their fur. Each evening after they were fed, Cian called them to lay by the campfire where he talked to them and brushed them carefully. When he found a tick, he dabbed it with alcohol, lifted the tick with tweezers and dropped it as a little fireball into the flames. The dogs came to expect their grooming each evening and were content to curl up on their oilcloth on either side of the tent as night fell.

The days passed into weeks and Cian felt the temperatures getting cooler at night. He ran his hand over the horses' backs often, talked to them and checked their horseshoes every evening. The pace was kept deliberately slow because of the terrain and the lingering heat of a long summer.

Then one night the drought broke and the rains and winds came. Draping himself and the horses in oilcloths, Cian dealt with the conditions, but his movement northward on some days fell to little more than a mile or so. He realized he had not kept track of the days and had to guess that it was now July or August 1813. It was also possible, he thought, that far behind him the Governor's road surveyors were already preparing to follow the trail into the Blue Mountains. Ahead of him there were no roads of any kind and no other horsemen.

As winter arrived in the high country, Cian was forced to focus his days on hunting and cooking, the earlier the better, with northward travel occurring incidentally. The higher peaks were snowcapped and temperatures hovered around freezing, so Cian kept the horses under oilcloths and allowed the dogs to rest inside the tent. The lack of northward movement on colder days allowed Cian time to think about what a sweet spot might actually look like, if and when he found it. It would be in the higher elevations, open woodland with lush grass and year-round running water. There would be no one else around to dispute his claim. The area would feel peaceful and appear beautiful. And that would be enough, he thought.

One clear, freezing day in mid-winter, as Cian looked down from a summit at the various creeks and river valleys angling away from him, he saw that some valleys drained to the west, all the rest drained to the east. The confusing maze of mountains he had been in for perhaps three months now, he realized, was part of a major range. That range ran north-south, and he was standing at an elevation and a location which was the dividing line between watersheds. The rivers running west flowed to what might be an inland sea. The rivers flowing east ran down to the Pacific Ocean.

Looking north, the dividing line weaved left and right from summit to summit. It was time to decide whether the sweet spot would be to the west or east of the divide. It mattered because if the land was worth anything it would produce a surplus that would need a market. The ideal market was Sydney, but Cian was now so far away it would take months to get there, even if a road was eventually built into the plains behind him. It might be possible to find a better connection, he thought, if a large enough river flowed directly east from the divide and down to the ocean. A trail might be created along its banks or a raft might be an easier solution. The problem was that he had no idea how far inland he had traveled. Such a river and such a trail might run for two hundred miles to the ocean.

Even though the concept of an ideal place was beginning to be defined in Cian's imagination, it was not seen in reality that winter. The cold rains came every few days, and in between storms

Cian followed the ridges, assessing drainages to the east and then the west. He would pause and look down into the valleys with the telescope, hoping to see something he would recognize as just right. Unmoved by what he saw, he would shake his head and wonder why he was being so particular.

Snow in the air and sub-freezing temperatures surprised Cian one morning. He spent the day in his tent wondering what he had committed to. He was gambling with his life, as much as the horsemen who had whooped down Mount York. There was no knowing where he was or how much snow would fall in the high country through winter. The idea of a sweet spot suddenly seemed like foolishness. Without good forage and hunting, he would soon be forced to lower elevations and eventual confrontation with those holding prior claim. What, Cian wondered, would Father Clare have to say about arriving at a point in life where the end of that life no longer seemed so remote. In an instant a thought came to him. Father Clare would probably say, in his common-sense tone, "Pray for the ship."

The cold months of September and October brought less rain, more sun and more movement northward. Lateral travel to the east and west was required when there was no other way but to follow safe elevations along the ridges. There were plenty of valleys below, most with creeks running through them on either side of the divide, but none seemed sweet enough. To claim a place and plant seeds, then realize life would amount to little more than subsistence as a hermit, caused Cian to look once at each valley and keep moving north.

When spring arrived and Cian was still in the high country, moving north between the summits, he camped for several days on a promontory looking west. Father Clare's words about being a wanderer all his life were gaining credence. He had done everything necessary to stay alive, to look after the animals, to avoid confrontation with the Aborigines and to be on the lookout for prime land. He wondered what he was doing wrong. Was there still a hidden anger from his hell in Ireland that had not yielded to prayer and solitary travel? He traced the lines of a square in the dirt floor of his tent, made it look like a box and then thought of the Liberty Boys in the Curtlestown lane. In his mind Cian dropped them into the box. O'Hanlon, standing with his men in their tall hats in the stinking dungeon under County Dublin Gaol. Into the box. The insane and vicious inmates of that gaol. The mad vicar in the dark outside the cathedral, the cruel faces of the barristers in the hanging court. Into the box. The lifeless eyes of Megan, Holly and Breen. Into the box. A lid went over the box. Nails were hammered down and the memories were trapped inside. Cian lifted his arms quickly, as if the memories might escape back into his mind.

"God, take it," he cried out. "Take this! It belongs to you. All of it."

Suddenly the strain on his arms was gone, as if his hands were no longer holding any weight. He wondered why he had taken so long to ask. Perhaps he hadn't believed mere words had any power, or more likely that his familiarity with the discomfort had gradually shifted toward despair. But now it was over. It was done. It was, after all, more than just speaking words. It had to do with a heightened concentration on need and complete trust that his request had already been anticipated. Cian leaned back on his hands and laughed, for the first time in years.

"They're not mine!" he announced. "Not mine any more!"

But right after the relief of deliverance, when Cian went outside to stoke the fire and search Win and Bonny for ticks, he stood up straight in exasperation. Bonny was expecting. He let out a sigh and talked to her, explaining he couldn't offer a warm home or safe place for her litter. If she had her pups while they were still wandering, they would have to ride in a box on the pack horse. And that would only work while they were nursing. What would he do with a litter of young dogs in the wilderness?

About a month later, after weaving back and forth on either side of the divide, still slowly moving north, Cian began allowing Bonny to sleep inside the tent on her oilcloth. She had her litter one cold, sunny afternoon. The eight healthy, noisy pups kept Cian awake all night. It was a bittersweet event. There was an implicit trust in Bonny's eyes, but Cian had nothing to show the proud mother that they would ever be anything more than wanderers.

The next day Cian built a box of the straightest, smoothest sticks he could find and lashed it onto the back of the pack horse. The pups on their oilcloth and folded blanket put their little paws against the sticks and looked out at the world from the swaying back of a horse. Cian turned around often to keep an eye on them. He realized the situation couldn't last more than month or so before the pups would need to run every hour and the pace northward would slow even more. On the positive side, the rains were less frequent now and temperatures were warmer. Spring was arriving.

Day after day, the excited yelps of eight pups echoed back and forth between the cliffs in the high country. Cian knew it was only a matter of time before the sounds attracted dingoes. A pack of dingoes would not only kill and eat the pups but Win and Bonny as well. In a feeding frenzy they would kill and eat a man. From that point on, Cian spent more time watching Win and Bonny than the pups. Both dogs seemed to share the awareness of danger and frequently froze to listen and sniff the air.

One afternoon Cian realized the inevitable was about to happen. He tethered the horses on a lightly wooded plateau, set up the tent earlier than usual and gathered rocks and wood for a square of four campfires. Bonny and Win, he noticed, were stopping often and looking behind them, whining. Cian understood the confrontation needed to occur at a site of his choosing. The horses were moved to shorter tethers next to the tent, one on either side. The dogs were fed the last of the wrapped meat, and Bonny was put inside the tent with the pups in their basket. Win was tied to a small tree near the tent entrance. Eight rectangular flaps were cut and secured as musket ports on all four sides of the tent. Wood was stacked beside the four campfires but not lit until dusk. Both muskets and both pistols were primed. Hunting knives were stuck into the poles at each end of the tent. The pups nursed and then, against their will, were put back inside their basket.

As night fell Cian's main concern was how to deal with the attack if there were more than four dingoes, or if his shots went wide. All the stories he had heard conveyed the danger. A pack of dingoes operated with speed, cunning and shock. They were hardy, muscular terrors and known to be unintimidated by tent walls. They were shrewd and capable of coordinating an attack from several directions simultaneously. If Cian was distracted by one dingo burrowing under a staked tent wall, two more would rush Win and tear his throat out in a second.

An hour passed after dark. Cian saw several dark shapes for a split second moving around the edge of the plateau, silhouetted against the firelight. All four campfires were in need of more wood. Cian weighed the risk to himself of going out to pile more wood on each fire. It would only delay the attack, he reasoned. It would be better to let the fires die down now, while he was still alert. That meant the attack could occur at any moment, but there was no way to know how many were in the pack and from how many directions they would come. Bonny whined and looked up at Cian every few seconds. All eight pups joined in with Bonny, making it hard to hear anything but fear. Outside the tent door Win was agitated, growling and pulling hard on the rope. Cian felt his pulse pounding and listened to his own rapid breathing as he waited, watching through the musket ports for shadows moving fast toward Win.

When the attack came, Cian knew immediately by the shrill change in Win's bark. Both horses whinnied and reared next to the tent, casting shadows from the dying campfires. But using Win as bait drew two dingoes at a pounding sprint across open ground, straight toward Cian's chosen musket port. Cian's first shot sent a lead ball through the head of the lead dingo. The deafening roar and bright muzzle flash startled the second dingo, which skidded sideways, twenty feet from Win. Pulling a pistol from his belt Cian fired and saw the ball hit behind the front shoulder, knocking the dingo flat. Win shrieked at the shock of the musket and pistol flashes just feet behind him. The horses whinnied and twisted as giant shadows next to the long sides of the tent.

Just as Cian turned to check the other end of the tent, Bonny's whining turned to savage snarling as she sunk her teeth into the snout of a dingo pushing under the staked canvas door. In a second, the surging dingo had forced Bonny backward and half its brown body was inside. Cian grabbed the knife from the pole above Bonny, reached over her, ran the blade in hard between the dingo's ribs and wrenched upward toward the spine. As the dingo withdrew, howling, another dim shadow, menacing snout and two eyes appeared under the canvas wall, four feet to the right. The cunning beast had somehow gotten around the shrieking pack horse outside the tent. Cian slashed the knife through the canvas, straight into the skull, behind the brutal yellow eyes.

Outside, at the other end of the tent, Win, still tied up, was fighting to the death with a fifth dingo. Cian pulled the pistol from the left side of his belt and aimed through the musket port. In an instant the blast blew a hole through the dingo's body. Win fell flat, whining at the shock of the sound and flash above him.

Cian glanced left and right, to both ends of the tent as he grabbed the second musket. Inside the tent, the noise was unbearable as Bonny and all eight pups barked furiously. Outside, the horses bucked and snorted. Two bleeding dingoes were crawling between the campfires, one on its belly, one on its side. From the gun port it appeared there were no other shadows moving around the plateau. Cian tucked a knife into his boot, primed a pistol, put it in his belt and went outside, carrying the second musket. He counted three motionless dingoes, then followed the two trying to drag themselves away in different directions. Each snarled and reared to turn on him, but Cian kept his distance and shot them both dead.

Bonny brushed against Cian's legs and circled around him, still barking. He bent down and held her. Then he tied her up next to Win while he dragged the five carcasses to the steepest side of the small plateau and shoved them over the edge.

At the tree by the tent, Win was whining and swaying in shock, so Cian untied him, brought both dogs inside and lit a lantern. With the canvas doors secured, Cian lay back on his saddle, pulled Win and Bonny close to him and talked to them. They responded with agitated yips and barking, getting up and circling restlessly until, having had their say, over and over, they fell against him, exhausted.

In the morning Cian packed the tent and poles, knowing he needed to get the horses and dogs away from the smell of dingo. He lifted Bonny up onto the pack horse next to the pups' basket and allowed Win to ride on the lead horse, in the gap between the saddle bags behind him. By noon they had descended into a thickly wooded valley divided by a shallow creek. Cian took some of the load off the horses on the creek bank and allowed them to drink and graze while the pups played in the water.

It was important to relax, even for a hour, Cian thought, to calm the animals but also to calm the feeling in himself that he was doing nothing more than wandering. At some point, he understood, he would have to choose a land claim from the abundance he was passing through. But up there in the high country, he was too far from civilization to be able to make any living other than subsistence. It occurred to him that he was becoming, in effect, a solitary Aborigine on perpetual walkabout.

Another month of wandering passed and the days grew warmer still. As Cian anticipated, the pups could now see well into the distance and demanded more play time. Now they were larger, their yips and barks echoed against the cliffs from two crude baskets lashed to the rig on the pack horse. Northward progress had slowed and Cian had no choice but to accept it.

One morning in November he was expecting to stop for another pup-romp at the top of a high ridge, urging the lead horse up and through dense forest, when he realized it was not a ridge but a summit. From the high elevation he could see for fifty miles. A thousand feet below him, patchy clouds hung motionless in the still air over three valleys.

To the west, the peaks of many more mountains filled the horizon. To the east, there was a wide gap between neighboring summits where forested slopes faded into an indistinct blur in the distance. It was possible the coast might be less than a week's travel away in that direction. To the north, three parallel creek valleys spread out below him, separated by forested ridges. One valley gradually veered west, one to the east, but the one in the middle ran due north. It was unusual, Cian thought, to see a fair-sized creek tending due north. There were more mountains to the north, about ten miles away, so the creek had to turn either east or west. If it flowed west, perhaps to an inland sea, it might be time to take the risk and follow it to lower elevations, with caution. If it flowed east, it might join other creeks and become a river flowing to the Pacific Ocean. Such a river could enter a natural harbor, a future port. Looking down from the summit, Cian could feel decision time was upon him. He ignored the yelping pups and spurred the lead horse down into the middle valley, through eucalyptus forest opening into grassy glens along the east bank of the creek.

Cian cantered the horse to a rise on the east side of the valley, hoping it would give him a better overview. He turned the horse under tall trees, held his breath and stared in wonder. The valley appeared to be about half a mile wide, the creek meandering through the center. The grass was as thick and green as any he could remember in Ireland. Even the wooded ridges on either side of the valley were lush and verdant. From above, warm sunlight turned millions of long blades of grass into a sea of green candles. For a moment Cian considered the possibility that after seven months of wandering back and forth across the great divide he had found the sweet spot he imagined might exist somewhere in the wilderness. There were plenty of tall trees for lumber and there was plenty of water, year-round. Turning to the left and right, he could see dense thickets of trees and bushes behind him, indicating springs emerging from the slopes below the timbered ridge.

The clamor from the pups brought Cian out of what seemed like only a momentary reverie. He lifted the dogs down, unloaded the horses and tethered them in the shade. Before setting up the tent, he settled Bonny with the pups near the horses and took Win up through the grass and trees to the top of the eastern ridge.

From the ridge, looking east, Cian could see the neighboring valley was just as favorable. In an instant, he could see how he could fence the hills and slopes of both valleys with runs for a thousand sheep. Perhaps two thousand. A large house and a barn, shaded by tall trees, would fit nicely in a dell with a view of the middle valley creek. Then the reality of reconnecting with distant markets that bought wool and lamb occurred to him. He chided himself for unwarranted exuberance when there was no known route to the coast, no established port and no sheep. Other than the horses, his only real asset was an idea.

That night Cian slept in his tent on the rise and woke at dawn with the commotion of the pups wanting to go out to explore. Over breakfast he drew a plan in the dirt next to the campfire and explained it to Win. The plan was to follow the creek northward along the valley and to discover whether it turned to flow to the east or west. If to the west, he would have to admit the sweet spot would probably be found somewhere else. His purpose was to produce a surplus in an ideal location no one else had claimed and then get it safely to the east, to a harbor on the coast. He was free to do this, as Michael Dwyer had meant, for the ultimate benefit of the new country, as well as for himself.

"If the creek turns toward the east," he said to Win, pointing to the plan in the dirt, "it might join a river or become a river. And if that river is navigable, we have ourselves an easy way to the coast. Which is what we want."

Win wagged his tail and appeared pleased that this had been decided. For a moment Cian considered taking just Win and the lead horse to explore the valley but decided against it, not wanting to risk leaving Bonny and the straying pups unprotected in dingo country. Instead, he left the tent where it was, lifted the pups into their baskets on the pack horse and followed the creek north, Win and Bonny running alongside through the grass.

A couple of miles to the north the valley became much wider as the creek joined a meandering river. Then came the moment of truth. The river took a great turn to the east, and then southeast. Cian, relieved at the outcome, began to ride at a good clip along the south bank through easy country, rolling hills and open woodland. It seemed appropriate to him, relieved as he was, to sing to himself the Irish tunes that matched his mood. Neither Bonny nor Win appeared to mind.

On his left, to the north, loomed another great line of mountains. To the south, the maze of mountains he had already crossed. But to the southeast the land descended gradually into hill country and in the far distance Cian could see, through the telescope, a relatively flat sea of green that might be part of a coastal plain. Turning around now and then he kept his eye on Win and Bonny, running behind the lead horse. They would be the first to notice if dingoes were pacing them on the ridges.

The riding was so easy compared to the trackless wilderness in the mountains that Cian estimated they had traveled more than ten miles by noon. He was about to rest the dogs and tether the horses when he thought he saw a smudge of smoke rising into the air, a mile to the southeast. The view in the telescope confirmed the plume of smoke. It was coming from the direction he intended to take. If it was an Aboriginal encampment he would face a quandary. There was no way he could risk a confrontation. He would be forced back into the high country. This would amount to the same outcome as if the river had turned west toward an inland sea. The lower elevations would be easier country for kangaroos and likely well populated with Aboriginal encampments. It was possible he was trapped in the highest elevations unless he could find something to trade with them.

Cian fed the dogs and let the horses graze while he decided what to do. Looking at the plume of smoke, he lifted Bonny and Win up onto the horses and began to take a wide berth around the site of the smoke. As he approached the valley from the south, he found the source of the smoke hidden by trees. Cautiously, Cian rode closer, remaining under lower-growing trees in case the Aborigines kept watchmen along the approaches.

At last he was close enough to use the telescope to see detail. Smoke obscured a clear view until the breeze changed. It was not an encampment. The source of the smoke was a black metal pipe rising from the center of a wooden hut. Cian gasped in surprise, thinking he was the only newcomer to the mountains in more than five hundred miles. Thinking of how he, living as a hermit, would react to strangers, he rode closer, as carefully as if it was an armed encampment.

There was cover behind trees about a hundred yards uphill from the house. Cian remained mounted and called out.

"Hullo, the house! Anyone there? Anyone there?"

When there was no response, he called out again and again. Suddenly, from about fifty yards away in the trees on Cian's right a man's voice spoke out, not in anger but apparent astonishment.

"Where in the blazes did you come from?" the stocky man said, leaning on his musket.

"The high country, up there," Cian said, pointing over his shoulder, as he recovered from his surprise.

"How is that possible?" the man asked. "There's no way over the mountains."

"I came over the Blue Mountains, west of Parramatta, then north along the divide," Cian said.

"You were the first man to cross the Blue Mountains?"

"No, not the first. I was in the crowd that came over after Blaxland found a way."

"A crowd," the man said, walking closer. "Where are the rest of them?"

"They all went west. Far as I know, I would be the only one to come north. My claim is about ten miles or so upstream."

"Well, ten miles is fine. I can live with that. What do we have here?" the man asked, walking closer and looking at the pups in their baskets.

"'Tis me family, it is." Cian answered.

Cian could see the man was delighted to see the pups. His clear brown eyes widened as he greeted them, and being of medium height, had to stand on his toes to pat them in their baskets. The pups responded with tail-wagging and whimpering.

"They are little beauties," the man said, as he picked up one of the pups, which pawed at his thick black beard. "Worth their weight in pure gold, they are. Allow me to introduce myself. Tim Austin, ex-New South Wales Corps."

"Please to meet ye," Cian said, leaning over to shake Tim Austin's hand. "Cian MacGerrity, ex-County Wicklow."

"Ah, then you'd know Michael Dwyer and friends."

"Not really," Cian said, "I kept me distance from all that. Probably why I'm here. I'd be here for the New World, not the old."

"Same here. Couldn't wait to get out of the army. What a cesspool of damned politics. Mutiny against the Governor. Always surprised Bonaparte didn't clean us out. Well, water under the bridge, I suppose. Now that you and your family are here, I should offer you the palatial comfort of my lean-to. Come on inside for a mug of tea. The dogs are welcome too."

"No dogs of your own?" Cian asked as he dismounted and lifted the dogs down.

"No," Austin said. "A minor oversight on my part, having to get out of Sydney in a hurry. The ship was leaving. So, I brought a dozen sheep up here, thinking I could handle them running around on my own. Now I've got forty and I spend all my days chasing them down."

"Ye say, ye brought sheep up here. Is there a harbor, a port on the coast?"

Austin was about to answer when they were interrupted by a clamor of dozens of sheep bleating from somewhere behind the hut.

"Well, now," Austin said, motioning Cian around the hut, "your dogs have found the sheep. While the water's heating, let's see what they're made of. Are they trained?"

"They were house dogs," Cian said, following him to a sheep pen in chaos. "I'd seen a few herders at work by the roads and they taught me a few things. No one would sell me their working dogs. These two were going cheap. I took a risk."

"Aye, haven't we all," Austin said, raising his voice over the noise. "Let's let a few out of the pen and see what happens."

Austin half-opened the makeshift gate to his main pen but the sheep were spooked by the two pacing dogs and eight wildly excited pups. All forty sheep blew through the gate in a panic, pushing Austin aside. Bonny and Win went to work instinctively, one on either side of the dispersing flock, nipping at heels, wheeling back and forth, until they had the sheep milling in a tight circle within three minutes. The untrained pups had surged right into the center of the melee and were quickly tossed on their backs by sheep hoofs. Unfazed, the pups bounced up and joined their parents on the outside of the flock.

"I thought you said they weren't trained?" Austin said.

"Beginners' luck it is, be sure of that," Cian answered.

Austin laughed, applauded the dogs and strode into the center of the flock. He seized the bellwether by the wool on her neck and dragged her back toward the pen. The other sheep began to follow in ones and twos. Then Bonny and Win grasped the plan and began nipping at heels until all forty sheep rushed back into the pen. Austin lifted the gate closed and shoved a peg into the hasp.

"I think you're going to be a wealthy man," Austin said, over the noise of forty bleating sheep. "You'll do the thinking, they'll do the work. Come on in for some tea."

They left the dogs circling around the sheep pen and returned to the hut.

"Now, meself it is, that's relieved," Cian said. "I bought them on faith, thinking I'd know what to tell them to do. Seems the other way around."

"Luck of the Irish. They're keepers," Austin said. "Now, you

80

were asking about a harbor?"

"Ye follow this river and it becomes a larger river? Can ye raft wool to the coast?"

"No. This river goes over huge falls then turns north into the mountains. The way to the coast is southeast then east, beside a shorter river. There's a decent harbor a bit over a hundred miles from here. You can get sheep in and wool out, if you trade for safe passage," Austin said, offering Cian an upended log for a chair, inside his two-room hut.

"Why not claim your land by the river, near the harbor?" Cian asked.

"Well, what I meant by safe passage is, it's occupied, you see. It's thick with encampments. I came up here because the Aboriginals don't contest these parts, at least for hunting. They've passed by, probably for ceremonies, up at the bend in the river."

"They know you're here?"

"I don't bother them, they don't bother me."

"How would ye get past them if ye want to get wool down to your harbor?"

"You trade. Give them clothing and things they want, for safe passage. It's worked the few times I've needed to get through. Funny though. Some of them are always friendly. Some of them are always furious. They stand next to each other, talking about two different things, as if the other man wasn't even there. They have hierarchies and boundaries we don't begin to see," Austin said, offering Cian a mug of tea.

"I've kept me distance, so far," Cian said, accepting the steaming mug. "Would ye be going through them soon, to look for passage to buy dogs for your sheep?"

"Not possible. I couldn't leave the sheep to go to Sydney. Your pups, as I said, are worth their weight in gold. Are you interested in a trade?"

"I would be," Cian said. "What would ye have in mind?"

"One ram for one pup. How does that sound?"

"Make it two rams for one pup. Four ewes for one pup," Cian

offered.

"I could live with that," Austin said. "I could train up three or four of these little beauties in a couple of months and save my back some damage."

"So where did ye learn to work a flock?"

"England. My family, it's said, have been sheep herders since Roman times. So the story goes. Northwest England, Cumberland County, near Rosthwaite. I was the youngest son of four, so off to the army I went. Second lieutenant was as far as I got and that was about all I could stand."

"How did you find this place?"

"I have land near Sydney Cove. I sold some of it to someone who wanted to build houses. Bought a small cutter and explored the coast. I liked the look of the harbor and these hills. Some of the Aborigines didn't like me so I traded my life for rope and buckets and pushed on up here. This land is what I wanted. On the way back I traded shirts and hats for safety and went back to Sydney. I sold the cutter and bought passage here with sheep aboard. The Aborigines remembered me at the harbor. Same plan."

"How far north of Sydney are we?" Cian asked.

"We're about three hundred miles north, as the crow flies."

"What would your brothers say if they could see what you've got here?"

"'We'll have some of that,' is what they'd say. They'd be over here in a flash if they knew. You can't do much with forty acres in Rosthwaite. What about you and Wicklow?"

"I have no family there now," Cian answered. "But I'm thinking me father would say, 'Make your claim.' So how is it you do that, when the government has no idea this place exists?"

"I've thought about claiming in Sydney," Austin said. "Been here two years and it's still an experiment. The stakes are out with my name on them. But with three or four of your pups I can expand the sheep runs I've got by a factor of five, maybe more. When I claim in Sydney, it'll be for all the land I can work. If I claim before then, everyone will know and I'll have a crowd arriving, disputing the watershed."

"How would a crowd go over with your friends around the harbor?"

"Bloodshed, probably. Sooner or later, someone would be an idiot. God help us."

The conversation with Tim Austin continued over mutton chops char-grilled on an open fire out in the sun. Cian found the man friendly and generous, unlike most of the aloof New South Wales Corps officers he'd observed on the roads and watch-posts around Parramatta. The pups banged around their legs, exploring every nook and cranny of the hut and yard and then ran back to the pen to growl at the sheep. Austin asked for two of the male pups and two females, in return for two rams and twelve ewes. All twelve would lamb soon. Cian agreed and began thinking of what it would take to cut timber and trim lumber for his first sheep runs in the middle valley.

Late in the afternoon, after the trade of pups for sheep, Cian was about to shake hands and leave when a thought came to mind concerning Father Clare.

"How often does a ship come to the harbor down there?" he asked Austin.

"Hardly ever. Only by arrangement. I ordered wagon parts and a few other things four months ago," Austin replied, reaching for a stack of papers. "I asked for a set date, arriving in the harbor just two weeks from now, if I've got my calendar right. It's a risk for me if they miss that date."

"I understand why," Cian said. "If ye do go to the harbor then, in two weeks, I'd be much obliged if ye'd ask the skipper to carry a letter to Parramatta for me."

"I can do that for a neighbor," Austin said. "Would you be willing to check on the sheep every couple of days?"

"I can do that, for sure."

Cian sat on a stump and wrote on paper supplied by Tim Austin, briefly describing his situation to Father Clare, mentioning the distance of the unnamed harbor from Sydney, Austin's hut and a diagram showing the route upstream to the middle valley claim. It felt out of place to Cian to describe to the priest his claim in remote wilderness, given Father Clare's apparent acquaintance with the Governor in Parramatta, the Sea Lords in London, Bonaparte's subjugation of Europe and the potential threat of the French navy to England and Ireland, as well as to New South Wales. "Find a way" had been Father Clare's final admonishment, and so Cian sealed the letter and handed it and the four pups to Tim Austin.

Cian followed the rolling hills in sight of the river, hoping to arrive in the middle valley before dusk. Win and Bonny worked each side of the flock while the four remaining pups looked on from their baskets. But by the time the flock reached the big turn in the river, darkness had fallen and the sheep refused to move any further. Cian fed the dogs where they lay next to the sheep, tethered the horses and hung two paraffin lanterns on tree branches nearby. It was a clear night, so he laid back on his saddle, pulled a blanket over him and fell asleep under the stars.

The pups woke him before dawn. All four of them had taken to harassing the sheep. Cian called them to follow him to wash by the river bank. As the pups splashed in the shallows, Cian glanced up at the dawn while he dried himself and marveled at the sense of peace in the air. In County Wicklow he had never known such a feeling could exist. The sun came up as he loaded the horses, and then he set Bonny and Win to work moving the sheep. By mid-morning he found the tributary creek and followed the valley to his claim. The tent was intact, the sky a spectacular blue and his freedom felt as if it was finally beginning.

His first task was to build a movable holding pen for the sheep, a jackleg fence of split logs. Eucalyptus trees of the right girth grew abundantly within easy hauling distance. Between hunting, cooking, checking the dogs and horses for ticks and other chores, it took Cian five long, hot summer days to finish the pen. When the last section went in and the sheep were finally grazing inside, he took Bonny, Win and the pups up to the top of the ridge and looked down on the beginnings of his claim. From his vantage point on the ridge, overlooking the middle and east valleys, Cian began drawing lines in the dirt, indicating the scope of the permanent sheep runs he intended to build.

The concept took advantage of all available water sources and allowed for a rotation of fallow runs. A gated weir and channel would divert creek water from upstream through the lower fields for crops and sheep troughs. On the slopes, springs would flow to sheep troughs for separate runs under the trees on higher ground. There was even a natural basin on sloping ground that if deepened would make a fine spring-fed pool for bathing. Not far from the pool, gently sloping land lent itself to a homesite, backed by tall eucalypts below the ridge.

For the next year Cian worked to make the plan a reality. Prospects for the flock improved and the pups matured out of their harassment stage to capably imitate their parents. Cian visited Tim Austin now and then for company and helped him assemble a wool wagon from boxes of parts. He leveled ground on the home-site and the tent became covered storage after Cian built his own basic two-room, wood-slab hut. The pool not only became a reality but a place of relaxation, lined with slabs of local slate. Stacked slate also worked well for the chimney he added to the hut, in anticipation of colder weather.

When winter came and snow covered the ground, Cian's pace of logging and trimming slowed, but he still made progress on the fences. Spring brought more lambs, and with the use of woolshears borrowed from Tim Austin, Cian tied his first wool bales. A patch of land near the pool now yielded potatoes, green onions and carrots from seeds he'd brought with him in the saddle bags. The dogs proved quick to alert Cian whenever dingoes came into the valley. He kept both muskets primed and handy and killed four dingoes during the second lambing season. Wallabies and kangaroos occasionally came close, but for the most part Cian had to follow the ridges to hunt them.

By the next summer, Cian was planning to look after Tim Austin's flock while Tim took passage to Sydney to sell property against debts and then bring back a boatload of sheep. During the passing of a year, Cian had not seen any Aborigines, either hunting or gathering for ceremonies near his claim, though Tim reported several groups had come up from the falls to the big bend in the river.

Around Christmas, in the hottest part of summer, Cian was taking a morning off from logging, submerged in the pool, his back against smooth slate, when he heard Bonny barking, far off in the distance. A moment later he heard Win and then the younger dogs. He got out of the pool, pushed wet hair away from his eyes, and ran back to the hut. He reached for the telescope hanging on the inside of the back door where he racked the muskets. Two riders were about a half mile away, both trailing pack horses. Neither looked like his neighbor. Unlike prospective squatters, who would be looking around, they were coming on with purpose, as if on Crown business, the business of Tim Austin's creditors, or the associates of Michael Dwyer. Whoever they were, they were approaching in a manner suggesting some kind of an inquiry.

For a moment Cian recalled a memory of approaching figures on a lane in Curtlestown and made himself dismiss it. He pulled on work pants, struggled into a shirt and began priming both pistols. The telescope showed both riders much closer, following the creek bank, looking up under dark, broad-brimmed hats toward the hut. Strangely, the dogs' barking had diminished, as if intimidated. Cian stayed low, moving behind shade trees to a position to one side of the hut. The riders dismounted, talked quietly for a moment and began walking uphill, side by side. Cian shoved one pistol into the back of his pants and held the other up as he waited behind a tree. The two dusty riders stopped about a hundred yards short of the hut and one of them cupped his hands.

"Hullo, the house!"

"Let me see your hands!" Cian called back. "Both of you! State your purpose!"

For a moment there was silence, then laughter. Cian gripped the pistol in his right hand and took aim at the taller figure.

"Cian MacGerrity!" the taller rider called out. "Our purpose, me boy, is to come across a little hospitality in these parts!"

It was Father Clare himself, up in the high country, a long way from the center of the world. Cian grinned, put the second pistol in the back of his pants and rushed barefoot to welcome him. The younger dogs swirled around his legs, giddy with the excitement of greeting new visitors.

It was Cian's intent to give the priest a great hug and to celebrate the surprise with his own laughter, but something happened as he reached his old friend. Cian's glance caught the eye of the second rider. He looked again, and again under the dusty brim. Her eyes and her unspoken greeting conveyed a feeling of recognition. Instantly he perceived she was genuinely glad to meet him. In the same moment, kindness and intellect radiated through her eyes as she smiled. Unembarrassed by his half-dressed appearance, she was perhaps ten years younger than him, strong and guileless, every bit his equal. It took another second to appreciate that she had ridden over a hundred miles from the coast, was broad of shoulder and very sweet. Cian's mouth must have been open in astonishment, because from somewhere outside his attention on her eyes, he heard laughter again and felt Father Clare's arm on his shoulder.

"Cian, happy I am to see you too," Father Clare said, still laughing as he hugged Cian. "This is Oriana Nolan, recently from County Cork."

"Oriana," Cian responded, holding the young woman's gaze as she threw off a worn rider's glove and offered her hand. "Pleased to have company."

"Pleased to meet ye, at last," she said, bowing her head slightly. "I feel as if I'd known ye for a year now. Father Clare, ye know."

Cian found it hard to imagine that anyone had thought anything about him in more than a year. Other than Tim Austin, he had spoken to no one and was growing comfortable with the idea of never having company. Now, he felt as if he, in wet, unbuttoned work clothes, was greeting visiting nobility. Her hand was vital, warm, a transmitter of subtle lightning.

"Ye don't say, Father," Cian said, and turning to Father Clare, "Ye've come from Cork? Here?"

"Ye managed it yourself. A stop in Sydney Cove and a visit to the new priest at the chapel ye built in Parramatta. Ye've come a long way, me boy. Glad to see all this, I am. And glad to see ye, indeed."

Cian felt so self-conscious under Oriana's attention, he reached for their horses' reins and began to lead the four horses to drink at the little stream that trickled downhill from the spring-fed pool. He looked back and smiled in gratitude at Father Clare.

"'Find a way,' ye said. I never expected it'd be yourself that found the way to me."

"Always the plan. Now, me boy, having found the way to this fair place, why not play the gracious host, enough to show us what it is ye've done?"

Cian left the horses at the stream, took them to the hut and opened the back door.

"I'd offer ye a grand room," Cian said, turning to Oriana, "after coming all this way. But 'tis still in the back of me mind and not yet built."

"'Tis grand enough it is, what ye've done with wilderness in a year," she said. "I can think of a few landowners in Cork who've done nothing with their land in five generations."

"Peace it is ye have here," Father Clare added. "The finest salons in London, Vienna and Berlin I've dined in, with their grandees, yet I felt no such peace as there is in this valley."

"Then come this way," Cian said, guiding them outside to the slate-lined pool near the hut.

Oriana laughed in amazement, set her hat aside and bent down to wash the dust off her face. Then Cian took them up to the ridge separating the middle and eastern valleys. Father Clare commented on the water sources, the sheep runs and shade trees as well as plans for expansion of the flock. He asked Cian about when he would file his claim in Sydney. As he answered each of

Father Clare's questions, Cian noticed Oriana's attention was still on him. She seemed to take in every word, looked around thoughtfully and then came back to his eyes.

At midday, Cian char-grilled wallaby steaks, threw in sautéed onions, boiled potatoes and carrots, and they dined in the sun, sitting on log rounds at a tree-stump table. Father Clare invited Cian into the storage tent after lunch and showed him the ammunition, medicine, books, tools and a variety of grain, fruit and vegetable seeds he had brought as gifts. Oriana listened as Cian pointed out terraces on the slope below the hut where fruit trees would thrive.

"Would ye gentlemen mind very much," Oriana said, standing between them on the future apple tree terraces, "if I took to the spa pool in this heat? A long ride 'tis been from the harbor and from Sydney."

Cian took Father Clare back up to the ridge and found it difficult to hide his sudden feelings about Oriana. She had arrived mere hours before, yet it seemed he'd known her intimately for many years. The discrepancy puzzled him and stirred a sense of urgency in Cian to find out why. At this point Oriana and Father Clare were visitors who could leave at any time, without resolving the puzzle of how he seemed to recognize her.

"The ship ye came in, to the harbor," Cian said, as they stood under a shade tree on the ridge, "when does it come back for ye?"

"We met your friend Mr. Austin outgoing as we came in," Father Clare replied. "By some special arrangement with the captain, a retainer fee, your friend said he'd be back in two weeks. He said ye were taking care of his flock and his dogs."

"I am. So ye leave in two weeks?"

"I do. Events there are in London and Dublin I'd best attend to. What is it you're not saying?"

"Would Oriana be returning to Cork with ye?"

"I'd have no way of knowing that, me boy. She's a young lady with her own free will."

"So," Cian began, "what does that mean?"

"It means 'tis no business of mine. But there is that which I can offer to ye. It has to do with your claim. The days are coming when ye'll have a thousand sheep and more here. Ye'll have apples and pears on these slopes. Wagons would take your wool and fruit and potatoes to the harbor. Peace and prosperity will become ye. And then what?"

"And then what? Isn't that enough for a man?"

"For some it would be, 'tis true. But not yourself. A new frontier there is, asking for ye in the years ahead."

"This is the frontier here," Cian said, confused. "Ye mean further west, or north?"

"'Tis hospitality I'd mean, anticipating the hopes of those who may come to these hills, needing the care of the Lord. A greater need there is now in old Ireland and not-so-merry England for the prosperity and comfort ye'll find here."

"Father, ye ask me, of all people, to anticipate for Ireland and England? I'd have me hands full enough to stay alive meself here. How say ye this, about hospitality?"

"Oh, ye may not be here by yourself. There comes a time when a man produces a surplus of goods, by the grace of the Lord, and a time when a man produces a surplus of goodwill, also the Lord's. Both gifts may be yours."

"Maybe. If I live long enough up here."

"The Lord will show ye the need when the time comes."

Cian looked down on the sheep grazing inside the long jack-leg run extending into the eastern valley. He was still confused.

"A farmer, I am. Up in the middle of nowhere. There be plenty of places for the Irish and the English to go. Why would they come here and need anything from me?"

"Middle of nowhere? Where you are, there the Lord is, though he keep a small distance when ye don't wash."

"But what would I have here to give to yon Irish and English?"

"The Lord has free will, as ye do, me boy. Such things will be shown to ye when he chooses. This I say to ye now. Be prepared."

"And ye say I wouldn't be alone?"

"I make no such assumptions. Entirely a matter of free will, for

90

all concerned."

"So ye speak of the future, that I be prepared for I know not what?"

"I speak, that ye welcome your soul's way home. Look at us now in these frail bodies. What then, when they no longer stand?"

The conversation sobered Cian and he sat in silence against a large tree trunk, next to Father Clare. Cian understood himself to be nothing more than a tenant farmer, with a little experience as a road planner and the great good fortune to be the first squatter in the middle valley. All of his good fortune could disappear if just one representative of the Crown found fault with him. Now Father Clare was telling him to see beyond his greatest dream of prosperity and peace to something unimaginable.

A few minutes later Father Clare suggested they stroll back down from the ridge, to brew a sample of Irish tea he'd brought with him, along with some honey from the beekeepers in the Hawkesbury Valley. Cian was still absorbed in his thoughts when they arrived at the hut. Oriana opened the wooden-slab door. He stood still and stared. Her dusty hat and riding gloves were gone. Her golden hair was brushed back and her blouse and work pants looked as if they were new. She tilted her head slightly and smiled, as if to say, "What are you looking at? It's me." Cian understood at that moment that Oriana had already made up her mind about Cork.

For the next ten nights, Cian slept on one side of the storage tent and Father Clare on the other. Oriana slept in the hut and tidied and reorganized the two rooms in a way that made the interior seem to double in size. Every day brought a new surprise concerning Oriana's expansive nature. She could split fence rails and set jackleg fencing, cook aromatic stews with herbs from the saddle bags she'd brought with her, and toss her long golden hair out of her eyes in a way that made Cian turn and stare in wonder. It felt more than wonderful to Cian that he was no longer bound solely to the dour disciplines of wilderness survival. Oriana caused a surge of excitement and more changes in him than he could understand. Instead of having to cope with heat, cold, thirst, hunger, shortage, fear and danger, Cian felt an unexplainable certainty, exuberance and joy the closer he came to her.

One day, when Cian was riding with Father Clare in the eastern valley, they stopped to let the horses drink from the creek.

"Me boy," Father Clare said, "I'd be speaking a week or so back about free will. A ship there is, coming to the harbor, bearing your friend Mr. Austin and more sheep. 'Tis a choice I'd make to be on that ship, to be about our Father's business in Parramatta and in Europe. Now, there be a choice ye have to make, afore me time comes to leave for the harbor."

Cian knew exactly what Father Clare meant. Both the priest and Oriana were waiting on his decision.

"Me mind understands the matter and the time," Cian replied, "but gives me no words that speak to it. 'Tis a thing higher than me words."

"'Tis a road ye plan. Your life. Who must know what it is ye want?"

Cian took a deep breath and looked into his old friend's eyes for strength.

"Would ye wait on the ridge for me, till ye see a sign?"

Cian rode back to the middle valley, tethered his horse and walked to the hut. When he opened the back door Oriana looked up from her work and held his look, as if she already knew.

Cian and Oriana MacGerrity were married in the sight of the Lord that day, next to the spring-fed pool. Father Clare left the next morning with just one horse, surrounded by a swirl of excited sheepdogs, until he passed out of sight among the hills. Neither Cian nor Oriana saw him again in that life.

Cian built a profitable business in the years that followed, exporting wool and fruit, continuing to grow according to a plan that in time ceased to be a frontier. The new frontier he gradually came to realize as infinite began to expand at home. Oriana's strengths included the ability to anticipate both his strengths and vulnerabilities in every endeavor they took on. Their intuitive cooperation made their successes seem natural. It was also natural for them to not only greet newcomers to the high country but to assist with material shortcomings, medical emergencies and pooled transportation to and from the harbor.

It was no wonder that the names Cian and Oriana MacGerrity became known for hospitality and encouragement by example, beyond their valley, even to folks who settled in lower elevations nearer the harbor. But, by mysterious means, their names also served to personify the New World at that time, becoming emblems of inspiration to tenant farmers and indentured servants in the Old World. Survival against want and tyranny held the attention of most until someone would strike up a story that began, "This was the time after the rebellion had failed . . ."

EPILOGUE

Father Samuel Clare returned in London in May 1815, shortly before Napoleon Bonaparte's final defeat at Waterloo, Belgium. Father Clare anticipated the economic downturn and increase in unemployment in England and Ireland after the end of the Napoleonic Wars. Representing no faction, he used the diplomacy of enlightened self-interest to encourage Parliamentary Select Committees, government bureaucrats and business leaders in London to invest in shipping, lumber mills, housing, harbor infrastructure and skilled labor for new businesses in New South Wales. Also anticipating legal conflict between the increasing numbers of wealthy landowners, emancipists and Governor Lachlan Macquarie's eventual successor, Father Clare moved discreetly in the halls of influence in London under various personas. He quietly encouraged the concept in Whitehall that representative self-government by an elected legislature in Sydney would enable just taxation, preempt insurrection and serve in the interests of prosperity for all. This was partially accomplished in Sydney when the first elected Legislative Council formed to advise the new Governor in

1824. After that date no records exist of Father Samuel Clare.

In December 1812, Joseph Holt sold his land near Sydney and left with most of his family to return to Ireland. His ship was wrecked on an Atlantic reef but the survivors managed to reach the Falkland Islands. Holt and others were stranded there for many months, reaching England in February 1814, via the United States. Joseph Holt then retired to Ireland but regretted leaving Australia. He died near Dublin in May 1826.

About the time Cian MacGerrity crossed the Blue Mountains in May 1813, Michael Dwyer was appointed Chief of Police for the town of Liverpool, southwest of Sydney. He served as Chief of Police from 1813 to 1820, during which time he owned The Harrow Inn and increased his holdings to 620 acres. In 1820, Dwyer was fired for alleged drunkenness and misplacement of documents. A lawsuit over land acquisition bankrupted him in 1822. He served a short time in debtors' prison, contracted dysentery and died in Liverpool in 1825. Michael Dwyer retains the status of a folk hero in Irish-Australian culture for his sustained stand against tyranny in the Wicklow Mountains, south of Dublin.

In September 1818, just after the birth of Cian and Oriana's second boy, Joshua, Governor Macquarie's Surveyor-General John Oxley passed a few miles to the north of the middle valley, unaware of the presence of the earliest unrecorded squatters. He did not see Tim Austin's hut or sheep a mile away in the hills. Tim Austin was in Sydney at the time, where he married, returning soon after with his bride. The river passing near Austin's claim was later named the Apsley River. A fine upland town named Walcha *(Wolka)*, once known as Irishtown, still thrives on rich, fertile land just west of the big bend in the Apsley River. The surrounding region has long been considered to possess some of the most spectacular and beautiful scenery in Australia. The unnamed harbor, 120 miles to the east, was named Port Macquarie by John Oxley. The trail east, from the high country down to Port Macquarie, became known as "The Wool Road" and later as the Oxley Highway.

Cian and Oriana had four sons and two daughters in their

ever-expanding home. Their numerous descendants live in every state in Australia. They prospered in the middle valley, becoming icons of decency to many in the upland area and exemplary names to the poor in Ireland. Their bodies died within a year of each other, in 1852 and 1853 respectively.

The soul of Cian MacGerrity returned to physical embodiment in 1920, born in rural Queensland. Prior to that birth, from a vantage of objectivity, his soul was shown the early warning signs presaging a foreign invasion of Australia, in what would become known as World War II. To thwart the tyranny the possible invasion would bring, he volunteered for the army in 1940 and served in North Africa and New Guinea, where he was severely wounded in jungle combat in 1943. He saw his country saved but never recovered from his wounds. His body died from complications after multiple surgeries in 1945.

More recently, the souls of both Cian and Oriana returned again to this lower world, to carefully chosen families and having no outer memory of each other. Tutored by angels and a saint they referred to as Father Clare, they had agreed in one of the universities of the spirit, one of the levels of heaven, on a way to recognize each other in this world of action and consequence. They are now both twenty-one and living in different cities in Australia, still in the care of the Lord, quietly anticipating something they can't describe.

THE CRASH

One abrasive Berkeley lawyer, one demanding
smartphone and a dangerous way of driving
meet the very long view of life.

THE CRASH

The art of driving while busy is not dangerous for those who practice the fluid motions of a tennis spectator—central vision to the left, peripheral vision on the mirror, central vision on the phone screen, peripheral straight ahead, central vision to the right. Christie Lemaire had exceptional vision skills and hand-eye coordination. She had practiced her art in and around Berkeley for decades and counted drive time as billable time, because she was working. Her consulting law firm in Berkeley filled a niche in national politics, supporting a woman's right to choose, advising wealthy Party donors, and predicting probable outcomes of legal challenges to the cause.

The problem facing the cause did not come from Christie, her firm or even the people of California, but from other parts of the country. There the popularity of the cause was no longer certain, even among young women. The meeting in Sacramento in just over an hour and a half would be about money. The action item would assess the right amount of money needed to produce the most persuasive message in the social media favored by young women.

The Party had recently agreed to make available the largest national database of this demographic group ever compiled. Years of recruiting effort had ensured that even young women who were in the United States illegally could participate. The majority of young women in targeted counties would agree with the message and assert their right to choose by selecting given options on their phone in their preferred language. Results would be measurable within minutes and independently verified within hours. National media would report the results, donors would be vindicated and certain candidates for public office would be inspired by a rolling series of such polls. This was Christie's cause, the farsighted work of committed experts, independent of the Party, well ahead of the election.

For Christie, arriving for a meeting such as the event in Sacramento, well ahead of all other consultants, was standard procedure. Traffic, she observed, was not bad westbound on University Avenue. Merging onto the I-80 by 11:15 a.m. would get her into a parking station near the State Capitol with plenty of time before anyone else arrived. Anticipating the northbound ramp ahead she turned the radar detector on.

The phone screen reconfirmed there were no scheduling conflicts. All calls were routed to voicemail and there were no new emails. Monday through Sunday Christie's phone held the key to her sixteen-hour days. She was her own chief-of-staff and knew the sequence and priority setting of every task, every hour and every billing code. When things had to change, a few touches on the screen rearranged priorities. Bickering and disputes with other highly credentialed egos in Sacramento would not be so easily controlled, she mused. *Some people need a little help to change their priorities.*

There would be plenty of time for that, Christie thought. Traffic was flowing easily, well above the speed limit coming down from the hills. All of the lights had been green since she left her office and the day was moving along. A quick flip of the visor against sun glare and Christie continued her practiced sequence of central and peripheral vision, alternating between the phone screen and traffic, until it occurred to her something was not quite right. Inside the span of a second her peripheral vision noticed that the traffic lights facing her at the intersection of University and San Pablo were red, which was strange because, as always, she only went through intersections on green.

100

Her central vision, now straight ahead, noticed an unusual absence of traffic in front of her. Her peripheral vision to the right noticed in slow motion the black grille of a truck with a white hood listing a company name, *Grenenger,* above the capitalized word, *ASPHALT.* Disbelief slowed time to a crawl as her mind processed the impossibility of seeing that black grille shatter the passenger-side glass and project the door and roof lining toward her eyes in an unstoppable crescendo of twisting metal pieces, screaming and bending against each other. Simultaneously her stomach seemed to leave its place in her abdomen and bulge toward her throat. Her small SUV, originally westbound, flipped sideways onto its roof so rapidly it became airborne, then southbound. The roof bounced on the surface of the intersection and then the rear was struck by the grille of the panic-braking truck. The second impact propelled Christie's SUV into the air, above the intersection, until it bent around a steel streetlight outside a music store in an explosive cloud of glass, metal and plastic shrapnel.

In the pall of smoke and shrill hissing of ruptured hoses Christie had no chance of seeing the out-of-control truck, a half-second behind her. Its tires were locked up in a cloud of white smoke, sliding sideways into the curb. Seams and vents in the asphalt tank ruptured and cracked open as the heavy weight shifted on the chassis. Then the truck's rear tires hit both the curb and the SUV, ejecting a fountain of asphalt in all directions.

Christie's phone was forgotten in the noise and chaos. She heard herself scream as the truck hit the SUV for the third time. As she tried to move her head, she heard groaning, over and over. Her body was bent sideways against the pushed-in passenger door and her head was compressed under the crushed roof. The car was pinned tight between the streetlight and the truck, which was now leaking hot, black, flammable fluid onto the street.

There was no movement in Christie's arms or legs and the shocking, pulsing pain in her neck and back began to phase into nausea and numbness. The deafening ringing in her ears gave way to silence. Her vision was beginning to fade as she thought she saw faces looking in, pointing and shouting through the steam, smoke and dust.

Oh, God, what are they saying? Don't stare at me, speak to me! Why are you backing away? No, can't you see, I'm not alright, you goddamn idiots! Get me out of here! For God's sake do something, fast! Where the hell are you going? Oh, God, help me, help me!

Their idiotic pointing and ridiculous unwillingness to look her in the eye reminded her for just an instant of the kind of summer intern she hated taking on as a favor to someone important. But the impulse of disgust faded as the effects of shock, the immobility of her body and the unending silence forced her to confront a frightening awareness. The sickening sense of dread now caught her whole attention, swelling in importance, addressing her with an immediacy and the severity of an awful, wordless knowing that for her the cause was ending.

Immobilized, staring straight up through a smashed passenger window into the glare of the sun, she saw only blinding white light. The light increased around her, shimmering beneath her and on all sides, quiet, irresistible, calming. Wide bright rings of moving light formed within great descending curtains of an aurora borealis. Her attention became fixed on a dazzling ovoid of white, gleaming with shining mother-of-pearl radiance in the center of a great sphere of light. Out of the silent descending shafts of light came the softest sounds of a pure, familiar music. Comforting voices in the thousands, quietened gradually as the face of a serene lady of immaculate purity appeared within the mother-of-pearl light. Christie felt a sudden leap of joy at the inexplicably familiar figure, who now regarded her as if they were old friends. But along with the recognition came a prompting, to wait in silence until addressed by this majestic being. Surely there would be an explanation from the lady in white as to why she would choose this time to appear once again.

Time seemed to stop. Soft light blazed from the calm lady's blue eyes and the tone of her voice was kind.

"Dear one," the lady said, extending her hand. "My daughter, come closer and be not afraid, for we have counseled together on other occasions when life and opportunity were being weighed."

"Weighed?" Christie whispered, wondering at the gravity of the angel's expression when everything around her was so beautiful.

"Indeed. Such is the condition again in your world. Your choice between life and death becomes more difficult now because of your condition. I refer to your hardness of heart. You have matured in that hardness since we last spoke. You are no longer the shorn lamb for whom God would temper the wind."

"I remember you," Christie said. "You're the angel, I remember."

"And I remember you, in both joy and in tears, my dear daughter. I set aside both now as you have come to a point of decision. I may no longer look away from the hardness and ignorance you have claimed. I am here as your starry mother to show you your choices. Great is the consequence of your decision."

"My decision?" Christie asked.

"Look at your hands, your body."

Christie glanced at her hands and saw they were formed of white fire. She turned left and right and realized she was no longer in her physical body. Instead, she was inside an ovoid sphere of white light. She began to guess the answer to her question even as she asked it.

"Why am I here?"

"The Earth must move on," the angel answered. "The standard has been raised. This world has known you, my daughter, over the aeons by many names. You are known in this life as Christie Lauren Lemaire."

"Yes."

"And for what are you known?"

Christie hesitated to respond. The kind lady's tone suggested some kind of warning, yet Christie had done nothing wrong to warrant it. In how many decades of driving had she missed a light? One mistake.

"I made a mistake," Christie admitted.

"The outcome of which has not yet been decided," the angel

said. "In your world firemen will arrive to cut you free and be unaware of the extent of danger beneath the vehicles. Your life and perhaps theirs hangs on your understanding of the mistake and your decision to correct it."

Christie pondered how missing a light could be of so much concern.

"How could it be so awful, other people in danger, because of a small mistake?"

"The mistake I refer to is not so small. I am sent to you because you see it not and you are indeed at the crossroads of life and a form of death you do not understand."

"My mistake . . . not so small?" Christie asked, not understanding. "Why were you sent to me?"

"I am an angel of hope, sent by Gabriel, archangel of the resurrection and the ascension. I bring hope. I bring counsel to you, which your human mind and emotions cannot withstand, for they are of the world. I speak to you in the objectivity of your soul, in an interval outside time and space and I bring hope.

"Will I die, because of this mistake?"

"You have free will. You must choose."

The angel extended both hands to Christie, perhaps to ease the gravity of the choice she was referring to. The touch of her warm palms and gentle fingers was comforting.

"Walk with me," the angel said.

The timeless interval had no horizon or physical point of reference and the shimmering aurora around them held no interest for Christie. Nor was her soul's focus on the deteriorating condition of her body inside a burning car in Berkeley, but on the holy face and mysterious meaning of the angel's words. Understanding the gravity of her mistake and the so-far undefined choice, related to life and death, was now paramount to Christie.

"What have I done?"

"I speak, not to condemn, but to comfort and console."

"Have I hurt anyone?"

"By worldly reputation," the angel began, "in the subjectivity of the personality by which you are known, you are considered something of a tyrant, a 'Berkeley Amazon,' to quote a pundit of your time."

"I've heard that," Christie said. "A reputation helps move things along. People get out of my way. I get things done fast."

The angel held her eyes on Christie, unmoved.

"That personality is in a perpetual defensive posture, unwilling to consider choices presented by others. It perceives no merit in others' opinions at any time. God sees cause and effect and merit over many lifetimes. You, in your objectivity, have the ability when prompted, to bypass the abrasiveness of your personality. As a soul you have an intuition of your original purity. That is why I address you in your objectivity, somewhat separated in this interval from the defensive ego below."

It seemed to Christie there was nothing wrong with being defensive about serving the cause effectively.

"I always need to move people to act," she shrugged. "They wait too long."

"I offer perspective," the angel said. "I offer the long view of your journey toward God. From this may come understanding and definition of the mistake. From this you may decide if you have hurt anyone."

The angel raised her hand and a thick book appeared in front of them, the pages turning by themselves, not to text but to a total immersion, three-dimensional movie screen.

"This is your Book of Life," the angel said. "It is God's memory of your every action, word, emotion and thought since God created you both, perfect in his image and likeness."

"Both?"

"Both," the angel confirmed. "God uses the polarity of male and female for expression. Each complements and reinforces the other. Form in the lower world appears in flesh and blood. At its highest point of origin, form is a nonphysical, magnetic flame. Love is magnetic between the twin halves, male, female. Love for God's creativity and love for each other."

"I don't have any . . ."

"You do have an 'other.' You were at your origin, twin flames, alpha, omega, perfect inside a divine ovoid. Then the descent into the lower, denser worlds and separation. This is him, at a point in time and space lost to your historians."

The angel pointed to a page in the Book, looking through a courtyard window onto an actual memory, complete with private thoughts and emotions. The effect of instant recognition was startling to Christie. Even more surprising was the unexpected rush of love, overridden by something between mild dislike and the urge to criticize.

"Yes, it's him," Christie said, surprised at her instant recognition. "It is him! I know, he's a priest. He's not supposed to talk to me. For him, it's forbidden."

"This is you," the angel said, pointing at the Book. "This is you looking at him through an open, upstairs window. This is how you felt."

The feeling in her chest felt like a sudden punch to Christie, an agony and an ecstasy combined.

"He won't talk to me," Christie said, looking down at the departing priest.

"He will."

"Where are we? I know this place."

"This courtyard," the angel began, "was in a temple complex in the city of Caiphul, the spiritual and administrative capital of Atlantis, east of what is currently known as the Bahamas. This moment occurred over 35,000 years ago."

"How was this recorded?" Christie asked. "How can it be replayed from so far back?"

"You remember this because your soul retains such memories within an inner, etheric library, not ordained by God for the waking mind. These memories would prove difficult if borne by your conscious awareness. The function of that awareness is to concentrate on the given task, each moment in the life at hand. Your soul's function is to concentrate on the blueprint of the divine plan you have abandoned."

"It's fascinating to see him," Christie said, still looking at the distant priest, "but he left without even acknowledging I was there. He didn't even look back. It was deliberate. He knew I was watching."

"You will not always be so separated, nor so dense in form," the angel replied. "This is the beginning of perspective."

The angel moved her hand over the Book. Christie adjusted her attention to a new view of the temple complex, to a set of terraces beyond the courtyard. Here, the angel presented the strangely familiar figure of the emperor and high priest.

"The Rai!" Christie said, moving closer to the book. "That's the Rai. I feel like I know him too, but how?"

"Yes, you know him. You have known him in many lives and yet you have not known him."

Christie heard the words but didn't understand the angel's meaning.

"He reminds me of Jesus," she said, then paused. "Why?"

Looking at the face of the ruler, she wondered how she felt so sure of Jesus' appearance. In her outer personality she was a militant skeptic of any opinion not proven by documentary evidence.

"The waves in his hair and his calm face and the way he's standing," Christie continued. "I just know. But here he's the Rai. And later, much later, he's an ordinary carpenter. Thirty-three thousand years later. How can that be?"

"May I speak of perspective?"

"Yes, please," Christie said, turning to the angel. "Tell me."

"Your historians rely on documented evidence, limited as it is. They do not seek access to the memory of God. Even if granted they could not provide evidence acceptable to their peers. They must wait. This perspective across the arc of time is expressly for you, as a soul of light."

"I understand," Christie said, turning to watch the Rai on the terrace.

"Do you?" the angel asked. "Do you understand the aeons of

time in which you have been tested? Are you aware of the results of your tests to this point? It is important you grasp the broad perspective of your Book of Life."

The angel passed her hand over the page and the scene changed again, to a mob riot in the streets of Caiphul.

"In the days before the Flood," the angel said, "before established history, the human lifespan was far longer. In this lifetime, four hundred and fifty years after the abundant living you saw around the temple in Caiphul, a revolt was instigated against this same Rai by his chief counselor, an agent of the Wicked One. You lived to witness it."

"They can't go into the temple," Christie said in alarm, watching the street scene unfold into an assault on the temple and an ultimatum for the Rai to step down. "How could this happen? The Rai could have turned them back."

"It was allowed as a test of the free will of the people, to offer proof they were able to discern the difference between right and wrong. Eighty percent of the people in a nation of ten million failed the test. Eight million sided with the chief counselor, who claimed the government was not supporting the people with sufficient subsidies. God supported them abundantly, yet eighty percent of the nation fell for the victim perspective of the sons of darkness."

Again the angel advanced the flow of time and space to another page and looked at Christie.

"The consequence of the coup was a slow decline toward anarchy. The Rai, whom you correctly perceived as the soul of Jesus, bowed to the free will of the people and left Atlantis with the two million people who still supported him. You and your twin flame were among the loyalists."

The open page showed Christie's personality of that time, together with her husband the priest, discussing the consequences of leaving everything they had built in Caiphul.

"Wait, it's him," Christie said, wanting to study the moment. It seemed both natural and insufferable that she had been so close to him, a priest. "I want to see him. I'm right next to him. Look at me. We look as if we were always together. What happened?"

"Your people, these two million, emigrated from Atlantis and settled in a land called Suern, spanning what is now known as India, Pakistan, Iran, Iraq and Saudi Arabia. You were among a holy people who became known as the Suernis."

The angel changed the scene to a temple by a ceremonial lake, in a town in northern India, many thousands of years before the Vedas were written. The culture appears stately and harmonious. Christie and her husband the priest retain their Atlantean turbans, robes and graceful manners. Gold and precious stones are standard features of spiritual symbols used in public architecture.

"We were the Suernis in India," Christie said, amazed as she saw their opulence. "But look at the gold everywhere on the buildings. Every army in the world would have come after that."

A slight movement of the angel's hand initiated a montage of the Suerni lifestyle from the perspective of Christie's soul memories. Central to the safety of Suern was the alignment of the will of the people with their Rai.

"The Suernis were the most powerful people on Earth," the angel said. "No neighboring armies dared approach them under the rule of the Rais. The Suernis lived in peace, in a seemingly magical existence. With little effort they could levitate and travel any distance. They spent most of their time in prayer and meditation and created food and materials by visualization, devotion and voice command."

"If we could do all that, what happened? Why have we forgotten?"

"Your people were very close to absolute freedom," the angel said. "For the next 14,000 years the Suernis lived peaceful lives of hundreds of years. Half of them passed their tests under the Rais' strict training. By devotion and obedience to God in the physical world they ascended to God in the celestial world, having no need to incarnate again."

"The other half . . . ?"

"You and your twin flame were among the one million who did not pass those tests. Agents of the Wicked One who instigated the corruption of priests and scientists in distant Atlantis eventually appeared among the Suernis. In Atlantis, the corruption led to wars then anarchy and barbarism. In Suern, it was more subtle. It began in the form of resentment and disobedience, but it led to starvation and finally genocide by invading armies."

The Book showed several disguised intruders surveying a temple gathering and initiating casual conversations. Christie strained to discern the words of the provocateurs among the people.

"No," she murmured, listening to the serpentine logic of victimhood. "They're dark. How did they get in?"

"Your national security was sacred under the Rai's sponsorship. For this the Rai required holy conduct from all Suernis. A few lost perspective and resented the purpose. The complainers increased in number and their accusations against the Rai caused the insurrection to be repeated. That which occurred long before in Atlantis found traction again in Suern."

"Oh, no, me too," Christie said quietly, observing her complicity as a complainer over a life of many centuries and a decline into decadence and starvation.

"About 13,000 years ago, a different Rai of Suern, Rai Ernon, saw that he had failed to turn around the resentment and died from despair. The people lost their power and began to starve. Farmers were brought in from a revived Atlantean civilization to teach your people how to farm and weave and live by the sweat of the brow. It is from this time that you and a once holy people, a certain influential million, developed an abiding resentment against God and his representatives."

"We were tricked by people who told us the Rai wouldn't allow independent thinking. If we couldn't tell good from evil then, how can we know now?"

"Ask God, if you want to know," the angel said. "Yet you have not asked with devotion. This was a turning that remains as a stuck record, an atheism within you and that certain million souls to this day. You were ordained to be shepherds and defenders of God's people, but when Suern fell into impotence and the corruption of the wicked returned to Atlantis, the whole world descended from resentment and decay into a long stone age."

"We allowed this?"

"You gave in to the Serpents. In the absence of the Rai the Chaldeans invaded Suern and a genocide occurred. And in Atlantis, by divine decree, the dominance of the wicked ended in the collapse of the mid-Atlantic ridge, closing that history in the flood of Noah."

The scenes appeared in rapid succession across the pages of the Book of Life. After a pause the angel continued.

"A long dark era. In historical times, your people reappeared in new bodies as the seed of Abraham, then as the children of Israel, expanding as that certain one million in Egypt. The Israelites were enslaved there for four hundred years as a teaching to assuage the debt of ingratitude to God, the abundant provider."

Christie studied the visual and aural record in Egypt at the time of Moses.

"We became the Hebrews? The Chosen People?"

"You were indeed chosen, as those in dire need of resurrection from resentment and ingratitude. A once holy and noble people fallen to slavery and avarice."

Christie now felt an ominous bell tolling somewhere in her solar plexus.

"You see yourself here," the angel said, "in the life where you were freed by God through Moses, yet you were among those who preferred the Golden Calf and a return to material Egypt. There are consequences, such as the loss of abundance and freedom, when tests of maturity and loyalty are not passed. Your people were the forgetful ones."

As the angel moved her hand over the page depicting the Golden Calf, there was a sharp resurgence of Christie's feelings against Moses, little different than her resentment toward the Rais of Suern.

111

"On the tablets that Moses broke," the angel pointed out, "were the sacred invocations that would have begun your return to the abundance and holiness of the original Suernis. Your body died in the Sinai desert and you did not see the land of Canaan until subsequent lives."

"Why? Why the waste of a life in a desert over a gold statue?"

"The carryover of resentment," the angel answered. "It does not dissipate at the death of the physical body. In each of your Hebrew lives you resented the prophets. As consequence for ignoring their counsel you were, by choice, vulnerable to murder, rape and enslavement by Philistines, Assyrians, Babylonians and then Romans. This was the unmitigated law for God's heirs, exacting in its consequences."

"It was impossible to remember six hundred laws every day. How could that be fair?"

"Fairness came as grace with Jesus. You recognized Jesus' face then, and you do now. But you didn't understand the immense advent of grace. Grace offered mitigation of the law, softening it by mercy. Mercy carried your accumulated weight of resentment, to buy time and new opportunity while you relearned gratitude and generosity. And so, as you see here, I wept. You were among the easily distracted who favored the thief Barabbas instead of he who carried your debt."

The scene in the Book of Life showed Christie in that embodiment in Jerusalem heckling Jesus from a distance and laughing about how he had walked into the Pharisees' trap.

"Oh, God, that was me."

The descending spiral of choice followed by consequence continued as page after page revealed new heartaches.

"Thirty-seven years later your twin flame was killed fighting Roman legionnaires in a militant uprising. You were forced to go to Rome as a cook for the Hebrew slaves made to build the Coliseum. After that holocaust and centuries of scattering, your people, once the holy Suernis with power over matter, reembodied as the warring founders of the European nations during the dark ages.

This was a truly dark, consequential time for you."

The Book showed a series of poverty-stricken lives in dark forests and damp, dirt-floor hovels in northern France and western Germany. Each short, squalid life was ended by sword, arrow, spear or starvation.

"It gets worse and worse," Christie grieved.

"Fearful, violent lives lived in misery, by the sweat of the brow and your absence from God and mercy. The repayment of every jot and tittle of error, the hard way. It took a thousand years of defiance and resentment before you yearned to escape from these rounds. Here, in dark-age Holland, you were robbed, beaten and left to die. With your dying breath, a plea to God for mercy and to be tested again."

The page in the Book of Life showed Christie at the end of that life on the muddy, straw-covered floor of a dark hut with few possessions.

"My God, what have I done?" Christie whispered.

"And so I brought hope," the angel said, turning a page in the Book. "In the 1030s, you were given a life in Poland, a difficult mission you volunteered for, in which you would persuade the Christian nobility to lighten the harshness of the feudal laws on the pagan people. You were given a grace of the Holy Spirit, in eloquence and presence to speak for mercy, against impetuous capital punishment, amputations, torture and blindings. The nobility were impressed by you but complained that your ideas would cause rebellion. In retrospect, you see the irony."

"Christian nobility?" Christie said, pointing to men on horseback outside a fortified wooden church. "They were warlords. Where were the priests that should have stood with me?"

"It was given to you to lead," the angel answered. "Let me show you."

A scene unfolded in a dark, candle-lit church in western Poland. Christie saw her soul in the personality of an unusually attractive nun fall to her knees, alone in the visible presence of the angel of hope.

"I appeared to you in a sanctuary in Gniezno," the angel said, "because the clergy of that time would not remind you that the grace of divine protection must be called for daily, then, as now. But you forgot. Your mind and emotions were distracted by threats from both church and state, and you despaired. The invisible priest who did stand with you against the corrupt bishop and the warlords was Rai Ernon of Suern. You were not raped or murdered, by grace of his intercession on your behalf."

Christie stared at the living record and wept quietly. The angel pointed to events on the next page.

"A rebellion among the people and an invasion from the west destroyed the nobility and a period of anarchy followed. You were enslaved by invaders but as you see, you escaped into a forest where you died of exposure a week before the Christmas of that winter."

The page of recorded soul memory in the Book showed the nun in worn, thin clothing, on her knees in the snow, her last mumbled words spoken to the sky.

"What was I saying?"

"In English your words meant, 'freedom, freedom, freedom.' Again, I wept, for you passed a test of loyalty, but not wisdom."

"Wisdom? No one helped me. I was alone."

"Help was available for the asking," the angel said. "There was no coercion to pray for help. Only enlightened self-interest."

The record showed angels of wisdom and protective angels waiting in concentric tiers above the despairing nun, waiting for instructions from her. The angel of hope moved the pages again.

"You see here, in a life as a noble woman during the religious wars in Germany, you allowed your despair of mind and emotion to foster cynicism. Thinking daily appeals for grace were unnecessary, you suffered betrayals—even rape, inquisition and torture—by a series of clergy corrupted by the wicked. The consequence was a soul condition that would now be described as a post-traumatic stress disorder. This affected your willingness to associate with other people."

"That probably still applies," Christie said. "Explains a lot."

"You became a something of an angry hermit for eight European lives in succession. By pain of this disorder, you perpetuated an error of equating cruel, corrupt and brutal men with all men. Even in the objectivity of your soul, you have not sought discernment or forgiveness."

"Forgiveness? When were men not brutal? Look at their faces."

The angel turned the page of another bitter life in medieval England to a series of new pages concerning a soul with a familiar face. It is the Atlantean priest.

"Discern, my daughter. Look again. There has been no contact with your twin flame for six centuries, so deep is your disdain against all his gender. He has looked for you."

"He has married, these other women. Many times! See . . . his wives, his children."

"Because you were hiding in forests and castles and caves, muttering against all men."

"How is he any different from all men? I wouldn't look at him, now or ever."

"He is no brute, dear one. You underestimate his capacity for forgiveness. And your capacity. I bring you the quality of hope."

"For me? Why? Look at these centuries. What am I worth, if I always fail?"

"Allow me to show you."

The angel lifted the book and turned it. The living page became a bright mirror, of the kind that reflects the subtle column of glowing vertical lights in the body celestial.

"This," the angel said, pointing to a glowing light near the heart, "is the infinite, tethered to the finite. It cannot be seen or touched in the body terrestrial, located behind the physical heart. It pulses in an interval outside time and space, similar to the divine ovoid of your origin. This etheric flame is the infinitely expandable fire of God. It is the same cool, unfed flame given at your origin and it continues even in the lower world."

The flame was delicate, tiny, about one-sixteenth of an inch in height and on closer inspection was actually three flames, blue, yellow and pink, intertwining around each other out of a white, glowing source.

"It's . . . it's so little," Christie said, straining to examine the glowing page.

"The one God in form," the angel said. "The same fire burns in abundance here in me and in all of the hosts of the Lord. When we are sent to impart hope or protection, healing, wisdom or mercy, even freedom, we impart the engrafted Word, God's fire in us to strengthen God's fire in you, in time of need."

"Is everyone's fire the same?" Christie asked.

"No, it differs in the detail. You are looking at your own, in this mirror."

Christie turned to the angel for more explanation.

"From the prayer of one woman, man or child, preserving this fire of God in the lower world, we are compelled by the law of intercession to protect and strengthen those who are named. Behold, God's infinite fire in you. This is your worth."

But looking closely, Christie could see that of the three intertwined flames the blue flame was more dominant and the pink the least.

"The blue part is taller."

"Your expression of God's will is unique to you. The pink is your expression of God's love. The yellow flame is his quality of wisdom in you."

Christie looked closer again.

"They're not even."

"They are out of balance," the angel agreed. "Ask for more opportunities to express both love and wisdom. God has a right to test you and you have a right to be tested, as Jesus was. When he ascended, this flame within him was nine feet tall, the resurrection flame, rotating at the speed of light.

"That was him. I am me. You know me. What are you asking me to be?"

"God will never give you a test you cannot pass. I am sent to ask that you order your life in such a way that these flames are

116

in balance. You have made a name for yourself in the world as the imbalanced Christie Lauren Lemaire, outspoken champion of a woman's right to choose. So, you shall indeed choose this day whom you will serve. Life or death, this day."

The angel paused to observe Christie's response.

"I want to live, of course," Christie said. "What are you suggesting?"

"Grace is offered to you, such that if you choose the long view of other souls' journeys toward God, life will be extended for you. You have seen the particular timing of an entry into the world, the need for specific parents. You have seen that the ordained place and key alliances cannot be altered without aborting the mission. Now hear the law. Do no harm to any soul for whom God offers life. This is balance. This is justice. This is mercy."

Christie realized the crash had precipitated more than a crisis for her current life. There were implications for future lives. The angel had brought her to face a binary decision, each with dire consequences. Death, with her reputation intact. Life, with her reputation shattered.

"Mercy, for who?" she asked, defending her place in the cause. "You are asking me to give up my practice, my clients and lose everything?"

"You may practice the law of the state," the angel stated, "but not at the expense of the law and grace of God's gift of life. Where they conflict, you must choose. Life or death."

"You know I would be ostracized. I would have to leave the state."

"Choose life."

"I would have no business, no connections, ever again."

The angel held her gaze on Christie, calm but firm.

"Choose freedom."

"Freedom? I'm no slave, to anyone," Christie protested.

"Choose now and let that choice be for that time when you yourself may yet need the portal of birth again. For in your imbalanced state you are neither ready for heaven nor deserving of hell.

This choice is given to you in recognition of a level of maturity, when there is no longer any excuse for ignorance. If you knowingly partake in the denial of life, then life may be denied to you."

Christie looked aside, then back at the mirror in the Book, depicting the tiny infinite fire in her.

"I'm not ready to make . . . decisions at this level."

"Daughter, I have heard the fear in your most private thoughts, of ending yet another life as an old maid, bitter at God and man. That old night is over."

Christie caught the look in the angel's eyes. There was no escaping or denying the private fear, or that it would be a perverse choice to die of self-inflicted bitterness.

"There are no good choices," she lamented.

"Your choice, my daughter, now goes far beyond the social, political and business aspects of the worldly profession in your current life. I recommend your private thoughts be extended, to the next 35,000 years in your Book of Life. Look forward. It is possible to transcend the lower world, by grace, long before then. It is also possible to fail. You are your own witness."

To Christie, everything in her soul memory over the past 35,000 years had indicated failure. How would any stretch of time in the future be different?

"You said you brought hope."

"Hope remains," the angel said. "All that is still to be recorded in your Book of Life hinges on the freedom that comes to you from illumined forgiveness."

The angel turned a page in the Book to show the body of Christie Lauren Lemaire, pinned in twisted wreckage at a smoke-shrouded intersection. Unconscious, the bloodied, dust-covered face was frozen in an expression of shock and despair. Christie stared and wept at the awful familiarity of observing her own broken body. She turned to plead with the angel.

"Change everything? Everything? What can I do?"

Calmly, the angel held her palms out toward Christie. A delicate violet and pink stream of pure light extended from the angel's glowing heart and hands to the same places in Christie's celestial body. A moment later, golden light rays emanated from the angel's heart, followed by a stream of white light.

"There is the pathway," the angel said. "Freedom and illumination have been extended to you. Hope has been imparted to you, by the engrafted Word. There is wisdom in forgiving God and man. Having seen and understood a broader perspective, it is the personality of Christie Lauren Lemaire with whom you must now reason. That abrasive personality is still a child, in pain and mortal fear. Comfort her, console her with the news that for you, God has chosen life, not death."

The long silence continued unabated while a stream of glowing, yellow-white metallic sparks shot out of the smoke and arced across her narrow field of view. Her right ear was still pressed against the passenger door and the crushed roof kept the top of her head from moving in any direction. Acrid fumes filled the interior and burned her lungs. If she coughed again the sharp metal in the roof would cut deeper into her scalp. A gloved hand came from nowhere and roughly clamped an oxygen mask over her mouth and nose. At first it wouldn't stay in place and she saw lines of her own blood dripping from it. The gloved hand tried again. Another hand reached in and kept it from falling. Gradually, a distant whirring sound came from the direction of the arc of glowing sparks and she could hear far-off shouts of men. They were rapid, desperate sounds, men screaming sharply at other men, something about the fuel tank getting ready to blow, about getting foam onto the right place, about the toxic smoke and heat from the asphalt fires.

Another voice from the other side of the car yelled, "For God's sake, get out of there, get out of there! It's going to go! Get out!"

The gloved hands stayed in place, unmoving in the smoke. She sucked in oxygen and heard the tearing and cracking of metal as the roof was peeled off. A loud hissing came from the underside of the car. A huge billow of white poured in through the broken windows, bringing in foam and steam. For a moment the smoke thinned enough for her to see flashing emergency lights and then earnest men's faces behind the gloves, checking on her eye movements. Loud commands came from one side about the careful removal of the buckled roof panel. Paramedics were being summoned and more men's faces appeared in the windows, each busy with their assigned task and loudly debating the safety and logistics of lifting her vertically or horizontally.

Someone else called out her name, "God, she's alive, Christie Lemaire. She's conscious!"

Suddenly, within the shouting and the chaos all seemed calm, so well under control. These men, who clearly knew exactly what they were doing, were going to take care of her. There was no need for a dummy who had just run a red light to worry about things they had already figured out. *God, they're a beautiful sight. Men have no idea how fine they look when they're intense and concentrating on things that matter.*

An instant later firemen lifted her bleeding body up and out of the smoking wreckage. Paramedics applied braces and direct pressure to the wounds and others moved a stretcher into position beneath her. For a brief moment she considered her phone. It was still somewhere in the twisted pile of junk that used to be her car. The thought of that controlling little rectangle, as the cause of all this fuss and a completely altered schedule almost made her laugh. *Serves that thing right. It's my life. Mine.*

Unable to suppress the laugh she coughed into the oxygen mask, realizing the persnickety little demon with all its demands would probably be crushed and recycled when the mangled mess finally went to the crane in the wrecking yard.

Free of that thing running my life. Don't need it. Think I'll take today off. Tomorrow too. Time to sit back and relax.

HERE IN THE SOUTH OF FRANCE

An almost-priest, a beautiful, angry woman
and an invisible château—revealed by the
light on a river, deep in the south of France.

HERE IN THE
SOUTH OF FRANCE

Roland Allevard put down the phone, got up from his desk, walked to the end of the hall and knocked on the door of the new assistant priest. The priest, Father Dupree, was new to the diocese but not new to taking command. Statements had been made to the staff during Father Dupree's first day in the office concerning new initiatives the bishop was about to undertake. Rumors had circulated among the staff that Father Dupree had been sent from Paris. Something important was afoot. However, there had been nothing from the bishop in writing.

It was unusual in the Diocese of Nîmes for anyone but the bishop to announce initiatives. At such times all staff and clergy received printed and electronic copies at least once. The Bishop of Nîmes was known for being careful and thorough, as was his administrative staff. According to custom and the demands of his office, the bishop was rarely seen on the lower floor of the administrative building. But as one of the business managers for the diocese, Roland had developed enough sensitivity to unseen currents in the office to allow that perhaps unspoken political considerations were involved in the new initiatives.

Standing outside Father Dupree's closed door, Roland believed it would be better for staff morale if the new assistant priest was not given authority to make changes on behalf of the bishop. The traditions of hierarchy had their place in the diocese. To Roland, it seemed more important to restore confidence among the staff that standard procedure had not been abandoned. If the senior priest, Father LeBlanc, would walk over from the sacristy immediately and spend time with the staff, explaining they were not being subjugated, the gloom might lift. But Father LeBlanc's hesitant footsteps were not heard. After a moment the door opened.

"Come in, Monsieur Allevard," Father Dupree said. "Find a seat, move some boxes and let's get started."

The room had been renovated after the previous occupant had died in there at his desk. The 150-year-old walls had been replastered and painted, and another wall had been knocked down to double the space. New bookshelves and a large new desk had been installed and there were still plenty of unpacked boxes stacked around the room.

"How can I help?" Roland said, taking a seat in the middle of the room.

"You can help a great deal, Monsieur Allevard. Considering the administrative talent pool we have here, you are the ideal man for what we have in mind."

Roland looked into the assistant priest's eyes. He wanted to know if Father Dupree was speaking for the bishop.

"Father, who are we talking about?"

The priest did not sit but paced behind his desk, picking up a book and pointing it at Roland for emphasis as he spoke.

"It's not who, it's what. We're expanding."

Father Dupree was a big man with a full waistline, moving energetically like an orator. He waved the book at the freshly painted ceiling, then at Roland.

"You have experience with cost-benefit analysis, planning departments, municipal zoning, in this and other dioceses. You're familiar with our vendors, you know this diocese well and you're discreet. Further, you're a lay minister, you're already thirty and so your path to ordination is overdue. It should be among our considerations, yes?"

"Yes, of course, Father," Roland answered.

"Good. This is important. What I'm about to assign you is

confidential. You will report to me and only me. We'll discuss your assessments face-to-face. How and when we move forward depends on your findings."

"With respect, Father, I have other assignments due this week."

"I'm transferring your assignments to Rousillon. There's room for adjustment within the budget. The matter at hand is of larger importance."

Roland shifted uncomfortably in his seat, understanding he was to be part of the bishop's new initiative, without the bishop or the senior priest being present.

"May I take notes?" he asked, expecting to document the experience.

"No," the big man from Paris said, as he paced. "You'll see why in a moment."

Roland again shifted in his seat, noticing a clinical odor from either the fresh paint on the walls or something leaking from one of Dupree's boxes on the floor.

"You are aware," Dupree said, turning to Roland, "of the eastern parts of the diocese—Les Angles and Villeneuve-les-Avignon. Yes?"

"I'm aware."

"We wish to consider the costs and benefits of the construction of a new church in that area," Dupree said, raising his eyebrows. "A large new church. That area is underserved, in our opinion. You are also aware, though, that just across the Rhone River is the diocese of Avignon, and that the diocese of Nîmes is a suffragen of the diocese of Avignon."

"Yes, Father. I'm aware."

"Good. Then you are aware that the Bishop of Nîmes and the Bishop of Avignon are good friends. Yes? And that congregants of our diocese in Les Angles and Villeneuve cross the Rhone to attend the nearest places of worship, which happen to be national heritage venues in the older parts of Avignon. They take their tithes and their children from our diocese across the Rhone. Were we to build a new church in Les Angles, to expand attendance here and better serve our local congregants, to retain them and their tithes, we would not want any strain in the friendship with the Bishop of Avignon."

"I agree."

Roland wondered why the two bishops would not discuss the matter themselves. He shifted back in his chair.

Father Dupree leaned toward him. "Then you see the delicacy of the matter and the importance of constructing a confidential cost-benefit analysis for a new church in Les Angles."

Roland did not see the point of discretion between bishops, nor did he see any written authorization from the Bishop of Nîmes.

"I'm sorry, Father, why would this matter be confidential?"

"The bishop contemplates success, Allevard. Until that is assured your assignment remains an unofficial concept. You will validate the concept by asking specific questions of the parishioners who stand to benefit."

"So I'm to ask unofficial questions," Roland said, "about the idea of a new church to serve Les Angles and Villeneuve. And I'm to begin with the deacons and the city planning departments. Then I approach realtors, donors, elders, parishioners, vendors . . . as if it was my own idea?"

"That's correct," Dupree said. "That's why you're the perfect man for the assignment. You're young enough, presentable, not yet ordained. The unofficial face of the diocese."

Roland drew in a breath as he resisted openly objecting to the priest's use of flattery.

"If the bishop's concerns are involved, shouldn't we be discussing this with him?"

"Absolutely. He expects results and we are to provide them quickly. There are two phases to the assignment. Your informal assessment, followed by the formal. Are you with me?"

Roland wondered whether he should challenge the priest to pick up the phone and call the bishop. But there was something hidden, a political concern, if hierarchy was appointing him to be the unofficial face of the diocese. Father Dupree stood upright waiting for him to agree.

"Do we have the bishop's letter of direction?" Roland asked, calmly.

Father Dupree sighed and looked up at his new ceiling, as if summoning patience.

"As I've explained to you, there is no paper trail at this time."

"At his request?"

"At his request. And so, based on the template you have used for new site assessments, for this and other dioceses, you are authorized to begin work today on the informal assessment, beginning with inquiries to the parties you mentioned, though your inquiries are to be of a general, not official, nature."

"And if the reaction is negative?"

"Then I am expendable," Dupree said, waving the book. "I would be transferred back to Paris and the bishop would know where things stand."

"With respect, Father, the parishioners will wonder if I'm pre-empting the bishop."

"You represent the bishop's concept, which he has not initiated at this stage."

Roland had been around church politics long enough to know when a non-answer should not be challenged. He shifted direction.

"How large is this new church to be?" Roland asked, controlling the dissent in his voice.

Dupree ceased pacing and lowered his tone.

"To be determined," he said. "There's another thing, Allevard. It should be obvious how crucial it is for the Church to demonstrate its expansion to the Muslim community. Our Muslim citizenry seem to consider themselves the only religious people in France. Yes?"

"Yes, Father, it would appear that way," Roland said, beginning to understand.

"Now, Allevard, I've recently served in Marseilles where forty-two percent of new births are Muslim. In Paris it's fifty-six percent of new births. Where does this suggest that France is heading, in your opinion?"

The scope of the initiative became clearer. Dupree plowed on.

"If we don't expand, how are we to be perceived? You already know. That consideration alone should be sufficient. Do you understand what is required of you? For the purpose of briefing me on your progress, you may keep handwritten notes."

Roland realized he had little discretion in the matter.

"How much time do I have?" he asked.

"That depends on you. I'll expect you in here for our first assessment meeting tomorrow evening at five."

And that was it. The assignment began immediately.

Back at his desk, Roland prepared a sequence of inquiries and contact details. He thought of calling Father LeBlanc for confirmation, but realized the senior priest would refer him right back to Dupree. As a confessor Father LeBlanc was fine. As an administrative authority he was prone to conspicuous absences.

The way forward, Roland decided, was not dissent. That would be pointless. Instead, he would push forward, develop an ordered task list and get it done as quickly as possible.

At the top of his contact list were the three deacons who worked with the poor, the elderly and the needy in the eastern parts of the diocese. They would each offer lists of parishioners, covering a cross section of the underserved parish. He would talk to those who crossed the Rhone to attend services in Avignon and those who stayed home. At the bottom of Roland's schedule were his municipal and professional contacts. They would bring up basic statistics for Les Angles, population 8,400, and of Villeneuve-les-Avignon, population 13,500. The planners would point out that the two towns comprised a small portion of the Diocese of Nîmes. But if the estimates held that almost 60% of the population were Catholics, then there was a potential for around 12,000 congregants taking notice of a new church.

The three deacons, all in Nîmes that day, liked Roland's "unofficial idea" and offered him their lists of leads, beginning with those who regularly crossed the river to churches in Avignon. The lists were extensive, the statistics promising, and no matter how unorthodox the methodology, Roland had to grudgingly admit that Father Dupree probably had a case for investigating parish interest in a new church.

Roland drove out of Nîmes about midday on A9 toward the northeast. When he reached Les Angles, he took the winding local roads through the suburban, middle-class town, down the long hill to the wooded waterfront along the Rhone.

The sight of the broad, tranquil river soothed him. The Rhone, in its silent, flowing majesty offered welcome contrast to the demands of Father Dupree's book-waving edicts. In the sunlight reflecting off the river, there were no financial calculations, political secrets or religious rivalries. Roland began to look at his watch and then ignored it.

Just a few moments of peace before the street-walking and door-knocking begins. Give me peace.

Hands resting on a railing, he stared upstream at the glass-still water of the Rhone coming slowly toward him from far-off Lake Geneva in Switzerland. The water, he imagined was pure, fed by streams trickling through quiet forests and glacial valleys far up in the Alps. In his mind, he began to trace the great river to its source. The journey upstream became serene beyond words, gliding over the broad river in a weightless state, heading buoyantly up to snow-covered heights. There, the air, too, felt pristine. No lists of busy people, who may or may not care about a new church, or demonstrations to rivals.

Without looking at his watch, Roland realized he had to get on with the task at hand. He returned to his car and drove to the address of his first contact. He worked methodically through simple questions in each interview, engaging parishioners in conversation and then finding ways to move on to the next contact.

The trouble, though, was that Roland began to notice a discouraging pattern in the responses among those he interviewed in Les Angles. It was subtle, surfacing as tones of indifference. Mostly, those he visited agreed a new church would be fine, but there was an unexpected lack of enthusiasm. Some wanted Roland to know they would be in no position to pay for it. Others liked the medieval architecture in Avignon. A few said they liked the drive across the Rhone and more than a few assumed a new church would be part of a shopping mall. They were ambivalent, as if it were a gift with strings.

Around dusk, as Roland was wondering what to say to Dupree at tomorrow's meeting, he found a parking space on a residential street outside his last contact for the day. He got out of the car and checked his notepad, considering the day had passed with little promise. The deacons' list indicated his final interview for the day would be with a married woman in good standing with the Church. No information about her family background was provided. He looked across the street. A blond woman in her early thirties was getting out of a car in the driveway. Last interview for the day, he thought, until he noticed the way the woman, lit from one side by the interior light of the car, brushed her hair out of her eyes and closed the door with authority. Roland paused, marveling for a moment how the Church seemed to have a knack for retaining attractive married women as congregants. Immediately he caught himself and remembered the standard mental caution. *If you're going to be a priest you set aside this mindset, now and forever.*

The correct way of perceiving any married woman in good standing was to appreciate that they were the real center of the family and therefore the parish. They brought their children into the pews and by persuasion, their husbands and their tithes. To reinforce the perception of the married woman as the indispensable center of the Church, Roland had expanded the standard concept to see each woman as a representative of the Divine Mother. Respectfully, Roland looked again at the woman and thought, *Mother Mary, one of your own.* He crossed the sidewalk to the edge of her driveway and called out to her politely.

"Madame, excuse me, are you Vivienne Montaux?"

"Yes," she answered, warily. "And you are?"

"I'm Roland Allevard from the diocese in Nîmes. How are

you?"

She turned away from him, with an edge to her voice. "I'm trying to get in my front door. Nîmes? Are you serious? Are you here to apologize?"

At first the woman had appeared to want to ignore him. Now she made a step toward him, one hand clearly tightened into a fist.

"Apologize? No, I'm here regarding . . . something else," Roland stammered.

"You people *are* something else," the blond woman said, clenching both fists. "I don't want to talk to you or anyone from Nîmes."

"Okay," Roland said, making light of her discourtesy. He thought over his own words and tone and decided to press on, as if he hadn't noticed her hostility. "I was wanting to ask your opinion about the prospect of building a new church in Les Angles."

The woman's face appeared to express disbelief, then anger.

"Idiots! You've got to be kidding! How dare you? How did you get my name and my address? How?"

"One of the deacons," Roland said, taken aback at her strident tone.

"You *people*," the woman said, raising a fist toward Roland. "I have been trying every way I can to get off your damn mailing lists, to get rid of you! Now you're here in my drive and you want to build a church? If I could, I'd sue you and the Vatican and your whole pack of lies, to get my life back! So don't ask me about building churches, now or ever, here or anywhere! Do you understand?"

Roland realized that he'd walked into the consequences of a clerical error and that this lady was someone who should not be on any deacon's list.

"Then I guess I am here to apologize," he said, lightheartedly shrugging off the deacon's error. "I'm not sure what happened to cause the situation you're describing. But I can listen, if you need to vent. I've got time, I suppose. It's the end of the day."

"No, for God's sake, monsieur. How would that help?" she said, fumbling with her keys. "You're not capable of understanding. I just want my life back. I don't think that's something you or

131

anyone can do. It's a little late for that. Good night."

And just like that she closed her front door as the street lights came on.

The next day in the neighboring suburb of Villeneuve, Roland pressed on with his visits and received tepid approvals for a new church from everyone he spoke to on the deacons' lists. The parishioners were saying, in effect, go ahead, build it and we'll attend because you're asking us to. It was not the stuff to demonstrate to the Muslims, the Protestants or anyone that the Church was overflowing with zeal. As if to rub salt in the wound, late in the day he accidentally bumped into his clerical error, Vivienne Montaux, who was coming out of a store in a Villeneuve strip mall.

"Hey, I'm sorry," Roland said, embarrassed, suddenly red-faced as he recognized her. "I'm not trying to pursue you. Really. Just having a not-so-good day. Two not-so-good days."

"You people don't learn," she said outside the automatic doors, pausing long enough to get her point across as a question. "Building a new building with the same message that the Church is infallible, because it's infallible? You know the Muslims are just like you? Infallible, with an attitude. I feel sorry for you, doing their dirty work. Quit while you're still sane."

Roland stopped as he backed up on the sidewalk, surprised yet again by her tone and opinion. He could tell she was serious. But her opinion could not go unchallenged.

"Are you saying you see us the same as the Muslims?" he asked, incredulous.

"Spiritual wickedness in high places. All about submission, monsieur."

"Oh, my God," he said, hands upraised, sincerely concerned for her lack of discernment. "Is that how you feel?"

"Like I said, I feel sorry for you. What a mess. Me too. Good-bye."

That did it. He stared at her in dismay as she made her way across the parking lot. *How do you offer consolation for the pain of living in the world, when the consolation is seen as the problem?*

Roland got into his car and sat for a while, stunned. He had faced two days of lukewarm agreement and no real dissent. This woman's dissent was certainly real and anything but lukewarm.

As Roland drove back to his office in Nîmes he pondered how disproportionate an impact Vivienne Montaux had made on him. In the office he brooded at his desk and took longer than expected to prepare a summary for Dupree at five. When the time came he knocked on the door and Dupree let him in to the somber office. Stacks of books and boxes remained on the floor. The odor of paint and cleaning chemicals remained in the air. Father Dupree's desk was covered with folders and he sounded busy.

"Monsieur Allevard with a progress report. Come in and take a seat."

Roland sat down slowly in the wooden chair and looked at his notes, such as they were.

"Begin," Father Dupree said, gesturing.

"I can't say we're in such great shape, Father," Roland said. "I've covered about half the deacons' contacts. The response at this point is not negative, but I would say it's . . . indifferent. We could build a new church in Les Angles without objections from parishioners but . . . and it's a little surprising to say, without much enthusiasm, so far."

"Why not?" the priest asked.

"I wish I knew."

"Then change your tactics. Get back out there tomorrow more like a coach, less like you're asking their permission." Dupree paused as the phone began ringing. "Contact everyone on the lists, and then give me some options for site locations, three, maybe four, with pros and cons. I'll see you in here at five, in two days."

It puzzled Roland, as he drove home to his apartment on the other side of Nîmes, that Father Dupree, the other priests and the bishop himself were not lifting a finger in public to help. This was a cause that would seem to warrant everyone in the diocese getting out on the streets, on the phone, email and social media. He wondered how politically sensitive the premise was, perhaps requiring plausible deniability. Or the assignment might have something to do with a test. It might be an initiation concerning his path to ordination, being among their considerations. Whatever it was, he faced two more days of interviews on his own, which were to be more like coaching parishioners to be enthusiastic about his unofficial idea. Then research on several site options would follow. This was the informal phase. *Would the formal phase involve more than one person? What on earth were they doing?*

Roland stared at the gas fireplace in his living room while he ate dinner and thought about the conversation with Madame Montaux. *She was an angry one. For what reason?* There was no time he could remember in his service with the Church when he felt so in need of clear direction.

No direction came for some time that night. He turned sleeplessly back and forth, fighting a sense of futility. In time though, he slept and a simple dream began with a sense of weightlessness and a flight path over a broad river, heading somewhere pure, up into the high country ahead. As he glided back and forth across the breadth of the glassy river he noticed he wasn't alone. Two great streaks of white fire flew parallel with him to his right, two on his left, two beneath him under the water and two in the air above him. They were elongated ovals of dazzling white light with a long, glowing luminescence behind. Glancing to each side he could see inside each streak of light was a living fire-being. These were sentient beings, each with an extraordinarily beautiful face. Now and then he noticed they were looking at his face. At last it came to him, as he flew above the river, that they were a type of angel the Church described as seraphim.

Why he needed an escort while simply gliding over a river wasn't clear, but he felt glad and comforted to have their silent company. He looked up ahead at the beauty of the wooded banks on either side of the calm water. Far off in the distance, on a bend in the river, he saw a great, tall château, wide and beautifully proportioned, bright pennants flying and hundreds of people walking along garden pathways and standing on terraces, looking out at him approaching them. The escorts banked to the right and left and disappeared in fiery white streaks. He tilted slightly away from the center of the river and landed lightly on his feet on a lawn a good distance from the château. It seemed as though he knew this place and felt welcome there even before anyone greeted him.

A friendly young man met him on a pathway and greeted him by name, saying he would guide him through the throng of students around them to where Paul was waiting for him inside. Paul, he remembered now, was the master of the château and was someone he looked forward to meeting. The château was more like a university campus than a palace for wealthy recluses. Here everyone was young, friendly and possessed of a light-hearted vitality and innocence, so different from where he had come, down the river.

Up a wide, rounded set of stairs his escort ushered him into the château through open, double doors. A simple feeling of gladness filled Roland, part relief at being welcomed to a place of beauty and part anticipation of an undefined event. In the foyer a very tall, noble-looking man in a tailored green coat and light-colored slacks greeted him and shook his hand.

"Very glad to see you again, Roland," the tall man said.

"It feels good to be back. I'm trying to remember what kind of class I'm here for this time."

"Today you're going to get to the details outlined in your last class. This is a step up, and for you it's timely. Events are unfolding and you may benefit from a wider perspective. Let's head for food and drinks in the garden, out by the rotunda. Then we'll need to come back inside and get to the workshop."

This was Paul. The man had a trimmed beard, short, blond, wavy hair, intelligent blue eyes, and he walked with an impressive bearing, lean and upright, the epitome of discipline. His voice was not gruff but kindly and melodic and he knew everything. They walked toward a marble rotunda surrounded by lawns and landscaped gardens. A feeling of both peace and alertness filled Roland as he looked around.

"I remember from the last time I was here, we're in daylight," he mused. "Yet I left Nîmes at night."

"The environment is self-luminous," Paul answered. "The electrons in every atom move at close to the speed of light."

"Then . . . how could I be here?"

"That would include your celestial body, even the atoms in the air. The terrestrial world moves much more slowly. Life and time and seasons there depend on solar cycles. That is the realm of debt."

Paul offered Roland a sparkling golden drink in a tall crystal glass and was straightforward about his reason for being there.

"The situation for you in Nîmes and Les Angles is coming to a head," Paul began.

"You know about that? I don't get . . . I don't understand why I'm out there on my own. Isn't this something that's important to them?"

"They know the money isn't likely to be available anytime soon. There are restrictions. Strong public support might help their case. They're not surprised by what you're finding."

"So . . . why?"

"They are afraid for France and the Church. It will play out, but not quietly. There are apostates in every religion who abandon God's gentle solutions for his sons and daughters. Court intrigue is an emotional intoxicant for those who prefer rivalry over brotherhood. Their courses are known and they are contained by that which they sow. That which is not predictable is your course."

"What do you mean?"

"On your previous visits you saw a number of paintings in the château, from the time when I was in the lower world, in the service of the Church. The Church has done and continues to do much good, but you are called to a higher purpose than administration."

"You mean ordination?"

"I mean God's gentle solutions for his sons and daughters. Whether that is accomplished through ordination is your choice."

Roland looked around at the pristine beauty in every petal of the climbing roses around them. Light shone from within the flowers as if they had an inner understanding of perfect form. He felt he was still hesitating, wanting more information for a calling that was supposed to be an innate passion. Paul invited him to walk through an arbor into an area of landscaped gardens.

"I'm still no closer to knowing what to do," Roland said. "Were you a priest?"

"In my final round of life in the terrestrial world," Paul answered, "I felt that higher calling, not as clergy, but as an artist. I wanted with every part of my soul to convey to my brothers and sisters the reality of heaven as their rightful destination. But there were many in the Church at that time who saw the reality of their position in the world as their rightful destination. What mattered to them was their rank relative to other men. This, they believed, would somehow provide them a permanence in heaven."

"That's a little close to home," Roland said, "if I'm looking at ordination. The men I know have given their life as a sacrifice."

"God is no respecter of persons. The men I knew had little knowledge of, or willingness to pay every jot and tittle of their debts to God, or to the living God in other people. These men of rank I served through my art, displayed in their chapels."

"What was your name in that life?"

"My name then was Paulo Cagliari, from Verona, but as I came from the Venice school of artists I became known as Paul the Venetian to some. To others I was Paulo Veronese. There was one high-ranking man, one particular bishop, who commissioned me early in my career to paint a certain large canvas. I needed the money, and in gratitude I made sure I attended one of his rare sermons. He was very strict and rule-bound, fire and brimstone in his sermon to that congregation, in Venice, in 1553."

Paul stopped for a moment and looked directly at Roland.

"I was given the gift to see through this rule-bound bishop. He was not trying to please God. He was trying to please his superiors in the Church. Their requirements may have included threats of hellfire and damnation in his sermons, but what he himself needed was the light of heaven."

"How could you have known that?"

"My attention was on God, not popularity with him or anyone else," Paul said. "I prayed and vowed that day to paint for the expansion of God in him. When he saw the completed work, he showed no reaction and continued with his strict service, without the joy of our Lord. Your soul, in that life, was that bishop. In every life since then, you have gravitated to various offices in various places in the Church because it was rule-bound and predictable. Direction for you was never lacking within the chain of hierarchy. I spoke to your soul long ago in a cathedral in Paris, warning you this time would come, when direction would not come reliably from the Church and you would have to seek it from God. You showed no reaction. Now your path of complacency, relying on institutional direction, is coming to an end."

"How could it be coming to an end? I'm willing to take ordination as the highest service to the Church."

"God is self-transcendent, always moving on and up, as you may choose to do, in his image and likeness. If you leave Church administration and take ordination, you should know that prior to this life you agreed to a path of inner direction from God. The difficulty of the mission would take you far from reliable Church hierarchy. If you chose a path other than ordination, it would be equally difficult. Outside the regimen of the Church, you would need a source of buoyancy from within. That is the path of joy. Anything less would end in disaster."

Roland put his hands on his forehead as his choices now seemed even more complicated.

"A path other than ordination?"

"There is one who is far from joy and adamantly disinclined toward direction from God or man. And yet she is very dear to God. Nothing less than the path of joy will save her from the orthodoxy of despair. There are many, far from Nîmes, for whom you may bring assistance and counsel through the pathway that ordination would offer. The mission to save this one daughter of God, close to home, through the pathway of joy is offered to you alone."

Roland looked at Paul in disbelief, hoping this was not going where he thought it was.

"You have very little recent practice," Paul continued, "in the kind, personal conveyance of joy. You would have to draw daily on the great reservoirs of joy God would willingly open. You co-created those reservoirs with God long ago and have not accessed them for some time. God offers you two opportunities to approach him. The choice is yours."

"Do you mean . . . ?"

"You are already well acquainted. Of course that's who I mean."

"Oh, no, but . . . no," Roland pleaded. "She's so fiery and angry. Angry at me, at the Church, at everyone."

"Not so. Most people get no response from her. She is afraid of losing her temper. The reason she made the effort to speak to you, even in anger, is because she felt safe. She too has been here, at the invitation of our Lord. Art has been her expression of God in other lives and other cultures. It would have been so in this life if not for decisions by strict parents, an arranged marriage, an abusive spouse, and clergy who rejected her requests for divorce for many years. It is a razor's edge that you would walk. It would mean shedding the joyless momentums of your institutional past and allowing her to breathe kindness. Who else can do that?"

"I may have felt a . . . no, I don't think I can do that, even for her."

"'Even for her?' She has needed you in very close proximity for a long time now. This daughter of God needs to gain your forgiveness for a betrayal. In a time long past, she forsook you for a wicked, charismatic ruler. You objected to his lawlessness and you were put to death. Yes, you were wronged but you withheld mercy and cloistered yourself in religious orders life after life, to convey to her the hurt of your non-forgiveness."

Roland looked at him as the error began to register. "How many lifetimes did . . . ?"

"What matters is the present. By the grace of God, she needs your forgiveness and you need her joy."

"Joy? I don't see any joy in her. She's predictably angry and cynical."

"She is in pain. That said, I'm reminded to inform you that you'll have some assistance in weighing your thoughts about her."

"Weighing my thoughts . . . about not bumping into her again?"

It seemed to Roland that Paul's smile meant he wanted to move past the conditions of fear and doubt to another subject. He gestured toward the fleur-de-lis pennants above them.

"You haven't remembered any of your previous visits here," Paul said, "because it might have caused your mental awareness some confusion. Tomorrow, when you wake, that forgetting will gradually be reversed. You'll remember some of what we've discussed."

They had begun walking through the bright, fragrant gardens again but Roland hesitated. The prospect of consciously remembering a discussion that would put him at odds with Father Dupree, Father LeBlanc and the bishop seemed fraught with danger.

"I can't have this conversation in mind at the office. It would be better if I didn't remember anything."

"As you prefer," Paul said. "But what if you do bump into her again?"

"Then I need to know the truth about something she said. Something about the Church being no different than the Muslims. That hurt . . . it did, and you want me to see her again? Say I didn't hear it?"

Paul turned and pointed through the trees toward the pennants over the château.

"There are Shia and Sunni Muslims and all kinds of Christian students here and in every one of the other universities of the spirit. And Buddhists, Jews, Sikhs, Mormons and Sufis. But no one when they're here has an interest in those divisions. We are one. The qualifications to come here have to do with the expression of the divine flame in the heart, not the religion held in the world. That drops away. They don't bring doctrines and man-made rules here. They have enough of the heart-fire developed to lift their souls to this level, while their body is sleeping. They

140

actually practice the spirit of their religion when they're awake. The fleur-de-lis is the unifying symbol of the heart-fire, the same divinity in each of them."

"But she sees no difference between the Church and Islam. They're not equivalent."

"The world's religions are integrated here, without competition. I, myself, am a student of yet higher levels of the one God, of whom there are more wonders than I can say. For you, this is the level of heaven that matches your willingness to gradually understand how the integration works. There's more to show you. Let's look at one of the galleries inside."

Paul invited him to take one of the curving paths back to the château. As Roland walked, he held his hand out to touch the leaves and blossoms on the fruit trees beside the path. Each touch felt like a conveyance of pure happiness.

"But if this is one of the levels of heaven, where are we?" Roland asked.

"Here in the south of France. That river is what you call the Rhone."

"And tomorrow, when I wake up, I'm going to recall being in a university in heaven?"

"Yes," Paul said. "With a sense of peace and an interest in coming back here, where you know you'll be welcome."

At the side of the château away from the river, they took a wide, semicircular stairway of glowing flagstones up to a garden terrace. Roland paused for a moment to look back at the beautiful gardens and then followed Paul inside. At the end of a long, carpeted hallway Paul pointed to a double doorway leading to a series of luminous gallery rooms. Hundreds of examples of fine art were displayed on the curved walls and in various nooks. The paintings themselves seemed to provide their own illumination from within the pigment.

"These gracious works are by students from every nation, every religion," Paul said. "Beauty and the love of God in man are the common factors. And look at these sketches. Da Vinci, Constable,

Monet. Progress to their current lives. Norman Rockwell studied here, before and during that life, and he still comes here, preparing for the next."

"And . . . I suppose I have to prepare," Roland said, turning to look at Paul. "When I wake up in Nîmes and have to go back to the parishioners in Les Angles tomorrow, what then?"

"It will play itself out as you remember parts of what we have said and what you have seen. You will know what to do. You will have the capability. There's something in this next room you need to see."

They entered a wide workshop area and in a nook with tall windows, looking out on fruit trees and landscaping, was a golden easel with a large, blank canvas resting on it.

"This is yours," Paul said. "You have a unique genius waiting to be expressed in drawing the image of joy in yourself. This is a joy that transcends the sense of competition, sees past it, to the common needs of kindness and respect, for atheists and agnostics as well as the devout. If God sees past the worldliness and politics of institutions and people to their unity, can you? Can you draw it? Every time you visit here you'll make a few changes. You'll perceive a new aspect of that unity and want to add it to the canvas. You may remember part of the concept tomorrow while you're at work in Les Angles."

"It's been a while since I stood in front of a canvas. It's so blank."

"Someone you know will, in time, be willing to help."

"If I have the nerve. I don't know how I'd even begin to explain this."

"Think of yourself from now on as a most welcome student here, not as a captive of a feudal setting in your world." Paul paused and smiled. "I'm gently reminded, I must ask you to pardon me as I have a class to teach in a few minutes. Remember your canvas. I look forward to watching for you coming up the river again this week. We'll have a few things to talk about."

And with that, Paul left him staring at the easel and the blank canvas. On the gold-framed canvas he saw the bright, broad river flowing just beneath him. The escorts formed up on all sides and he began slow turns over the sun-glinting water before forgetfulness overcame him and he woke up in his dark apartment in Nîmes as the phone alarm chimed.

The drive from Nîmes to Les Angles and Villeneuve that day felt strangely relaxed. Although the deacon's contact lists rested in folders in a briefcase on the passenger seat, they didn't carry the same stress as they had on previous days. Those days now seemed to have come and gone long ago. Time and priorities had somehow been altered. The response of parishioners to a potential new church probably would not alter much in substance from earlier interviews, but to Roland it didn't seem to matter as much now.

What did matter to Roland as midday passed was a recurring image of Vivienne Montaux in his mind's eye, even while he listened earnestly to parishioners' opinions. By mid-afternoon he realized with unease that there was an unexpected and unexplained attraction there. Even lay ministers are trained to recognize and deal with it. But, unwanted as it was, the image of her face and eyes wouldn't leave his mind. Further, his mind was distracted from zoning maps by thoughts of looking at a blank canvas on a golden easel and gazing out through a window at beautiful gardens. It was as if he was experiencing a dream while he was trying to shape pros and cons for potential church sites. And a melody kept circling around his inner ear, "No need of moon or star by night, or sun to shine by day . . ."

By five, Roland had stopped all attempts at work and sat in his car thinking. What he felt was almost like remembering a movie, about being in a fabulous château and listening to a story about a wayward bishop. It felt exciting, vital and about freedom and he wanted to experience it again, but it wasn't a movie. Then without warning, a sudden intrusion of the opposite kind, the feeling of condemnation that warns, "You're in trouble now," made him sit up in the seat. Roland recognized the feeling as a premonition of impending disciplinary action. This was an institutional hazard that he'd learned to live with in the office in Nîmes. It would float up from nowhere, even if he'd done nothing wrong. At this point, he realized with shock, he had done something wrong but couldn't describe it. It had to do with crossing some kind of line of respect. Or perhaps he was no longer so afraid of disciplinary action. If that was the case how would he be able to confess his thoughts and feelings, even to Father LeBlanc? There would be a long silence on the other side of the confessional. Then the platitudes.

Uneasy with his thoughts and feelings, Roland remembered some of the cautionary statements in a ministerial text. "When a candidate for ordination finds he has separated himself from willingness to submit to confession . . ." it began. This was a career-ending admonition. But instead of trembling in fear, something in him pushed back. Vivienne Montaux's comment about submission came to mind. Did she mean submission to God or submission to man? Surprisingly, Roland felt no qualms about the hypothetical idea of confession to her, when he found deep resistance to confession to the clergy he knew. This was a moment, he realized, when an entire career in faith could be broken. He sat in his car as dusk fell and rested his head on the steering wheel.

"God, help me," he said.

As night fell over Les Angles, Roland made himself stretch and get ready for the drive back to Nîmes. Thoughts of sitting in the center of Father Dupree's office came to him and he didn't take the most direct route to the highway. Taking his time around the winding streets of Les Angles, he remembered the turn he'd taken to Vivienne Montaux's home two nights before, and out of curiosity wondered if her car would be in the drive by now. It was dark and no one would see him on that particular street, so he cruised by and noticed with surprise that he was slowing and then stopping to look at her car, parked right there in the same drive he'd stood on. Stunned at his own behavior, he pulled over to the curb, several houses past hers, and waited for something to happen, for someone to tell him to leave. It felt ridiculous to keep the engine running, wasting fuel while he collected his thoughts, so he turned the key off and sat there.

144

What am I doing, he wondered, *start the car.* But competing thoughts pushed back, wanting to resolve the inner conflict concerning confession. Softly, a mysterious phrase came to mind several times, "And yet she is very dear to God." The concept of Vivienne Montaux as a daughter of God made him wonder if confession to such a one was as valid in God's eyes as confession to clergy. It was a crazy idea, and he wondered if he was losing it after a lifetime of strict discipline. He got out of the car in exasperation, thinking to walk around it and burn off the tension. Then, waiting for something to happen, he heard a stern voice calling out from behind him.

"Selling churches to the gullible at night now?"

It was her voice. He spun around expecting to see her on the sidewalk under a streetlight, but her voice came again from the center of the street.

"Night sales? Really?"

Hands on her hips, sweatshirt sleeves rolled up, she was out jogging in her neighborhood, veering toward him, then jogging backwards. She was breathing hard between phrases.

"I hope my neighbors tell you to go home and get a life. No offense."

"None taken," he gasped, trying to think of something to say. "I was going to knock on your door down there. I guess I came to see you, not the neighbors."

"Oh, no you don't. I've got no time, no anything for you people."

"Please, I'm not 'you people.' I think I need . . . I think I do need a life. There's no way I can go to confession like this."

She shaded her eyes against the streetlight above him.

"Maybe you're already insane. Maybe I should call the cops to help you out." She held up her phone. "Right here."

"You're very kind," he said, trying to think on his feet. "What I wanted to ask is . . . would it be okay for me to talk to you on another, better day, not about the Church, but about a place I go for painting lessons. I thought of you and wondered if you were a painter."

"You wondered if I was a painter?" she said, incredulous. She kept moving and stretching. "Me, a painter? I don't paint. I haven't for a long time. You're with the Church in Nîmes. Why don't you want to talk about your Church any more?"

"Because I've come to the place where I take ordination or I don't. That's why. And maybe, for the neighbors, the middle of your street isn't where I would normally be thinking about confession."

"Are you serious or are you messing with me, in the middle of the street?"

"I'm serious."

"What a mess," she said, jogging in place under the streetlight. "What do they do to people? As if I didn't know."

"It's not the Church, it's on me. My fault, my choice."

"What am I likely to tell you?" she queried, raising her hands. "Yes, you're right, no one talks about this in the middle of the street. You want to push buttons about confession? Walk with me down to my place while I'm cooling off. As if I'm going to know what to tell you." She clenched her fists, then seemed to think better of it. "What makes you think I'm a painter? How would you know that?"

Surprised that she was even giving him any time at all, Roland said the only thing he could think of as they approached her drive. "A guess."

By then she was near her front door. She broke the silence.

"A guess? Look, I don't know why you'd ask me, of all people, about the messes the Church makes. I said I felt sorry for you at the mall yesterday. I didn't mean to demean you. It's like I wanted to grab your collar and shake some sense into you, everyone like you. Ordination? Oh, my. At least you paint. At least you've got something going for you."

Roland looked at her blue eyes and decided to risk an explanation. He held his hands up as if trying to sculpt something in mid-air.

"It's not going for me," Roland admitted. "It's a difficult

assignment. A blank canvas staring at me. My painting teacher told me to draw something that I can't even describe. It's probably going to take a while before I can even imagine it."

She seemed puzzled at the assignment and looked at him carefully.

"Why don't you paint something simple, something easy first? Who is your teacher?"

"To explain that would be like a confession, and I can't go to the diocese. Not now."

For the first time Roland noticed the beginning of a smile.

"A guy like you going to the dark side for art lessons?"

"No, not like that," he said. "Maybe, if I could think of the right words, how to describe the assignment. Think of a mind-stretch to ideas never imagined, at least by me. It's meant to make me stretch beyond what I think I am."

"I don't even remember your name," she said, shaking her head slightly. "How do I feel like I already know you?"

"My name is Roland Allevard."

"And you know my name," she said, hands on her hips. "You know I'm skittish about the Church. Never again. Look, were you really going to knock on my door? You're really not selling churches?"

"No, I'm not selling churches. I needed to talk to someone. I can't ask questions in Nîmes."

"Then you're in a bad place," she said, pausing for a moment. "So, if you actually can't talk to them, if you're for real, maybe we can talk . . . on some better day. But why me? I can't even help myself."

They looked at each other in silence for a long moment. Roland felt his pulse surging, thudding in his ears and chest. Looking at her under her porch light he realized that there was something more than attractive about her face, and as the word *beautiful* came to his mind, it seemed she blushed. She seemed less agitated and more thoughtful as she spoke.

"I just normally don't have anything to do with men. I don't understand why I'm talking to you. You're with the Church and everything."

"I could be starting my life over again soon. You've been there."

"You remembered?"

Roland realized that she was folding her arms because she was probably getting cold.

"Yes. I'm not about to forget. But you shouldn't get chilled. Maybe, instead of talking out here, would you mind if we could talk in a café somewhere, say tomorrow or the weekend, somewhere in town?"

She hesitated, staring into his eyes. It seemed she was thinking between each word.

"Okay . . . okay, a café. Geneve's. When?"

"Now?"

At this she did laugh. She turned away for a moment and looked back into his eyes again.

"You actually aren't so crazy, are you?"

"No, I'm not. But I do need to talk. Just to you. About how you decide when you don't know what to do."

"I can listen. I can do that. But about deciding?"

"How about, how you decide what goes on a blank canvas? Beyond what I can imagine."

"I might have a few suggestions. Maybe a few questions, like who is your teacher? Wait here while I change."

Within two minutes Vivienne, dressed in a long-sleeve sweater, jeans and boots, pulled her front door closed, waved her keys and agreed to meet him at Geneve's in Les Angles.

Geneve's was not crowded that night, and they were shown to a corner table with a single lit candle. Vivienne ordered a bottle of local white wine she had heard about. The moment after Roland ordered soup and cheese for both of them, Vivienne eyed him carefully.

"Tell me," she said, "why you think I'm a painter?"

"Blue and green paint under your fingernails."

When she smiled and appeared to relax a little more, he asked her about her painter's list of important things. Lighting, Vivienne insisted was the right key to the mood and tone of the story that a painting should tell. Her favorite painter was Monet because of the calming effect of still water, lilies and the harmony of natural colors and proportions. Their conversation revolved around their interests in art until Vivienne became more somber.

"Is it true you have no one to talk to about ordination?" she asked.

"It's not something you question at the diocese. For a lay minister it's considered a fait accompli."

"But if you're actively questioning what you'll do for the rest of your life, surely that means you shouldn't do it."

"Ultimately God decides."

"What happened to free will? Why bother asking anyone's opinion, including me?"

"I don't know. What if God offered his position on it through you?"

Vivienne smiled, as if the thought was beyond anyone's imagination.

"I don't think so," she said. "I could only offer a very subjective opposition to anyone giving their life to an institution full of dead men's bones."

"Well, that's charming," Roland responded. "If you're talking about the veneration of bishops and relics, look past that at what a priest represents to God. Look at what a priest can do for a community over decades."

"But you're not alone with God in that institution," she said, leaning close for emphasis. "There are certain men crept in unawares. They masquerade under apostolic succession and claim infallible authority when they are not only fallible old men, they are Machiavellian men. How can you tell the good from the rotten? By what they do. By who and what they tolerate. By who and what they don't speak out against!"

Roland looked around and motioned for her to lower her voice.

"Keep it down. They'll think we're stoners. We're actually talking about what I've spent my adult life doing. I serve God in the people, not the conspiracy theories you're seeing."

"It's a Cosa Nostra, Roland. They won't leave you alone with God and a little parish somewhere. You have to agree to support their system. This is the system that imprisoned me with a monster my parents and the parish priest chose for me."

"How do you administer something so worldwide without a system?"

"Your system has no checks or balances," she said. "It's an oligarchy that protects itself. When I went over the priest's head to the bishop, the bishop chastised me for faithlessness to that monster, my parents, the Church and God. I was the villain in the eyes of an ivory tower hermit who had no understanding of what a holy family would look like. And why was he so blind? Because the system had imprisoned him in ignorance. It gave him authority over thousands of families who had issues that he had no experience in. Worse, he had no real interest. He was stuck in a mindset from a thousand years ago because the Church is stuck in that mindset. Why would we give credence to an institution that died a long time ago? It's been rotten in high places for a long time."

"And what about all the saints?"

"They were saints because they endured persecution by members of their own order. What about the pedophiles? Who is it that tolerates them?"

Roland found himself smiling in spite of the verbal drubbing his vocation was receiving. Clearly Vivienne was wounded and speaking subjectively, but the debate was lively and he couldn't help admiring her spirit. He thought of an open-ended question just to hear her voice.

"If it's so bad, why hasn't the whole institution collapsed?"

"Because there are good people in it too. Just not in charge of anything much. Look, take you for instance. Say you became a priest and you had to deal with people like me. You're celibate, so you don't have a clue what married life takes. You don't have children so you don't know about the changes that happen in people who do. You're not unemployed, so you don't get what happens when people who identify with their job go and lose their job. You hear the words from their mouth, but you're not actually required to get the pain between the words. So you pray over them with platitudes for twenty years and you become a bishop. You're still as incompetent at counseling as you were when you started. But now you have more title. Their system rewards incompetence and ineffectiveness."

"Okay, now we're getting somewhere," he said, smiling again. "Just the advice I needed."

"Roland, don't you see? You can't reform it. You can't go to a quiet corner of it."

"You make it sound heartless, when there is a heart in it."

"I think it's your heart, at your level of the Church. You don't want to look at what's under the rocks on the levels that exist above the pastoral care you'd so generously give to your imaginary parish. Above that sweet parish, you enter into a coliseum that's survived for two thousand years by politics, intrigue and usury. You think it's all cleaned up now? They are bankers! If Jesus walked into the Vatican, he would turn over the money changers' tables."

"And you think if I became a priest, I'd have to deal with people like you?"

"People just like me. They want experience, competence and integrity as well as a genuine heart. I'm trying my honest best to rescue you from a huge trap. You deserve better."

"I asked for this honest best, didn't I?"

"I told you I wanted to shake you by the collar. I think, just looking at you now, I'd do it a bit more gently."

There was a tenderness in her tone and Roland admitted to himself that he was enjoying talking with her more than anyone he could remember. A week earlier, he might have bristled at the insults to the Church. Now, he simply wanted to know what she was thinking.

"And so, where am I now?"

"You have free will and you have to decide about the reality of that parish. Look, I don't mean to be so blunt or to cause any pain."

"You're okay."

"Okay?" she said, cupping her hands around the candle flame. "I'm messed up. It's kind of funny, me confessing to a priest, after all this time. I never thought I'd confess again. Maybe I should think about what you said about painting."

Her comment reminded Roland of his unfinished assignment. His mind shifted to a memory of a blank canvas in a gold frame. Remembering the untouched fabric of the canvas, he felt himself gliding back and forth in the sunlight above the Rhone. And as he felt he was in safe company, he looked into Vivienne's eyes and spoke his mind.

"I've been thinking about that blank canvas. It's flat, two dimensions. What I'm seeing is in three dimensions, and I'm traveling into it. I'm weightless, time is standing still. How do I draw that?"

"What are you traveling into?" Vivienne asked.

"Going upstream, gliding just above the Rhone," he said, motioning with one hand.

"Go on," she said

"It's mid-afternoon, I'm over the river. The light is golden and the air is so still. Taking my time going up to the high country. Banking left and right in an easy rhythm. If I wanted to I could touch the water. I looked upstream at it a few days ago and wondered if I was in heaven."

"I'd like to see that," she whispered. "I'm seeing it already. The further you go upstream the greater the peace."

"Maybe, some day, I could show you where I was standing before I left," he said.

"I'd have to think about that," Vivienne said, looking at the candle on the table between them.

"Why?"

"You're going to decide," she said quietly. "You have to decide about your life."

"I do have to decide. You're right. Very soon."

She turned, opened her handbag and studied the screen on her phone.

"It's getting late . . . look, the time," she said. "Maybe we should go."

They left Geneve's together and talked for a while by her car. Roland could tell by her tone his decision about what he would do with the rest of his life seemed important to her. She resisted meeting again but gave him her business card and asked him to let her know if he decided to enter the clergy.

"It was good for me to talk to someone other than myself," Vivienne said. "I'm sorry if I was blunt, a little pent-up. I'd like to offer my respect and say good fortune before you take your vows. I'm not really as discourteous as I sound."

Roland realized that she had made up her mind about him. He could only wish her a good night and watch her drive away. Had he stood in the street outside her home a few hours ago or years ago? He started his car and drove back to Nîmes in a daze. Without really focusing, he put the key in his apartment door, walked to his bedroom and stood still, staring at nothing. *What is happening to me*, he wondered. *What have I done?*

He lay back on the bed and pondered his decision about ordination. The more he looked at the opposing definitions of responsibility, the more he realized that he was no closer to a decision. Vivienne in her honesty had made valid points from her perspective. Father LeBlanc would make valid points from his perspective. He, Roland, still had to decide what to do for the rest of his life, and Father Dupree would likely expect a decision soon.

The thought of Father Dupree motivated Roland to redirect his attention toward something more peaceful. What came to mind was a view through golden light just above the Rhone. Gliding back and forth above the river in shafts of sunlight, heading toward the château in heaven, he had no recollection of leaving his sleeping body in Nîmes. Within moments the escorts, protective seraphim, appeared as brilliant streaks of white light. They settled into formation just ahead of him, behind him, above and below, coursing onward in straight lines through the water.

The bend in the river, obscured by trees along the banks, curved around to reveal the towers and bright pennants of the château. Then Roland saw green lawns and gardens and students on the balconies, in conversation between classes. This time, instead of being unsure where to alight, he looked to a balcony on the river side of the château. Paul was outside, leaning on a marble balustrade looking down at the water. He raised an arm and beckoned Roland to the balcony. The escorts sheered away, left and right and Roland stepped down onto glowing flagstones.

"Well, it's good to see you again," Paul said. "We have much to talk about."

Paul gestured toward the balustrade and they stood together looking out over a river in heaven. Roland took in the fragrance of the flower gardens and noticed the geometry of the lawns and trim pathways. In the distance he heard the laughter of students from all over the world, far from their sleeping bodies. Roland thought about Vivienne before he spoke.

"I should thank you for the invitation, even though I don't remember it," Roland said. "I did remember, consciously remember, what you told me when I was here last."

"And so, what now?" Paul asked.

"I talked with her for quite a while," Roland said, seeing her in his mind's eye. "You were right about painting. She thinks the lighting in a painting tells the story. I could tell she was seeing afternoon sunlight on the Rhone as I was talking about it. It was as if she needed permission to be allowed to go. I'd like to show her the view from here."

"What have you decided about the best path for you?"

"I haven't. Too much information now. Too many points of view."

"You have a range of career choices, all practical paths

ordained for you. All have rewards and difficulties. You are familiar with two of them. Ordination or church administration. If there was a third path there would be the question of what you would do to pay your way."

Roland rested his hands on the balustrade and tried to imagine a third path. To identify with anything other than the institution that met all his needs was something he had never considered. At first he recoiled from the insecurity.

"I have no idea," he said, looking out over the river. "Vivienne was right, at least about being unemployed. I've never been unemployed and I don't like the sound of it."

"Who have you been speaking to, about business, during the week?"

"There was a clerk," Roland mused, "and a city planner I spent time with. I suppose I could apply for a position in a planning department, in a place like Les Angles. The planner said they had a vacancy. I have five years' with the Church in that line."

"And your heart? You have a generous heart that should be engaged in the needs of the people around you, by doing and prayer."

"What do you mean? And stay on with the Church as a lay minister?"

"Let's go inside," Paul said. "There's something you should see."

They left the balcony and entered the château via stairs leading through gilded double doors, past several cozy, lamp-lit reading rooms, through more embossed double doors and onto thick carpet in an ornate great room. Paul indicated their way ahead, across the great room and up a series of tiered, wide marble stairways. At the top, another set of open double doors led into a carpeted oval foyer. This was the entrance to a formal dress-circle hallway, arcing to the left and right. The marble walls seemed to be luminous, lit from within the stone itself, inlaid with precise gold borders and fine fleur-de-lis in gold relief. Further along the curving hallway, another marble-arched entrance opened to a high-ceiling amphitheater. In the center of the amphitheater was a broad, clear, reflecting pool. Above the pool, without any visible support, an enormous, majestic, violet-colored flame silently rose more than six meters, two stories high above the reflective water. The flame did not give off any heat or flicker but did change hue in part, to rose, then pink and shades of purple and back to violet. Roland gasped in silence. The effect of the flame seemed familiar and comforting but he couldn't explain why. Paul spoke quietly to him.

"This is the Liberty Flame. Our God is a consuming fire. It's been here, not seen in the terrestrial world for over twelve thousand years. It's an aspect of God's presence and radiates with other flames like it around the world for a reason. It consumes the accumulated energy of cruelty, confinement and constrictions that people place on other people."

"How is it suspended above the water?" Roland whispered. "There's nothing to burn."

"It's an unfed flame, brought here before the Flood. You have a miniature version similar to it in the area of your physical heart. It too is suspended, unfed and a consuming fire."

"How does it radiate around the world?"

"Its radiance penetrates matter, through every atom, every emotion, every thought in every person of God. It's for transmutation, activated by holy prayer, adjusted by the intelligence and compassion of God. Any minister, any person in any religion has unlimited access to it by prayer. You name a burden and ask for God's will to adjust your prayer. This is what I wanted you to see."

"And transmutation, what is that?"

"The process of changing behavior like usury and cruelty to a higher form. Gently."

A few minutes later Paul ushered Roland out of the balcony area to the oval foyer and allowed him to catch his breath.

"I thought this was a university," Roland said.

"It is. There are dozens of universities and retreats like

156

this in the celestial world. Each has specific purposes. All are interconnected by bonds of love. There are two in Paris, another in Bingen, on the Rhine in Germany, Fátima in Portugal, Crete, Archangel in Russia, several in China, Africa, the United States and Canada and so on."

"How is any of this physically possible?"

"It's not terrestrial. Here, mental activity, emotional activity and spirit all move at far higher frequencies, without the density and lethargy of the terrestrial. Even the material elements here move exponentially faster at the subatomic level. And there are still higher levels, beyond light speed, all the way to formless spirit. Do you remember the words from one of your Church hymns, "The Holy City"? "And all who would might enter and no one was denied; no need of moon or star by night or sun to shine by day, it was the New Jerusalem that would not pass away."

"I remember it."

"You are here in your celestial body in one small part of the New Jerusalem. The terrestrial world you're going back to, will, over the centuries, become more congruent with the celestial worlds. Tens of thousands, and then millions, will come to these universities while their bodies sleep. It will change the terrestrial world gradually, by individual free will."

"So how will the world's bad actors, the dictators, the really violent people fit into that?"

"Earth will move on without them. At the end of their natural life they'll be given opportunities on other worlds, in other solar systems more suited to their state of evolution."

"What would Father Dupree or Father LeBlanc say if they knew about this?"

"Their time will come. Perhaps you will be instrumental on their behalf. Now, there's one more thing for you to contemplate."

Paul led him down a set of marble stairs, along a carpeted hallway to a familiar set of double doors and into the luminous workshop. There in the same nook, overlooking trees and gardens, was the golden easel and the pristine blank canvas. This time there was a painter's console standing next to the easel, equipped with an array of pencils and a pad for sketching. Paul invited Roland to approach the canvas and imagine.

"Think of what brings you joy," Paul said quietly. "All that God can make of joy and grace combined."

Roland stepped toward the console, picked up the sketchpad and the nearest pencil, and began to see the glassy beauty of the Rhone, winding gracefully through the woods in golden sunlight. Wondering if Paul had caught his thoughts, Roland turned toward him with a smile but Paul was no longer in the workshop.

Alone with his thoughts and beginning to enjoy the freedom to imagine beauty Roland began his first sketch in heaven, weaving the pencil across the pad as the broad outline of the river he saw in his mind. There the light, shafting down in amber and gold, told the story of a decision made in joy. Bright seraphim formed up protectively around him as he glided back and forth over the liquid gold reflection of the sun's rays, in an ecstasy of understanding what to do with his life. Over the river, it seemed as if the freedom from doubt would last forever, until the phone alarm chimed and Roland woke around dawn in his apartment in Nîmes.

On the drive that day from Nîmes to Les Angles and then Villeneuve, the car seemed to hover above the road. A gentle rhythm and sound of solitary bells signaled a crystal clarity in Roland's mind. A clear plan and sequence of tasks began to appear in his mind's eye. He had an obligation to finish what he had started for the Church, and he intended to complete it on time.

In a parking lot in Villeneuve, he laid out his collection of municipal zoning maps across the dash. He selected three plausible sites suitable for a medium to large church, easily visible and close to main roads. Pros and cons for each option were completed by midday, and before he began the trip back to Nîmes, he stopped near Geneve's in Les Angles, glanced at its outdoor patrons, busy waiters and through the doorway to a certain corner table inside.

"Thank you," he whispered.

At five he was at the diocese offices in Nîmes right on time and knocked on Father Dupree's door. The big man opened the door and looked at Roland for a moment, as if he didn't recognize him.

"Ah, yes, Allevard. What do you have?"

At the priest's request Roland laid out the completed task report on the desk. It was formatted in the diocese's official administrative style. He waited for Dupree's response.

"Fine. This is what we wanted," Dupree said.

"I wasn't able to find demonstrated strong support, but on the whole it could work."

"We have sufficient information now to add this case."

Uncertain as to the priest's meaning Roland wondered about sensitivities concerning the effect of a new church in Les Angles on the Bishop of Avignon, across the river.

"Will the bishops agree?"

"The bishops have already agreed, Allevard. We of the Church in France have already agreed, and we will apply to the highest authorities in the Holy See to establish the case that we must expand with the necessary means and without delay. Without delay, Allevard. There is no case for further accommodation with the courts and false allegations. We have what we need from you concerning this assignment and we thank you for your effort. Rousillon has been informed. Tomorrow you will return to your regular duties."

"Thank you, Father."

As Roland got up to leave, Dupree waved him back.

"We will need your summary application for ordination in the morning, to be on the safe side, as far as timing. You will be pleased to know, with that eligibility, you may receive an invitation to attend a sealed conference in Paris. An understanding will be conveyed to the body of the Church in France. This is a matter of historical significance and an event that will set the sails for your place within the Church. Read the summary application carefully this evening as it will require a number of properly written submissions, preparatory to the time of ordination."

159

Roland took the application packet from Dupree's hand, hesitated and then gave it back.

"Thank you, Father."

Father Dupree held the packet up and stared at him in disbelief as Roland let himself out of the office. At the main office door and again in the parking lot, Roland walked briskly, listening for sounds of the priest's pursuit and protests. He started his car and drove out of the lot, half expecting to be flagged down by anxious deacons with an urgent message from Father Dupree. No one came out into the parking lot.

That evening, Roland left his apartment in Nîmes and took the A9 northeast to Les Angles to meet a friend at a café called Geneve's. Geneve's normally doesn't take reservations for weeknights, but that evening they made an exception for a certain corner table, on the grounds that an important decision would be conveyed there.

Across the river, a few kilometers from Geneve's, there is a little waterfront business near Avignon where tourists and even people from Les Angles can rent a canal boat for a day, or maybe for a weekend, and travel at their own pace up the Rhone River, looking for châteaux that may or may not be visible to human eyes. They can take sketchpads and draw details of things that matter, because they're beautiful. They can stop at cafés and restaurants in towns along that smooth, serene river, just talking to each other, being kind to each other and forgiving each other for things that in this world need a great deal of time and trust to be explained.

CONTINUITY

A city's greatest hero passes a torch of consecrated power, strengthening a new generation and burning an old elite.

CONTINUITY

I had the pleasure of attending an unusual annual police awards ceremony in New Winchester this week, at the invitation of New Winchester Chief of Police Frank Garrett. You may accept the notion that annual police awards are not expected to be controversial and that they are predictable, insider recognitions for locals. From my perspective, this event is still resonating at my very core.

Why did I attend? Multiple invitations are extended to me in advance every day of every week. My choice each day is based on the value I perceive in those who will be participating. I have known and respected Frank Garrett for many years as one of the most balanced law enforcement officers in the nation, and so I took him seriously when he asked for my time. When he invited me to this event and told me his keynote speaker was going to be the great Gideon George, I knew I had to be there. Gideon George is the quintessential, straight-news journalist of the old-school type and had not spoken in public for over a decade. He didn't have to travel as far as I did because he is a New Winchester local, but given his age I understood this might be the last time anyone heard him in public.

Due to a security problem at the airport, the chauffeur was delayed, so I arrived late and found myself squeezing into a full gallery of spectators on the second level of New Winchester's sharp new City Hall. Frank had invited a bunch of out-of-town journalists, including myself, and the best of the local New Winchester scribes were also in attendance. The mayor was there with the police commissioner, just about the whole Chamber of Commerce, the city commissioners and all sorts of important people I could not recognize. Front and center, of course, was a full house of young city and county police officers, who were probably wondering why there was standing room only at their insider ceremony.

The awards themselves took place first and then Frank announced his keynote speaker, Gideon George. Everyone in the gallery who knew Gideon stood to offer a standing ovation as the old man came out slowly into the lights around the podium. None of the younger police officers had ever heard of him and so they were the last to get up, clearly not understanding who they were applauding or the reason for the barrage of camera flashes. Suspecting this was going to be newsworthy, I turned on my recording mike, even if only as a final acknowledgment of Gideon's contribution to journalism. I, myself, did not understand I was about to get more than I bargained for.

Gideon George gripped his hands on the wooden trim of the podium and surprised me with the sharpness of his demeanor. He looked carefully at the audience and cleared his throat. When he began to speak he looked left and right, addressing the police officers, but every now and then he turned and looked up at me. Directly at me. As he commenced, Gideon's introduction and salutation was brief, as is his style.

Ladies and gentlemen, thank you. Please be seated. I am here tonight to fulfill my duty to the men and women who are the police officers of this city, where I have been very grateful to live for most of my life. It may seem unusual for a journalist to state his duty, but I trust you will shortly understand the meaning. I'm grateful to Chief Frank Garrett for the invitation to speak. The Chief understands why I have to speak. The time is now.

Many of you are aware that this new building is named for a former New Winchester police captain, Jake Byrne. You know of

Byrne Boulevard and Jake Byrne Plaza in the business district. You may be aware that Jake Byrne was the most famous police officer in the history of New Winchester and is recognized as a hero and an icon in shaping the identity and character of the city. My duty to you this evening is to explain Jake Byrne's role in how the city's character was reshaped.

First, it's important for you to understand Jake's background. He was born here in New Winchester in 1920 in a part of the city that doesn't exist any more, thanks to him. That area used to be known as the Wallace Blocks, a decent enough neighborhood in the 1850s but not so nice by the time he was born. Rail and freight-yards in 1890 were followed by a maze of factories, crowded row houses and petty crime. By the time Jake was ten there were four territorial gangs in the square mile around the Wallace Blocks, and their shifting status in fights was the constant topic of conversation at the Catholic school he attended.

Jake was recruited and kicked out of two of those gangs where he learned how to fight "mean." He took his frustrations out at the local Y and became a strong amateur boxer. Jake may have gone to a Catholic school but he was no saint. Those school years were the years of the Great Depression, and like his father, mother and older brother, he found there was only factory work when he left school. He was not tethered to anything important in the gangs or the low-paying, dangerous factory jobs. He was going nowhere by the time of the Japanese attack on Pearl Harbor in December 1941. That event seemed like the greatest, most exciting thing at the time, he told me, but he had no idea how it would change him.

It was his father who suggested Jake apply for officer training school in the army, and so he became a second lieutenant in 1942, a lieutenant in 1943 and shipped out for England in 1944. Jake's unit went ashore at Normandy a week after D-Day and got chewed up in the Battle of the Hedgerows, the maze of French farmland just behind the allied beachhead. Between Normandy and crossing the Rhine into Germany, he became a captain, was wounded by bullets and shrapnel three times and lost 240% of his company. That means, between visits to field hospitals, Jake saw all of his company killed or seriously wounded almost two and a half times over, in less than a year of infantry combat. He told me that leading young men around new obstacles day after day and through that much blood, agony and loss aged him in ways that don't count as years. By the end of the war in the summer of 1945, he was traumatized but wouldn't show it.

Coming back to New Winchester, the way it was in 1946, did not help. Jake's parents and brother no longer lived there because criminal gangs had taken over during the war and the turf fights were now at the mafia level. It didn't help that without war production, factories shut down and unemployment made for a surplus of mean, young men in a decaying urban wasteland. The mafia types didn't trust many of them, and the police didn't know how to control them. Jake was furious at the police and the city for not doing something. To him, New Winchester was in a pre-anarchic situation, similar to what he knew had transpired a few years earlier in Nazi Germany, a breeding ground for lethal armies of useful idiots. When Jake applied to join the police force in 1946 he was not exactly a rookie. I am sure he had to restrain himself, to hold back from interviewers the dead-serious authority of a combat infantry captain, the type of man who was not about to accept anarchy in this city.

Jake could not and would not tell anyone in 1946, or at any time since then, except myself, sworn to silence until now, that the mission-oriented, trusting relationship with his conscience changed when he got back and saw what had happened to New Winchester in his absence. When Jake became a police officer, there was a disconnect between the street cops and their superiors at precinct levels. Jake was a street cop who was mad at his superiors and in a position to take out his feelings on the money men and gang leaders who he held responsible for the impending death of his city. He was this close to becoming a vigilante in uniform. Taking out opposing leaders was what the government had trained him to do as a combat infantry officer in France and Germany—identify

166

enemy decision-makers and take them out, fast, no questions. He could have done it in New Winchester as an under-supervised rookie and gotten away with it for a while, because of the practical absence of ranking superiors on the street and the frequency of murder among rival gangs and their enforcers.

To his precinct officers in 1946, Jake was just another rookie, but in practical matters he was an experienced recon-scout and killer, now working in a civilian setting with an untreated trauma disorder. Within a few months of becoming a police officer, Jake had identified a list of gang leaders and mafia enforcers in about a square mile area of slum housing and factories. He planned to personally eliminate these individuals, knowing he could get away with it in the chaos. But something unexpected happened to Jake Byrne. That square mile included the dangerous area around the Catholic school he had attended as a boy. He was on patrol there one night and separated himself from the other three officers to take a break. The self-examining conscience that saved his life in combat had kicked in during the patrol, and he couldn't stand listening to the banter of the other patrolmen while he was planning murder. At the time, he had an attitude that could take or leave police regulations. He needed privacy to think through the pros and cons of his systematic plan to save New Winchester by execution. Knowing the school yard well, Jake jimmied the lock to the chapel door at the back of the school and sat alone in the dark near the altar. At some level, his conscience was uneasy with the systematic plan and the reflection on his father if he was caught. He lit his cigarette lighter as a candle and said out loud, "What do I do?"

He didn't expect any kind of answer from his conscience, but he got one anyway, and it was vocal, as clear as a powerful man speaking behind him.

"Follow the law."

It was this stern three-word directive in the dimly-lit chapel that changed Jake's mind about being alone with his conscience. It shocked him. The sheer power in those three spoken words followed him from then on, and there was no way he could think about getting away with murder when he felt what was likely the eye of God probing his every thought.

The beat cops in New Winchester at that time went about in squads of at least four and more often up to twelve for force protection. Gang factions would usually exceed this number, and taunts between gang lookouts and police often led to chases, directly into ambushes.

Gangs had so little respect for the police that they regarded the cops as rivals and were always eager for confrontation. If the cops had billy-clubs, gang members would bring baseball bats. Nothing else was more exciting in New Winchester at that time than fights, the bigger and more brutal the better. As a rookie, Jake took part in his share of these fights, as if the cops and gangs were equals. The disrespect for law enforcement and its ineffectiveness disgusted him. It was what had motivated him to plan to take matters into his own hands. Chastened against that course, he pursued seniority, going over his superiors and taking a new, systematic and legal plan directly to the Chief. Within a year he was promoted to lieutenant.

I entered this account in 1947, just after Jake had become a lieutenant on the street. I was a journalism graduate who saw the near-anarchy and the police in paralysis. Police patrols at that time were predictable and ineffective, ridiculed by the gangs and even by myself. The only police officer who impressed me was Jake Byrne. Jake had something going on in the Wallace Blocks that was hard to describe. It was a mixture of unpredictable patrols and selective arrests, as well as apparent disappearances on his part. The rumor in his unit was that Jake was going undercover among the gangs and that the Chief knew. To me, this guy, Jake Byrne, was going to be in the news one way or another, so I attached myself to him to get what was sure to be tragic news, before anyone else. I made sure my editor knew he was mine, got my news copy in on time, and I had the beginning of a career writing city crime news.

The thing is, Jake didn't turn up dead in a vacant lot. He would look for me, spell names and facts for me and told me where to find corroborating witnesses. I knew what he was doing but the facts always checked out. Pretty soon I had a genuine working friendship with Jake, who saw I wouldn't write opinion, just facts. That friendship lasted all our professional lives, and we were personal friends right up to his passing this year. Jake's wife passed on a few years before him, and that's why I'm here tonight.

On the strength of almost forty years of our professional and personal friendship, Jake invited me to his home after his retirement in 1985 and asked me to listen, ask questions and take confidential notes. The content of those notes that are now here on the podium were not to be released until after his passing and that of his wife. He asked that they be released first and foremost to the police officers of New Winchester. Part of Jake's motivation was that after retirement he began to spend his time weeding, pruning and planting in the rose garden on his corner lot. His time by himself in the garden was hardly private for more than a few minutes before well-wishers would come by and want to praise his career and achievements. He was a self-effacing man and eventually left the garden to someone else, and he called me in to set the record straight, for you. As Jake saw it, he was no hero and no icon.

Jake Byrne was also not religious. A Catholic upbringing was an indifferent thing to him, because it occurred during a time when he saw church and state authority figures as ineffectual. No one had any effect in turning around the decay that destroyed the Wallace Blocks and the rest of the inner city. What mattered far more to Jake was the inner relationship he developed with his conscience during combat in France and Germany. He trusted it. It was genuine. It kept him alive and helped him get a dirty, awful job done. He didn't think of it as an aspect of God or anything beyond the personal survival smarts he expanded to help the men in his company.

When I attached myself to Lieutenant Byrne in 1947, I asked him a leading question about his rumored undercover activities. I remember him looking right through me and ignoring the question. Only after his retirement, with me sworn to secrecy until after his passing, would he tell me about those years. The matter had to do with the expansion of his conscience.

As a lieutenant, Jake had new authority to develop an increasingly detailed map of rival mafia and gang hang-outs and sources of income within the decaying, core square mile and low-income areas around it. Other officers knew of Jake's map but were not that interested in making use of it. Safe, predictable patrols and regular shifts were more important to them. The labyrinth of narrow, century-old streets was confusing, dangerous and impenetrable to other officers, as well as to Jake. It bothered him that criminal suspects would so easily escape arrest by his patrolmen by disappearing into hidden tunnels and sewers inside and under the maze of old brick row-houses and factories. It was New Winchester at its dirtiest and ugliest, and there was nothing that could be done about it.

One night in the Blocks, during a downpour, Jake got separated from his officers, who were in futile pursuit of suspects. He stopped running in order to get his bearings and stood alone in an alley. Instead of trying to locate the name of the alley, his thoughts went to the larger question of how justice could ever prevail in such a hostile and unrepentant setting.

He stood still and asked his conscience out loud, "What do I do?"

This time there was no vocal answer, just an image in his mind's eye of fire engines and ladder trucks entering a burning neighborhood. The visual response puzzled him until a week later he heard sirens from all over the city. Jake's unit was called to assist civilian evacuations from the Wallace Blocks area. The fire destroyed six blocks of housing and factories, leaving over two hundred people homeless and many more injured, and it bankrupted the under-insured corporate landlord. Fortunately, no one was killed.

In the weeks after the big fire in the Blocks, while the courts and newspapers debated whether it was arson or accident, the area declined and more people moved out. The mayor and city commissioners visited with reporters in tow, including me, and they vowed to rebuild, to add more police patrols and a new fire station, but nothing happened. The city still taxed the Wallace Blocks, but now no one actually owned it.

Within a year the blight had encompassed all of the Wallace Blocks. Few wanted to live there, and no one wanted to buy the derelict district to make something of it, so it fell into ruin.

The fire and decay changed the dynamics of the impenetrability of that square mile. Some gangs quickly disappeared, others took advantage. They set up shacks inside the blackened ruins or occupied empty buildings as bases for robberies and crimes they committed in surrounding areas. Jake also took advantage, redrawing his map several times.

In the summer of 1948, Jake was with a patrol in the Wallace Blocks investigating and inventorying abandoned buildings. A radio call came to Jake that robbery suspects were likely to return to that area after dark. Officers were positioned out of sight to arrest the suspects and recover stolen goods. Jake chose to wait it out alone in a lookout post on the ground floor of an empty row house. He spread out his map on the floor and cupped a flashlight over it. Unlike the war in Europe, where his unit gained ground and moved closer to Germany each month, no ground and no progress was being made in the square mile of hell at the center of old New Winchester. The decayed urban area would not give up its crime and death culture, and there was no hope that piecemeal arrests would change the Blocks for the better. Jake could have torn up his crime map in frustration at the ineffectiveness of his work. In resignation, he bent over the map and waved his hand just above it, as if to magically erase the slums and the poverty-mindset and replace them with gardens and functioning businesses.

A memory came to his attention from his school days when a priest told him face to face, "Man proposes, God disposes." It didn't matter what the priest had referred to, the idea came to him to propose to God the erasing of the square mile of hell and let God figure out how it would be done.

171

Jake spoke out loud in the front room of the empty house, "God, I propose tearing down this whole area and rebuilding it with something better! Not my will but yours be done. Amen."

Immediately he felt the urge to expect that nothing good would ever happen and countered the fatalism by repeating, "Not my will but yours be done! Amen!"

Sheltered from most of the neighborhood noise, Jake stood still long enough in the empty house to gain an impression that there were people there in the Blocks who were not able to leave. He had given no thought to the remaining residents or even the resident criminals as people who may be trapped because they had no livelihood and nowhere else to go. It was a complication he had not anticipated so he proposed another idea.

"God, I propose you find a way for everyone here to leave, to get free of this place."

Another impression came to him. He was to walk through the blighted area alone, block by block, in uniform. He told me he laughed. That would be suicide, he reasoned. The image persisted and Jake resisted. Common sense seemed to be on his side and he decided to push back.

"God, I propose you explain to me how that could be safe."

The image that came to mind was from a captioned stained-glass window in a nave in the church where his parents often took him as a boy. The image was of Archangel Michael. Still alone with his street map in an abandoned house in the Wallace Blocks, Jake thought he was being tricked. He reacted defensively.

"I don't believe that's who you are. If you're the devil, you're not welcome here. You have to leave, right now. Right now! Get out of here! If you're a holy person, show yourself. Show yourself! Show me who you are!"

Nothing happened for a moment, and then Jake began to see a bright blue form. It was without any doubt for him the visible presence of Archangel Michael, the one Jake thought was confined to the Old and New Testaments, standing a few feet in front of him. This was the person, not the stained glass portrait. The tall, strong, young man looking directly into his eyes was an authority any military man would recognize. The man appeared to be about twenty years of age with shoulder-length blond hair and blue eyes and was covered in blueish armor. Jake gasped as he felt an expansive pressure in his chest, an ecstasy that was exhilarating and peaceful at the same time. Light increased from within and around the figure until Jake could not look at him without shading his eyes. Even that was not enough and he lost his bearings in the room, backing up and falling to his knees in the open front doorway, hands cupped around his eyes. He was not afraid, just mystified and almost blinded.

Jake called out into the light, "Why come to me? Who are you?"

This time there was a vocal response, "I am Michael, Archangel of the Lord, servant of the Christ in you."

Each syllable spoken by the archangel resonated in Jake's chest as if an octave of bells were being gently touched inside him. There was no pain or fear, only amazement. No man, woman or child he knew had ever spoken in that way to him. The quality of voice left him feeling uplifted, even though the words were pronounced with authority and power.

Awareness of the presence of the archangel faded, and the next thing Jake knew his patrolmen were lifting him to his feet, thinking he'd been attacked. He was barely conscious, so an ambulance was called. Jake was unhurt, but the patrolmen could not have known that.

I was listening to police radio that night and heard Jake's sergeant make the call to the dispatcher. I could have kicked myself for not being out with the patrol. If Jake was dead, my career was in trouble. Guessing where he'd be taken, I got to the nearest hospital as the ambulance brought him in and waited until the nurses would let me see him in an observation room.

Jake was sitting on the side of a bed. I asked him how he was doing and he said fine, he just needed time to think.

"To think about what?" I asked. "About who hit you?"

"No one hit me. Man proposes, God disposes, Gideon."

I couldn't get any sense out of him and thought he had some kind of concussion. Much later he told me that he was barely in his mind, trying to figure out why he felt so different. A part of him was in complete peace and in a sense of trust that all was well. His mind, though, was restless with unresolved questions. Jake's experience as a boy in a Church school was sufficient to drill into him that there are mysteries of God that only the priests are qualified to deal with. Everyone else should stand clear because they could be in jeopardy of their mortal soul without knowing it. This was what he was wrestling with when I spoke to him. Based on that experience, there was the possibility he was in trouble with the Church for a doctrinal infringement, some blasphemy he didn't understand, and he was not about to tell anyone anything. But the more he relived the encounter, the more he felt comforted, and after a while he set aside any concerns that he was in jeopardy. Still, he kept his thoughts to himself, and I'm sure he would not have spoken to a priest, even if one had been called.

The hospital released Jake that night and he went home and sat in his apartment living room. He was unmarried at the time and had to figure out what to do and whether to believe his own memory. As the expansive feeling of peace faded the questions and doubts crept in. Jake's problem was not in the heart but in the mind. As his mind applied its reasoning, it identified four problems. First, he had proposed an idea to God and God had given him an answer. He didn't like the answer because it was too dangerous according to police protocol and common sense. Second, angels did not appear to people in 1948. Angels and archangels belonged in the Good Book and had no business speaking with people who had been warned in church that the devil could appear as an angel of light. Third, the notion of "servant" was no longer an acceptable social concept in 1948. Why would an archangel talk about being a servant? Archangels were in charge of legions of angels and could do anything they wanted. Fourth, Christ and Jesus he understood to be synonymous, but he did not understand the reference to himself. There was no one to talk to about any of it.

Flipping through a Bible his father had given him didn't help, so Jake made another proposition.

"God, I am proposing you help me clear up this doubt and confusion." Within seconds he was asleep in his chair and woke up with sunlight coming in the window.

The precinct had given Jake some time off, so he drove over to the church where the stained-glass image of Archangel Michael was still in the nave. A deacon greeted him and Jake asked if there were any prayers to Archangel Michael he might borrow. The deacon showed him one but said it was restricted and could not leave the sanctuary. Jake read it and understood why. It was titled, "The Pope's Prayer" and it proposed to God that Archangel Michael protect the supplicant and enter Armageddon for the binding of Death and Hell and the casting of the Devil into the lake of sacred fire. It was strong stuff with vivid wording no priest had allowed him to see as a boy. He memorized it as best he could and thanked the deacon.

On the drive home, Jake tried to repeat his memorized prayer but could only remember the first two lines. For someone who had no interest in prayer, he thought it was a good enough start, because those two lines were a proposition that got to the point right away. Still, it made him wonder, "Why me?" Why would God send Archangel Michael to him when he hadn't prayed or gone to church in years? This was the same archangel who had long ago thrown the proud rebel archangel Lucifer and Satan and a third of the angels out of heaven, down into this lower world, to live out their remaining time either as men or demons. They were collectively "the Devil," but what was Jake to God?

The rules of the relationship with God appeared to be that he, Jake, had to initiate every move with an idea, spoken as a proposition that some would call prayer, and then he would get unspoken direction in a cryptic, economical image or concept. He was free to agree with it or not. He wondered what would happen if he ignored the direction. Then he wondered what would happen if he followed it. What if, he wondered, if he kept saying the parts of the

175

prayer he remembered and followed the direction. But no police officer in their right mind would walk alone in uniform around those narrow streets, past those burned-out buildings and vacant lots where tribes of vagrants lived and squabbled with the remaining residents over nothing. His gun and uniform would be worth more as trophies to those hoods than his discarded body. Jake wondered if he was crazy, deluded to even consider it. He'd seen it happen to men in France, men who muttered prayers instead of sighting their rifle. Was it belatedly catching up with him, three years after the bloodshed?

For a week Jake did nothing out of the ordinary as he thought it over. Then he received an order from the Chief to go to a high security section of the city jail to interrogate a certain murder suspect. This individual was suspected of murdering one of the many Wallace Blocks gang leaders as well as three of his allies and then taking over the gang. The meanness and cruelty of the man made an impression on Jake. There was no remorse, only defiance. The gang's income and purpose had been redirected to serve the needs of this monster. He had sacrificed any dissenters, setting them up for mauling and torture by neighboring gangs. There were no remaining renters in the blocks that this criminal controlled.

The Chief's problem was that there were no witnesses in the Blocks willing to confront the gang leader in court. Everyone knew the prison was overcrowded and complete sentences were seldom served. Jake's job was to interrogate the suspect, then find and protect witnesses who would be willing to testify.

Jake arrived at the afflicted section of the Blocks in a convoy of squad cars. There was plenty of force protection. Jake and his men moved among the fire-ruins and derelict buildings calling for witnesses. The vagrants and gang members retired to the tunnels they had connected to the sewers, a kind of below-ground slum. This was the domain of the king of the rats. It infuriated Jake that he had fought and won a war to free the people of Europe from tyrants and three years later people in his own city were living like cavemen.

Finally Jake cornered about a dozen miscreants armed with crowbars and knives in an abandoned row house. Whispering the first two lines of the prayer under his breath he held his troopers back and advanced alone toward the entrance. The closed front door was sagging on one hinge. Instead of kicking it open, Jake dropped his peaked police hat behind him on the street, lifted the damaged door open, and stood in the doorway to confront them. He looked them over and again called for witnesses. They remained defiant and suspicious, almost sub-human in their filth and degradation. They were of the same mean, low character as the individual he had interrogated in prison, differing only in degrees of brute strength. Someone needed to explain where they were headed.

Jake spoke clearly, without threatening them. "Winter is coming. None of you will survive here. Your only chance is to leave the Blocks now. If you go into the city, you will have to surrender your meanness, serve your brothers and sisters, sacrifice your time and energy in work and be selfless. Surrender, serve, sacrifice, be selfless. Maybe you'll have a chance."

He left the Blocks without any witnesses, knowing the gang leader would have to be released within forty-eight hours if the district attorney had no case to stand up in court. The situation reinforced his view that the city itself was criminally negligent in failing to evacuate and condemn the entire square mile of degradation. Someone had to do something to explain to the city fathers where they were headed.

Jake brooded over the city's failure and how to get the commissioners' attention. Squad cars continued to be called into the Blocks for serious crimes two or three times a day. Frustrated, he proposed to God that he be shown the best way to get the city's political authorities to act. Two weeks later his patrols were directed to arrest robbery and assault suspects near Juniper Street in the Wallace Blocks. Positioning his men to ambush suspects, Jake returned to his patrol car and radioed the dispatcher. All was ready.

Time passed. He visited each patrolman's position, then withdrew to an alley to wait. As he waited he quietly repeated his two lines of the prayer and found his frustration shifting toward a sense of urgency. The time had come.

The Wallace Blocks, with no parks and few sidewalks, were laid out in 1850 as inexpensive homes for industrial workers. The area was bounded by a rectangle of four main streets intended for passage of occasional supply wagons. These streets ran north-south and east-west, with narrower lanes and alleys connecting them. Gangs blocked and held these alleys as territorial boundaries and fought over turf encroachments for over sixty years, between 1890 and 1950. Jake knew the dirty, infamous streets in detail, and while he waited he kept thinking over his idea to clear the whole square mile of desolation and replace the slums with something the city could be proud of. Then, in an instant, his thoughts of merely contemplating images of improvement changed to a sudden knowing of what he had to do. With a surge of confidence and without announcing anything to his patrolmen, Jake began walking north on Juniper Street, right down the centerline, speaking under his breath, over and over.

"Saint Michael the archangel, defend us in Armageddon, be our protection against the wickedness and snares of the Devil . . ."

As he walked up Juniper Street, the two prayer lines became second nature, and another part of Jake's mind, observing the residents and others who came to windows and doors to look at him, determined he would find a way to get them out of there and find them something better. The city, he reasoned, should create a new housing inventory, offer every renter several work and housing options in other parts of the city or in the suburbs, then float a bond to buy the bankrupt Wallace Blocks and condemn the buildings. Even if it were only a few blocks at a time. The concept was so obvious he couldn't imagine why the mayor or city commissioners had not already done it. They needed a push, and he was going to provide it.

At the intersection of Osage and Juniper, Jake turned west,

walking down the centerline of a dirty street with no moving traffic, only derelict trucks and sedans that served as bedrooms for the homeless. No one had come near him, though maybe a hundred people were watching his progress in amazement.

At Eastlake Road, Jake turned south and continued on unmolested until he neared the intersection where he would turn east on Ash. About fifteen hoods, known police-haters, were waiting in the alleys and lanes for him. Jake recognized them and raised his right palm toward them, continuing down the centerline of Eastlake. None of the bad guys moved from their alleys. In Jake's mind he simply sent them the message "It's over, you're leaving," even as he spoke the two lines of his prayer.

A crowd of twenty-five to thirty people watched from the middle of the street behind Jake as he turned east on Ash. Residents had never seen a lone police officer walking the centerline of their street. Their common experience of a police presence began with flashing lights, squad cars braking aggressively, lots of yelling, a dozen or more officers, fights, screaming, blood and handcuffed people cursing or face down on the street. A lone officer on the centerline, with some kind of purpose in his stride was clearly unprecedented to them, as if it was a sign without words that something was about to change in the Blocks.

When Jake returned to the area where he had left his patrol they came running toward him demanding answers. The robbery suspects had avoided the scheduled ambush and the officers were confused at Jake's unannounced disappearance and reappearance. He was obviously not undercover.

But it was Jake's patrol report on the centerline event and possible city negligence that got the attention of the Chief and the police commissioner the next morning. That report began a cascade of political inquiries by the mayor, who discovered that the city commissioners had been sitting on a recommendation to buy the Wallace Blocks from the bankruptcy receiver and then pay to demolish the buildings. No commissioner had wanted to be on public record for raising taxes or proposing a substantial new bond to the voters.

I covered Jake's testimony in front of the mayor and city commissioners, where he proposed the creation of a new rental housing inventory and job listings in the newer parts of New Winchester and its suburbs. Jake had already had clerks in City Hall unofficially tally available rental vacancies, and this made a powerful case to the do-nothing politicians. I lobbied my editor for front page photos and copy coverage for Jake's proposal and its political ramifications, and it worked. The newspaper received hundreds of letters supporting Jake and quite a few announcements of new candidates for commissioner positions at the next election.

Jake, though, didn't waste a second, even as he was promoted to captain. He knew the politicians would squabble and waste time over what to do when the Blocks and surrounding areas were eventually condemned and torn down. He was already ahead of them with the same determination that poured through him when he walked the Blocks alone. Using his willing clerical contacts at City Hall as his unofficial research department, Jake came up with six variants on a district-wide street layout and rebuilding program for the square mile that included the Blocks. His enthusiasm was contagious as the effort spread above the clerical level. Mid-level managers began making unofficial inquiries to national banks, hospital corporations, pharmaceutical companies, office-tower developers, national retail chains, shopping mall developers, architectural, engineering and landscaping firms. And Jake supplied me with summaries, sketches, photos and maps, just as "conversation starters," as he put it. Much of it made it onto the front page of the paper, and it was a high point in my career. It was also a great time for New Winchester, which hadn't had anything really new or exciting happen in the city for more than fifty years.

The year 1950 turned to 1951, and Jake, still a police captain, kept setting precedents as an accepted if unusual backdoor factor in the redevelopment plans for New Winchester. I had attached myself to Jake when he was a street operations police lieutenant in 1947 and seen his expertise develop in terms of tact and diplomacy with rough people in dark places. I had to change my own expertise in order to follow Jake as he entered city politics via support from the Chief, the police commissioner and the mayor. Jake was a natural at transferring his diplomatic skills with street people into effective influence within the political class. You could call it bandwagon popularity, but there was something unique going on when at Jake's suggestion the police commissioner invited him to make a new round of evacuation and relocation presentations for the Blocks to the mayor's circle, then to the city commissioners and their financial friends. I could not gain access to those meetings. Jake was smart enough to refer me to the official city spokesman for comments and primed me with the right questions to ask him.

It was just after this time that the city took control of the Wallace Blocks from the court-appointed receiver and condemned the area. This gave the go-ahead for relocation of the remaining residents to private and city rental inventories. A demolition and redevelopment bond was passed by the voters, and the bulldozers took down the hundred-year-old desolation. Decayed neighboring areas within the square mile around the Blocks were also bought by the city and condemned.

I looked out at a vast swath of inner New Winchester from the top floor of the newspaper's building one morning in spring of 1951. It was open, free, bulldozed ground that had recently been the center of hell in our city. That day our photographers provided the photos and I provided the front page copy telling the story of how one man had changed New Winchester for the better. The residents of the city felt the tide of change, and a surge of public recognition appeared for Jake. I suppose I was the one who began the hero-story around Jake Byrne and it is fitting that I am the one to now add new information to the public record about Jake.

Although it appeared that little redevelopment occurred between 1951 and 1954 there was a lot going on behind the scenes. Acting on Jake's backdoor suggestions regarding the best mix of parks and gardens with banks, hospitals and retail centers the city fathers did a fine job of negotiating with developers, national corporations, the state and the federal government. These were the years prior to the Eisenhower interstate freeway project, and New Winchester got in on the ground floor with its petition for urban freeway development.

Jake was not always shaking hands in the halls of government. The city fathers had no exposure to the faces of the vagrants and criminals removed from the Wallace Blocks to low income housing or to prison, but Jake remembered them. He was fully aware of the momentum the city was gaining in redeveloping its inner identity, but he also knew that vagrants and criminals resurface in other parts of a city and reoffend unless redirected.

Accordingly, Jake visited the prisons and with the help of the wardens reviewed the records of inmates in order to prepare them for some level of success in reentering the city. His reputation preceded him in working with wardens, social workers and religious orders. I know, because I followed him into some of these meetings. Jake was always self-effacing and kept the subject on the best interests of the at-risk individuals as well as the taxpayers. I heard him counsel prisoners with the same simple formula they seemed to retain and think about: "Surrender your meanness, serve your brothers and sisters, sacrifice your time and energy in work and be selfless." By rationing his time with them and keeping the conversation short, they were more likely to remember the few words he spoke.

The year 1954 was a milestone for New Winchester. Construction crews broke ground on a dozen new building projects and freeways at about the same time and City Hall announced an historic record low for violent crimes. Jake resisted calls for election to public office and instead exchanged some of his street time for classroom time, training new police officers. In 1956, New Winchester had its first new shopping mall, a glitzy galleria that gained national attention and a lot of appreciation in a city that had no real reason for much self-esteem in a century.

In those giddy years, the sky seemed the limit for the new New

Winchester. Christmas season 1958, though, was the most important to me personally because of something that happened to Jake Byrne. I was with Jake inside the new shopping galleria when he took a turn that I mistook for a kind of mental or emotional breakdown. Many years later I began to understand what happened, but only after my own emotional breakdown in the 1970s, after the end of the Vietnam War. When Jake and I sat down together after his retirement, he explained that his emotions in the galleria had connections with combat events just before Christmas 1944. These events, during the Battle of the Bulge, concerned being outnumbered, starved, surrounded by German forces for weeks, and forced to leave his dead and wounded in the frozen forests of Belgium.

We were riding the escalator together to the upper levels of the galleria. I was looking at the fantastic atrium and the Christmas lights around us. Jake was looking at the dozens of infants and toddlers with their mothers coming in and out of the retail stores. When I turned to look at him, I saw his eyes were wide, his face frozen in either shock or amazement. I couldn't tell. Then I saw tears in his eyes, and he sat down on a bench in a children's toy department in Macy's and put his head between his knees. I asked if he needed help, and he shook his head and said nothing.

In 1985, after his retirement, Jake explained that the "conscience" that had preserved him in combat and told him to follow the law as a rookie, then had appeared in person to him in the empty row house in the Blocks, never spoke or appeared to him again. But the prompts of conscience, in terms of instructive images, original ideas, determination, persistence, patience and tact did continue in the privacy of his own mind at opportune moments. At the time we were in the galleria, Jake's "conscience" silently conveyed to him the concept that the infants and toddlers he saw were representative of the rapid return of some of the war-dead to new bodies and new families. This event in Macy's occurred just thirteen years after the end of the war—the baby boomer generation coming in. It was the answer to the question all war survivors ask themselves: why did I make it back and so many fine men didn't?

Jake was smart enough to avoid asking clergy that question. What mattered to him in the galleria was that his men had not been lost. Although he believed he had abandoned them in the forest, an infinite power was returning them as our greatest asset, children. For Jake, patience was necessary with such mysteries—eventually the opportunity and the answer would present itself at the right time as knowing evidence. There was, of course, no documentary evidence or corroborating witness for the return of the war-dead to us in 1958 or in any year—not for a hard-news guy like me—and Jake knew that, so he didn't respond to me at the time.

I had to process that entire survivor equation by myself, alone, just as Jake did. In 1968, while Jake was training rookies in New Winchester, I received what I thought was a promotion from my newspaper to a higher salary and a foreign news desk in Saigon, South Vietnam. I took military transport and went up Highway 1 to report on the Marines in Da Nang and the far north, and I got in on the full fury of the Tet Offensive. For whatever reason, I went back in 1969 for another tour of duty and came home in shock. I had seen so many American and Vietnamese deaths, so much horror and disorganization, I tried to cope by sheltering inside my straight-news reporter role. Emotionally, I shut down, to save myself.

No one from the paper met me at the airport, but Jake was there. He hugged me, said welcome home and didn't say anything else. It took me fifteen years of quiet grief to know what Jake knew about the war-dead returning for renewed opportunity. They don't remember what the survivors remember, and that's a good thing. I say that as I look out on this audience now.

I happened to ask Jake about the pain of those who come home, the survivor equation, right before his retirement, and the questions I asked were probably instrumental in why he felt comfortable confiding in me. When we sat down together, I took pages of notes on his career insights, and then I had a few questions for him.

Why had he resisted calls for election to public office? His answer, and I quote: "I would have been too proud of myself. God did the work. I offered up a proposition for holding elective office. There was no answer, and I took that as a no. Fine with me. Never liked politics." Unquote.

Why were there no further appearances by the archangel? Jake's answer: "No need. I learned how economical God is with communication. Once you know and trust that unmistakable call to attention, you obey immediately."

Why not release these insights to the public now (in 1985)? Jake's answer: "I don't want to offend the Church. They do good work. We're all brothers."

What action did you take if you proposed a concept or a plan to God and there was no response or you didn't agree with the response? Jake's answer: "No answer from God is an answer. I would know instantly if a change was needed. If I didn't understand, I could ask for clarification. Usually I got the fact that I didn't see all or know all and so I should trust, obey and wait for things to unfold. When your will matches up with God's will, change happens. It's not always what you expect. Look at the city then and now. I wanted to agree. I wanted to cooperate. It's far better than I expected."

Did God communicate to you through conversation with other people? Jake's answer: "For sure. Not all talk is chatter. If your conscience is awake, you hear people's needs and you act. You also hear about what you need to do and you act."

Did you feel privileged or special having access to this proposal and response connection? Jake's answer: "It's standard procedure for everyone. Police especially."

Why do you feel God is economical with communication? Jake's answer: "I don't think God wants to prolong your infancy. There's more joy in finding answers for yourself than in getting stuck in the demanding baby-bird posture. Feed me, feed me! Take the hint, figure it out and grow."

How do you want police officers to respond when this information is released? Jake's answer: "Continuity. What one man can do, others can do, too. You will be tested."

Jake was economical with his speech and made every word count. Reading between those words, I found Jake had a great love for this city, his fellow officers, the people of New Winchester as well as what he called "the expanding union of the universe." He may not have expressed this love often in words, but he surely expressed it in more enduring forms through what he did. What Jake Byrne did with his life was exemplary, more than anyone else in New Winchester's history. What he expects from you is that you become exemplary.

Ladies and gentlemen, you can see I'm an old man and more than ready to pass this bright torch from Jake Byrne to you. If there's one word you take away from this event tonight it is . . . continuity. Continuity. Thank you for your kind attention.

Gideon George acknowledged the audience as everyone in City Hall stood to applaud. Moments later, Gideon turned and walked slowly off stage, and the gallery erupted immediately in commentary. The tumult was to be expected. When a major media figure known for his reticence and careful choice of words offers such a candid description of so much personal history, he himself makes news. I found myself less interested in the opinions of the important people in the gallery around me and more interested in the expressions on the faces of the policemen and women on the main floor below me. This event was for them. How would they cope with the intractable conundrums of our time in the absence of Jake Byrne? This event was about what they would make of Jake Byrne's concept of continuity in an era of lone-wolf terror attacks, side by side with a full-blown surveillance state. Who would follow the law?

Many standing in the gallery around me contested perceived omissions or ambiguities in the testimony, but I had no stomach for argument or conversation with anyone. Too often during Gideon's speech, I had felt him looking directly at me. It was as if he was holding me accountable for how the young police officers would accept Jake Byrne's expectation of continuity. I pondered the purpose in Gideon's repeated gaze and remained in my seat almost unaware of the noise on all sides. I certainly wished these officers well, but knowing what I had known for a long time they were irretrievably inside the surveillance state. And the state had a strange record in its reception and reaction to terrorists.

I was still in my seat thinking about this conundrum of our time and Gideon's challenge to the police officers, when a series of unexpected turns began to unfold. A swirl of movement on the main floor caught my eye, and there in the middle of it was my old friend Gideon, who had not retired to rest in a reception room but was handing out manila folders and shaking hands with a large crowd of police officers. I had so underestimated Gideon that I stared down at the main floor in amazement and felt the sudden urge to get out of my seat and find out what was behind the frequent eye contact.

The main level was packed shoulder to shoulder, and I had trouble making my way to Gideon. Frank Garrett saw me, shook my hand and spoke close to my ear.

"Don't leave," he said.

"What's going on?" I asked.

"Gideon needs to see you. This way."

Frank showed me into a private reception room and drew the curtains closed on a night view of the New Winchester skyline.

"I'll be leaving," Frank said. "This is between you and Gideon. I'll let him know you're here."

I stood in the center of the room after Frank left and wondered if I was being viewed on one or more security cameras. Moments later Gideon knocked and came in to shake my hand.

"I had my eye on you up there," he said, grinning as he locked the door.

"I got that," I replied. "It's good to see you looking so well."

"I feel pretty good," he said, before pausing. Then he looked me in the eye, as if he was reading my thoughts. "Don't record this. Memorize what we say. The room is clean."

"What's going on?"

"What did you think of the event tonight?"

"I'd say you got the attention of more than one young Jake Byrne out there. Mission accomplished, from what I could see. They got the continuity."

"Did you?"

"Did I? Sure."

"No, you're not seeing it yet," Gideon said, patting me on the shoulder. He kept looking me in the eye. "All these years you've been the impeccable insider, always discreet with your sources. You know far more than you'll say and far more still than you'll print."

"Well, yes, of course. We both do."

"But you know far more than me about the cycles of war and national debt and the ones we don't name. You know their faces. You know our debt is more than the public knows. You know who, what, when, where, why and how. They have collateralized the republic, without the people's permission. The wars and the surveillance state are about control, more than the public knows. You know why. And your brothers and sisters are helpless because they're clueless."

"Don't go there, Gideon."

"It's like the status of control in the Wallace Blocks. Jake Byrne knew what would happen if he went in there alone. You cannot go in there alone and live."

"What are you saying?"

"There are dozens of cops right here who are going to take up Jake Byrne's relationship, and they're going to adapt it to our time. Dozens. There's only one of you, free to move with the ones we don't name."

"I survive because I don't antagonize them, I listen to them. Let's not rock that boat."

"You survive because they use you. Invisible powers need ways to communicate their power and some of their intent to the rest of us. Your blogs are one of their ways."

"Gideon, they own the money behind the media, the government, the banks. I'm not Jake Byrne. How long do you think I'd live if I outed them?"

"Not long if you outed them on your own. The timing is not yours or mine. The same Providence that created the universe will not continue to share power with them. They were given a certain amount of time. It will end. The Wallace Blocks ended according to God's timing. Jake Byrne cooperated at the city level. Here's the global level."

"Who is this coming from?"

"Jake. Jake Byrne. He was aware, way past the city level. He was aware of you."

"So I schmooze with plutocrats and . . . you're saying?"

"You volunteered to tell the truth. At the right time, the right way. There is no one on earth as uniquely positioned to prove to an unsuspecting people that their birthrights have been quietly sold to foreign interests. You've been sitting on the written proof for years."

"Okay, it's all there for a rainy day. But how do you know I volunteered for anything? How would Jake Byrne know about my private life?"

"How did Jake do what he did? He had an understanding and kept it private. This is where you choose if you want to agree, if you want to cooperate."

"God almighty, Gideon. I'm happily agnostic because it means no complications."

"So you die at a very old age with this complication: you never got around to telling the people who screwed them and why and how and when. But you wrote plenty of gossip and witty stuff about plutocrats who wanted publicity. Just nothing important about the ones we aren't allowed to name."

"How about the complication of dying at a not very old age."

"Depends," Gideon said with a smirk, "on how much a faux agnostic like you wants to cooperate with the power that created space and time. The presence of the archangel that came to Jake spans galaxies. The embodiment of the will of God. He forced the proud down here and he takes them out of here when their time is up."

"I think, to explain it to myself, you're informing me I'm already involved."

"You're already involved."

"How? It's just me. A high-fallutin' money wit like me. How am I going to know?"

"It's not just you. You're not alone. Time and events will confirm for you what to say, when the timing is right and how it's distributed. The communication may or may not be economical, or concerning wit."

"You knew about this when we worked in Boston."

"Well . . . I'll be in touch." Gideon clasped my shoulders. "You've shown courage getting this far. Propose to God that a sense of peace and comfort go with you. Keep this private."

I left the event after saying farewell to Gideon and flew out of New Winchester deep in thought.

On the flight home I looked out of the window at thirty-three thousand feet and could not avoid hearing my conscience. It reminded me that I was indeed the impeccable insider. I had always been discreet with sources. So discreet that over time I had withheld my hand, procrastinating the exposure of evidence, to preserve a safe and privileged life. I had been positioned to discover far more than Gideon knew about the managed cycles of war over the centuries, the expansion of fiat currency, unrepayable national debt and perpetual surveillance. I knew the sullen faces of the hidden ones, those of extreme privilege, the global governors.

Inside the world of print, both Gideon and I knew so well that no one crossed the ones we do not name. Yet he was holding me accountable for receiving the torch from Jake Byrne, without excuses for my safety, my reputation or my lapses into agnosticism. It occurred to me that if you think the eye of God is upon you, it is.

A FORTUNATE MAN

In 101 B.C., in a forgotten battle against
pirates, a mere moment in the war of aeons
between the sons of light and the sons of
darkness, death yields once more to life.

A FORTUNATE MAN

As far as Theron Dimitris was aware, none of the slaves aboard the cargo ship *Hypatos* could swim. His own inability to swim had been a fear suppressed since the age of fourteen. Strong and mature for his age, he began adult life at fourteen with cargo duties. The work required care, loading urns of oil, wine, jewelry, perfume, copper and marble slabs from warehouses into the holds of ships in the Athenian port of Piraeus. Overseers and trusted slaves accompanied the cargo to destinations around the Mediterranean, returning to Athens with goods from Egypt, Persia and India. Four years of seafaring had not eased his fear of the sea.

Now eighteen, on his fifteenth circuit of the eastern Mediterranean, the rumors of danger now regained his attention as four Cilician pirate ships approached fast, out of the remnants of a storm on the port side. These sea-wolves from the southeast coast of Asia Minor were known across the Mediterranean as slavers and ransomers, mockers, torturers and ruthless thieves, unrestrained by the absent Roman navy. The crew and slaves of the *Hypatos* watched in silence as the pirates turned into the wind and raced out of the storm at the trailing edge of dusk. It became clearer each moment the Cilicians would catch up with them. A blustery, moonless night had been forecast by the navigator. A few minutes more and the *Hypatos* and the other five cargo ships in their convoy might have escaped into the dark, just one day west of safety inside the harbor of the Egyptian port of Alexandria.

The Athenian captain, Galenos, a shrewd naval veteran, gave orders that they would fight to win, and he instructed the archers to hide under tarpaulins and behind the deck cargo. The heavily laden *Hypatos* was larger and slower than the other five ships in the convoy and not built for speed or maneuverability. Only the element of surprise would help the *Hypatos* escape into the night. Waiting under cover, Theron remembered hearing other slaves' stories about encounters with Cilicians. The stories said, if anyone on board resisted when the grappling irons were tossed onto the deck they would be run through with a sword or thrown into the sea alive. Slaves were considered worthless for ransom and too much trouble for resale if they were wounded. If a slave spoke, wounded or not, he would be beaten and thrown into the sea. Now the mercenaries, the crew and all the slaves were armed, not only to resist, but to kill every Cilician attempting to board *Hypatos*.

The wind-filled mainsail of the leading pirate ship could be seen over the cargo covers, approaching at a brisk speed, white spray breaking over the bow. Heeling over in the gusty wind, the four Cilician ships' sails glowed orange in the rays of the setting sun. Theron and the other slaves, officers, crew and mercenaries gripped bows, cudgels and javelins and waited out of sight, each in their appointed position in the lengthening shadows behind the rows of cargo. Everyone on board *Hypatos* knew the consequences of capture. Survivors would be sold and transported to a short, painful life under the overseers' whips on a Roman plantation in Sicily. For those who resisted, an even shorter life in the darkening sea, on a windy, moonless night.

The leading Cilician pirate ship turned quickly, preparing to board what must have appeared to them as slow-moving, easy pickings. Seconds before grappling hooks were thrown by Cilician skirmishers, Theron, the other slaves, the crew and the mercenaries rose up from behind the deck cargo and took aim at the closest boarders. Yelling and cursing, the pirates threw their hooks, leapt over the handrails and found themselves looking straight toward arrow-tips coming out of the last dazzling rays of the sunset behind *Hypatos.*

Theron's first arrow took a pirate in the throat, and in the volleys that followed every pirate with a grappling hook or raised sword on the first and second ships was killed. Within a minute, the captain had ordered a dozen of the archers to begin firing pitch-laden, flaming arrows up at the pirates' mainsails. At close range the burning pitch spread on impact. The pirates' sails burst into flames and then black smoke erupted from a mass of reed-covered bales and other stolen goods tied together around the mainmasts.

On the port side of *Hypatos,* the first two pirate ships collided, stern to bow, as their sails disintegrated and flaming debris fell on their helmsmen and crew. But five grappling hooks still held *Hypatos* to the lead pirate vessel, and while attempts were being made to cut the ropes the out-of-control pirate ship heaved sideways in a large swell and hit *Hypatos* below the waterline. The cracking, groaning and splintering of timbers was audible even over the shouted orders and screams of the wounded.

Surprised by the organized resistance, the surviving pirates retreated from the flaming debris in confusion. But bound by one remaining grappling hook *Hypatos* continued to grind against the hull of the first Cilician ship. The pirates' mast, engulfed in flames from the burning bales, sagged and toppled on top of the grappling hook, touching off flames across the cargo covers and up into the mainsail of *Hypatos.*

Although Theron could no longer see the other two pirate vessels or the five escaping cargo ships in the dark beyond the flames, he noticed the odd tilt of the deck and realized *Hypatos* was taking on water. The recently detached pirate ship began sinking by the stern, its bow angling upward, still in flames. Panic and fearful yelling set in among the slaves and crew who couldn't swim. Theron shouted to every one of them who would listen to grab wooden boxes or buoyant debris and jump with it into the water. It occurred to him he was yelling as much to calm his own fears as anyone else's. He found an empty wooden crate, but like most of the other slaves resisted going over the side until he could no longer stand upright.

Minutes of commotion ensued on the slanting deck before the *Hypatos* heaved suddenly to port and began to capsize. Everyone, dead, dying or still living, was thrown into the crimson-tinted water as the sun finally disappeared. The second pirate vessel was still afloat, burning from bow to stern in clouds of black smoke. A few minutes later, it too rolled over and the last points of light went out as the flames were extinguished and darkness on the sea gradually became absolute.

Some distance from the snuffed out light, Theron held onto the empty wooden crate, alone in the water. He could see no horizon between the black of the sea and the moonless black of the sky. Rising up and dropping down with each wave, he called out repeatedly for anyone to respond to him, believing some survivors might still be clinging to debris close by. But there was no response, only the slapping and tugging of each dark passing swell against the slats of the crate.

According to every sea story Theron had heard in his eighteen years, he believed there were always survivors, no matter how great the disaster. Now the absence of comforting voices near him became surreal, silently mocking his certainty of survival. *I'm in a dream,* he thought, *This is the dream I feared, being on my own in the sea.* In the dream waves smacked his face and salt water stung his nostrils, as if someone was trying their best to wake him up, slapping him to get up and to get back to work.

Sometime later in the darkness, he began wondering if he might fall asleep in the dream and enter another dream where he was actually awake. In that dream he imagined he would be picking olives in the master's grove and looking forward to the evening meal. There would be plenty of the master's rough red wine, kalamata olives, onion-flavored bread, slabs of tasty cheese, sweet cream and conversation about incidents in the day's work.

The crest of a dark, unseen wave submerged his face, and Theron realized he was in danger of losing his grip on the crate.

He looped his rope belt tightly around a strong rib on the crate, then around his waist, and waited for something to happen. For minutes nothing changed except the rising and falling motion of the waves and the rasping tone of fear in his breathing. He was getting tired. There was nothing to see in the dark, not even his own hands. He was hungry and thirsty, and to survive he had to stay awake all night.

To keep himself occupied, Theron imagined what he would do and say when a ship passed by in the morning and he was hauled on board. He would tell the crew he was a sailor, just like one of them, and he would never even hint at the things those who are born slaves give away by their servility. His freedom to leave any ship's company with full pay at the port of his choosing would be taken for granted. A port such as Piraeus might be his choice, and from there he would pay whatever the fare was to ride in a cart all the way to the agora in Athens. He would be indifferent to the noisy crowds and would think it was his right to take his freedom, to do whatever he wanted and go where he wanted. In fact, he would keep going inland from Athens, to the interior, to the foothills of Mount Olympus, where it was safe, far from the sea. Perhaps with his sailor's pay, he would buy a small olive farm in the hills and sell baskets of olives in nearby villages, without any obligation to get close to the sea again.

Night passed, the wind dropped, and dawn spread over a glassy sea, reflecting sunlight harshly in his eyes. Hunger was not the issue any more. It was thirst and fatigue. Fear grated in his throat as he breathed. No one, alive or dead, was in sight. The debris field from the sunken ships had dispersed during the night. No ships were close by. The awful sound of each wheezing breath began to dominate his awareness, as if he was obliged to listen to someone who was afraid, dying under torture. He tried to stop breathing, just for a moment of reprieve from the wheezing. Panicked, he gasped and then convulsed as he flailed in the water.

Night fell again, and with the darkness came a sense of despair. Dizziness and hallucinations came and went until, with a

197

start, he felt water washing over his face. A tug on his belt alerted him that something was wrong with the crate. He could no longer see it but he could feel it pulling him down. The wood in the slats of the crate had been absorbing water, and what once supported him now conspired against him. He was supporting the crate. He pulled the rope around his waist loose and let it drift down with the crate into the darkness beneath him.

Now he had to focus on the effort of treading water. Fatigue and delirium moved in rhythm with the swells. Up and then down, the pitiless cadence of an impersonal motion he could not influence. He coughed out the water stinging in his nose, but not fast enough. Every wave covered his head and every gasp took in salt water. Without being able to breathe or regain the strength to surface, he began flailing again. His lungs felt like they would explode and his fingers clawed upward but felt nothing but water. Pressure increased in his ears and sinuses as his forehead and eyes felt like they would explode. This was the agony and fear he had dreaded. He wanted to let out a long, loud cry in bitterness and anger against the blackness, but water filled his lungs, and at the point of asphyxiation by salt water he was no longer conscious.

Separation from the body terrestrial began. The faculties of celestial consciousness belonging to the soul took over. Theron's human faculties had no hope of escape from the hostile environment of the open sea, but a familiar memory of origin came to rescue his soul. Superficial thinking ceased, but awareness of an expectation occurred. He looked upward, certain that somewhere in the distance a point of light would appear and draw closer. He stared at it, reached out and tried to pull it to him until he was inside it, flying along within it at a master speed, in bright sunlight, leaving fear, pain and desperation in a dense, slow-moving, lower world.

For Theron's soul it was a reflective homecoming, accomplished countless times before, this time tinged with relief but also, so much regret. So little had been accomplished in eighteen years of constraint, resignation and humiliation. Most of the men he had served were free-born and still alive, squandering their freedom on the demands of the body. He had wasted his short life on people who thought nothing of wasting their own lives. The inability to go where he wanted, to do what he wanted, now made the quality of freedom as vital, as essential as the gifts of life and opportunity. What he craved most was another opportunity, a real chance, this time with the freedom to choose to do something worthwhile, with no one to hinder him.

As he wondered how he could make his case for another opportunity, he noticed a white, sandy beach in the distance. His attention was drawn to an old man with a horse and cart in the dunes. The silver-haired, silver-bearded old man appeared amiable and somehow familiar, even from far off. As Theron circled and looked down, the old man left the cart and walked toward the beach. Drawn to him, Theron descended through iridescent shafts of sunlight and stood on the sand. The old man shouted in recognition and held his arms out.

"Oh, my, you're here, you're here! Yes, my boy, yes, I've been waiting for you," the old man said, as he hugged Theron. "I'm so glad to see you."

"Diogenes," Theron said, as he remembered. Emotion overcame him and he held his old friend for a long time.

"There, now, an ordeal. You're through it now," the old man said. "The others are not here yet. I understand what you've been through, but I don't think they will. They simply can't. But for you, the episode is over. It's over, done with. Now, now you might want to consider a place to rest for a while, a good while. When you're ready to plan, I'll be ready to help. Do you want to stay in the port with me? I have room."

"I want to get as far away as I can, into the interior. Hills and mountains, solid earth. As far from the sea as possible. I want to forget everything, be by myself."

"I have somewhere in mind. Come on."

They began walking up the dunes toward the horse and cart.

"I'm glad," Theron began, "to see you again, but . . ."

"But you feel some resentment. That somehow there's no justice. My boy, the law is just. But you, you especially, will see the law transcended by Grace."

"I don't want to go back to see anything. I don't want to go back, ever. Here, I can do what I want."

"There's work there in the terrestrial that must be done by someone, my boy. The others will need you. They will depend on you and you on them. And in your maturity it will be given to you to lead."

"I'm sorry but I don't want to see them. Not for a long time."

"Take the time you need and rest."

"I want to be alone, touch firm ground every day, see dust coming up around my feet and feel safe. I'm not ready for anyone needing me, depending on me, telling me what to do. I'm nothing. I don't want to talk to people, except maybe to you, now and then."

"That is perfectly fine with me. Talk to me when you need to," the old man said, glancing up. "Well, bless me, will you look at that beautiful day. Hardly a cloud in the sky. You're going to enjoy the peace and quiet."

Feeling cheated out of a full life and holding an abiding grudge toward the sea, Theron exercised his freedom to say nothing. He could have asked Diogenes what he had been doing around the port and where their circle of friends were in the world of change but he chose silence as they climbed up into the cart.

The horse drew them along on a rutted road up into the wooded hills. The day was clear, sunny and perfect for contemplation. As they crested the line of hills the old man pointed forward, down through the roadside trees into a valley of olive groves and open woodland. It was warm under the bright sun and the shady groves to one side below the road looked inviting. They stopped in a hollow in the valley by a wooden hut surrounded by white oaks, not far from a creek-fed pond.

"Like it?" the old man asked, gesturing toward the hut. "This land, the hut and the pond are yours if you want."

Theron got down from the cart and looked inside the hut. It was clean and tidy, as he would have kept it himself. On a small wooden table there were linen cloths covering slabs of cheese and bread, a bowl of olives and a jug of wine. The old man followed him inside and picked up the two stools by the table.

"I thought you might be hungry and a bit thirsty. Take a bowl and a cup and let's sit outside and eat by the pond."

Theron looked around at the peaceful setting under the trees. He understood Diogenes had been kind enough to prepare the place for him and he was grateful. But Diogenes, Theron remembered had no need to return to the terrestrial world. He was free, while Theron was not.

"You were a free man when you came here, weren't you?" Theron asked, as they placed the stools in the shade next to the pond.

"I was, in every sense of the term. No debts to draw me back. But I wouldn't move into the upper worlds when I understood the debts your parents faced. Or what you faced. Eat up. That cheese has a good tang to it."

"Where are they now?"

"They have gone back. They're not slaves this time. They're free-born, in the northern forests among the Angles, away from war. That was their plan."

"They'll be in wars," Theron said. "Where there are wars there are slaves. There's no protection from it. They were free and then they weren't. I want to be free to choose what I do, all the time. The unending peace."

"There is no peace in that world unless you expect it in your prayers. You'll learn. And I want to ease your sense of injustice. You did well. You ran the course. You paid the debt and the way is open for consequential work."

"Work? I prefer to stay right here. Right here. Do you own this land?" Theron asked.

"It's yours, for as long as you want."

"Are the olive groves mine to harvest?"

"Everything you can see. There's a small market village over

201

that hill. They trade for olives."

"That's just what I want. I can be free here. I can decide what to trade and when to trade."

"As it should be," Diogenes said, tossing pieces of cork bark into the sun-dappled pond. "What's also important is what you do with your thoughts while you're here. This is an interval given over to rest and for imagining ideas about where you might want to go next."

"I don't think I want to go anywhere but here. This is perfect. I could be an olive grower here forever."

"Well, I come up to the village from time to time for olives and fruit and things. I'll look in on you. But if you ever want to talk about your travel ideas, you can hike down to the port. Everyone knows where I live."

"I don't think I'll be interested in any kind of travel for a while. A long while. Nothing to do with the sea. Far from the sea. Count on it."

"Here," Diogenes said, tossing Theron a few pieces of cork bark, "throw these in and see how long they float."

Theron absently tossed the pieces in one at a time and looked up through the trees at the dazzling blue sky. Fluffy white clouds had appeared in interesting shapes far out toward the horizon and their gradual unfolding into ever-changing new shapes peacefully took his attention. He felt himself relaxing and thought he could begin to undo some hurt there. By the time he looked around Diogenes had gone.

The days passed into weeks of an idyll so wonderful, so saturated with peace without anxiety that Theron lost all interest in memory or imagination. To him, past and future were sown with pain and so he avoided all thought other than what he saw in front of him. He filled his days with simple routines around the olive grove, pruning, raking leaves and twigs, picking ripe olives and walking down to the village with a basket strapped to his back. The people in the small market there were always welcoming and friendly. But their small-talk was mostly chatter and hard on his ears. He was just as pleased to walk the winding path back home to the hut with a jug of wine, sticks of bread and a round of cheese in his basket. Walking was a pleasure in itself, taking his time, watching puffs of dust kick up from his sandals.

The days were soft and carefree among the olive trees. In the midday heat he rested on the flattened grass by the shaded pond. Sitting comfortably with his back against his favorite white oak, Theron sometimes involuntarily felt a warm, glowing feeling in the center of his chest and wondered what brought the exhilarating joy out of nowhere. It was a bubbly feeling of exuberance, an expansive feeling radiating across his chest as if a sparking flame was being turned in circles in there. He accepted it as confirmation he was where he should be.

At night in the candlelit hut, Theron would play harmonious melodies on a simple flute he had traded for olives in the village and would feel the same pleasant, uplifting glow in his chest, vibrating in agreement with each note. He couldn't control it, but how could he resent it as an intrusion? Sometimes his thoughts would ponder what Diogenes meant about travel ideas. Why, he wondered, would anyone want to leave a perfect olive grove and such calming music by a beautiful pond to go anywhere else?

Then, one morning while Theron was picking olives on a hillside he noticed wisps of dust through the trees and was glad to see Diogenes coming by to see him. He gave his old friend a welcome hug and during their conversation by the pond, over bread, olive oil and cheese, Diogenes again brought up the subject of travel.

"I know you're happy here and would stay here forever but have you ever thought about traveling again?"

"I don't see why I would need to, or want to."

"What if there were people far from here who needed to see you and would benefit greatly by the blessing of your good company?"

"Then you should invite them to come here to see me," Theron said.

"I know you would be hospitable to them," Diogenes said with a smile, before he grew serious. "They are unable to come here, to these hills, and need you to go down to them. They're encumbered by debts that were not expected."

"I could, but I don't want to have anything to do with the sea."

"If they depended on the sea for their living, as you depend on this land, would you be as hospitable, to help them?"

"There's always some other way to do what you're asking. I'm not interested in the sea."

"Do you remember why?"

"Drowning. I drowned. I don't need to remember."

"You're free to choose not to go to sea again. But there are other people who are not so free. They risk exactly what you experienced, every time they go out to sea. They still go."

Theron smiled, guessing what Diogenes was getting at. "They shouldn't go," he said.

"Take a look at the pieces of cork bark you tossed into the pond the last time I was here," Diogenes said. "Keep them in mind."

"Why did I have to drown?"

"You didn't have to," Diogenes said. "It was not the will of God. The God of all cosmos preferred you lived a long, prosperous life as a free man. It was your free will not to trust God with your life, before, during and after each voyage. You made no request for assistance. Daily prayer, in enlightened self-interest, could have made you a free man."

"But I was born to never have a free will. I lived a short, poor life as a slave and I drowned. There was no man or ship in sight. How would any request have helped me?"

"Look back and remember a life in Egypt when you bought, owned and mistreated slaves. In your life as Theron you were humbled. By your loyal service over eighteen years, you repaid those you had mistreated long ago in Egypt. Your soul didn't baulk at the opportunity to repay the debt. Your personality, comparing itself with others, was resentful. God measures all things to the finest degree, even service. You drowned because your personality was preoccupied with self-pity. This, then, self-justified not asking

God for protection, from Cilicians or the sea. Ignorance of the law of intercession is no excuse. You must ask. You must ask."

"You say ask. Are you meaning ask Zeus, the capricious?"

"No, no, those are concepts made in the human image. Outside time and space is perfection. Who created time and space for us? Who created cosmos for us? The one God, creative spirit within all matter, from the stars to your fingers, penetrating time and space. His spiritual fire is more concentrated within his people than in all the matter on Earth combined."

"You're saying there is one, outside and inside space and time? Can the name of this one be spoken?"

"I am that I am."

"That is the name?" Theron paused. "That is the name, the creator of the cosmos? Who is I?"

"Think about it."

Diogenes handed Theron the remainder of the loaf of bread as he said farewell, climbed up into his cart and waved as the horse took him down the path to see a friend in the market village. It was dusk when Diogenes passed by and waved again on his way down through the hills to the port. That night Theron did keep their conversation in mind, wondering what the old man was referring to about people far away who would benefit greatly by his company. Still, Theron thought, it couldn't be anything more than speculation because he offered no details. He put the idea out of his mind and settled down to play his flute in the candlelight inside the hut.

Days, weeks and months passed by in a peaceful blur involving occasional work picking ripe olives for the market, raking twigs and leaves in the grove and sitting against a tree tossing cork bark at leaves floating in the pond. One day he arrived with a basket of olives at the market in the village and was about to trade when a traveler stepped into the shade of the shopkeeper's tent and asked if he could taste the olives. The traveler liked them and offered to exchange a measure of olives for an urn of salted anchovies in garlic, herbs and oil.

"I've never tried anchovies," Theron said to the traveler. "That's a strong taste. I like it. Where did you get them?"

"In the port," the traveler said. "They're from Hispania. Expensive for such small fish."

Theron looked again at the traveler and wondered why he recognized him but couldn't remember his name.

"I'll trade for them. Where do I know you from?"

"Egypt," the traveler said, stepping out into the sunlight.

"I was recently in Alexandria," Theron said, "but I was confined to the docks. It must have been somewhere else."

"When I knew you in Egypt you lived in the pharaoh's palace," the traveler responded.

Theron looked the traveler and searched his memories, something he rarely chose to do, especially concerning Egypt.

"I've had some unpleasant lives in Egypt," he said. "Help me remember."

"A long time ago I helped you with a dream about seven fat cattle eaten by seven lean ones and a second dream about seven full ears of corn eaten by seven thin ears. It was God's way of warning you that seven good years in the fields would be followed by seven years of famine."

Theron stared at him as his soul's memory looked back through his many lives of regret. His eyes widened at the traveler. This man knew him in a life he did not regret.

"Joseph?" Theron asked. "You're Joseph, son of Jacob?"

"The last time we served together," the traveler said. "It's been a while. I'm recognized by people now as Jesus of Nazareth, from Judea. I haven't forgotten your trust and your generosity. You were a man of God then and now. You were gracious to my father Jacob and all my family. You're not forgotten."

Impulsively Theron put his arms out and felt his heart expand and burn for joy as if he was hugging a long lost brother. He held the blue-eyed man by his shoulders and laughed for the first time in a long time.

"So you're here to remind me that not all my Egyptian lives

were errors best forgotten. I've lost track of time in the world. How long has it been since then?"

"As the world measures time, almost two thousand years since you saw Egypt through that famine."

"Mainly your contribution," Theron said, wiping moist eyes. "Time just collapsed when I remembered you."

"Things have changed for the better. Too much to talk about here. Are you walking to the port?"

"In that direction," Theron said, "to my place by the olive grove, just over the hill. Do you live in the port?"

"I'm on my way to see an old friend, Diogenes. Do you know him?"

"He's my teacher, my sage, my rescuer all rolled into one. Of course I know him. I should invite you to dinner at my place tonight and we'll go see him together in the morning."

Jesus, or Joseph ben Jacob as Theron remembered him, accepted Theron's hospitality. As they walked the trail back to the hut among the olives, Theron pondered the mystery of his last short, bound life as a Greek slave. A profitable life of good decisions almost two thousand years earlier as a ruler of Egypt stood in contrast with most of his lives. He asked his friend Joseph, or Jesus as he remembered to address him, his opinion concerning the apparent mismatch in worldly position.

"God is no respecter of persons," Jesus said. "Titles and position mean nothing in the greater context."

"The context of what?" Theron asked.

"The greater context of war between the sons of light and the sons of darkness."

Theron drew in a breath, associating that war with endless pain and endless loss. He was surprised that Jesus would mention it.

"I find I avoid the subject for obvious reasons," Theron said.

"They bring war, and we bring peace—by the hand of God through us."

"Which hasn't worked too well for us—my last life included."

"They squander, we grow," Jesus said. "By the cycles of justice and mercy, they will be no more and we will outlast them."

Theron liked Jesus' spirit. He seemed bold and unafraid but how practical was it to wait for an implacable enemy to weary?

"My brother, when would that be?" Theron asked. "I don't see it anytime soon. You were a mystery in Egypt and you're still that way. How do you just say, we'll outlast them?"

"Take an urn of water. Let's say it's filled by God with water of life once every day—but only for those who love God. For those who don't, they sustain themselves by taking it, by force or deception. Either way their debt to God for misuse of power increases, life after life, and its weight guarantees their soul's mortality."

"When immortality is what they want most."

"They are self-defeating. Time is not on their side. They're depressed and furious at the futility of a long, drawn-out war they can't win."

Theron looked up at the trees overhead and then at his dusty feet on the trail. Over the long term he admitted Jesus had a point. But his memories went far back into the past when pain and defeat at the hands of the sons of darkness was almost guaranteed in every life.

"Do they know they can't win?" Theron asked.

"I don't think they want to know," Jesus said. "They are depressed. They know the law but deny it. Every jot and tittle of that water of life must be accounted for."

"And when they're bankrupt?"

"There is a final judgment by sacred fire, consuming everything unlike itself in them. God takes no pleasure in it. They were beautiful when he made them and when they took their free will. Their entire agglomeration of misused energy returns to the source, purified."

"And what about us?"

"Rough diamonds."

They considered the ironies of the terrestrial world as they walked under the trees. The greater context of a war spread over aeons was obscured by the immediate threats of accusations, lies, pain and loss. The sons of light couldn't see the context, or any progress and the sons of darkness, cunning, blind and demented, squandered their time and energy in vengeance. The just outcome was inevitable, the long duration unnecessarily tragic and painful for God in man.

"Why does God allow it? Get rid of them now," Theron suggested as they crested a hill and looked down on his olive grove in the valley.

"They have the freedom to turn around while they have time. They can ask for help. If they're sincere they will be protected from those who are not."

"After all the harm they've done?"

"Petition God to make that judgment."

Inside the candlelit hut that night over dinner Theron listened to Jesus describe his recent last life, full of mystery and great purpose, in the Roman province of Judea. There were many parallels with his life as Joseph, though the life in Judea was even more exemplary, as the public personification of God, inside time and space.

In Theron's last life, Greek culture celebrated the caprices of the Olympians as possessors of attributes humans could understand. Here in his hut Theron was sharing bread, cheese and olives with a man without caprices, who sounded and felt to him like a friend or an elder brother. Yet Jesus had been the chosen instrument of God, anointed to carry the weight of the peoples' errors for thousands of years, as needed. There he sat, at a rough wooden table in a humble hut, a source of mystery.

Theron was moved that such generosity and cooperation between God and man could be imagined, let alone possible. The sparring culture of the envious Greek deities didn't lend itself to productive partnerships between heaven and earth. The gravity, courage and humility of his friend reminded Theron of Diogenes' promptings about getting on with the job and traveling again, within Jesus' greater context. He wondered, as Jesus looked at the candle and spoke calmly and thoughtfully, how his friend could be carrying the weight of the world's infamy, its spoiled and blackened water of life, without the appearance of strain.

The next morning, while Jesus prayed under the tree by the pond, Theron packed wine and food in his basket, including olives for Diogenes. Soon after, they began the hike through the hills to the port, talking about progress in the greater context. As they climbed, Theron looked down at the valley and thought there was a chance he might not see it again for a while.

When they entered the outskirts of the town around the port, the first person Theron asked was able to point him in the direction of Diogenes' home. The old man's home was a large villa on a wooded hillside with views out over the port. Surprised, Theron knocked at the double doors on the uphill side of the villa, and a servant let them in. Diogenes embraced Jesus and Theron and ushered them through the upper floor to a vine-covered balcony with a view of the bay. Theron offered his gift of olives, Jesus the sealed urn of savory anchovies in oil, and Diogenes' servants brought cheese, bread, wine and fruit. As they sat down to share the feast on the balcony, Diogenes was direct.

"Have you thought about traveling again?" he asked Theron.

"I've been thinking," Theron answered, "about the others. Are they back?"

"They've been and gone, twice," Diogenes said. "You chose not to see them. They saw what had to be done and went back."

"You should have reminded me of the plan," Theron said.

"My boy," Diogenes said, "I'm not a miracle worker. I'll remind you now. I have a portrait."

"Can I see it?"

Diogenes passed a large portrait of a young lady to Theron. He held it and studied it. The young lady was familiar, attractive and someone he remembered trusting. Theron's interest increased when his attention shifted to the people standing in the portrait behind her. All seemed to be focusing their attention on him, as if they were aware of him right there on Diogenes' balcony.

"Looking at them, it feels like they're thinking about me, right now," Theron said.

"They are patient. They are very patient," Diogenes answered. "When you travel you won't see them for some time. There are other people you'll see first, if you agree."

"You're saying there is a plan? One that doesn't involve the sea?"

"That's what the enemy expects," Jesus said, "that you'll hide from the risk of pain. You have a number of choices. One does involve the sea and those you recognize in the portrait."

"By experience," Theron said warily, "I find it difficult to remember such choices when I am in the world. They seem like a good idea here. There, they represent effort and I try to avoid them."

"You'll be aware of me with you," Jesus said. "Even when your mind is busy and you've forgotten what I look like, I'll be with you."

"I'm asking to be kept away from the sea."

"You will be protected," Jesus promised.

"And her?" Theron asked, indicating the portrait.

"Someone whose life and opportunity depends on your thoughtfulness. It would behoove you to anticipate others' needs."

"How will I find her?"

"Let's consider Diogenes' suggestion," Jesus began.

Theron listened to the plan as it evolved and was adjusted. He asked questions and accepted the wisdom in the advice he was being offered. The plan involved risk and he would face the sea every day, but there was purpose toward the greater context. He would be born to loving parents, grow up as a free man, a Roman citizen, a person of no importance in the world. If the plan worked, if he remembered, he would see the eyes of the girl in the portrait face to face. He looked deep into her eyes in the portrait, as if she was face to face. The one word that came to his mind was, *hurry*.

"Where is she now?" he asked.

"She's with her parents, still in her mother's womb," Diogenes answered. "She accepted the risk that you might not be compatible in age."

"Will I recognize her?"

"She will recognize you, at the right time and as service is rendered," Diogenes said.

The old man stood up to signal enough questions had been asked and a decision was needed. Diogenes looked out over the port and turned to face Theron.

"Theron, she is key to your purpose. The time you spent alone in your valley seems to you to have been no more than a few months. You have rested. In the world where change is effected the passage of time since your former life has covered 343 years. She will not survive without you."

Theron nodded and looked at both of them. "I understand. It's time."

As summer began in the third year of the reign of Emperor Philip I, some citizens of Hispania Tarraconensis had reason to doubt that the Pax Romana would last indefinitely. At that time, in the quiet port town of Emporiae, a healthy fourth son was born to Artemon and Xeno Isocrates, hard-working Greco-Roman maritime merchants. On the day Xeno gave birth and laughed with joy at having a fourth boy, another rumor of imperial scandal in Rome came belatedly to the boy's father, Artemon. Artemon maintained suspicions about the men who became emperors of Rome and kept himself informed through conversations with merchant ship captains in the port.

That morning Artemon had acknowledged being blessed with another son, but for business reasons his sensitivity to potential threats to the *Pax Romana* took precedence. The latest rumor, said by a merchant ship captain to have originated with a disillusioned senior officer in the Praetorian Guard, hinted that the previous emperor, Balbinus, had been murdered by a faction within the Praetorian Guard. This had followed the assassination of Emperor Pupenius a few months earlier by that same Guard. Officially, no mention of conspiracies was tolerated in Rome or the provinces, because the Senate intended to avoid insurrection among the legions.

Artemon had listened to the ship's captain and grimaced as he looked east over the sea toward Rome. He took the business of the Senate in Rome seriously, as having a direct effect on his own business. He was not hesitant to enjoin the captain in his cause for political change.

"When you get to Rome," Artemon said with determination, "find that senator of yours and tell him it must be law that the legions are loyal to Rome, not to their conniving generals. I had a fourth son today and I will not allow those sleepers in the Senate to endanger my family or my business. Do you hear?"

"I hear you, my friend," the captain said, "but all they want from you is garum, not instructions. They were, are and will be above listening to you or me."

"Then you're safer here than there," Artemon said in frustration.

Artemon meant it when he considered his northeast corner of Hispania safer than Rome. The *Pax Romana* had been a reality in Emporiae for well over two hundred years. No insurrections, no coups and very little crime occurred in the beautiful harbor town, part Greek, part Roman. Problems came to Emporiae from the outside.

Later that evening, safe on his upstairs balcony overlooking the cargo ships in the aqua blue harbor, Artemon could see at a glance the beauty and proportion of his fourth son. The baby nursed strongly with Xeno, and Artemon felt he could more or less take his family for granted while he focused on commerce. He had three older sons, equally handsome and growing fast. The eldest, Evaristus, now eight, was strong and assertive and showed promise of being a fitting heir to the family business.

The threat Artemon perceived was the fragility of the *Pax Romana* in Rome itself where most of his produce, garum condiment, was sold. As he noted to Xeno, in the eight years prior, four out of six emperors, Balbinus, Pupenius, Maximinus and Severus Alexander, had been murdered by conspirators in the Praetorian Guard or the army. A fifth emperor was said to have committed

213

suicide, and the sixth killed in battle against a rival general in Africa. Six emperors in eight years did not indicate stability. Civil war in Rome, Artemon told Xeno, would damage commerce in Emporiae.

Three days later, a concerned Artemon and his wife Xeno took the infant boy and his three brothers to the Temple of Asclepius, in the Greek part of Emporiae, to dedicate the child to the god of good health. Xeno had asked her husband if he would name the boy Alcaeus, meaning "strength." Artemon had agreed, and the infant was held up toward the sun as his name was pronounced.

One clear evening that summer, Artemon came home as usual from the jetty after directing his workers to haul the day's catch into the warehouse. He sat in his favorite chair under the shady vines over the balcony. Xeno was nursing Alcaeus in the easy chair next to him. Looking out at the sunset over the harbor he said that this was the happiest day of his life and to hell with Rome. The day's catch was a record, the men were cheerful, he now had four strong sons and he was grateful to Xeno. Xeno mock-punched his chin and kept nursing.

"The sea," Artemon said, "the sea will always provide, even if the harbor can't or the Senate won't."

"We're doing well enough," Xeno answered. "We can't complain."

For all its magnificent history and scenic appeal, the white sand beaches, turquoise blue water and sheltered harbor, Emporiae was in slow decline and they knew it. Competition from larger ports to the south, Tarraco and Barcino, with deeper harbors and easier access to the Via Augusta and the Via Domitia north into Gaul was now a fact. It meant Emporiae was becoming a secondary destination for shipping. And yet, there would be no decline in income for Artemon and Xeno. No matter what scandal occurred in Rome, Roman and Greek merchant ships would continue to tie up in the harbor at Emporiae and buy every urn of garum that Artemon and his peers could produce. The empire's appetite for garum was increasing.

Garum was a fermented, savory fish sauce, prized as a flavor-enhancing condiment across the empire. Like wine, garum was graded and marketed on a continuum from basic to gourmet, depending on taste and quality. The garum made in Emporiae was a thick broth, derived from sun-dried, salted anchovies. While anchovies were common in the waters off northeast Hispania, garum from Emporiae was graded as expensive in Rome, because of the artisan method of gourmet processing. The warehouse Artemon owned near the harbor was full of drying racks, stacks of salt, urns of piquant garden-grown herbs, lemon-flavored olive oil and garlic. With four growing sons, Artemon planned to finance an expansion of the warehouse and buy a second, larger fishing boat. His sons would eventually work for a share of ownership rather than wages so a down-payment and loan for a second boat could be easily serviced.

The problem with Artemon's logical plan was his youngest son. Alcaeus, he discovered, did not like being anywhere near the water. The boy would cry and make a scene when hoisted aboard their fishing boat, even when it was still in the harbor. The crying would stop promptly when they returned to land. Artemon and the three older boys were mystified at first. Although Artemon became resigned to the strange behavior, the older boys were disdainful and relentlessly teased Alcaeus with horror stories about giant leaping fishes pulling him out of the boat and dragging him down into the depths of the sea.

As Alcaeus reached four years, Xeno began to teach him the simplest ways of handling fishing nets and finding holes that needed repairing. To everyone's surprise the four-year-old took to the nets and even began helping his mother with small mending jobs. With practice and praise, Alcaeus improved his techniques and was considered precocious as a net mender by age five.

But that winter Xeno caught a chill and developed a fever the physicians from the Roman part of town couldn't bring down. With no warning or explanation, she died a day later, without regaining consciousness. Artemon paced around the house in tears, talking to himself for three days. A friend's wife came into the house to feed and look after the four stunned boys. For five-year-old Alcaeus the unexplained loss of his mother became a trauma. Artemon followed an agreed principle and had the body cremated in the Roman manner. But to little Alcaeus, there was no reasonable explanation when he saw that his mother had been reduced to ashes and that the urn with her ashes in it was being taken out to sea by his father. Why would he take her out there when it was obvious the sea was unsafe? How could his father not see she wouldn't be happy there?

Net mending in the warehouse became Alcaeus' place of refuge from views of the sea where his mother had been taken. It also kept him separated from his elder brothers, who mocked him as often as they could for being afraid of the sea. Artemon, for his part, softened his views of Alcaeus and saw how dedicated and useful the boy was. He would come by and talk to Alcaeus while the other boys were cutting and racking fish. Artemon would sit back against the stone wall and tell the boy history stories about Emporiae, about how old the town was—827 years old, as far as Artemon could tell. He told Alcaeus about the proud Greek people who had founded it after their great journey from the other end of the sea in Asia Minor. They were the best seafarers in the world, from a seaport like Emporiae called Phocea. Artemon would help Alcaeus pronounce names such as Phocea and then explain how Phocea itself was a colony of the much older Greek sea port of Athens. Alcaeus, who often said he liked the sound of his father's voice, would sit up straight on his bench, wide-eyed as his father continued the story of how the Phocean Greeks founded other sea ports like Messina in Sicily and Massalia in Gaul. But Emporiae was the only Greek colony in Hispania and though they were Roman citizens now, it had all been started by their great ancestors the Greeks, 827 years earlier.

"Where did the Greeks who founded Emporiae build their first temple?" Artemon would ask Alcaeus.

"Palaiapolis," the boy would shout, standing up to point to

216

what had once been a rocky island, where the colonists built a fortress and acropolis. Over eight hundred years later, the old town on the island was now joined to the mainland by a sandspit.

"What happened soon after Emporiae was founded?" Artemon would ask again.

The five year-old would then say with absolute certainty, "The Persian king invaded Asia Minor eight hundred years ago. The Greek people had to leave Phocea and they sailed their ships all the way to Emporiae, the safest harbor in the world."

His father would smile, then burst out laughing. "I love this boy," Artemon would say, over and over as he hugged Alcaeus.

Alcaeus knew the next story from multiple tellings but would ask his father to tell it again anyway. Artemon would then recall the days of the terrible Hannibal, the fiercest Carthaginian general from north Africa, who brought his hundred thousand men and elephants through Hispania, passing dangerously close to Emporiae. No one could stop Hannibal, who took his elephants north into Gaul and over the mountains to attack Rome. The Romans sent their best generals and soldiers out in a fleet to cut Hannibal's supply route through Hispania.

Artemon would ask Alcaeus, "Where did the Roman army choose the best harbor to land, where they knew they could find good seafood, supplies and friendly people?"

The boy would shout, "Emporiae!" And then would add, "And that was how Emporiae came to have a Roman part and a Greek part, side by side."

Artemon and Alcaeus grew closer as the boy grew taller. Artemon chastised the older boys for teasing their young brother and pointed out that they were spared net mending because of Alcaeus' fine work. When the boy turned ten, Artemon allowed Alcaeus, with one of his brothers, time away from the warehouse and the sea to follow his evident interest in the wooded hills west of the town.

Rolling hills rose gently behind Emporiae and folded into valleys dotted with olive groves and open woodland. Clear, shallow creeks ran through the valleys, and in places where two creeks met Alcaeus would push through the long grass to watch the water mingle. In one such place he placed rocks and watched the water flow around them. He added more rocks and wondered if he could make a pond. Over many visits and forays for rocks under the trees, Alcaeus created a small pond that became his favorite place of meditation in the hills, brother or no brother. He found strong straight sticks, tied them together with layers of white oak bark and built a shelter from the sun. Although at least one of his older brothers was supposed to accompany him up into the hills, they didn't think much of the pond and often abandoned him and returned to the town.

By the time Alcaeus was fifteen, Evaristus, now twenty-three, was expecting a deal with his father in the form of a loan from a money lender to buy a large, used fishing boat, needing only minor repairs. The prospect of becoming a boat owner and expanding their father's business preoccupied all three of the older brothers. Business was consistently good with frequent large catches, but obtaining the cash needed to maximize a down-payment was their primary topic of conversation, followed by conversations about girls.

In the winter of Alcaeus' sixteenth year, he was busier than ever, repairing the largest collection of nets the family had owned, making sure they were always folded in the correct order on his father's boat. One gray, rainy day Alcaeus was repairing an old, frayed net in the warehouse, imagining he was sitting by his pond in the sunshine, when he heard the wind beginning to shriek outside around the tiled roof. He straightened up to listen to the eerie sound and noticed it was almost dark. His father and brothers always came back early on winter days, well before dusk. They were usually loud and boisterous in the warehouse when they came in. All he could hear was the wind, howling strongly now through a driving rain.

Alarmed, he ran outside into the storm, down a pathway and out onto the soaked harbor beach as daylight faded. There were no fishing boats tied to the jetty. He ran as fast as he could along the beach and up onto the stone jetty that defined the harbor. From the end of the jetty Alcaeus could see a short distance out into the rain and spray flying up from the churning waves. Two women ran up behind him and stood looking out into the rain, saying nothing. Alcaeus caught the anxious glances the women exchanged and realized they were thinking the same thing he was. There was nothing he could do. He sank to his knees on the rough stones and thought of his mother, still out there. Then he remembered his father's kind voice, the history stories, the visits his father had made to the pond and how they would share wine, cheese and bread under the bark shelter. Now his father was late, very late getting home. Darkness fell and the women left, crying. Alcaeus knelt alone on the jetty in pitch darkness, rain and wind whipping his face. A horrible, familiar feeling came over him.

No one told him to go home and get dry. He couldn't remember walking home, getting up in the morning or going to the warehouse. But he waited there for the sound of his father's voice. Hours passed with only the sound of the wind whistling in the eaves.

A man he didn't recognize came in around mid-morning and told him the news that had spread around Emporiae. Four fishing boats and their crews had been lost at sea. Others were wrecked along the coast. It was a tragedy and a disaster for the whole town. After the man left, Alcaeus sat in a daze listening to the remnants of the storm. Some time later he heard another man's voice in the warehouse, calling out his name. He stood up. An older patrician gentleman stepped between the fish racks and introduced himself as Publius Gallienus. Alcaeus knew of him as a Roman money lender and lawyer who conducted business from his mansion at the wealthy end of Emporiae.

"Alcaeus, I apologize for letting myself in," the tall, silver-haired man said. "Perhaps your father mentioned my name regarding a possible business loan. It appears there will be no loan. I'm sorry, very sorry. I heard you lost your mother too, some time ago."

219

"Eleven years ago," Alcaeus said.

"There is nothing I can do about your father or your brothers or their loan now. But the fact is, you are the sole heir to your family's home and a substantial business."

"I'm not a fisherman, sir."

"Neither am I. I am a lawyer as well as a lender, and under the circumstances I offer my services for free to help you, in memory of your father."

"How?"

"The law says you are considered under-age as a property owner, and yet the property is yours and no one else's. Your case must be argued before the magistrate. You need legal documents proving all this is yours."

"I don't know anything about legal documents."

"They are necessary. If, for example, you were to rent this warehouse or your home to a fisherman, documents signed by reliable witnesses would be needed first, stating you are the legal owner of the land and both buildings."

"Did my father have these documents?" Alcaeus asked.

"He did," Publius answered, sitting on a bench. "Those documents were filed with the magistrate of Emporiae long ago. Now they need to be replaced."

"Doesn't anyone remember him?"

"Your name will be on them so no one could take the warehouse or home from you. If you don't make garum, you will need to earn money from somewhere to repair the buildings and buy food."

"How do you know he didn't survive? He could have washed ashore."

Publius nodded and extended his hands toward Alcaeus.

"It's possible," Publius said. "In case he didn't, you may want to consider renting the warehouse to a fisherman. If you did, you would have steady income. However, another document would be needed. This would be a contract between you and said fisherman, to ensure rent was paid to you on time. As you are under-aged that document would also be signed by witnesses known to the magistrate."

"You said you could help me."

"I did. I knew your father well, Alcaeus. He was a fine man, the backbone of the town, as far as I am concerned. I would do it for him. And you could learn a few things about the law. As far as your father or brothers go, I'm afraid I have no answers for you there."

Alcaeus accepted the generous invitation and visited Publius in his mansion at appointed times in the next week. He caught on quickly as he studied examples of deeds and contracts Publius showed him. Many were older contracts between suppliers and the military. But one patent contract Publius had crafted for a multi-arrow catapult inventor caught Alcaeus' interest.

"Look at the terms," Publius said, "further down, at the bottom of the page. If the inventor didn't meet the quota for delivery each month he could lose exclusive rights. The army could appoint other manufacturers."

Alcaeus absorbed the new information like a sponge, even when Publius could not control his coughing fits and had to leave the reading room. Publius, for his part, was good to his word, securing Alcaeus' legal rights with the magistrate and soliciting a short list of reliable tenants.

An established Emporiae garum producer, Sosigenes Kletos, an old fishing friend of Artemon, made it known to Publius he wanted to be at the top of the list. Publius advised Alcaeus to offer fair terms. Within a day Sosigenes agreed to rent the warehouse and its equipment and pay Alcaeus for net mending services.

Twelve rough fishermen and garum makers under Sosigenes' employment moved into the warehouse during the next week. It was a strange, surreal change for Alcaeus, listening to the somber, gruff fishermen barking orders in impatient tones. His brothers' teasing and his father's tender questions and stories now seemed like a dream only he retained. If, in the days ahead, he forgot the sounds of their voices or the looks on their faces, he felt they would be as lost as his mother, somewhere at sea. For the first time he closed the door to the room he used for net mending and worked unseen. A thought began gathering momentum that it was his fear of the sea which had caused the loss of his family.

Then something more ominous began to occur around Alcaeus' garum warehouse and in the factories on either side. Fresh fish, tools, clothing and money were being taken whenever the fishermen were absent. Sosigenes confronted Alcaeus about the theft as complaints from the men increased. Alcaeus pointed out places where warehouse tools were missing.

"Why would I take tools from the warehouse?" he asked Sosigenes.

"Ah, it's not you, boy," the old salt answered. "I'm thinking I might know who or what it is that's taking them. There's been some break-ins in the Roman part of town."

"What it is? You mean who it is."

"There's some things in this world, looking like people, I don't think are people."

Nothing was resolved until Sosigenes' men set a trap one night and the thief was caught. Alcaeus was called to the warehouse by Sosigenes. As the owner, it was Alcaeus' responsibility to send for the magistrate's soldiers. He held a lantern up to the thief's face to take a good look. The thief was no older than himself but had the strangest, most dangerous black eyes and bitter face Alcaeus had ever seen. The magistrate's men were notified, but before they arrived the thief locked defiant eyes on Alcaeus. In a split second Alcaeus discerned an inner world of rage and anarchy, a violent, unstable whirl of energy and fury that defied logic. He wondered how such a one could survive for long in a world dominated by Roman order and law. It seemed to Alcaeus he was witnessing a young, walking dead man in the light of the lantern, dead because he had nothing in common with this world.

"A good flogging is what this one needs," Sosigenes muttered.

"A good hanging from the end of the jetty would be better," one of Sosigenes' men suggested.

The magistrate's soldiers arrived about the time the fishermen were agreeing to lynch the captive. An officer directed soldiers to chain the strange thief and took him away before Sosigenes' men could act.

"You better tell that creature," Sosigenes called out to the officer, "if it can understand, we'll hang its carcass on the rocks if we catch it here again."

"Where did he come from?" Alcaeus asked Sosigenes as they watched the soldiers leave.

"I heard there's wild men living in the swamps north of town where the river comes out. Never heard of anyone living there in all my days. Miserable, stinking place. Some are saying it's the Iberi coming to take their land back. I say they came up from Hades and we hang them all."

Alcaeus heard nothing more about the thief as the days passed, but his thoughts remained with Sosigenes' more probable comment about the swamp men being Iberi. Eight hundred years ago, when Greek colonists founded Emporiae, they lived on an island off the coast for safety. After twenty years of cautious trading with the Iberi, the Greeks began to establish a new town between the harbor and the locals' village named Indika. But the Greeks found it necessary to build walls around Emporion, as they called it then, to keep the thieving locals out of their homes and businesses. The walled relationship continued for three hundred years until Roman legions arrived to cut Hannibal's supply lines from north Africa. The Romans found welcoming Greeks in Emporion and suspect locals on the other side of the Greek walls. Without hesitation, the Roman legions leveled Indika and set up a military logistics camp and barracks complex where the Iberi had lived for a thousand years. From Emporiae, Rome conquered the rest of the Iberian peninsula. But it took over two hundred years of intermittent war and rebellion to subdue the various Iberian tribes. This was the prelude to the *Pax Romana* that some of Emporiae's citizens thought would last forever.

Alcaeus remembered his father talking about the *Pax Romana* and its structural weakness, in which the legions' first loyalties were not to Rome but to their generals. Artemon had lamented the delay in the news of scandals and disasters, which arrived far too late if effective warning was ever needed for Emporiae. Ten years earlier, Artemon had told Alcaeus, three Roman emperors had died in the same year. Emperor Valerian had been captured in battle against the Persians, and Emperors Aemilian and then Trebonius Gallus were killed by their own troops. Two years prior, Hostilian had died of plague and Trajan Decius was killed in battle by eastern Goths. Each disaster had occurred far away and was old news when it arrived, but it had worried Artemon.

What if, Alcaeus wondered, Sosigenes' comment was not so flippant and the appearance of the swamp men was an omen to be reckoned with? How would he protect the warehouse? It was at such moments Alcaeus deeply missed his father. Artemon would surely have had something to say to the magistrate about the swamp men. Meanwhile, Sosigenes' men were calling the thief Cati, or the wildcat, after a predatory creature that had not been seen in those parts of Hispania for centuries.

The incident made Alcaeus feel vulnerable. If the warehouse was targeted for theft again and the thieves were lynched by fishermen, Alcaeus would hear from both the magistrate and vengeful swamp men. His fears were confirmed when he asked Publius about property owner's responsibilities. The magistrate, Publius told him, would not send his scarce soldiers to be ambushed in the swamps but would only respond if a Roman citizen was murdered.

Alcaeus found himself avoiding his net mending room in the warehouse whenever possible. He reasoned he didn't have to listen to the men cursing each other during the afternoons or cackling about their vigilante plans. He planned his days to work alone mending nets whenever the men were at sea. When they were in the warehouse he would be in the hills meditating by his pond.

Sitting against a white oak by the pond, Alcaeus often found himself thinking about his father and brothers at sea in a storm too severe even for their skills. He couldn't shake the feeling that somehow he might have helped them. One day, hunched over in a low mood under the tree, he questioned how he could still feel responsible. He tossed cork bark into the water in frustration, trying to hit pieces floating in the center of the pond. Watching the pieces float in a group, an idea came to him in an instant. He sat upright and imagined each piece as a person in a storm at sea. Then the thought occurred to him, if enough cork bark was enclosed in something like fish netting and worn like a vest it might help a fisherman stay afloat much longer in a storm. Stunned, he stood up by the pond and realized he could have helped them. For almost seven years he had watched cork bark float on the pond he had made and didn't connect it with flotation at sea. In remorse he ran down the trail through the hills, through town and straight into the warehouse. Outside the net mending room several large baskets were used to store scrap netting. He took off the vest he was wearing, laid scrap netting over it as a template, reached for a knife and cut four outlines the same shape. Then he stitched them together at the sides and bases, leaving the shoulder sections open.

The next morning Alcaeus went up into the hills with a basket on his back. Instead of laying back in his shelter next to the pond, he foraged for chips of cork bark. When he couldn't find enough, he began cutting chunks of bark off a white oak tree with a fishing knife. Pressing enough cork bark into the basket to fill it, he hiked back down to the town to begin his experiment.

Trial and error showed the vest was too small when the layers were padded with cork, so he had to cut larger pieces from scrap netting. The process took several attempts before he had a wearable vest bulking with cork pieces, sealed inside fish netting with stitching at both shoulders. The last step was to enclose the front with rope ties. Then came the moment of truth. Who would test it in the harbor?

Alcaeus couldn't bring himself to ask one of Sosigenes' humorless fishermen, and no one else he knew would do it. He reasoned if someone who couldn't swim was willing to test it and survived the test, then the idea might be worthwhile. That someone would

225

have to be him.

When Alcaeus entered the shallow turquoise water at the sandy north end of the harbor, the vest tightened across his chest and his breath began rasping in his throat. Hands shaking, he sank slowly into the water at waist depth. Now breathing heavily, Alcaeus was surprised and then shouted in relief at the instant buoyancy. The cork vest looked ugly, but it worked, and no one witnessed his fear.

At the warehouse, Alcaeus used all the spare netting he could find to make a series of cork vests, each a little less awkward and bulky-looking than its predecessor. Then it occurred to him that he could sell them, and he asked Sosigenes if he would be his first customer. The old dog laughed at Alcaeus.

"Nah, that thing would be worthless to me, boy. You're thinking of your father, I know. If there's a storm coming, I'll stay in harbor. Besides, everyone working for me could swim cross the harbor when they were this high. They'd throw these things of yours overboard as a waste of space. Space for your feet, your nets and baskets of fish. That's what we need on the boats. More space."

Chastened by the ridicule, Alcaeus gingerly asked other fishermen around the jetty if they would be interested in trying a vest and received similar responses. Thinking the problem was not efficiency but appearance, Alcaeus looked through the warehouse for anchovy netting with the smallest openings. If the openings were tighter, the cork pieces could be smaller. But all the anchovy netting was needed for garum fishing, so Alcaeus decided to put the idea on hold. Fine netting would have to be purchased from another port where a surplus existed. With a new design in mind, he threw the prototypes into an unsightly pile in his net mending room.

That afternoon, word came to Alcaeus that a Roman merchant ship bound for Massilia was tied to the jetty. Massilia, the biggest Greco-Roman port in southern Gaul, would have the netting he needed, so he followed the path down to the jetty and called up to a sailor on board for permission to see the ship's master. The sailor told him the captain was meeting with merchants in the Roman part of town. After filling an order form for the tightest anchovy netting in Massalia, Alcaeus asked the sailor if his crew would wear a buoyancy vest. The sailor had never heard of the idea and was reluctant to speak for his captain. He suggested Alcaeus come back in the afternoon, but as his captain went by the book he should not expect anything. It was yet another disheartening response.

Alcaeus returned to the warehouse and hoped the captain would return to the ship before dark and make a decision. Ten experimental cork vests were tangled in a pile in the net repair room, a waste of space and effort. Until he had the tightest netting the vests would appear too bulky and would not sell.

On a whim, to clear the space, Alcaeus stacked the prototypes in a netting cart later in the afternoon and pulled it down to the jetty. No one answered when he called from the bottom of the gangplank, so he stepped aboard and called down below. Still no answer. The sailor he spoke to earlier was not on duty. No one appeared to be on duty on the entire ship. Disheartened at the ongoing series of rejections and after dunking himself in the harbor for nothing, Alcaeus took the vests out of the cart. There he paused, looking up at the ship and realized how sorry for himself he sounded.

"I can't use them," he thought. "Maybe someone else can make something out of them."

Alcaeus carried them forward, raised a hatch and dropped them down into a stack in the ship's open hold.

Two nights later Sosigenes told him that Cati, the strange, dark-eyed thief caught near the warehouse, had escaped custody, seriously injuring one of the magistrate's guards, and was hiding out somewhere in Emporiae. A mansion in the Roman part of town had been robbed. Food, clothing and weapons were taken. As night fell, Sosigenes ordered four of his men to find positions out of sight around his boats and the warehouse. Alcaeus promised the old man he would lock the doors and shutters on the house.

During the night, Alcaeus woke with a start to the sharp sounds of fighting and cursing outside, somewhere near the harbor. By the time he reached the warehouse, the thief had been caught and beaten. Sosigenes' four men though didn't stop there. They decided the thief would hang from the mast of Sosigenes' largest fishing boat. When Alcaeus got close enough to the cursing thief, he could see it was the black-eyed wild man, Cati. As foul and terrifying as the thief was, Alcaeus resisted the lynching. Something he sensed within the wild man would be let loose on Emporiae if the law was flouted and local men became anarchists like Cati.

"You cannot murder him!" he called out to the fishermen. "I will call Sosigenes and the magistrate. Let the law decide whether he lives!"

The fishermen ignored Alcaeus and dragged the thrashing creature to the boat mast and threw a dock rope around his neck. Alcaeus moved toward them with his fishing knife raised.

"I'll cut that rope!" Alcaeus warned. "Go call the magistrate's men!"

"Boy," one of the fishermen snarled, "go back to your house."

But in the momentary distraction the creature Cati struggled loose of the rope and the four men's grip on his arms. He reached the side of the boat in what seemed like one enormous bound and turned for a second, out of their reach. The voice of the dark anarchist shot out as a combination of a hiss and a growl.

"I'll remember all of you. One by one."

Then the monster was over the side and swimming in a frenzy out into the dark harbor. The fishermen turned their furious eyes on Alcaeus.

"What have you done now, boy?"

"Let the law judge," he responded.

The next morning, the magistrate representing imperial justice in Emporiae sent armed couriers to Sosigenes with a note of censure warning him that his attempt to preempt the provincial courts of Rome would not be tolerated. Sosigenes had known nothing about the event until his angry men had woken him in the night.

After the aborted lynching and the magistrate's censure, Alcaeus' relationship with his tenant Sosigenes began to sour. From that point, Sosigenes and his men rarely spoke to Alcaeus in the warehouse and began taking their net mending business to other warehouses along the harbor. Still, Alcaeus retained enough income to live on as long as Sosigenes kept the terms of the rental contract for the warehouse. To avoid the tension Alcaeus began spending almost every day in the hills, his cork vests and net repair business permanently on hold.

Summer passed into autumn, and Alcaeus assumed his order for netting from Massalia had been lost or disregarded by the sailor or captain of the Roman merchant ship. He kept himself busy hauling lumber up to his shelter by the pond, expanding the shelter and enclosing it in preparation for winter. While Alcaeus worked on the shelter, he wondered whether he should see Publius Gallienus about renegotiating his rental contract with Sosigenes. He now felt queasy every time he entered his own warehouse. It was time, he decided, to end the contract. But how? Only the sale of the warehouse would accomplish the freedom he wanted.

The best idea, Alcaeus thought, would be to ask Publius if he would finance Sosigenes' purchase of the building. With part of the proceeds, Alcaeus hoped to pay Publius to take him on as an apprentice in law. But when Alcaeus knocked on the door of Publius' mansion, a servant told him the lawyer was unwell and would not be seeing visitors for some time.

That winter became another low point for Alcaeus. He avoided conversation with Sosigenes and avoided mentioning the buildup of trash around the warehouse. Uneasy about his future, unable to relate to the sea-loving fishermen his age, Alcaeus lived as a teenage hermit in his family's large house. His financial security depended entirely on the dubious goodwill of Sosigenes. If Publius remained unwell and would not see him, Alcaeus had no one to turn to for advice if Sosigenes reneged on the contract.

In a town dependent on fishing, Alcaeus now lost any interest he once had in the fishing business. The townspeople of Emporiae took little interest in him, other than an obligatory nod in public. He realized one clear, cold day in spring by the pond that he was a hermit in his own town because the townspeople considered him cursed by misfortune. From their perspective, there was little to refute the perception. He was an unlucky orphan, a loner and a silent misfit who did no work. It made Alcaeus uneasy to think there were converging similarities between his situation and that of the wild man, Cati, who had been recaptured and was now back in the magistrate's prison.

That same day, as Alcaeus walked the trail down from the pond, he noticed a long line of people leaving town via the main street. A bystander told him it was the funeral procession for Publius Gallienus. As Alcaeus watched the procession head toward the crematorium and cemetery north of town, he felt his lifeforce draining out into a bleak horizon with no future, no safety and no reason for being alive.

The day after Alcaeus' eighteenth birthday, spent alone at the pond, he was leaving the house when he overheard a garum fisherman mention a big Roman merchant ship, *Heraclion*, in the harbor, bound for Massalia in southern Gaul. Hoping he might be able to place another order for finer netting, Alcaeus strolled down to the jetty and waited at the bottom of the gangplank for a sailor to invite him aboard to see the captain. When no one appeared at the top of the gangplank, he called out. The ship's first mate came up out of a hold toward the stern. The man leaned over the rail, stared at Alcaeus and without comment turned and went back down into the hold. Remembering a similar incident a year earlier, Alcaeus concluded he would be better off alone in the hills and trudged off the jetty. He tried to laugh at yet another rejection, muttering to himself about his reputation as the hermit, now spread beyond town to ships' crews.

Suddenly a man's loud voice called out from the jetty behind Alcaeus, "Sir!"

Alcaeus had never before been addressed by a term he associated with men his father's age. He glanced over his shoulder, wondering if there was some miscreant on the jetty behind him, closer to the ship. A group of ten or twelve people appeared along the railing of the big ship. For no apparent reason, they descended the gangplank and approached him as he stood at the town end of the jetty. Thinking at first he had somehow insulted the first mate, Alcaeus looked around for a line of escape to the nearest warehouse facing the harbor. The group continued to approach. A big man leading them held up one hand and they stopped on the jetty. They began murmuring and continued to stare at him. To one side of the big man, a girl with braided, golden hair and high-cheeked Saxon features was called forward. She nodded affirmatively, then spoke softly in good Latin.

"Yes, that's him. It's him."

The whole group seemed to gasp at him, then babble at the same time, making no sense to Alcaeus. The big man held up both hands this time, and there was silence as he walked forward. Broad-shouldered and lean, he moved with a soldier's confidence. Alcaeus thought again of running for the nearest warehouse but could see the man's knife remained on his belt. He noticed the man's graying beard was trimmed in the style of the wealthy, and more important, his brown eyes appeared almost kind, not furious. The man stopped well short of Alcaeus and enunciated clearly, as if he were an aristocrat.

"Young man, my name is Aetius Archias Marcellus, merchant of Massalia, citizen of Rome. This is my daughter, Laelia. It appears my daughter remembers you from our visit last summer. It also appears you were the instrument of God and knew our need before we did. You, by the grace of God, are the reason we are alive. We are here to express our gratitude."

Alcaeus hesitated, then stammered, certain the merchant was confusing him with one of the acolytes at the temple. At the same time, he was aware of the girl's eyes on him.

"I'm not sure you have the right person," Alcaeus said. "There's a temple to Asclepius in town. There are priests at the temple. You could talk to them."

The fair-haired girl turned to someone behind her and advanced toward Alcaeus carrying one of his prototype cork vests. She was about his age and would not take her clear blue eyes from his.

"One of our ships was in Emporiae last summer," the girl said. "My father, my brother and the crew were in town. I was aboard, checking manifests. I heard you calling. I saw you drop our vests in the hold and didn't know what they were. Our ship sank in a storm near Sicily, and all ten of us survived because of the vests. We thought you were directed by God. You knew of our need before we did."

Alcaeus' face turned bright red as she looked at him. They were his vests, but he was certain he knew nothing about directions from any deity. To Alcaeus, no one in Emporiae needed direction more than he did. And in front of a crowd of strangers, there was nothing he could do to hide the expression on his face. The girl's eyes were beautiful to look into. He wondered how she could appear serious and joyful at the same time. Compared to any woman or girl in Emporiae, she was the embodiment of a goddess, direct, authoritative and bold in conversation. But Alcaeus didn't know where to begin. He couldn't claim credit for saving these peoples' lives. Yet here were ten or more grateful souls waiting on a profound word from the deity who directed him. Finally the big merchant rescued Alcaeus from the profound embarrassment he was experiencing.

"Young man," Aetius said, "may we ask your name?"

"Alcaeus Isocrates."

"Son of Artemon?"

"Yes, sir."

"I heard of your loss. My condolences. I counted your father as a friend. Would you do us the favor of accepting our hospitality on board our ship?"

Again Alcaeus didn't know what to say to people who thought

he had saved their lives in a storm at sea. The girl with the alive eyes, Laelia, stepped forward. A slight smile on her sun-burned face hinted at the possibility that she was less deity and more girl than she first appeared.

"Please, Alcaeus," she said, courteously. "We would be honored."

Bold in speech, she was also bold in her manner. Her skin was warm as she gracefully slipped her arm around his and gently tugged Alcaeus toward the gangplank, as if she already knew him.

Alcaeus accepted the gesture as they walked together but found it difficult to rapidly adjust to these sea peoples' gracious perception of him. His self-perception had for many years included being the object of his brothers' taunts, afraid of the sea, as well as an unfortunate orphan and a loner. Being the center of attention for someone so attractive put him in a role for which he had absolutely no preparation. He wondered, for just a moment, if they were being polite to set him up, planning to turn on him, as his brothers did. To maintain his focus, he told himself to look down at the treads on the gangplank, feel them underfoot and not embarrass everyone by tripping on them. After a few steps across the deck he was ushered down a stairway.

The bustling group gathered in a lantern-lit great room below deck. Servants hurried to set and fill cups on a large table. Several kitchen people peeked out of the galley to catch a glimpse of the mysterious guest. Plates and bowls of char-grilled seafood, aromatic bouillabaisse, sizzling sautéed onions, fresh vegetables and herb-garnished condiments were placed on the table next to the drinks. Aetius raised a cup, turned to Alcaeus and announced a toast.

"In the presence of our honored guest, hear us, God, we are grateful! We thank you for your fiery presence in us and for your tender intercession in our deliverance at sea and on land!"

The rest of the crew raised their cups and loudly echoed the toast. Alcaeus remained confused as to who they were addressing. He didn't understand the reference to their deity. But he did grasp that these gregarious and confident people were seafarers, quite comfortable with their life, confined on a cargo ship that would soon be far out at sea. He was ready to leave, to go back into the hills to the pond, when Laelia touched his hand and invited him to sit.

"Please, make yourself comfortable. Would you like something to drink?"

She placed a cup filled with a golden liquid in front of him, added more to hers from a decanter, and served him a bowl of char-grilled seafood topped with lemon garum. Bold as always, she looked into his eyes.

"My father said something to the effect that you might not be used to having a lot of people around. I'm not sure what he meant."

"I suppose he's right," Alcaeus said, hesitating. "I'm not sure I understand the reason for being a guest here. Everyone seems friendly, but I don't know that I deserve . . ."

"I think everyone here sees what my father sees," Laelia said. "You deserve our gratitude and you're worth the celebration."

"Your ship, you were on it when it sank off Sicily?" he said, changing the subject.

"Yes, I was. That was the *Hermes*. She was our fastest ship. She had garum from your factory on board, as well as goods from Barcino and Tarraco going to Rome. I couldn't accept we were going to lose it all. Then I saw how high the seas were and realized we could lose our lives in minutes. I didn't understand what your vests were until that moment. They were still in the forward hold. In the water I remembered your face and thought God had decided to save us through you."

"By God, you mean Jupiter or Neptune?"

"God, the one God," she said. "I am that I am."

"I don't understand."

"The creator of all of cosmos and us."

"Forgive me," he said, "I'm a little lost. My family were Stoics and Greco-Roman."

"My family's Greco-Roman, at least my father's side. His father was from Achaia in Greece, his grandmother was Gallic, from Massalia. My mother is Gallic, from Lugdunum. Our home and our warehouse is in Massalia."

"Is that where you go from here?"

"No, we have cargo to load in Barcino and Tarraco. Some of it is going to the army in Narbo, some for consignment in Massalia. After that the rest of the shipment goes to Rome."

"You're not afraid of the sea, of storms?" he asked awkwardly and then tried to recover in a low tone. "No, no, I didn't mean that."

"No, I'm not afraid of the sea. But I was afraid of you," she said, "until I saw you again. I saw you on our deck when we were in Emporiae last summer. I had been sleeping and didn't know if you were a high angel from God or if I was dreaming. I thought I saw a being not meant to be seen by people, and I was afraid to say anything. I was trembling. You looked like you had come from heaven and you looked so stern. I couldn't tell anyone."

"Stern? I don't know how you thought that," he said, smiling at the unusual idea. "I'm just me. I'm not much of anything. All I have is a warehouse that belonged to my father. But I don't go in there or work there now. A tenant is in there with a dozen of his men. We don't talk any more."

"Where do you work?"

"I spend a lot of time in the hills. That's where I got the idea for the vests."

"Don't you manufacture them and sell them here?"

"I need finer netting to make them less bulky. No one in Emporiae is interested. I came to the harbor to place an order for netting from Massilia."

"Come to Massilia with us," she said, her eyes widening. "You could use factory space in one of our warehouses. I know the kind of netting you need."

Alcaeus looked around the table and took in the laughter and camaraderie of the crew. It was a friendly atmosphere, but these were people with boundless courage. He felt confined to a compromised situation in Emporiae and unworthy of their fearless company.

"I can't leave Emporiae," he said, knowing she was inviting him to take a sea voyage. "This has been my family's home for hundreds of years. I have a big house and the garum warehouse."

"They'll still be here. Just while you develop the vests. You would have a much bigger market for them in Massalia. You could look for wholesalers in the port, come back here and manufacture them."

"I don't travel by sea," he said, avoiding her eyes, "any more."

"How do you . . . Oh," she said softly, and then paused, "the sea. That's why you created the vests. Your family. I understand."

"I could have saved my family," he said. "I didn't think of it in time."

"You saved us. You saved this family and our crew."

"I'm glad," he said, able to look at her again. "It's good that I've done something."

"You have. But what will you do with your business in Emporiae? You said you live by yourself in a big house. You don't get along with your tenant. You don't have much of a market for your vests here. Come with us and take a look at Massalia. There's a hundred times the market there."

"Not by sea."

She touched his hand and moved closer. Alcaeus noted her warmth, her kindness and the effect her eyes had on his pulse. When she spoke there was no guile in her voice. Laelia was utterly unlike anyone he had ever known in Emporiae.

"There's no danger now," she said. "It's mid-summer. There are no storms this time of year. Stay below deck and be with family. We would treat you like family because you treated us like family."

"You're very generous, but . . ."

"Let me ask my father," she said, getting up and drawing her father into the conversation.

Aetius pulled up a chair and listened to his daughter summarize their conversation. Whether it was the warmth below deck, the good food, or the good company, Alcaeus felt a new, welcome sensation. It was difficult for him to describe it in terms of safety or freedom from anxiety. To him, it was simpler to think of Laelia's words, "There's no danger now." Those words mattered more than anything—so much so he had to restrain himself from crying at the sense of relief from a loneliness that he had long thought he deserved for losing his family. At that moment he realized his loss was abnormal and Laelia's bright, confident, generous world was the way life should be lived.

As the conversation developed, Alcaeus was aware of Aetius calmly observing him and Laelia. When Aetius seemed to understand his situation, probably drawing from memories of his commercial friendship with Artemon, he leaned forward and spoke in his calm, deep voice.

"We would be pleased to offer you a safe journey to Massilia. And back if you want it. You're bright and young and you have good ideas. Your father understood that Emporiae's decline has been occurring since he was a boy. The harbor looks scenic, but it is slowly filling with sand. Massalia is growing. Unless you're producing garum like your tenant, Emporiae doesn't have much to offer any bright young man."

"I have a warehouse and a home here," Alcaeus said. "It's all I have. If I leave for any time, Sosigenes could renege on the lease. I have no one to represent my deed in front of the magistrate. Sosigenes could claim ownership and that I had abandoned the deed. His men would be witnesses for him. No one in the town would argue with them."

"If you have the deed, you could sell the warehouse to Sosigenes at a fair price," Aetius responded. "You could sell the house to him or any of his men. That would give you capital to start fresh in a growing market where you could develop your ideas."

"I could, but I don't know anyone in town I could trust to help me," Alcaeus said, thinking aloud. "I'm eighteen now, so I suppose I need to start talking to business people and find out what the warehouse is worth."

"There are lawyers in Emporiae who could represent you. I know of two I would recommend. What else is important to you here?"

"Nothing much. A pond in the hills where I go to think."

"Here's what I would propose," Aetius said. "I could take you into town today and introduce you to a lawyer who knows businesses here. He could draw up a fair bill of sale and have it presented to Sosigenes. These things take a few days to conclude. We leave Emporiae tomorrow for Barcino and Tarraco. When we return, within a week, you would probably be a moderately wealthy young man with a future—if that's what you want."

"I would need to decide in front of a lawyer, decide today?"

"Today, before you and I see a lawyer. The ship leaves tomorrow."

Alcaeus felt a wave of heat rush through him. He had casually strolled down to the harbor thinking he might be able to place an order for netting via a ship bound for Massalia. Now he had to decide in the next moment whether it was he who was bound for Massalia, leaving hundreds of years of family heritage behind in Emporiae. He felt Laelia looking at him and glanced at her, wondering what she was saying without speaking. His eyes held contact with hers, and an intangible transfer of excitement and elation flowed across the short distance between them. *I know*, he decided. *I'll go wherever that joy is going.* He turned to her father.

"I would be grateful if you could introduce me to a lawyer," he said, in his calmest tone.

Laelia stood up, blue eyes moist, beaming at Alcaeus and then turned to her father. She seemed to restrain herself from saying anything.

"There's plenty of time left in the day, if you're ready," Aetius said.

"I'm ready," Alcaeus answered, glancing at Laelia.

"I'd like to go with you, Father," Laelia said.

Aetius would not allow Laelia to accompany him to Alcaeus'

family home or to the warehouse. The merchant walked quickly around both floors of the home, without comment. He then instructed Alcaeus to take him into the warehouse, introduce him to Sosigenes as an investor from Malissia, interested in buying leases on seafood factories in Hispania and then give him the tour. It worked. By the time Aetius was ready to leave, Sosigenes and all his men had stopped work and were standing in place with their mouths open.

The introduction to the lawyer in a mansion in the Roman part of town went smoothly, with several knowing nods from the lawyer as Aetius laid out prospects for the sale of both properties. Arrangements were made for the lawyer's agent to visit Sosigenes with instructions to vacate or counter-offer.

On the way back to the harbor Alcaeus heard a commotion coming from a side street leading to the magistrate's office and the prison facilities. A gang of six inmates were being marched in chains to the harbor. Armed guards propelled them with obscenities and the flat sides of their spears. Alcaeus stopped to watch the death march. Last in the line of six he recognized the wildman, Cati, at the same moment the convict saw him. Without hesitation Cati turned his black eyes toward Alcaeus and hissed, like a snake and a cat in hideous combination. Alcaeus recoiled in his feelings but tried not to show any visible reaction. The dismal parade clanked on toward a waiting Roman navy ship in the harbor.

"I see your acquaintance with one of the sons of darkness," Aetius said.

"Not of my choosing," Alcaeus responded. "I would guess he's not long for this world."

"I agree," Aetius said, lowering his voice. "They have their cycles of decay, disintegration and, in time, the death of the soul. That one has nothing left to lose, nothing to hide. It's the ones who want to hide their darkness, their commitment to revenge, early in their decay, that are the most dangerous. We think we can trust them, paragons in high places in the empire. They exist, for now."

"How can you tell who is who?"

"By what they do, not what they say."

When they returned to the gangplank of the big cargo ship at the jetty, Alcaeus stopped, trying to think through the coming sequence of events.

"What do I do tomorrow?"

"The lawyer's agent will brief you at your home in the morning. Follow his instructions. Let him do the talking to Sosigenes. We leave for Barcino early in the morning and will dock again in Emporiae in five days. But in the meantime, I think someone is expecting you'll stay for an evening banquet."

As Alcaeus looked up at the ship, sun-burned Laelia appeared and leaned over the side, blond hair blowing in the breeze, free of her braids. Aetius glanced up at her and started laughing as he took hold of the gangplank. Alcaeus took in the unspoken communication between father and daughter and it reminded him of wordless moments of understanding with his own father. Alone for two years, without that understanding, Alcaeus wondered if it had been the cause which made him appear stern, unsociable.

That night, Alcaeus stared at the ceiling in his upstairs bedroom, thinking of Laelia for hours. It surprised him that he felt the same warm glow in his chest by seeing her in his mind as being in her company. Eventually he fell asleep, pondering the generosity of Aetius, who was surely a buffer against the harshness of the world.

When the lawyer's agent arrived in the morning, Alcaeus was ready. He had seen Aetius' ship, *Heraclion*, leave the harbor after dawn and then prepared himself for business. The agent was quick and efficient in explaining the documents and then went out alone to the warehouse to negotiate with Sosigenes. The sound of Sosigenes' protests could be heard clearly, all the way to the house. In a half hour the agent returned with news that Sosigenes had agreed to buy the home and warehouse for a sum of money Alcaeus could hardly believe. The agent appeared unmoved. Alcaeus signed the documents and then he was alone again for four more days with his family memories.

After one last visit to his pond in the hills, Alcaeus spent his time packing the few possessions he wanted to take with him. The agent came by with more documents for the sale of the home and warehouse, with promissory notes made out in Alcaeus' name. No one else in town came to visit.

On the final day, Alcaeus watched for the big ship to enter the harbor and was ready at the jetty as it docked. He looked up at the *Heraclion*, hoping to see Laelia, and when she appeared at the ship's rail he was surprised at the leap of gladness he felt to see her. She came down the gangplank to greet him and looked into his eyes.

"I was thinking about you," she said. "You haven't changed your mind?"

"I'm ready to go," he answered, brushing his fingertips against hers, aware that they probably had an audience. "I'm ready."

Laelia showed him to a cabin downstairs, arranged his belongings and brought him refreshments.

"I've gathered some books I hope you'll like while we're under way. If you're more comfortable down here, I'll be around to keep you company."

"I've been thinking," he answered, "maybe I could keep you company on deck for a while, if you wouldn't mind."

"I'll keep an eye on you," she said lightly, then became more serious. "I wanted you to know that we were in the water off Sicily for two days in the sun and two nights that were completely dark. I had lots of time to think about my chances without that vest. I'll never forget it came from you."

The next few days passed in a bright blur of blue skies, a calm sea, banquets in the evenings, music and singing, a friendly crew who knew what they were doing, and Laelia's eyes on him often. The crew seemed content to leave them alone among the ropes in the bow. There they talked for hours about ideas for manufacturing useful things, Gallic songs, great seafood and amazing and mystical stories about her God. Above all, Alcaeus noticed her generosity, kindness and the light-hearted feeling she conveyed in everything she did.

When they docked at the Roman military port of Narbo in Gaul, he helped deliver cargo ashore and load goods for Massalia. Work completed, he went with Laelia and the crew on a tour of the local seafood serveries along the waterfront. It was like a dream in heaven to be accepted as part of a large and happy family. When there was a day's delay waiting to load important cargo for Rome, Alcaeus felt his time in heaven had been extended. The time ashore with Laelia made him wonder what he had done to deserve such good fortune.

Three days later, when the ship began to approach the entrance to the great harbor at Massalia, Alcaeus remembered Aetius' comments concerning what the bigger Greek colony could offer, compared with Emporiae. He stood in the bow with Laelia and took in the details of the far larger setting and the greater opportunities Massalia held. The hills and ridges in the distance were dotted with trees, temples and the villas of the wealthy. Around the port itself, he surveyed a vast built-up area of crowded housing, narrow lanes, smoking chimneys and far more noise and traffic than Emporiae.

Feeling pleased at this first journey away from his ancestral home, taken in such comforting company, Alcaeus noted with relief he had survived a voyage by sea. But he wasn't prepared for the look of concern on Laelia's face as they moved closer to the docks. He turned to see what she was looking at. A squadron of naval ships were hoisting anchors and unfurling sails. Agitated crowds were milling and arguing on the wharves. Aetius left the helmsman, leaned over the side and shouted out to dockhands who were berthing the ship. Alcaeus couldn't hear the extended response from the wharf below the ship, so he watched in confusion and waited until Aetius came over to speak to them. Laelia pressed against Alcaeus' side as her father stood in front of them.

"Merchants, captains, the military," he said in a grim tone, gesturing toward the crowd on the wharf next to them. "They are concerned at the news. An invasion. Uncounted Franks and Allemanni have bypassed the legions in Gaul and crossed the eastern Pyrenees into Hispania. There are no legions close enough to stop them. They have overrun Emporiae. It has been looted and burned. Two naval ships were in the harbor. The crews witnessed the attack. The Franks and the Allemanni are moving south down the Via Augusta in great numbers. If they sack Barcino or Tarraco we will feel it here. If more come eastward there will be war here."

Alcaeus heard Aetius' words amid the turmoil on shore but had trouble believing what had been said. He knew of the nomadic Franks who marauded and pillaged in the rainy forests far to the north, but they were checked by the legions in their garrisons along the Rhine. Did this news mean the hordes had broken through the legions or gone around them? How could the generals in Gaul and Hispania allow this? The *Pax Romana* in Hispania had its beginning in Emporiae and been a fact of life, taken for granted for over two hundred years. Now waves of Franks, the most mobile raiders among the Germanic tribes, had penetrated southern Gaul and crossed the Pyrenees with no notice and no one to stop them. Alcaeus thought of the mansions in the Roman part of town, doors shattered, Frankish swords raised over his neighbors, the town in flames. The people of Emporiae had no defense, no garrison, no escape. Few, if any, could have survived, except by swimming out to sea. Now, more Franks could be on their way to Massalia. He felt Laelia's hand tighten around his.

Aetius left them standing there, went to the rail and called down to two centurions on the wharf. Alcaeus couldn't hear their response but he did hear Aetius direct the crew to extend the gangplank. While the men pulled the gangplank into place Aetius crossed the deck quickly and addressed Alcaeus and Laelia.

"No crew will leave the ship. They're waiting on news. If these centurions receive orders to march, we may have to leave for points east."

"Father, if there are Franks coming, we have to bring Mother on board!" Laelia insisted. "How much time do we have?"

"Wait here," Aetius commanded.

Aetius descended the gangplank and tried to reach the two centurions at the center of the anxious crowd on the wharf. Soldiers were called to create a perimeter around the centurions. Junior officers came and went, dispensing orders and bringing new information. From the railing in the ship's bow, the constant interruptions to the officers' huddle seemed grim. It was hard to tell from a distance if they were naval officers waiting to embark or commanders about to join a nearby legion. Alcaeus watched in silence as he realized the life he had lived in serene Emporiae was now over. If Massalia was in danger, who knew where safety could be found? At last Aetius turned their way and beckoned them to leave the ship and join him in the noisy crowd on the wharf.

Laelia led Alcaeus down the gangplank and turned with a wry smile as she stepped onto the worn planks of the wharf.

"Welcome to Massalia. Welcome to Greek Gaul."

They joined Aetius, along with other captains and crew, on the outside of the crowd now packed around the two centurions. Aetius turned around to speak to Laelia.

"It seems there was a huge battle with the Franks on the lower Rhine. Tens of thousands of Franks escaped. Large numbers evaded the legions by moving south into Gaul. They traveled away from the roads, from the north to the south of Gaul. Uncounted thousands, all in eastern Hispania now. Only one legion there, far to the west."

"Are the Franks near Massalia?" Laelia asked, over the noise around them.

"No. There's a legion west of Massalia. They won't come here."

"And Emporiae?" Alcaeus asked.

"It's gone, looted, burned," Aetius said. "Barcino is next."

At that point two merchants near them, apparently from Barcino, shouted over the crowd at the centurions. The taller one could be heard more clearly.

"What the hell are you standing here for when there are Franks at the gates of Barcino?"

The younger centurion tried to reassure the merchants.

"We have a legion embarking in Narbo as we speak. Another legion, already in Hispania, I'm sure will be marching west to Barcino."

This didn't satisfy the worried merchants who complained even louder about the risk to their families, their businesses and their city. The older, sword-scarred centurion stepped forward and was brutally realistic.

"Those two legions will not get to Barcino before the Franks," the veteran said. "That's why Barcino has walls, to buy time. The bastards will leave for the mountains when the legions arrive. But it's going to take time to get thousands of Franks out of there."

"How much time?" the taller merchant demanded.

"Two legions chasing thousands of Franks and their loot around the Pyrenees? They're going to try to escape back into Gaul with it, not die for it. But if these thousands hide the loot and scatter, take up raiding around Hispania because they can, it could take a while."

The candid admission by the senior centurion brought an uproar, not just from the two Barcino merchants but from every other businessman on the wharf with investments in Hispania.

"What happens to traffic on the Via Augusta and the Via Domitia for the next ten years while your two legions are figuring out where they are?" another merchant demanded.

The shouts of distressed merchants increased, demanding more legions and cavalry be sent from other provinces. Aetius motioned to Alcaeus, Laelia and the rest of the officers and crew to head back to the relative sanctuary of the *Heraclion*.

"When can we unload?" Laelia asked her father. "The merchants must have seen us arrive."

"We wait until the chaos subsides."

They made their way through the crowd on the dock to their guards at the gangplank and up to the main deck of the *Heraclion*. From the ship's rails they saw the effects of the news taking place several blocks away. Local riff-raff were taking advantage of unguarded warehouses within sight of the docks. Looters carried barrels of wine and oil away on their backs while naval soldiers on the docks prepared to board ships bound for Barcino. Alcaeus stared out at the mayhem. Nothing like this had ever occurred in Emporiae. Until now. Aetius returned from briefing the *Heraclion*'s officers and stood at the rails between Laelia and Alcaeus.

"Are you thinking about Emporiae?" Aetius said calmly to Alcaeus.

"I can't believe it," Alcaeus replied.

"You're alive. You're alive. Sosigenes and the rest are gone."

"The world is filled with savages," Alcaeus said, dazed by everything he had heard and seen.

"Not quite," Aetius said. "There is some news you haven't heard."

"What is it?" Laelia asked.

"More detail about the battle on the Rhine," Aetius said. "According to a legate I spoke to on the dock, it appears the Governor of Germania, General Postumus, crushed the Franks at Empel. If I know Postumus, it won't be the last."

"How could thousands of them invade Hispania if they were defeated in Germania?" Alcaeus asked.

"My guess is they knew Postumus would pursue them to the north. The Franks are opportunists and shrewd. Many of the survivors headed south, knowing he wouldn't take legions away from the frontier. Looting Hispania, where he has one legion, is their idea of revenge."

"You know this general?" Laelia asked. "You called him Postumus?"

"I knew him when we were officers in Colonia Agrippina. The same legion. He's Gallic, very smart, the best of the best."

"What can he do against the eastern Franks and Allemanni, if they cross the upper Rhine?"

"He will stop them cold. He'll divide them before they can mass and surprise them day and night. I remember him saying that he would take out a generation of barbarians if he ever

246

became governor."

"What does this mean for Hispania?" Alcaeus asked.

"The Franks will disperse there as raiders. I'm afraid, the best that can be done now is to force each raiding group back into the Pyrenees with the two legions that will be assigned.

"Why not send ten more legions to Hispania?"

"Postumus will need all his legions in Germania now, on the upper Rhine. The tribes there don't farm. They hunt in the forests, live off the land and swarm like hornets toward anything unlike themselves. Postumus will get the job done. We will, too. This is where we see opportunity when everyone else sees panic."

"Father, you see opportunity at a time like this?"

"I do. I have a friend in Bonna on the lower Rhine who makes wagons for the army. He knows his business. I know the sea and maritime trade from my father. I know there's a market for Gallic lumber in Massalia that goes begging, especially now. I could sell more lumber through this port than anyone. But I need wagons, lumber wagons, to get it in quantity to Massalia from the forests in northern Gaul."

"But what if the Franks have other ideas?" asked Alcaeus.

"I'm counting on Postumus to stop them. When he does, I'll need special wagons. I don't want to go to the Rhine to buy them. I want to build a factory in Gaul and make them here. The army can send me plenty of starving Franks as lumber cutters and haulers. There are plenty of oxen in Gaul. But I need an inventive young man with brains and good fortune to go with me to see my friend in Bonna, to learn the fine points of building heavy wagons. Would you be interested?" Aetius asked, as he looked at Alcaeus.

"Me?"

"You, as soon as I can confirm that Postumus has the Franks in hand, well east of the Rhine."

"Say yes," Laelia prompted, stepping around her father to press next to Alcaeus. "Please say yes."

Alcaeus almost laughed at the waves of emotion sweeping through his feelings. He realized he was already at home with family, after what seemed like far more than eighteen years of loneliness and loss. Standing at the rails of a merchant ship in a port seized with chaos, he was with family—family who saw hope and fortune when others throughout the port saw fear and uncertainty. He wondered how he deserved the warmth and beauty of Laelia next to him and the leadership and kindness of Aetius.

At that moment, just before he was about to reply to Aetius, a man with wavy, light-colored hair down on the dock next to the *Heraclion* walked into Alcaeus' line of sight and turned to look up at him. The man, who seemed strangely familiar, smiled briefly at Alcaeus and stood there on the dock for a moment. A thought came to Alcaeus from nowhere he could recall. *You'll be aware of me with you, even when your mind is busy and you've forgotten what I look like. I'll be with you.*

Alcaeus looked down again to the dock, trying to remember how he knew the man with the smile, but couldn't find him again in the crowd. In a split second of reflection, Alcaeus pondered whether the strangely familiar presence was always close by. If so, it appeared that he, Alcaeus, was rarely sensitive enough to notice.

"Alcaeus?" Laelia said, nudging him.

"Sir, yes, yes," Alcaeus said, turning to Aetius, "I would be very grateful for the opportunity. I couldn't be happier. I'm ready to go when you are. I'm just trying to stop laughing and crying at the same time. Will Laelia be going to Bonna?"

"I haven't asked her yet," Aetius teased. "I'm a busy man, but I suppose I'll get around to it in a while."

And so Aetius did. As for Alcaeus, within a year he had exceeded the engineering standards of the army's preferred wagon-maker in Bonna and developed a new, articulated heavy lumber wagon in Aetius' factory in Lugdunum, the largest city in central Gaul. This was the hometown of Laelia's mother and location of more friends and relations of the family than Alcaeus dreamed could exist.

When Alcaeus and Laelia were married in a Christian ceremony in Lugdunum, just after the first of the new line of articulated wagons began leaving the factory for the forests, a crowd filled the city's largest chapel and spilled out onto the streets. Word of the marriage had spread throughout Lugdunum.

As Alcaeus and Laelia left the chapel in a specially decorated horse-drawn wagon, the streets throughout the city became lined with people wanting to catch a glimpse of the young man from Emporiae, who had not only brought employment for many wagonmakers but economical new ways to build roof trusses, hay balers and grain silos. It seemed, many said, that he had been born with an unlimited source of useful ideas and unlimited good fortune.

THE MAN ON THE MOUNTAIN

A spectacular mountain in Oregon, *The Lightning Rod of the Cascades*, hammers the unprepared but permits a stunning preview of the Promised Land.

THE MAN ON
THE MOUNTAIN

South Shore Boulevard runs along the high south side of Lake Oswego. It winds down through towering forest and slows traffic to twenty-five as it crosses three, two-lane bridges over fingers of the lake. Residents who take this meandering drive home or to work appreciate its beauty, day or night, gently uplifting the soul and reminding them why homes along the waterfront begin at $6 million.

Late on a Monday morning in October, three Lake Oswego residents, Shane Brist, Augustus Cousins and Benjamin Lorroway, were westbound on South Shore, heading out on a mountain climbing trip to Mount Thielsen in the Oregon Cascades. Each held a reverence for the beauty of Lake Oswego, and none of them spoke as shafts of sunlight angled through the trees along the water's edge, sparkled on the glass-still surface of the lake and reflected off boat-docks, left and right, as they crossed the bridges.

Once a year, these three wealthy men managed to cajole family and partners at work to accept that this was their week off, just the guys, going to the mountains. Two years earlier they climbed Mount Adams. Last year they climbed Mount St. Helens, and while the crowds and the crater itself were spectacular, they generated more laughs camping and staggering around by their bourboned-up selves somewhere in the woods. They had laughed at the absurdity of their good fortune, the high stakes in their careers that had made each of them wealthy, and recollections of more than a few outstanding shared memories. The bond behind their friendship came from shared triumphs on a conference-winning football team at a major West Coast university twenty years earlier. There they had been idols and girl magnets, so much so that none of them remembered their triumphs on the academic side of graduation.

Shane became the conscientious one, the former back-up quarterback rolling straight through his Masters in Electrical Engineering into an entry level job with a supplier to Boeing. That was followed by eight years at Boeing itself, then a huge, risky jump to become one of the three junior partners in a start-up engineering design firm in a Portland suburb. That start-up was now a successful, privately-held player in classified aerospace equipment.

Augustus, who preferred to be called Cuz, from his last name, took his business management degree and followed his father into home construction. From there he became a partner in a successful commercial and residential construction company. The success of his company was due in part to Cuz's workaholic ability to pull frequent all-nighters. That ability had surfaced in response to a nightmare marriage and a worse divorce.

Ben graduated with a degree in business and finance, and over the years worked his way into sole ownership of a retail investment franchise in an office tower close to home in Lake Oswego. Of the three, Ben remained the most athletic, a dedicated cyclist, but at age forty-three was beginning to lose a twenty-year surgery battle with his knees.

In fact, all three were forty-three years old. All were comfortably well off, all were African-American, successful in their professions and well respected by their peers and clients. That was the absurdity that made them laugh. Each of the three had teen memories of friends, no better or worse than them in intellect, who had succumbed to the god-awful, un-nameable disease of the streets. For whatever reason, many of their teen friends had identified with Los Angeles street attitudes, broken laws and spent the best years of their young lives behind bars.

In contrast, Shane, Ben and Cuz had seen tens of thousands of fans stand up and roar in partisan support when they came out of the tunnel onto home field. Shane, Ben and Cuz were not only living the American dream, they were IRS-certified members of the top one percent in the wealthiest nation in history. Yet for them, privilege and waterfront real estate came with an edge. They were aware that for some mysterious reason they were exceptions. They had avoided the disease, and they quietly encouraged each other never to take it for granted.

They were also aware that over twenty years had passed since the experience of being girl-magnets and campus favorites. Now, they were in close and surreal proximity to middle-age. Each held the opinion that discussing such an unwelcome concept as getting older was off-limits in the company of spouse and children. That was their purpose in taking a week off once a year, so moorings remained intact and changes could be rummaged through, without the knowing smirks of wives who never aged and teenage children who knew everything.

On that Monday morning they were ready for something different, far more spectacular than Mount St. Helens, a climb where there would be no crowds. It was Shane's idea to climb Mount Thielsen, a non-technical climb, but still a difficult and dangerous hand over hand ascent to the summit. The approach and ascent would take about eight hours round trip in the unpredictable weather of the southern Cascades. However, it was Ben who had researched beyond Shane's basic climbing notes, topographical maps and gear list and informed them that as visually dominant as Mount Thielsen was among other peaks, it was said to be struck by lightning more often than any other mountain in the High Cascades. This topic began hours of conversation in the comfort of Shane's new, navy-blue Denali as they reached the interstate entrance and headed south.

"What were you thinking, Brist?" Cuz asked. "Ten million mountains in the state and you pick this one."

"Too late, Cuz," Shane said. "We're committed. Can't turn

back. This is the one."

"Like hell it is. I'm not getting fried for no good reason."

"Lightning's good for your hair, Cuz. Getting a little gray up there, and on the sides. Straighten that right out. No more gray."

"Hey, you need to hear this, Cuz," Ben said, from the back seat, "about Mount Thielsen, the 'Lightning Rod of the Cascades.' Even has its own Wiki page. Listen, 'Thielsen's spire-like top is hit by lightning so frequently that some rocks on the summit have melted into a rare mineraloid known as lechatelierite.' Mm?"

"Nice, Brist," Cuz said. "Rare mineraloid. That's what we need."

"And Cuz," Ben continued, "this is talking about decisions you have to make at a certain point a couple of hundred feet below the summit. You're going to like this. 'Wind whips through this notch below the summit carrying dust particulates from scree slopes, affecting visibility at times. Avoid getting too close to the right side of the south face. The exposure and drop is severe. A slip means injury or death. If injured, rescue is difficult and may be delayed.'"

"Lightning and injury and death!" Cuz said. "This is what we signed up for, right?"

"There's more," Ben said. "That was about going up. This guy is saying, 'Rope is recommended for the last eighty vertical feet of ascent, as well as for the descent. Coming down is where people fall and die.'"

"Better and better, Brist," Cuz said. "Thinking all the time."

"We don't need rope for the summit," Shane answered. "It's just hand over hand and we take it easy up there."

"If you can see your hands, assuming visibility isn't being affected up there, at times. What if we get up there and we're inside a cloud?"

So the conversation went, back and forth as they passed through Salem and the broad expanse of the Willamette Valley. By the time they reached the exit in Roseburg and headed east up into the foothills of the Cascades the conversation had covered multiple topics and come around again to Shane's motivation for choosing Mt. Thielsen.

"You know," Shane countered, "someone with a sense of perspective listening to you, both of you, would begin to detect a failure of imagination."

"I can imagine getting struck by a bolt of lightning," Cuz said, "without any problem. My failure is I don't like what I'm imagining."

"Okay, so imagine this," Shane said. "Four years before we were even born Dr. Martin Luther King Jr. set up the life we're into right now. You heard that name? We never even saw the man, but the more I look at it I'm thinking we owe him something for what we've got."

"What's that got to do with us getting blown off a mountain?" Ben asked. "Hate to say he wasted his time on us. He'd be saying we're acting like fools."

"Electrified fools," Cuz said.

"Come on. We're not going to get blown off anything," Shane said. "Think about what I'm saying. We all know guys who were in hell while we were playing in high heaven. I'm saying they never got what the good Doctor meant. He talked, but they didn't hear it like it was important. What he said was, this country has a creed and a conscience and we have to expect everyone's going to live up to it. We are living the good life because of him."

"We did it ourselves, man. I don't remember him doing anything for me," Cuz said.

"Our folks got what he meant about a creed," Shane said. "He set up an expectation that meant something to them. They passed it on to us because they believed it was true. Fifty years ago there wasn't much reason to believe it. Our folks did anyway. For us it worked. For the guys we knew who went to hell, it didn't. Why are we the ones who are okay with getting the job done?"

"I don't know," Cuz said. "There's luck, there's folks who don't pay attention, you listen to smack."

"But why don't folks pay attention? I want to know why."

"You're asking us?" Cuz mugged. "We're the fools going up a mountain with your fine self to get electrocuted and you think we're going to know stuff even God can't figure out."

"What I can't figure out is what you're talking about," Ben said. "What's the good Doctor got to do with us going to get electrified on this particular mountain?"

"Okay, you guys can think what you want, but the Doctor is important to me. When he said he'd been to the mountaintop and seen the Promised Land it was metaphor, it was rhetoric, but it was the vision people needed. It was an expectation of freedom from hell. Some of them ran with it. Our folks did. That's why we're sitting on this leather and taking a week off to do whatever we want."

"Like getting electrocuted," Cuz said.

"Cuz, you've seen the photos," Shane said, ignoring the comment. "Mount Thielsen is some kind of mountain. It's like this legend, this monumental peak you just want to stare at and you think this could be *the* mountaintop. Oh, forget it. I just figured you guys would feel the same way."

"No, you're right. This is the mountaintop. Lightning and *everything*," Ben said. "Definitely no failure of imagination there."

"Yeah, thanks Dr. King," Cuz said.

The conversation continued in the same vein for a while until Shane decided to ask Cuz why he had accepted the invitation to climb Mount Thielsen, without reservations.

"I don't know," Cuz answered, "what else was I doing? Finishing up the project in Tualatin. Everything's under control. Got a manager there, knows what he's doing."

"But Cuz doesn't know what he's doing. No, he does not." Ben teased.

"What do you mean?" Shane asked.

"Cuz is running mighty scared, he is," Ben continued. "Going to the mountain to get electrocuted so he won't have to go home."

"What's going on Cuz?"

"Damn right I'm scared. You would be too."

"What's going on Cuz?" Shane asked again.

"Laurie set a date and she's starting to tell everyone," Ben answered for him. "Right Cuz?"

"Seriously, you're getting married again?"

"No, Brist," Cuz said, "you can't say that to anyone. She's acting like I asked her and I don't remember saying anything. I was asleep, maybe. So, you know, it's a non-issue."

"Except now he *can't* sleep," Ben said. "Hell, he can't remember anything he didn't mean."

"So, you love her or something?" Shane asked.

"You make it sound like I'm supposed to know. I don't know. How am I supposed to know that? I don't trust myself. I'm the worst picker of women since Henry VIII. Jennine just killed me and I'm not going through that again."

"Electrocution can be fun, Cuz," Ben said. "This mountain is your ticket out."

"That the truth, Cuz?" Shane teased.

"Gentlemen, you're entitled to your idle gossip but tonight I plan to consult my expert counsel, Jack Daniels, about the subject of relaxing for a week. Join us tonight, if you care to."

"Five, maybe eight-hour round-trip tomorrow, Cuz," Shane said, "assuming you can walk straight."

"Brist, look at him," Ben said. "That face is the definition of marriage fear."

"Damn right. I don't know how you maestros did it. I got this one week to figure out the rest of my life," Cuz said. "One week."

At that moment the mountain came directly into view behind lesser peaks and conversation ceased. They turned off the highway toward Diamond Lake, arrived at the trailhead parking lot soon after, and began unloading. Being late in the season and late in the afternoon there were only three other cars in the lot.

They followed the Howlock Trail, then Thielsen Creek Trail, toting backpacks, a tent and a bearproof cooler, and found it easy going up to the Meadows Campground. Only two tents were up in the campground so they had a wide choice of campsites. After selecting a secluded site and dumping the gear, Shane called the other two over from the campfire.

"Hey, look at this."

Ben and Cuz came over to where Shane was standing at the high end of the campground. There, framed by tall firs, was Mount Thielsen in the distance, the summit 2,700 feet above them, the once-volcanic spire bright orange and white in the light of the setting sun.

"Oh, my God," Cuz whispered. "No one should be going up there."

"People do, now and then," Shane said.

"Look at it. Are you nuts? It's straight up."

"Totally doable. Right, Ben?"

"Whatever you say," Ben answered quietly.

At the campsite the six-man tent was set up in a few minutes, and while Cuz began cooking, Ben and Shane went into the woods for more firewood. Shane noticed as he left the campsite that the other two groups of hikers had packed up and left. On their way back with their first load of wood Ben caught up with Shane.

"Hey, listen," Ben said. "Looking up at Thielsen, I'm thinking I've got a problem. If you can make it up there tomorrow, I can. But getting down is something else. I can't cycle hills worth a damn any more. I've got another surgery coming up. Plastic knees is what I'm hearing."

"Why didn't you tell me?"

"Because I can't believe it's me I'm talking about. In here, in my mind, I'm like senior year in college. In my knees and my shoulders there's this old man, this stranger with issues and pain and doctor's appointments, and it pisses me off. Come on, I'm not going to tell you or Cuz how I'm feeling till I'm coming up on ninety-six. But this is a real mountain."

"We could have gone somewhere else."

"It's okay. I'll hang out here. Cuz will be fine if we take the bottle from him."

But after dinner Cuz kept the bottle and drank a quarter of it. Shane was scrubbing pots and pans when he heard Ben arguing with Cuz by the campfire. He thought Ben was trying to take the bourbon away from Cuz for the night but it turned out that Ben wanted his quarter of the bottle. By the time it was dark they were both wasted, half in their sleeping bags, still laughing and toasting each other in an incoherent babble.

Shane held a lantern in the doorway of the tent and couldn't help laughing with them as they attempted to make sense of each other's toasts. When they started jeering him, he left to put out the campfire and secure the food and gear from scavenging bears in the night. As he did so, he thought about the next day's weather forecast. It called for a warm, clear morning, perfect for climbing, with the possibility of a squall coming in from the coast late in the day. If he and Cuz started no later than nine in the morning, they would summit around noon in clear weather and be back at the tent before the squall. The following day projected squalls early in the morning.

Sunlight woke Shane, and as he sat up in his sleeping bag to check his phone, he could see the cell service was out of range. Cuz and Ben did not respond to being shaken. They were not moving. Thinking the aroma of breakfast would improve their condition, he got the campfire going and began cooking and making coffee. He checked the tent. Still no movement. He shook them again, describing the benefits of breakfast, but got no takers.

Over coffee Shane realized that he had to make a decision. It was possible neither Cuz nor Ben would want to make the climb any time that week. The mountain had scared them. The following day could be a rainout with lower temperatures and maybe snow at higher elevations. If he was going to summit, it would have to be that day and he would have to climb by himself. The climb itself was not technical and he was apparently in better physical and emotional shape than either Ben or Cuz, so there were no basic concerns there. It was simply safer to climb in a group and more fun with good company. The thought that clinched his decision was that the good weather forecast for most of the day was likely to encourage other climbers out on the trail, and if he felt like it he would join them. But by the time he made his decision, cleaned up dishes and left a note it was approaching nine. Time to get moving.

The trail became one with the Pacific Crest Trail up to the junction with the Mount Thielsen Trail. That was the standard approach for campers. At the junction, Shane was rewarded with a closer view of the mountain from a different angle. The trail below the treeline was a study in sunlit natural beauty every upward step, but he also noticed a line of gray clouds on the horizon, indicating an approaching squall, much earlier than forecast. Without removing his backpack he quickly took photos with the phone and moved on.

In fifteen minutes, gusty wind began to buffet Shane's face, the rain slanted horizontally into his eyes and lightning flashed inside the clouds around the summit and over the eastern face. He was above the treeline now, crossing a moonscape of gray rocks, feeling the full fury of the wind and rain and the dazzling lightshow, and somehow it all seemed wonderful.

"Dr. King!" he shouted into the squall, "This is great. This is what I came here for. Climb this mountain with me, lightning and everything!"

Thinking of Cuz and Ben who were missing the lightshow and the exhilarating experience, Shane pressed on up toward a summit completely hidden in the storm. *Onward, upward,* he told himself, but fifteen minutes later he was aware of a lessening of the wind, the rain tapped only gently on his face and then no more lightning. Soon there was no more squall. The sun broke through and now at a higher elevation Shane saw glimpses of the awesome summit spire between fast-moving clouds. Far out across the valley to the west, an endless fir forest extended to the horizon, thousands of feet below.

By the time Shane reached the steep boulder gully leading up to the notch a couple of hundred feet below the summit, he was scrambling for handholds and testing loose rocks for footholds. The higher he climbed, the greater the effort it required. His pace slowed as he methodically looked and tested each upward move before he made it. But it matched his need for a challenge, and he realized he was going to make the summit around noon in clear weather.

True to form, the mountain raised the level of difficulty as Shane began the final ascent to the summit. The air was crystal clear, the sunglare dazzling, the view amazing and the amount of concentration needed made for thoughtful pauses as he weighed every move. He could see why some veteran climbers recommended ropes. He could see why there was only one way up unless you were an expert technical climber. Handhold by handhold he moved upward, pressing himself against each rock face to reduce the relentless feeling that gravity was tugging him out into thin air. He resisted the temptation to look at his watch or to look down behind him. One such glance produced instant vertigo, followed by a minute of controlled breathing as he calmed himself and stared at the grains in the rock three inches from his eyes. *Keep moving,* he told himself, *one hold at a time, and don't look down again.*

It took Shane longer than he expected and it demanded more respect for the mountain than anticipated, but gradually he realized he had developed a rhythm and a technique that was safe and kept him moving up. When he looked up for yet another handhold and saw the next hold was the summit itself, he let out a whoop. He had done it. He and Dr. King, who he had invited along in spirit. There was no one else on the mountain.

Taking his time and breathing deeply, Shane surveyed the panoramic view in clear sunshine. The drop-off was as severe as advertised, straight down for thousands of feet to the forest floor. The forest stretched out far below in all directions. To the north he could see Mount Howlock and South Sister. To the east, the view stretched into drier eastern Oregon. To the south, he could see the famous Crater Lake, Mount Scott, Mount McLoughlin and in the distance, snow-capped Mount Shasta in California. To the west, Diamond Lake, Mount Bailey, and beyond that to the Coast Range. He held up his phone and carefully took overlapping panoramic shots at every point around the compass. Sitting on a volcanic rock 9,182 feet above sea level, he reached into his pack, took out a bottle of water, stood on the high point of the summit and raised it as a toast to Dr. King.

"To you, Dr. King, for getting me here, for all the good that's come to me, my family, for great parents who listened to you. This effort, this view is for you! This is for the Promised Land and what we make of it now. What *do* we make of it now?"

For a long while, Shane stood on the mountain top and contemplated his own question. It had come out of his mouth without forethought. It begged another question, which asked for a definition of what the Promised Land was said to be and what happened when one thought he had arrived. Time seemed to stand still in descending alpine sunlight as he pondered the question. *What were the limits of the Promised Land?* Eventually he noticed that the gentle breeze tugging at his hair was now and then a strong gust of wind. On the horizon another squall was approaching. He checked his watch and realized an hour had passed in contemplation at the summit. *No more daydreaming on the mountaintop,* he thought. *Time to go.*

The descent from the summit to the notch took longer than the ascent, looking down for places to change the position of his feet and taking even more care than looking up for handholds. It was painstaking, careful work, and while he concentrated on safety, the squall moved in on top of him. By the time he reached the notch he was inside the cloud, with wind gusts tearing in from the west, pulling hard at his parka. Turning his back to the flying grit in the wind he found shelter behind boulders and wondered whether he should wait it out. But this was a colder wind than the squall in the morning and it occurred to him it may be more than a mere squall. To protect himself he moved further down among larger boulders until the effect of the westerly wind was not as severe. As he sheltered there he realized he had moved in the opposite direction to the route he took up through the gully on the west face. If he moved downhill through the boulders and then turned west into the storm at a lower elevation he would be back on track.

A short distance downhill, the boulder-strewn slope gave way to talus and then fine scree, an almost sand-like slope of light volcanic rock pieces that moved easily under his boots. The scree moved so easily he realized he could boot-ski down through it at remarkable speed, slaloming more than five hundred vertical feet down a fold in the mountain, protecting him from the blinding gale behind him on the now hidden summit.

As the larger talus material reappeared and slowed his pace Shane figured he would traverse around the south face of the mountain until he recognized the unmarked route up the west face. If he descended further and ran into the uneven treeline anytime soon, he was not sure it would be a reliable guide in helping him meet up with the Thielsen Trail. Though the wind was less severe at that elevation, he was still inside the cloud with less than fifty yards visibility. The plan, he confirmed, was to stay above the treeline to maximize whatever limited visibility was available. But at that moment the cloud around him lit up like a million stadium lights. He was so close to the source of the lightning he couldn't discern individual streaks. Thunder fell on him with the deafening pressure of heavy, sonic weights. Sheets of lightning flickered and played around the summit, hidden in a gale and surging cloud just a thousand feet directly above him.

The pressure and proximity of such intense light and shattering sound made him gasp for breath as he staggered between boulders in what he considered to be a westward direction. After a few hundred yards of pressing on into the maelstrom, he stopped, dazed, to consider why he was moving so slowly. Pain radiated from his knees, down to his ankles and up into his pelvis. Facing backward to the wind, breathing deeply within the hood of his parka, Shane recalled Ben's words concerning the difficulties of the descent. Ben had casually mentioned that practiced climbers differ from weekend warriors in the strength and flexibility of their joints and tendons. A five-hundred foot vertical boot-ski descent through scree had just overtaxed his knees, joints and tendons, which had not engaged in downhill skiing for years. Now he was not only staggering—he could barely walk. Around him lightning and thunder continued without letup. This was no passing squall. This was the next day's storm, twelve hours early. It was getting colder, snowflakes were whipping through the air, and Shane found himself shivering inside his parka.

He had no choice but to keep moving forward into the storm on the assumption he would recognize the unmarked Thielsen Trail if he crossed it and that it would not yet be covered by snow. Unable to lift his feet normally without pain shooting through his knees, Shane found a way to shuffle one foot forward, then the other, making slow progress toward a trail he might not be able to recognize. Looking downslope he noticed visibility had improved to about a hundred yards. Patches of scrub and windblown trees could be seen. As he was wondering if he was lower in elevation than he intended, he noticed furtive movement at the edge of his peripheral vision. He was not elated. The blurred shape was not that of a man. He stood still and watched for more movement. The shape moved again between distant low bushes, indistinct in the flurries of wind-whipped snow. It was not a wolf or a bear. Whatever it was he could feel it watching him.

Pulse pounding in his ears, his breathing suddenly faster, Shane remained still. When there was no more movement, he glanced left and right, looking for a possible line of escape, and then realized the futility of his situation. The shape moved again, and this time he saw what it was. A hundred yards away, a full-grown mountain lion was stalking him, apparently wary. Shane remembered the bear-spray was still in Cuz's pack at the campsite. As the gale and grit blew around him and lightning struck amid deep rolling thunder, Shane began to understand it was just a matter of time before the mountain lion attacked.

From its initial position downslope the mountain lion continued to move in a wide arc, possibly attempting to position itself downwind to read Shane's scent. Shane, with no other options, looked for fist-sized rocks not yet covered by snow. He knew it was a pathetic excuse for personal defense but there was a chance several good hits on the lion could defeat its will. Shane decided his will to survive was stronger than the lion's, and that by conserving his strength, calming his breathing, and making accurate throws, the lion would feel the pain and withdraw. The irony for a former quarterback, making precise throws with volcanic rocks to save his life, just above the treeline on the side of a cloud-covered mountain, held no amusement for Shane. He could barely bend to reach the rocks on the ground.

The creature was now downwind reading his scent. Shane was not about to waste his only advantage of range. The first rock landed two feet away from the lion and bounced over it as it crouched behind a wind-tousled bush. The second and third rocks were equally close. The lion slunk close to the ground and hid behind another bush. A fourth rock hit the left flank of the lion, making it get up and move ten yards closer. In the course of another dozen throws Shane hit the lion two more times. It simply shook off the effects with a quick ripple of muscle under its fur at the point of impact. It hunkered down in a low profile and its narrowed, yellow eyes seemed to be reading his emotions, his breathing rate, waiting and watching.

Shane's pulse was now elevated to desperation. His mouth was dry and he could feel the awful unblinking concentration in the lion's eyes, of its will boring into his will. He was facing a practiced killer, an expert reader of emotions and intent, a perfected athlete so attuned to the needs of its own survival in a harsh setting that the outcome was horribly predictable and less than a minute away. The lion kept moving in a low, creeping motion, maneuvering between bushes, positioning itself to maximize speed between obstacles when it was ready for a final attack. The attack would be swift, three hundred pounds of hard bone, claw and muscle accelerating to forty miles an hour. It would smash him flat against the rocks on the ground behind him, the concussion knocking him out so he wouldn't even be aware of his neck being broken by sharp teeth. His throat would be torn open by razor claws at the same time and his successful life in praise of Dr. King would be over in about one second of crushing impact and blood-soaked snow.

"Oh, God, help me here," Shane murmured. "I need a knock-out hit or something. Come on, I need a hit between the eyes now. Give me something. Give me something. Hit it between the eyes."

He steadied himself, centered and timed the next throw as the lion rose. It was a good throw but not good enough, grazing the lion's skull. The lion crouched and went to ground, fifty yards away. Suddenly Shane was so incensed at the near miss and the unacceptable and imminent end of his life that he lurched toward the lion with his arms raised, yelling at it. The unexpected display disturbed the lion. It moved ten yards to the left, back in the direction it had come from. Shane could see it behind a bush tensing on its pads, the tail flipping back and forth in apparent annoyance. At first the attack had seemed impersonal, a wild predator following nature's course. Now Shane perceived a different, more elevated concentration in the lion's murderous eyes, the flicking tail and tensing body motions indicating a kind of hate for him.

The standoff lasted all of thirty seconds before the lion moved back toward a more direct line of approach. It crouched there, simmering, staring. For the first time Shane heard an ominous, low, guttural growl and saw the lips pull back, the yellowed teeth visible from fifty yards. This was personal. Shane was aware he was losing the strength to resist. There was probably only enough time for one rock aimed at the lion's eyes if its next move was a forty mile an hour charge, claws extended, teeth bared. They stared at each other, one weakening, one furious.

Seconds passed. Shane saw the lion's tail straighten, the shoulder muscles bulge and ripple as it rose quickly, its yellow eyes moving fast toward him. Simultaneously something blue moved from the right of Shane's hooded vision toward the lion. The lion looked toward it, suddenly shifted the momentum of its accelerating body and lost its footing in a shower of loose rocks and snow. A man in a blue t-shirt and jeans moved briskly from the right behind Shane, appearing out of nowhere, striding across the snow toward the surprised lion. The stranger raised his right hand and addressed the lion as he strode, speaking only one word.

"Go."

The lion backed up, turned tail and quickly ran away into the wind and snow. The man turned his gaze from the disappearing lion and regarded Shane in silence. Shane looked at the man. He was clean-cut, short-haired, wearing a blue t-shirt and jeans in a freezing snowstorm. He was African-American, about Shane's height but somewhere in his mid-to-late twenties with an athlete's build and intelligent eyes. He was also the most handsome man that Shane, a former girl-magnet, had ever seen. Seconds from experiencing a gruesome death, Shane found his mind stuck in neutral, his body still shaking from fear and surging adrenalin. No words crossed his mind. He simply stared at the man's clear, brown eyes, not knowing what to say. The handsome young man broke the silence.

"Shane Michael Brist."

Shane nodded weakly and said nothing, wondering if the lion had killed him and he was entering some kind of afterlife. He looked around for his bloody body on the ground. He clenched the fingers in both hands. They worked, he was still alive. The man in the blue shirt spoke again, in a tone that was respectful and kind but unmistakably that of an authority.

"My dear friend, my brother. We should get you off this mountain. The wind chill will be sub-zero here within a few minutes."

"I can barely walk," Shane said. "My fault, on me."

"Begin to walk," the man directed. "That way."

To his surprise Shane realized he was able to move without pain in his knees, and he turned to the man who was now walking next to him.

"Ha! I can walk. I'm actually walking okay. How is this?"

"If you were able to see," the man said, "you would notice there are what you have heard described as angels before you, to your left, to your right, beneath and above you. There are angels around your knee ligaments and tendons enabling you to walk. You'll remember them in their absence. In the meantime, your friends at the campsite are concerned about you."

"Yeah, I bet they are. *I'm* concerned about me. What about you? No parka?"

"No," the man said. "No parka."

"How? It's cold, man. Can't survive up here like that."

"Only a fraction of my person is here."

"Where is the rest of you?"

"With the rest of you. This part of you is an outpost. The perfect part of you is beyond time and space. Keep walking in that direction."

"Okay," Shane said, confused by the stranger's words. "The part of me that's inside time and space is wondering how you turn up, like when I don't think I'm going to live another second. You're in jeans, a t-shirt . . . How do you . . . do you live up here?"

"No," the man said, "I was with you on the ascent. I was interested in your thoughts about the Promised Land."

"Oh? So how would you know what I was thinking? I was the only one on the summit."

"I've been interested in your thoughts and wishes for hundreds of thousands of years."

"Okay, good to know," Shane said warily, glancing out of his hood as they pushed forward into the blizzard. "Look, I really appreciate you helping me out with the mountain lion and the knees and everything, but who are you? Who do you work for?"

"I am Afra," the man said, modestly. "My name means, 'a brother.' You have also known that for a long time."

"Afra, huh? Like the continent?"

"Like the continent."

"Okay, you're saying hundreds of thousands of years. And then you're saying we know each other?"

"We're brothers and old friends, and a lot rides on you remembering me."

Shane slowed his pace, noticing his hands and voice were shaking. All he could see ahead was blizzard. The man walking next to him looked and sounded real but Shane was beginning to wonder

270

if he was hallucinating. He decided to challenge the man, to see if there was a way to prove he was still conscious.

"I don't have any brothers or sisters," Shane said, trying to keep his voice steady. "I'm an only child. And all I can recall is that I'm forty-three, not hundreds of thousands."

"Your terrestrial body is forty-three."

"Right, okay. So give me a clue. How is it that you seem to know me?"

"I know your thoughts. You asked a question in your toast on the summit, saying, 'This is for the Promised Land and what we make of it now. What do we make of it now?' Well, brother, was that question rhetoric or do you want to examine your choices?"

"That was for me, man. I seriously didn't think anyone was listening. I didn't expect anyone to debate my private thoughts."

There was a pause in the conversation as sheet lightning flashed around the clouds above them and the concussion of thunder hammered on Shane's ears. Afra, right next to him, appeared unmoved.

"My brother, I can walk you safely down to your campsite and that will be the end of it," Afra said, as the thunder rolled away. "Or you can spend your time on this trail suspending your agnostic disbelief and your worldly skepticism. You can decide right now if you're going to spend these few minutes examining your choices as a mature adult."

"Okay, you saved my life. You read my thoughts. I don't understand who you are or where you came from."

"Listen to the sound of my voice," Afra said, over the noise of the wind. "You, as a soul, have heard it before, in the briefing you wholeheartedly accepted prior to entering this life. You understood then that I would approach you, seen or unseen, at around the midpoint in your active life. I would ask your permission to present you with the choices for the second half of your life. This is that moment. I'm here to ask, are you ready? My dear friend, I find you're unprepared."

"Alright, forgive me for being unprepared. I'm grateful you

helped me out, but everything you're saying is outside my frame of reference. If you actually knew me, you'd know I think like an engineer because that's what I am. No one I work with or live with talks about hundreds of thousands of years and accepting a briefing prior to this life. Talk to me like an engineer. That's what I'm used to."

"I know what you're used to. You and I also accepted it was possible you would become attached to the first half of your life. You and your wife on the waterfront of Lake Oswego, you want the girls to go to Stanford, your company to go on the NASDAQ. Now there are new options. There is a second half of your life."

"So, wait . . . You're saying the second half of my life could change completely?"

"Some perspective before the options. As a conceptual engineer with a security clearance, you're a journeyman. It's not your best work. But long ago you had the beginnings of real mastery with the practice of the choice that stands before you. Your conscious mind restricts access to what your soul remembers. Just stop me if you prefer not to hear it."

"Okay, read my mind, read my soul, go ahead," Shane said, shielding himself from the steadily increasing snow. "But if you know everything about me, you would know I've got a family and I'm not going to risk all that for something I don't understand. Why would I?"

Shane held the flapping hood of his parka and looked at Afra, trying to read the man's eyes. They were calm. He appeared focused and unaffected by the storm.

"Something important," Afra said, "that you can consciously understand concerns the plans of the senior partners in your firm. They have received a buyout offer, and you will not have much of a choice as to the outcome. No NASDAQ listing for you. The negotiations include the valuation of a design you brought from concept to prototype. From here on, you would be assigned oversight of its development with the buyout company. Or you could do something else. There are plenty of developers at Boeing. Developer or not, you will be offered a generous buyout package, which, within reason, would meet all your material needs for the rest of your life. No mortgage, no debt."

"How can you know this?"

"You will be financially secure for the second half of your life," Afra said. "Now, you say you admire Dr. King. Are you aware how financially insecure Dr. King was all his life? Are you aware how many dozens of times he went to jail for what he believed in? Are you aware he had four children and wanted them to go to certain universities? Let's keep that in mind as we examine your choices for the second half of your life."

"Wait, come on, why are you talking about me and Dr. King in the same sentence? There was no one like him. No one had his kind of vision, back then or since."

"Now we're getting somewhere. You've noticed that about the diaspora," Afra said, with a smile. "Well, Shane Brist, you were, still are and always will be Dr. King's brother in spirit. What you do about that is up to you."

"Hold on a minute," Shane said, as he slowed to look for better footing on the rough, snow-covered ground. "Dr. King was a major public figure, a theologian. He made great marches and speeches in front of a quarter of a million people. He fought with the FBI and the Klan and he knew everyone. He's our history. What's that got to do with me?"

"Dr. King only got so far before his life was cut short. Where's the follow-up? Where's the vision, so our people don't perish? Why are our people starving for freedom from narcotics, freedom from self-destruction, freedom from abortion, freedom from crime, freedom from poverty, freedom from false pastors and false politicians? Where is their freedom from ignorance and selfishness? Where is their path to holiness?"

"I don't know. Not my call."

"It is," Afra said.

"You're kidding," Shane said, throwing back his hood. He was having trouble keeping up. "Why are you talking to me? Dr. King knew everyone. I only know about a dozen people. People cannot and should not know anything about me. What I know is classified. I have a security exposure. I have an FBI file. Why are you looking at me like that?"

"Shane Brist, you are my brother. I've loved you as a brother and a friend for a long time."

"You keep saying that. How can that be?"

Shane stopped where he was on the trail in exasperation. His legs were trembling, his mouth was dry, and he felt as if he was going to pass out. He turned to Afra.

"I can't keep going," he said, panting, bending over to catch his breath. "I must be alive because I feel so bad. I don't think I can stand up much longer. My feet . . . can't feel them."

Afra stood in front of him and held his shoulders.

"Listen to me," Afra said. "It's clinical shock. It will pass. Shane, you may not stop walking. Look at me. Listen to my voice. Ask questions, keep talking."

"I'm shaking. I'm freezing, man," Shane said. "What's the matter with me? My legs are not doing what I tell them. How am I going to get off this mountain?"

"By obedience," Afra said, "plain and simple. You're fighting me by doubting I'm standing in front of you."

"I see you in a t-shirt, here on the mountain, in a blizzard. Am I even alive?"

"Close your eyes and stand still," Afra said. "Imagine the sun burning through the clouds. Look up at it."

Shane stood still in the blizzard and tried to imagine the sun shining onto the desolate moonscape around him. It felt foolhardy at first, seeing an imaginary sun and staring at it, as if he actually had passed on and was trying to find his way in a post-life dream. But gradually he felt a glowing warmth in the center of his chest where there had been an aching, crippling chill. The ache dissipated and the warmth spread down his arms. His abdomen relaxed and the warmth could be felt in his knees. Shane opened his eyes and looked into Afra's calm, brown eyes.

274

"What's happening?" Shane asked.

"Heart to heart resuscitation," Afra answered. "The God-given flame in me is infinite. Yours is not. Not yet."

"Thank God, I can breathe again," Shane said, noticing the dread of dying alone on the mountain was gone. "My feet, my toes. I can feel them."

Freed from the fear of freezing in place and dying where he stood, Shane began to realize that he had no trust in words. He had not believed what he heard but reverted to customary dismissive mockery. For him, it had taken a transfusion of light to prove the man in the blue t-shirt had saved his life for a second time. If so, why would the man take the time?

"Why me?" Shane asked, over the noise of the wind. "Of all people, why save me?"

"You're not off the mountain yet. Close your eyes again. Notice the warmth around your heart. Go into it, like going into a sphere. It's bright and warm in all directions. Now expand it, wider than you can spread your arms. This is what you'll walk in, all the way down the mountain."

"I'm seeing it. I'm inside it. Will it break if I walk through it?"

"It goes where you go. Concentrate on being in it. Your feet will do the rest."

"Why didn't I think of this before?" Shane asked, marveling at the dissipation of pain and dread.

"It's your creation now. I'm not doing all the work. Your turn. Now, walk."

"Don't doubt," Shane said to himself, "just walk."

"This sphere will take you to safety. All your work."

Shane felt as if he was riding a gentle wave that moved with every step. He reflected on the effort Afra had taken to shepherd him and realized that he was in the middle of something too sublime to be described to ordinary people like himself. If this was what it took to save his life in sub-zero windchill he would take it. He tuned out the gale-force gusts tearing through the clouds just above him and saw himself in bright sunlight.

"Cut me some slack," he said, turning to Afra, as they gradually picked up the pace, "for not believing you. If I'm alive, I'm in some altered state. I like it. I couldn't hear you before."

"I noticed," Afra said, smiling. "Nothing matters more than keeping your concentration."

"Can I ask questions as we walk?"

"Ask away."

"I don't get how you can remember hundreds of thousands of years back. I can't even remember what I had for breakfast."

"Is that a question?"

"No, tell me who I am to you. Tell me why you picked this time and place to save my life. And what's this about the second half of my life?"

"All your questions are related," Afra said. "I'll tell you, while we're strolling along here in the snow and the wind. Bright sunlight for you. Stop me if you're not following."

"I'll try to keep up. Who am I to you?"

"You, as a soul," Afra began, "were an angel of light, an angelic teacher of the celestial body of men, including the soul part of me. I couldn't see you or know your name, but you taught me by signs in the heart, encouraged me, passed the engrafted Word to me. You took pity on me when I was living in Africa, before what is considered known history. I was an ordinary teacher of village children and I was persecuted for teaching truth about the coming of the fallen ones, the rebel angels who fell with Lucifer and the Watchers."

"Were they close by? Could they hear you?"

"They could," Afra said. "Their agents and spies ignored me because I had no estates and was no threat. But to me it seemed like their headquarters was in my part of Africa. I knew what they were. They were prisoners here in 'reform school,' here on this Earth. Because of their residual wisdom they assumed they were the wardens and we were their prisoners. Eventually, they couldn't ignore their own reaction to the truth."

"Why antagonize them?"

276

"Someone had to tell the people. I looked for someone smarter than me, to hand off the responsibility. Very few volunteered."

"Where was I?"

"You were observing from angelic heights. I didn't know you then. I did what I had to do, alone, I thought. I walked across west Africa and I spoke. For all my walking, all my speeches about the destructive effects of voodoo, the poisonous, inverted music of the fallen ones I was ignored, then ridiculed, then beaten up. My family abandoned me as an embarrassment, an idiot. I didn't worship the kings of voodoo. To me the glamor of the wicked was foolishness. In that life I died alone, with few believing my warnings. You saw my predicament from the angelic realm and you were moved. By authority of the Son of God you volunteered to incarnate as a man like me in Africa, in what is now Ghana. You were my younger brother in my next embodiment. You brought the power of your voice, your strength and your wisdom. You were my younger brother from heaven, and I knew you were an extraordinary gift from God."

"And what happened?"

"You, the rescuer from heaven, got stuck in Africa, life after life. You got angry with the injustice of the voodoo mafia because you were persecuted too, by the profane who protected the wicked. Anger keeps people stuck here. It's like a mist, a rotten smell everywhere. That's why Africa is still the Dark Continent. Headquarters. So many hundreds of thousands of years of cruelty, treachery, brutality and every form of slavery. The fallen ones thought only of revenge against God and payback against their rivals. A volunteer from heaven and an exposer of the wicked? You and I and a small remnant were on the receiving end of their revenge."

"You're saying these were actual people, living in Africa? I thought fallen angels were some myth from before the beginning of time."

"Before the beginning of known history," Afra said, warming to the untold history. "They were Luciferians, the most intelligent of men. Over hundreds of thousands of years they destroyed every civilization on Earth, for revenge. In heaven they were once a third of the celestial teachers of men. That third turned on us. There was war in heaven. In their pride and their impatience they reasoned that God had created men with zero capacity to become Christ. They figured they had a better idea. For their error they were made to become men, the object of their profanity, under the same laws of gravity, time and space and mortality we lived under. They hated their confinement in physical bodies. On Earth they lived and died as resentful, powerful, vengeful men, tribal leaders, witch doctors, slavers, warlords. Their former wisdom gave them advantage over ordinary men. They are still here to this day, in high places on all continents, not just Africa."

"Did they have children?"

"Yes. And just like men and women, they died. God gave them repeated opportunity to come back into new bodies, life after life. Back to the scene of their cunning, their cruelty and their rivalries. Another chance to turn it around."

"What if they didn't give a damn?"

"A lot of the lower ranking angels did. They realized they had been duped by their leaders. By grace they found their way back to their first estate, just like men and women do. God gives them a certain amount of time."

"A certain amount of time. What happened to you, in Africa?"

"I walked across west Africa again in that next life, with you in support. I spoke everywhere I could. I made the slavers and the witch-doctors mad at me, and I was crucified by a mob, my own people, despite your efforts."

"Crucified, like Jesus?"

"Like Jesus. And like Jesus, I proved the Luciferians wrong about our capacity to become Christ. It's blasphemy to them and no one can mention it, let alone aspire to it. They want total control. They can't stand people getting independent and free of them forever. The profane change the subject, but the fact known to God is that I was the first of many to ascend from Africa. That was then. There are not too many with that option now."

"So what does that make you now, hundreds of thousands of years later?"

"In Christian terms I am described as one of the saints robed in white. In Buddhist terms I'm known as a bodhisattva. That's someone who has taken a solemn vow not to leave Earth for higher service until all sentient life is free of the causes and effects of the wicked."

"You saw everything that happened to Africa over all that time? How could you have been so patient?"

"When you have no more debts to God or man you don't have to live in the confines of time. I live and move in successive levels of heaven. Outside time you live by the cycles of God's creativity through you. In higher service it's joyous, it's buoyant, it's exhilarating. But my creative problem as a bodhisattva is my heart's attachment to the pain of our people. They have copied the pride and anger of the wicked for so long that they think it's theirs. They behave like the wicked. They've forgotten who they are."

"Well, what can you do about it? Can you stay here?"

"No," Afra said. "I have a certain dispensation, by authority of the Son of God and by the law of intercession. I may appear to be in charge of your safety and your direction. But without your continuing permission to sponsor you, I must withdraw. You have free will and you have to be responsible for every choice, so think carefully before you choose. I have already won my freedom. Your victory has to be yours. I mentioned the second half of your life. Let me show you something."

In an instant, Shane felt himself rising upward, straight up through the storm over Mount Thielsen, far above Oregon and the West Coast until, from a position far above the forty-fifth parallel, he was looking at the northern hemisphere of Earth, from the North Pole to the equator. Directly in front of him was the continent of North America with dusk approaching. He turned and looked directly into Afra's clear brown eyes, right next to him.

"From your celestial body," Afra said, "look at the African diaspora in North America. This is where our people have the best platform for freedom. This is where the creed Dr. King spoke about still lives. Look at the concentrations in the urban areas on the East and West Coasts, around the Great Lakes and spread across the southeast."

"I see."

"Now, look more carefully at those concentrations. Focus in. Tell me what colors you see."

"Grays, mostly grays. Some reds, some orange. They're tiny."

"Look for blues, yellows, pinks, whites, greens, purples, violets."

"Okay, I see some of each, here and there. What do they mean?"

"Those are our people's auras, the hidden lights of the soul, at this moment. One of the indicators of what they have become. It doesn't mean they can't change and grow. God's people in the African diaspora of North America. I want you to remember they're there, they exist. There are bright-colored people right there who aspire to holiness, who have no leader and you are looking directly at millions of them now. Remember this, remember it. They are holy."

"What about the grays and the reds and the orange ones?"

"They can change, for better or for worse. But remember the mountain lion? Remember when it let you know what it thought of you? There are a few, not many, but some of our own people identify completely with those colors of spiritual death, anger and pride. They imitate the wicked and would turn on you. They would tear you to pieces. Our own people have done this before, long ago and not so long ago."

"You're showing me this, but who am I to do anything about it? I'm an FBI-classified engineer. I'm the least public person anyone could imagine. Dr. King had degrees in theology and qualifications to the max."

"And you have none? You would not be here looking at the remnant if you were not qualified. It is given to you to lead, but not alone. Others are qualified. I will show them the same remnant from this perspective. You will not be alone. The old era has passed since the time of Dr. King, and a new era began after you were born. You now live in an age where martyrdom is not to be expected or feared. True brotherhood, being your brother's keeper, is expected."

"That's not new though."

"Understanding our strengths is new. Look again at the colors in the diaspora," Afra directed. "What bright colors jump out?"

"There are more blues and more violets than the other colors."

"Now, we're getting somewhere. Those are the God-given vibrations and purposes of the African people. We're students in God's university. We have a double major in blue and violet. God's colors represent divine gifts and talents. They differ from each other because they vibrate at different frequencies. Blue and violet are more common in our auras. They indicate strengths that African people are called by God to master. Our contribution to the one orchestra."

"What do you mean strengths?"

"From the one light, many colors. Within the blue frequency there are certain energetic ways for God to express himself. Blue vibrates with the qualities of God's will, strength, power, identity, leadership, the blueprint for form and then action. It charges, it makes things come together. It gets things done through leadership."

"And violet?"

"Violet is the freedom to erase and start over, if what we just created turns out to be a mess. It's the clean-up, learn your lesson, freedom from being stuck with your mistake. God knew we would need it. I'm not talking about the frequencies of visible light. I'm talking about light you create in your imagination. Visualized light. That's how God creates and uncreates. With light, love and voice."

"You're telling me here because it's a secret?"

"It's been public knowledge for almost a century."

"How does it work?"

"To uncreate anger and a sense of injustice from a thousand years ago, or from yesterday, you create that color while you pray. You pray to be free from anger. Anger is energy misused. Your anger and other people's anger. You persist until you're free."

"If it was that easy, why are there still problems for everyone?"

"I'm talking about taking one lifetime to clean up thousands of lifetimes."

"So, it's work," Shane said. "You've got to work at this. People will think it's endless."

"It's incremental and the problems are finite. Here's why it's worth a lifetime's effort. Look again at the diaspora. Now look at North America with all of the other peoples mixed in: European ancestry, Asian, Hispanic. Lots of death culture, anger, pride, self-ishness. That's the majority of the people today. If the remnant, where you see the bright colors in all groups, were to humbly accept the strengths God gave them to uncreate error, watch this. Add the energy of created violet and holy prayer, light, love and voice, over a lifetime."

High over the Northern Hemisphere, Shane watched Afra raise his right hand and place his left hand over his heart. Gradually the murky gray mist over the continent began to dissipate. The bright colors grew brighter and were joined by pinpoint lights around them. Years passed in a matter of seconds, and the bright colors became patches, then coalesced, bridging across the continent until the whole landmass glowed as if hundreds of millions of jewels were lit from inside.

"We saints," Afra said, regarding the glowing continent with both hands raised, "can simulate the future until we're violet in the face. It's you who have the authority on Earth. Let me show you what authority means and why you should want to become unspotted from the world. Look up, above the continent, into space. Look up at the stars. There are more stars across the universe than there are grains of sand on Earth. All of those stars are ensouled by sons and daughters of God. They have no terrestrial bodies, no error. They are pure co-creators with God, creators and stewards of solar systems and planetary homes. That is why you are important to God. That is your future. That is how the universe expands."

Speechless, Shane turned to look at Afra, who drew in his

extended hands and nodded to him. In less than a second, Shane saw the view of outer space and the jeweled continent fade and a broad expanse of Oregon forest appear below him. Suddenly he was in it, walking an unmarked trail through the forest in heavy snow. He turned quickly to see if Afra was still walking next to him. He was, his skin no longer brown but translucent violet. There was no buildup of snow on his hair or shoulders. Shane looked around at the treeline not far below them. He was no longer in his bright sphere of sunlight and winced as the gale caught him unprepared and drove snow into his eyes.

"I'm right here," Afra said.

"Have we been walking in this while we were up there?" Shane asked, as he brushed the snow out of his hair.

"Our terrestrial bodies were. We've been making some progress."

"I'm thinking about what you just showed me. Why doesn't anyone talk about that? Why don't we know?"

"You will find, during the second half of your life, that few have any interest in knowing."

Shane looked back toward the hidden summit behind them as dazzling, violet-tinged lightning shot around inside the clouds and thunder rolled a few hundred feet above them.

"Of all the colors," Shane said, shouting over the thunder, "why violet, as the eraser?"

"As your mind's eye images it, violet has the highest frequency, the shortest wavelength and the most energy."

"I'm seeing what? What exactly am I imaging? I don't know what perfection looks like."

"Think of the light in a violet-colored campfire or a single violet candle. You're in a peaceful sanctuary, a calm place," Afra said, glancing up as thunder continued to roll.

"And then what?" Shane shouted.

"Before you were created as a soul, God's perfect concept of what you would be was imagined as divine intent. That intent was pure desire, memorized at the highest frequency of light God created. Seeing that frequency while you pray overwrites the mistakes,

283

known or forgotten. Violet has the energy of original intent, more than enough to overwrite the slower vibrating frequencies. Original intent will overwrite anything unlike itself, like frequencies of gray and red, the memories of guilt, anger, the sense of injustice. It erases and changes trapped memories back to the original pattern. But you have to get it started."

"Okay, that's alright for people who pray. What I've seen on cable is like watching entertainers. It's like a show on stage with an audience."

"What about your sphere of bright sunlight? It comes after some thought," Afra said. "It's about getting a burdened feeling out of your mind. You talk to the one you trust. You could say, 'God, in the name of the Christ, forgive me. Transmute all that is not of the light that I have ever imposed on life and all that has ever been imposed on me."

"Transmute?"

"To change something to a higher form."

"Can I add details, in private?"

"Add details, in harmony and objectivity."

Shane walked in the snow for a while in silence as he digested the deluge of new information, realizing there were worlds of mystery beyond the certainties of engineering. He wondered how far into this realm Dr. King had explored before his life had ended too early. He brushed snow out of his eyes and wondered about Afra's seemingly infinite patience.

"Personal question, if it's not too private." Shane said, "Is your wife, I mean, you know, in heaven with you?"

"The term is twin flame. She is a child, an old soul, currently living in the United States."

"Okay, I thought . . . so you've been waiting."

"More than a few lifetimes," Afra said. "Up ahead, look to your right and left."

"The Trail!" Shane shouted, running forward. "The junction with the Pacific Crest Trail. You did it!"

"I keep my promises. Now, brother, as you were once my coach,

284

I will be with you, through the Holy Spirit. You won't see me or hear me. Do not expect voices or any such thing. You have faculties in your heart, a non-physical flame you will feel as a gentle warmth, rotating and expanding when I or Jesus or an angel of light is with you. Just as it was for the apostles on the road to Emmaus, when Jesus walked with them."

"Will I remember any of this? Will I think it was a dream?"

"You will remember it," Afra said. "Another thing to keep in mind about Dr. King. He is not in embodiment now. But his soul will be returning, with great energy and a great work to accomplish for the diaspora and for all Americans. He will return after your time, and he will look to your example and the sacred change that will come through you. He will cite that work as his inspiration, if by your free will you decide to take it on. For the second half of your life."

"The second half of my life will be an inspiration to *him?*"

"Make it an inspiration. He will note the sacrifice of a comfortable career. He will note the dedication of financial resources to the cause of freedom. You will define the meaning of freedom and the means to freedom for all Americans. He will stand on your shoulders as you are now standing on his. This is the continuity of brotherhood, for the love of God's people."

"How long have you known you were going to talk to me about this?"

"Half a million years—but not until you were ready. Speaking of brotherhood, look downhill, on the trail."

Shane brushed snow off his forehead and eyelids so he could see better. He put one hand up to block the snow from flying into his eyes. There in the distance, on the snow-covered trail up through the forest, he saw a blur of figures trudging uphill. A moment later he could tell it was two men moving slowly up a long incline, heads down against the blizzard. He felt sudden shooting pains in his knees and stopped moving to get a clearer view. As the two men came closer he staggered down the incline toward them.

"Cuz! Ben! Is that you? Is that you?"

The two men stopped, flipped their hoods and looked up.

"Oh, my God!" Cuz yelled into the blizzard. "Shane! God, he's alive!"

"Shane!" Ben yelled. "He's hurting, man. Shane, stay there! We got you! He's been fried, man. One lucky dude."

As Ben and Cuz reached Shane and crushed him with bear hugs, his knees collapsed and he fell to the ground. They pulled him up by his backpack, put his arms around their shoulders and lifted most of the weight off his legs.

"Thank God, thank God, you're alive," Ben said. "You get hit? You're crazy, you know?"

"You need water? What do you need?" Cuz asked, as the trio pushed through the snow, dragging Shane's feet, moving step by step down Mount Thielsen Trail.

"Guess I'm okay. Just the knees," Shane said. "Good to see you guys. Where's Afra? He was right behind us."

"Who?" Ben asked.

Shane made them stop while he turned and looked around. There was no one behind them. His swollen knees ached with the effort of turning around and he remembered being told he would notice the angels in their absence. He turned again and faced downhill as they continued the descent. *Where is he?* Shane wondered. *He was real, I know it. Talk to them.*

"Thank God you came up," Shane said, thinking Afra might have had a part in their arrival. "Thought you guys were out of it."

"We can't believe you're still alive," Cuz said. "We saw the whole thing from the tent in the campground. The cloud just covered the whole mountain and then it blew up from inside. Just one massive explosion after another. Wham, wham, continuous lightning. Thunder like it was never going to stop. We felt it shaking our brains down there. You were inside the thing. How can you hear any more? How are you even alive?"

"Had help," Shane murmured.

"Help? Look," Ben said, "we've been feeling real bad about the whole electrocution thing. It was this big joke yesterday. This morning we get the note, we see the clouds, the lightning, explosions. What do we do? You're gone."

"Today wasn't funny," Cuz said. "We didn't know what we'd find coming up here."

"You did good. You did great."

"Well, you don't look so great on your feet, mountain man," Cuz said.

"Okay, he's going to live," Ben said, "and no pressure or anything, but did you get up there and get photos?"

"I got photos," Shane said. "Full three-sixty panorama."

"So then what happened?" Cuz asked. "What happened on the way down?"

"When we get to the truck," Shane said, unzipping a spare key pocket in his parka, "Ben, the key."

"Okay," Ben said. "So what happened?"

Shane thought for a moment as he adjusted his weight on their broad shoulders. *How can I tell them or anyone what happened,* he wondered. *How can I even begin to translate what took me so long to believe, even while it was happening to me? There are just not enough words in the English language or any language to explain what happened. How can I give these guys a straight answer? What do I say?*

And then, as he pondered his situation he felt a warm, burning glow rotating in the center of his chest, expanding outward. *Okay,* he thought, *this is yours. Your words.*

"When we get to the truck," he said, looking to both of them, "and get the heat going, maybe we should just sit there for a while and not drive right away."

"Why not?" Cuz asked. "We're all packed up. It's going to snow all night."

"It's okay," Shane said. "The truck can handle the snow. We've got the whole week."

"So what's going on?" Ben asked. "Something happen up there? You see the Promised Land?"

"Better if you're sitting down. I've got something to tell you."

OUR LADY

America's most effective and competent president in over 150 years stands with a free people to applaud the nation's greatest First Lady—ever.

OUR LADY

Governor Robert Gillis was a rare commodity among U.S. presidential candidates of recent times in that it was widely recognized that he possessed qualities of leadership, integrity, humility, strength and competence, all at the same time. A successful business executive and popular state governor, Gillis also had a reputation as a practical man and a master negotiator. He was careful to select fights he could win, and consequently, was always known to win. Even more remarkable was Gillis' successful passage through his party's presidential primaries, where the party faithful were predicted to choose a polarizing ideologue to stand up to the opposing party's polarizing ideologue.

The reason the predictions were wrong, media pundits suggested, was that the remarkable Robert Gillis had the blessing of a non-polarizing personality and an independent mind. He gained media attention and public favor by avoiding controversial social policies and obligatory antagonistic rhetoric. During debates and interviews, instead of barbed responses to barbed taunts, Gillis would call his opponent on the taunt and advise him to return to the electorate's core issue, which, according to Gillis' assessment was economic growth. The combination of perceived virtues created Gillis' only actual disadvantage, which was an on-and-off moodiness among fickle, perhaps envious, media commentators who accused him of being Wall Street funded and therefore crooked and too good to be true.

The same commentators inverted his economic record as

a state governor, claiming evidence of malfeasance without producing any evidence. They claimed he had failed to release sufficient numbers of violent criminals from state prisons and so on. Ignoring the calumny, Robert Gillis outspoke his primary opponents on the most effective ways and means of creating economic growth and surprised the pundits by winning the right to represent his party in the presidential election. It was at this point that the opposition media pundits accelerated the too-good-to-be-true mantra and began in earnest to discredit him, trolling for Wall Street connections, scouring school records and Eagle Scout logs for any scandal they could find or manufacture. None were plausible, which made them even more cynical and made Robert Gillis even more remarkable in the public mind.

Polls indicated that those who would decide the presidential election were among the broad class of independent voters, the ones who took no part in the initial choosing of party candidates. They included a small core of a few million independent and well-informed voters. Outnumbering the well-informed were many tens of millions of low-information, low-interest voters. But dwarfing even these millions of casual, maybe-voters were close to a hundred million eligible citizens who in most past elections had chosen not to vote at all. Two months before the big day in November, these masses were unaware of the candidates and unaware of the consequences for themselves that would be set in motion by the outcome of the election.

At that time, the September polls showed Robert Gillis running a tied race with his well-funded opponent. The opponent was a traditional populist, skilled at suggesting blue skies and a chicken in every pot for everyone who would vote for him. It was working. Gillis stuck to his core point of strong economic growth and how it could be achieved. But as predicted by opposition media spokesmen, Gillis' "method of growth" message sailed over the lowered heads of a hundred million low- and no-information voters who remained distracted by electronic media and disinterested in consequences. The two presidential campaigns remained locked in a tie, and in early September it looked like the outcome would be a low-turnout, inconclusive election, hinging on the organizational capacity of each party to get their base supporters to mail their ballots or get out and vote.

Then, seven weeks before the big day, someone extraordinary stepped forward for Robert Gillis during a press conference, to break the tie in the polls for good. Her name was Vicky Gillis, and she was an instant hit. At first sight on the evening news, she was beautiful, even by celebrity standards, but what made her so magnetic was how she elevated the definition of celebrity. Most beautiful women are camera-aware with a "look at me now" aspect to their femininity. Vicky Gillis upended that convention in a few moments on news broadcasts with a combination of perfect proportion and symmetry in face and figure, as well as a projection of steadiness, purity, moral strength and a personality that seemed to say, "I see you and I understand."

Though she chose not to speak at her husband's press conference, her eyes conveyed an evident awareness of the people. By that light in her eyes, Vicky Gillis was recognized by the public intrinsically in a few startling moments as the nation's moral authority. What made those moments unique in the history of the nation was that tens of millions of people confirmed the same feeling at the same time. It was said by several media commentators after the press conference that the nation had at that instant decided on its First Lady. It remained a formality for the electorate to confirm in November that her husband, merely a successful state governor, might succeed in becoming President of the United States.

Attention remained on the First Lady-elect as if the nation was impatient to get closer to the authority they recognized but couldn't quite define why. It wasn't that Vicky Gillis had been invisible before that initial press conference, but her role as an analyst kept her in a campaign research bus while her husband's strategists maintained the growth message would carry the election. But early in September forecasters showed Vicky that her husband's economic growth message had been heard and understood by all who had the capacity to understand it. She also knew that there were a hundred million Americans who did not have an enlightened self-interest in understanding it. Rather than dismissing them as willfully ignorant, selfish, stupid or among those who had stopped trying, she brokered a campaign meeting with Robert and the strategists and suggested it was time for her to step in and break the tie.

To gain the attention of the hundred million eligibles who didn't intend to vote, Vicky Gillis began appearing at press conferences, events and on the evening news. She was unlike any lady the nation had seen, First or otherwise. She was radiant, confident, observant, well-spoken, unusually beautiful and kind in a way that intrigued voters and non-voters. These citizens had paid scant attention to her husband's virtues or ideas about growth. They flocked to Robert Gillis' campaign events just to stare at her. Light seemed to emanate from her face in a way that sensitive people could almost feel as a kind of gentle breeze, expecting everyone else could feel the same sensation. Her blue eyes had an awesome authority, a knowing sense of the people's condition, conveying the impression she knew about the chronic struggles in everyone she saw.

Media commentators and producers made the most of the unprecedented shift in the campaign story. Political analysts condensed the highlights of Robert Gillis' speeches, often involving thousands of competent words about strong economic growth needed to lift everyone's net income, followed by contrasting video footage of the dignity of Vicky Gillis simply looking a crowd or a camera in the eye. The impression the public gained from her was that as remarkable, virtuous and competent as her husband's strategists said Robert Gillis was, it was she, the wise, discerning lady, who would oversee the way the nation was run.

Even opposition media anchors who had concocted the too-good line for Robert Gillis noted that late-September polls showed double digit increases in the percentage of independents who definitely intended to vote. No one had ever seen anything like it where public opinion and private emotion became so quickly attracted to a lady who appeared to the people as the feminine personification of America, as true and beautiful as they secretly imagined she should be.

Then came the event in mid-October which confirmed that the presidential election would favor Robert Gillis. It began as a formal campaign speech at a major university. At the end of the speech Robert Gillis had the astuteness to step back to the guest chairs behind the podium, take Vicky's hand and walk forward to the edge of the auditorium stage with her. The crowd, which had politely applauded his economic growth speech, understood the gesture immediately and jumped to their feet and roared. The news footage was repeated for days on every channel, as an implicit pact between the people and the next president, that he and they understood the spiritual leadership of the United States would be in her hands. Based on this event, a seminal point in a gradual change for the electorate from decades of cynicism to trust based on discernment, a media pundit aptly described her as "Our Lady," and to most of the nation it felt right.

As election day approached, Vicky realized there was affection behind the appellation, but she had her own ideas of what Our Lady meant. To her it meant an awareness of historical exemplars who had personified qualities of care and kindness and had exercised the clarity of mind to know how and when to apply them. She kept portraits of Mother Mary, Kuan Yin, Mother Theresa and even the Statue of Liberty to remind her of those qualities. But the media's affectionate term could also be viewed as an invitation to vanity, so she would change the channel when network anchors mentioned her. What mattered far more to her, close to election day, was the change in the electorate away from cynicism to a trust that could not be betrayed.

President Robert Gillis took the oath of office on a cold January day in Washington, D.C., with network anchors giving equal time for commentary about the influence of Our Lady standing next to him. Their teenage son and daughter, rarely seen in public, remained inconspicuous with the Secret Service in the background. The post-election presidential honeymoon began immediately with high expectations and national optimism focused on the First Lady. The stock market remained buoyant, fuel prices dropped and political analysts began paying attention to the new President's economic agenda.

The analysts noted that President Gillis' agenda had the advantage of narrow majorities in the House of Representatives and the Senate. However, the President took nothing for granted and his skills as a negotiator were exercised from his first day in office, drawing opposition moderates into his legislative process. The horse-trading quickly became productive and word began to spread that the new President was probably going to get more useful legislation accomplished than several of the last presidents combined. The stock indexes moved up, Treasury Bond prices increased and the dollar strengthened against the Chinese yuan.

But during this time of busy optimism, with a new administration that favored fair trades and bipartisan deals with Congress, an unexpected event occurred. A House bill with no important co-sponsors was presented to the House Finance Committee chairman by an unlikely contributor, an independent congressman named Mike Storch, calling for an audit of the Federal Reserve. Many similar bills had come and gone in House committees over the years, but as a formality Storch's bill was given debate time in committee. It gained a life of its own in a political environment increasingly unsympathetic to the behavior of the big banks.

Like previous audit bills that had ultimately failed, Storch's bill passed the Finance Committee by a narrow bipartisan margin and was placed at the House Speaker's discretion. The Speaker's discretion gave it a low priority on the legislative docket for that session of Congress. No date or notice was released for debate or a vote on the bill, but it attracted media attention because three notable political analysts calculated that it might pass narrowly in both the House and the Senate. No other similar version of an audit bill in the previous hundred years had been given any chance of passing both houses of Congress. The reasons for the political failure of similar bills were obvious but unmentioned by the media. The leadership of all Congresses since 1913 had been dependent on campaign financing derived in stepped-down forms from Wall Street banks, the actual owners of the Federal Reserve system. If Storch's bill was narrowly passed by the unusually independent Congress, attention would then turn to the White House, where President Gillis would have to decide if he would sign the audit into law.

The prospect of an audit of the Federal Reserve had never before been considered likely or even possible, for the obvious and unspoken reasons. Now though, in the first year of the new administration, media commentators warned that a national political taboo could soon be broken with potentially devastating consequences. Retaliation by the Fed and its founding Wall Street banks could come in multiple forms, with a downward economic trend likely as punishment for the nation. Re-election problems would fall on those in Congress who voted for an audit, particularly the leadership. The bankers' message would be harsh enough and clear enough to ensure the next Congress delayed the audit indefinitely. The only person who could stop the confrontation and the slide toward the abyss was President Gillis. With one sentence from his press secretary, President Gillis could indicate a veto was likely, the whole scare would dissipate, and his legislative agenda could continue harmoniously. Instead, the President made no comment, and Storch's bill, soon to have a legislative number, remained on the House Speaker's docket for a vote sometime in the spring.

President Gillis avoided comment on the audit issue for a reason. Buried within the horse-trading details of several important pieces of legislation Gillis wanted Congress to pass was an expectation that he would accept certain legislation Congress wanted him to sign. Both branches of government had presented their wish lists early. Storch's bill was not anticipated in that term by the House Speaker and therefore not named in early negotiations with the White House. It was just there as an add-on, and the President decided to deal with it later. In the meantime, his silence on the matter was noted in high places on Wall Street.

The First Lady, too, was aware of the progress of Storch's bill. Vicky had her own White House staff, whose administrative functions included preparing briefs on all bills that passed committees in both houses of Congress. She agreed with her analysts that an unusual bipartisan change in sympathy had occurred in the relationship between Congressional leaders and Wall Street. None of the partners would speak about it because no financial relationships existed between them. The reason behind the bipartisan change of mood was that the Wall Street banks had brazenly broken a century-old agreement. The written part of their agreement originated in 1913 when Congress had, by an unrepresentative vote, transferred its Constitutional duty to manage the printing of the United States' money to a private central bank. No Congress since 1913 had found it necessary to demand the law be rescinded. On the grounds that control of the money supply was too complicated for Congress to handle and that the delicate process had to be free of political influence, the private central bank retained control of the right under law to print as much as it wanted, when it wanted.

The unwritten part of the century-old agreement was that the banks would not encroach on foreign policy. Except for the short tenure of President Kennedy, they had encroached for more than a century without challenge, gradually usurping U.S. monetary policy and foreign policy. Now, according to the Speaker of the House, they had gone too far, colluding with the Saudis to lower the price of oil to the point where Russia was threatened with economic collapse and possibly civil war. The Russian government in turn had protested to the Gillis administration and indicated Russia would retaliate against the oil and banking cartel by launching a conventional war to occupy the Baltics. Lithuanian, Estonian and Latvian authorities had by mid-February already identified and arrested dozens of Russian intelligence and plain clothes military in their capitals. NATO, meaning the U.S., would be forced to engage Russia tank to tank, close to Russia's home turf.

The mainstream news media, controlled indirectly by the banks, switched focus away from the honeymoon with the White House to photos and footage of fires in the Baltic capitals, bloody foreign terrorist attacks in Europe and the Middle East, and coverage of domestic celebrity outrages. News networks found easy money covering the chaotic marches and sensational arson of West Coast leftists and anarchists in their skeleton suits, assaulting police with Molotov cocktails to protest the next trillion dollar war. The Chinese military also seemed pleased at the prospect of an expensive military distraction for the U.S. in Europe. The Chinese navy expanded their intimidation of the Vietnamese in the oil-rich South China Sea and paraded several of their aircraft carriers within sight of Vietnamese shores. In the U.S. there was no mention of Mike Storch's bill in the mainstream media. Even Congress was uneasy about the consequences of what they may have provoked. A long, expensive and unpredictable war with Russia while China took advantage and dominated its neighbors would be one of several lines of punishment if Congress persisted with an audit of the Federal Reserve.

In the White House, Vicky knew her husband's promising legislative agenda and bipartisan relations with Congress would be derailed and consumed by disaster if the banks pushed Russia to conventional war in the Baltics. They discussed their concerns quietly in the mornings over breakfast and late at night after their two teens were asleep. The President understood the danger of the conundrum he faced: Veto Storch's bill and lose the respect of this Congress and any hope for his agenda or a second term. Do nothing to protect the private central bank from Congressional oversight and risk the big banks' provocation of the next trillion dollar war. The credit to pay for such an unnecessary, avoidable war would have to be borrowed from the banks themselves. Meanwhile the global economy would be devastated and China's military would rise, all on his watch.

299

At breakfast and in the evenings in the residence Vicky was often quiet, letting Robert develop his thoughts on the epic coercion over Storch's audit bill, seeing her role more as listener. Robert was clearly frustrated at appearing to be President but feeling like a bystander.

"I never understood the passivity of our predecessor," he said, pressing his fingers to his forehead. "Now I'm starting to get why he would party and golf and campaign instead of govern. The banks wanted him out of their way, and he accommodated them. For God's sake, Vicky, the bankers do a deal with the Saudis to pump way more oil than the world wants, until the price of crude goes under what it costs Russia to produce it. The Saudis and the banks break Russia for priming Iran's nukes. Iran presses on with their nukes anyway. Russia sends infiltrators into the Baltics as a warning to us to control our banks. The banks and the Saudis send their Chechen terrorists into Russia. The Chechens never had the kind of money they have now. Thousands of jihadis ready to die for something or other in Russia. So I'm okay with this because the banks stand for free enterprise?"

"Why bankrupt Russia?" Vicky asked.

"Because the BRICS 80 want to take out the dollar as reserve currency. The big banks are punishing Russia for leading the BRICS. Putin gambled on funding an oil economy at his price point and lost. If they go to hyper-inflation and spin out of control, Russia's nukes go to God knows who, like Iran. Come on, you don't back dangerous people like Putin into corners. This is not our foreign policy. I did not authorize any of this!"

But there was worse to come. That night Vicky became aware that the Gillis administration's honeymoon had ended. It was more than a shift in the fickle media. It was more personal, concerning indications of a prelude to assassination. The fear began with a penetrating sense of condemnation, almost making her sick in the evenings while she listened to Robert. And then, in the middle of a Monday night in mid-February, the nightmares began.

The nightmares were variations of the same assassination

theme. There would be a build-up in the dream of knowing Robert was being hunted, stalked, betrayed by his inner circle, the Secret Service ordered to stand down, and then he would be shot dead a few feet from her. Sometimes in the nightmares the bullets would come from far off, sometimes from close quarters, from guests, friends, mercenaries or the unseen. The fifth nightmare that week was the worst, a premonition that the assassin was a jihadi with a vest, waiting for the president, somewhere in a crowd. In the dream she scanned a vast sea of faces expecting she would recognize the culprit until the explosion came from behind, from a place she had already checked. Always, there was the torment of helpless premonition. No matter what the precaution taken, the betrayer or the hidden assassin would take aim or dial a number.

Vicky said nothing to Robert, even after five nightmares in a week. She would stifle her cries, hunching over on the side of the bed or sobbing into a towel in the bathroom, praying for help. Then, on a Saturday morning, when she missed a formal breakfast with Robert and foreign dignitaries to catch up on sleep, she staggered to a bathroom mirror, took note of her appearance and her misery and decided to act.

As soon as she felt able, Vicky called Robert's Chief of Staff, Jon Douglas, and arranged a private meeting at ten that morning. There were two purposes for the meeting. The first was to request that Jon arrange a noon appointment with the head of the Secret Service, followed by a meeting with the Deputy Director of the FBI two hours later. The second purpose was to allow Mr. Douglas to talk while she intuitively assessed his qualities of loyalty and trustworthiness.

Twenty minutes after ten, Jon Douglas passed the test without being aware he was being tested and agreed to arrange meetings with the Secret Service and the FBI. Next, Vicky spent an hour with her children, listened to Robert talk international politics over coffee, then went downstairs at noon to meet with the Secret Service.

That private meeting with Harry Brownlee, the head of the

Secret Service, must have become etched in his memory, because his answers regarding the rehabilitation of the Service did not satisfy the First Lady. She knew that the rumor about Kennedy's Secret Service detail being ordered to stand down was untrue, but why, she wondered, had the rumor ever existed. And why had the Secret Service descended to its nadir of integrity and efficiency during the previous presidency? The kind, beautiful lady the public knew gave Mr. Brownlee a list of questions that forced him to reveal unresolved budgeting, staffing, leadership and morale issues inherited from the previous administration. Harry Brownlee left the meeting with an understanding that he was on a short leash and would be hearing from the Secretary of Defense.

At two, Vicky met with Dan Grenenger, Deputy Director of the FBI, in a Secret Service office downstairs. Vicky began by asking Mr. Grenenger to clarify the Department of Defense chain of command above the Secret Service. Mr. Grenenger deferred to the Secretary of Defense and offered to schedule a meeting for Vicky to go over the budgeting and organizational structure. But Vicky wasn't about to let Mr. Grenenger go. She began to list from memory the historical sequence of assassinations and attempted assassinations by poison and bullets of seven U.S. Presidents and the investigative conclusions concerning those responsible in each event.

"You could take the conclusions at face value or see conspiracies behind every one," Grenenger said.

"You're aware of the work of the Warren Commission regarding Kennedy?" Vicky asked.

"I've studied the transcripts."

"There was no compelling reason for a certain bank to have one of its vice presidents appointed to the board of that investigation, was there? What would a bank official know about investigating criminal activity such as a presidential assassination?"

"Well, ma'am, that question has been raised a number of times over the years."

"Strange how those questions are raised and dropped, Mr.

Grenenger. I'm not dropping this, so I'll be direct. On behalf of the President, I'm authorizing you to construct a complete and accurate dossier on the activities of the first and second United States Banks and the Federal Reserve affiliates in relation to written and unwritten understandings with every President of the United States from Washington to the present. You'll report to me, and your work on the dossier will be confidential. When can it be completed?"

"Ma'am, we have files that address that history. I can have one of the chief archivists compile a complete dossier in twenty-four hours."

"What is this chief archivist's name?"

"That would be Benjamin Atherton. He could meet you here and follow-up with any subsequent questions."

"When?"

"Monday at nine, if that would be convenient."

Vicky nodded without satisfaction. Dan Grenenger had passed a test of scrutiny and for now Vicky let him go.

Monday morning could not come soon enough for Vicky after two more nights of repetitive nightmares and exhausted dozing on the bathroom floor. The strain was beginning to show, and even Robert, as busy as he was with diplomats and State and Defense Department officials, noticed her changed appearance.

But Monday morning did arrive, and still disturbed and anxious, Vicky decided not to improve her diminished appearance and dour expression. As she looked at herself in the bathroom mirror and then at the crumpled pile of towels on the floor, she realized she didn't care how she appeared. The millions of people who kindly thought of her as Our Lady didn't have to know how brittle she was. Without makeup or a smile, she dressed in sweats and went downstairs via a service route before nine to meet the FBI archivist, Mr. Benjamin Atherton, in the small Saratoga Room.

Saratoga was a lamp-lit reading room, decorated in white and gold and used for photo-ops, with its three walls of books, a fine desk, several leather chairs and a fireplace. She opened the main hall door ten minutes early, expecting to be alone, but a young man in a suit and turquoise-blue tie got up from a leather chair to face her.

"Mrs. Gillis, good morning," the young man said.

"Benjamin Atherton?"

"No, Mr. Atherton was not available when Director Grenenger called. I'm Joshua Cord from archives. I have the dossier you requested."

Vicky gathered her thoughts and looked carefully at the tall, serious young man. The situation was precisely the bait and switch in responsibility she had been concerned about. This man, Cord, did not have the same vibration she had come to expect from expressionless FBI officials. He appeared to be disciplined, trim and without obvious guile but did not exhibit the rigidity of hardened ex-military personnel. Cord returned her gaze without apology, apparently expecting her to answer him.

"Call Grenenger," she directed. "Get him in here now, or I will call him."

"I understand your concern, Mrs. Gillis. Neither Mr. Grenenger nor Mr. Atherton have the capacity to answer your concern or to offer a solution."

"A solution? I expected Atherton with a dossier. Get Grenenger now. I'm calling security."

"Mrs. Gillis, I am security," Cord said, moving a step closer, before she could bolt for the door. "The nightmares have to stop and the cause behind them has to be stopped."

"What would you know about that?" she said, glaring at him. "Are you responsible? Are you responsible for this?"

"No, I'm not. Your suffering is unwarranted and should not continue. You have to be informed in order to take corrective action."

"If you're not FBI, who are you and where are you from?"

"Mrs. Gillis, I am here to assist you, the President and the nation. The President made a verbal pact with a representative of the Federal Reserve last June, prior to winning the primary. The agreement covered indirect campaign funding and endorsements in return for a hands-off policy and acceptance of an in-house minder. This dossier shows an almost identical pattern with primary winners from both parties going back to Woodrow Wilson's time."

"How could you possibly know about verbal pacts made by the President?"

"It's fact, Mrs. Gillis. My recommendation is that you ask the President."

"I don't understand how you could know any of this, unless you are from one of the banks."

"That's not the case. The President's safety is paramount. Your well-being is equally important. My task is to secure both. After you speak with the President, I will meet with you again."

"Wait, wait a minute. You're setting my schedule? You're telling me my husband hasn't been forthcoming with me? Who are you, Mr. Cord?"

"Good morning, Mrs. Gillis. We'll meet again this week," Cord said with a smile and a slight nod as he turned and exited by a white, gold-trimmed door, a service door Vicky knew was always locked and alarmed.

Vicky paced across the plush white rug in the room, calling the FBI's Grenenger and then Chief of Staff Jon Douglas, but got voicemail for both. She considered calling the Secret Service but decided to calm down by listing the surge of questions that came to mind. First, Director Grenenger needed to explain a few things concerning his archivist, Mr. Joshua Cord. Her mind filled with a sequence of anxious questions that she had to have answered immediately about an impertinent archivist who knew far too much. But as her pen touched paper at the polished desk in the Saratoga Room, a strange feeling of peace came over her and the charging rush of apprehension and anger gently evaporated. She took a great breath of air and let it out slowly. Within seconds she had transitioned from apprehension to calmness, a tangible change with no apparent cause, and she pondered what had come over her. Whatever the unknown source of relief, it was welcome, and she recognized that some kind of benign assistance had intervened and now seemed to direct her attention away from her twenty anxious questions to the dossier that Cord had left for her.

"Thank you," she whispered, "for whatever just happened."

Thinking of the equanimity of one of the real Ladies, Mother Mary or Kuan Yin, she pulled a leather chair up to the desk, adjusted the reading lamp and began to read about the unfortunate Woodrow Wilson.

The information in the dossier was both eye-opening and frightening. It was clearly her responsibility to summarize and present it properly, but obtaining the undivided attention of the President of the United States during a protracted international crisis is a tall order, even for a First Lady. Vicky had to wait until close to midnight that evening to get her weary and pensive husband to listen to her. By that time she had made a handwritten summary of the contents of the FBI dossier. The nature of the contents meant the confrontation she had to have with him in the residence would not be easy. It began as Robert sank back into a sofa with a drink in one hand and his phone in the other.

"Robert," she said, hesitating, "there's something I've been meaning to ask you. I need your full attention. Give me your phone." She took the phone and left it in the bathroom with the tap running and the door closed.

"Oh, come on. You don't have to do that," he said. "I need to look at the thing."

"I'm sorry, but I have to have your attention. Listen and tell me: did you at any time make a deal with Manden?"

"What kind of deal?"

"A Clinton-Greenspan deal. The same kind of deal every recent president from Johnson on has made with the bankers."

"Why are you asking?"

"Because you did, didn't you? You made a deal with those Luciferians and you didn't ask me. They came to you and you

306

didn't ask me because you knew exactly what I'd say. I trusted you and you didn't tell me. You wanted to be in this place so badly that you sold out for their approval. You sold me out too. You sold the sovereignty of the country to the devil, like Johnson and Nixon and the others before you."

"Oh, God. No. Not right now, Vicky. They have a mandate to walk the line between inflation and unemployment. If I hadn't agreed to a general understanding, I would not have won the primary. Appleton or Gerrard would be President, and what good would that do anyone? They're clueless hacks and they'd go along with anything. If I hadn't dealt with the prerequisites, I would have been a non-starter."

"You complain about bankers running our foreign policy. They're like the imams vetting the candidates in Iran. What was the fine print on their mandate? A nod and a wink? You've sabotaged your own presidency, Robert," she said, standing in front of him.

"You are way out of line. I've done no such thing."

"You let them box you into a corner of their making. You thought you could bargain with them, on their terms. You deceived me, the public, and the people who voted for you, and you deceived yourself."

"Vicky, when I was governor . . . It's just better you don't know how laws and sausages are made. I shielded you from that because you never understood what it takes."

"No, Robert. You don't understand what it takes! What you have done is unacceptable. If you welch on your expedient understanding with those creeps, they will kill you as surely as they killed Kennedy. They will discredit your presidency and reverse any good you think you might get past them. And if you go along with them, you'll get to explain it at the end of this life. But long before that you'll face the judgment of the public."

"Vicky, come on, just calm down," Robert replied, unmoved. "You don't get it."

"I get what lying is, in the form of withholding the truth about dealing with the devil. They want to destroy the United States, Robert. Unrepayable national debt. Unending wars. Permanent hostages to the money changers. Just coincidences? Robert, if you let this stand, I will leave you, I will leave this White House, and I will tell the public what you have done. I keep my word. I will not tolerate my husband betraying my country."

"That's fine, it's okay, just relax and listen. I'm going to try to reason with you."

"No. That is the beginning of weaseling, explaining the unforgiveable! I will leave you if you let this stand!"

"No, you won't! You won't!" He waved his finger, warning her.

"How did that quote from Woodrow Wilson begin?" she asked, leaning in toward him. "I am a most unhappy man. I have unwittingly ruined my country. A great industrial nation is now controlled by its system of credit. We are no longer a government of free opinion . . . but a government by the opinion and duress of a small group of dominant men." Duress, Robert. A small group of dominant men. So, who is your Edward Mandell House?"

"I don't know who or what you're getting at. Why are you so crazy with this?"

"Woodrow Wilson had a bankers' man in his house. With you it's Preston Lepke, isn't it? He's their man in your house. Our house. Yes?"

"Okay, he's their guy. It's the way to communicate with them. So what? You just don't understand where you're going with this. Knee-jerk responses have a way of becoming self-fulfilling disasters because they lead to stupid, unnecessary words that shouldn't be said. Big unnecessary mistakes!"

"I'm not making any mistake, Robert. The long line of sell-out presidents stops here. Right here."

"Look, if I'm going to indulge your well-meaning, very caring kind of help, I've got to get you to face some sense of reality. These people have meant business for their sole benefit for hundreds of years all over the world. You fail to give them what they want, they end you and have some other country invade yours so every future

308

president gets the message about who controls the money. He who has the peso has the say so. You don't fool with these people the way you're so kindly suggesting I fool with them."

"I'm not being unreasonable," she said, lowering her tone. "I'm letting you know that I'm going to become involved. Nothing public. I want to help you, but you can't let this stand."

"How? This is centuries old. How are you going to hold down a million moving pieces when you don't know what you're doing? Even career people at State and the CIA don't know where you would start."

"I don't know either yet. I don't know."

"Vicky, I know you want to help and I know I'm in a hell of a place, but we've got to be careful. I've got to play for time and I can't assume what Kennedy assumed."

"I understand the danger. But we can't stay paralyzed, all tied up like we were in the campaign. We're going to break the tie soon, because we don't have a lot of time. Somehow. For now, you're so worn out you've got to get some sleep."

"Don't do or say anything without checking with me," he said, rubbing his eyes.

Although Vicky dreaded the thought of being trapped in sleep, in yet another nightmare, she could see Robert needed rest and encouraged him to get to bed. But that night there were no nightmares, and she woke in the morning with Robert's alarm, surprised at sleeping straight through the night unharmed.

That morning Vicky began wondering about the mysterious Mr. Cord and his promise to meet after her confrontation with Robert. She called Grenenger's number at the FBI. A receptionist answered saying Dan Grenenger wasn't available but would return her call. Instead, on a hunch she asked to speak with Joshua Cord in archives. A moment later Joshua Cord answered.

"I read your dossier, Mr. Cord," she said, uncertain where to begin with someone so forward and apparently above etiquette.

"I hope you found it interesting. May I ask if the President read it?"

"No, he has not, but as it turns out your assessment was correct. I'd like to know how you became aware of that."

"Mrs. Gillis, I'm aware that a fatal schism exists within the Russian government at this moment. Russia's errors may permanently change the world in the next few days. Corrective action is possible if it's taken immediately."

"Are you suggesting you have ideas to assist the Russians?"

"Action may be taken immediately to assist the President of the United States."

"In what way?"

"It would be better if it were explained face to face."

"If I agree, are you prepared to explain who you are?"

"I am prepared to explain the reason for the action that you and the President must take without delay."

"Without delay? Are you now an advisor to the President and myself?"

"Mrs. Gillis, I'm waiting downstairs in the Saratoga Room."

"I just called you at the FBI."

"The timing and sequence of the necessary action is crucial, Mrs. Gillis."

Vicky hung up and called the Secret Service, asking for the daily guest entry log and an officer to check on her in a few minutes in the Saratoga Room on the main floor. She then hurried downstairs, went directly to the reading room and opened the door with a shove, wanting to get to the bottom of this mystery. Joshua Cord, tall, athletic and calm in a three-piece suit and a peach-colored tie, stood up to greet her.

"How did you get in here?" she demanded. "There's no log of entry for you. I checked."

"Good morning," he said, pausing to look into her eyes. "It's good to see you. Please, be seated and be comfortable. This information requires your full attention. It is to be conveyed to the President."

Vicky was used to being treated with deference and as an authority, not with instructions from an authority. In an instant she realized Cord had taken the role of authority in her house, the White House, exactly the conceit she had rushed downstairs to fight. But as she began to bristle, ready to verbally slug him, she noticed the fireplace was lit. The fireplace was almost never lit in the Saratoga, yet layers of crackling logs were pleasantly alight and an aromatic tang of woodsmoke touched her nostrils. There was a golden glow from the reading lamps on either side, and she appreciated the softness of old leather under her hand as she pressed on the back of the armchair Cord had suggested she sit in. All the fear seemed to go out of her, just as her curiosity about Cord had evaporated several days or weeks or years ago. Yet she was alert, and her curiosity extended to what he had to say. She sat down in the armchair without anxiety and leaned forward.

"Alright, what information are you referring to?" she asked.

"The situation in front of the President began long before the current bill to audit the Federal Reserve. You're aware from the dossier that the first President, Washington, prohibited bankers or bank stock owners from holding public office or influencing public officials. The risk of usurpation of sovereignty by bankers applied then as it does now. King George had Parliament enact the Currency Act to provide continuous interest payments from the colonies to the Bank of England. That was the cause of the War of Independence. The Currency Act guaranteeing perpetual interest payments reappeared inside the United States as law under another name over one hundred years ago. Usurpation of sovereignty has led to a form of national bondage. An audit of the Federal Reserve will change nothing."

"Congress thinks it's important. What are you saying?"

"There are a few hundred dominant men involved. Baiting them with an audit will unite them against the President. The intimidation techniques, overt and covert, have already begun. Effective action to correct the usurpation requires rescinding the Federal Reserve Act, the law that empowers them to print money and collect interest through the government. The President must unite the leaders of Congress to rescind that law as a national priority. The President must unite the people by informing them of what that law has and will cost them in freedom, opportunity and annual taxes, where they will pay the interest and principal on the national debt indefinitely. The President must, without delay, engage the Attorney General to secure effective prosecution of these men, for fraud and conspiracy against the United States."

"Prosecution of bankers? They'll retaliate, they'll destroy the economy. Look at what they're doing to Russia."

"There can be no delay concerning Congress, informing the public and ensuring swift action by the Department of Justice. That is the urgency you must convey to the President. As we speak, Russia is in default on all domestic and foreign accounts and could soon break up into factions. The survival of the Russian economy, its nuclear security and the lives of tens of millions of Russians hangs on the choices of vain, greedy and incapable men in the Kremlin. One faction favors the sale of Siberia to China. It would change the world and the Kremlin would probably fall. Another faction favors a nuclear first strike on key financial capitals in the West. The Kremlin would certainly fall."

"Nuclear war? Because of the banks' deal with the Saudis, to push down the price of oil?"

"The bankers don't accept dissent, and Russia's fate is their warning to all. The Currency Act has expanded in complexity and now covers most of the world. George Washington was in a similar position to your husband. It's complete independence, requiring resolute national action, or complete and continuing domination by the few, if good men do nothing."

"Yes, but even good men baulk at risks. And uniting Congress is like herding cats."

"Washington had the same predicament. The uniting cannot be done by human will alone."

"What are you proposing?"

"The office held by your husband is the same office held by George Washington. It is simultaneously a secular office and a spiritual office, ordained then and now by the same Providence to whom Washington appealed."

"I can think of a few presidents who placed no value in that."

"The office elevates the officeholder, according to the aspiration of the man. Both the President and yourself would be well advised to aspire to the cause of independence as held by George and Martha Washington. The United States has not had the equal of a President and First Lady, in combination with a loyal Congress, since the days of the Washingtons. A better time to win national independence from these dominant few may never come again."

"Why come to me? Why didn't you go to Robert?"

"It is a matter of soul attainment, of surrender, service, sacrifice and selflessness over many hundreds of thousands of years. The President does not yet trust in God to the same degree. You are a daughter of God, whose heart flame has proven sufficient in constancy over time, where God may trust in man. You have been called by God to take dominion over the Earth, beginning with yourself. To that end you have been instructed by God, "Command ye me." In the matter of the nation's independence, it is given to you to command God, by the assent of the incumbent President, as the first President did, with and without Martha."

"Do you mean pray with Robert, or have Robert present?"

"The President is reluctant to pray, let alone command God as an heir. You have for many lifetimes perceived the love in that relationship. He is not yet able. Therefore, as First Lady you may accept the responsibility to lead in his presence."

"What about the people? Aren't they involved?"

"They must be. The President would be well advised to address the people, requesting the support of those who would pray, according to their free will. Those of every religion and every conscience would be exhorted to ask for the will of God to prevail in a time of global crisis. The international situation is in flux and could not be fully divulged without causing excessive fear. The request to pray for the will of God would be offered as a matter of trust between the people and their President."

"And Congress?"

"Those who are most afflicted, most compromised by guilt, are the leaders. If the President were to meet in complete privacy with the Speaker, the majority and minority leaders and whips of both houses, he would confront their fear. They have compromised their souls in exchange for financial support and see no way out."

"Is there a way out?"

"These leaders are rare men, similar to that of the first Congress in Washington's time. The Speaker, leaders and whips have accessible consciences. All nine are sons of God. None will be free of their financial bondage without the vision and leadership of the President."

"What should he say?"

"This second dossier," Cord said, handing Vicky a bound folder, "shows the credit history of all 535 current members of Congress. It is consistent with previous Congresses. About one third were bankrupt at one time. There were strings attached to their financial path into Congress. All members were and are dependent on bank-influenced political action committees for election and re-election. They despise their situation but live with it for lack of an alternative. The President should comfort them and provide them with their challenge."

"That is?"

"Their condition and that of the people was created by legislation. It must be undone by legislation and lawful prosecution. If the fate of the leaders seems similar to the 'hanging together or hanging separately' Ben Franklin observed, it's because previous Congresses have not learned from history. Both the leaders and the people must hear the voice of this President and trust him."

"But if they don't believe what you're saying about a way out because they're afraid of retaliation, and they can't or won't talk about it, what then?"

"That is the test of this people. Discernment and trust may now be placed where previous Presidents have not merited trust. As for you, by these dossiers and your own discernment, you have

314

sufficient understanding of the way out through legislation and the loving command. If it is your free will that this nation be independent of these men, then on behalf of the people, you speak it as a command to God, to be adjusted according to the will of God, as a decree fitting the heirs of God. This is the purpose to which you and the people were born."

"Who are you?"

"I am security. You are secure. Your family will not be harmed. Those who were hidden and would do harm have been reassigned and will be exposed. But I cannot do for you what you must do for the nation and what the people must do for their own freedom."

"I'm trying to put what you're asking into some kind of plan."

"You have sufficient understanding to effectively inform the President of the course that is his duty to take. You have sufficient favor in the heart of God to command on behalf of the people that your nation be delivered from harm."

"Isn't there someone else, someone clearer thinking, who can do this?"

"It has been given to you to lead. In humility lead the President. In humility speak for the people."

Overwhelmed, Vicky slid forward off the chair onto her knees and pressed her forehead against the rug. Her eyes filled with tears and she had difficulty forming words in her mind.

"How can I . . . command God when I can't think of the right words to say to you?"

"Have mercy on God, Immanuel, imprisoned in the density of his people. Speak with the authority of a merciful heart. Prepare the President with sufficient information, without interruption. There is a chapel not far from your room. Enter it, alone with the President. Instruct the President that you speak on his behalf and in the name of his office and that he must offer amendments, authorizing your prayer and command, as you conclude. Request that your petition be adjusted according to the will of God, because you do not see all or know all."

"When?"

"Now."

"Robert isn't easily pulled away from the . . ."

"The President will respond to your request."

"Now?"

"Right now."

Still on her knees, Vicky reached out with one hand to steady herself against the chair. She bent her head low, trying to think of what to say, questions to ask so as to have more information about how to put the situation into words Robert could understand. A distant rapping sound made no impression on her. It came again, accompanied by the sound of a door opening and the far-off voice of someone saying something about the Secret Service.

"Mrs. Gillis? Ma'am? Oh, my God. Ambulance, no, house doctor, get the house doctor! Fast! Saratoga Room. Get him in here!"

The next thing Vicky saw was the concerned face of the President of the United States, her Robert, hovering over her.

"Vicky . . . Vicky, come on, come back around, tell me what happened. Tell me, please tell me what happened. God, oh, God, I didn't mean for this to get so bad. Don't let this happen to her, not to her."

"Robert," she whispered, barely conscious. "It's okay, it's okay. Get me upstairs. We have to talk."

During the next hour Vicky had the undivided attention of the President of the United States in the residential wing of the White House. Too awed to speak, he simply stared at her and listened to the information. The children had come and gone, returning to their homework, reassured that their mom was just overtired.

Sitting in an armchair in the bedroom, Vicky regained strength by the minute as she encapsulated the briefing, working with every word before she said it, careful to provide an interpretation Robert could understand and accept. Within the hour, Robert understood the concept but could not accept the risk.

"This Cord," Robert said, "Joshua Cord, did he show up on the entry log?"

"No. The Secret Service checked. No record at the FBI."

"How can someone come and go past the Secret Service?"

"I can't explain it."

"I can't put you at risk like this. What Cord is talking about is suicide. You've got to understand, one step down that road triggers your nightmares. There are people you will never meet who are prepared to prove that they are the wardens of this planet, not just this country. Their rule, Vicky. Goddammit. I knew it when I was governor."

Vicky could see Robert's frustration and decided not to allow him to continue justifying his helplessness. Rather than contesting it, she changed the subject.

"Do you remember me telling you about the eight monks who prayed the rosary every day in a house a few blocks from ground zero at Hiroshima? Not even the smell of smoke on their clothes. Not a hair on their head was harmed. It's that immersion we're going into. It's still printed on our money, 'In God we trust.'"

"We trust? We need evidence! Cord has given you nothing."

"What evidence did Washington have? Trust, request, one step forward."

"You're asking me to step off something very high into nothing but air!"

"You're a good man, Robert," she said softly, touching her fingers to his hair. "But evil triumphs if good men do nothing. You are President of the United States. You're sworn to uphold an office you think is secular, limited by the Constitution."

"For God's sake, Vicky, it is! What are you saying?"

Vicky remained seated on the bed and kept her voice calm as Robert paced the bedroom.

"I'm trying to tell you what Washington figured out," she said. "Lincoln and Kennedy got it intuitively, not consciously. The office gives the officeholder direct access to Providence. The office is holy. It's a secret that protects itself against profane presidents. Whatever the profane gained from the office was limited by the person they saw in the mirror."

"Cord told you that?" Robert asked, seeming not to expect an answer as he pressed his fingers together. "What would Washington do? A prayer to save us from the abyss? From Congress and the audit. The Baltics, mad Russia. France and Spain this close to anarchy. No credit. No anything. Goddamn chaos."

"The office won't accept defeat or limitation unless you do. Humor me. Play the role of Washington. It's easy for you. You're feeling what he was feeling. In his day the wardens of this world were King George's bankers. Providence gave him the power of independence from them. Profane presidents let them back in. Providence will give us independence again, if you match Washington's faith."

"Vicky, look at me. I'm not Washington. It's me, the same me you married before we got here."

"You married the office, as well as me. Holy matrimony. In the sight of God, then and now. We stepped off into nothing but thin air, for better or for worse. Cord came to me and trusted I would explain your office to you. You, the officeholder of the Presidency have direct access to the same Providence that Washington did. He proposed, God disposed."

"That's all good, but Washington was the prayer in the thicket type. What wording would you have me propose?"

"Take a breath," Vicky said. "Calm down. I understand why you're edgy. Cord was not talking about direct confrontation. He was saying, you propose a course of action in the presence of God, then let God take on the confrontation."

"I still don't know what to propose. Tell me what I need to say."

"With your permission," she said, standing up and turning him to look at her, "and in your presence, in the sight of God, I would propose a petition on your behalf in the chapel. If you agree, it would be as if you were making the proposition to God as the officeholder. You would add additions and amendments. As President, you have to speak too, even if you agree with everything I say. You would have to ask for the will of God to amend ours."

"This is between us and God. It goes nowhere else."

"Your office represents the people petitioning God."

"What exactly are you going to say, that I can agree to?"

"We're going to ask for help in resolving the things we can't see, like uniting Congress, protecting you and holding the wardens at bay."

"Alright. I agree to that. Then what?"

"We'll know," she said. "One step at a time into thin air. Let's go."

"Go? You mean right now?"

"Right now. It's time."

As they approached the chapel, Vicky glanced at Robert to assess his emotions. He seemed to read her intent and squeezed her hand. She closed the solid door silently behind them and lit two white candles, and they stood in front of the small altar, Robert on her right. Our Lady drew herself upright, focused on a single candle flame and thought of the millions of low-information and no-information voters. Then she took a breath and began to speak with fervor.

On the basis that judgment is reserved for the Son of God, Vicky called out loudly for the intercession of the Son through the person of Jesus the Christ. She asked, for and on behalf of the people, for national sovereignty to be reclaimed from the few dominant men of global finance in the United States and elsewhere.

Vicky firmly requested that Jesus name the names of the dominant few and judge the records in the Book of Life of their actions over the millennia. Their misuses of power and control, she asked, were to be returned to them spiritually, as divine justice, according to God's will. This, she proposed, would act as a constraint against any expansion of their concealed progress toward totalitarian control of the United States and its people.

Next, Vicky asked for God's assistance in sustaining the resolve Congress would need to rescind the Federal Reserve Act of 1913 and to justly administer the nation's money supply, accountable to the people and the Constitution.

In conclusion, she asked that the people be made aware of the generational encroachments on their freedom and abundance, that the gold standard in currency and personal behavior be restored, and that unjust national debts be nullified, according to the will of God.

Vicky lowered her head in silence and waited for Robert's amendments. Robert glanced at her, wide-eyed, paused, then turned back to the altar. He seemed to gather his thoughts, assessing his level of agreement before he began to speak.

"By the authority vested in me and in the Office of the President of the United States," Robert said, "let this petition be accomplished and adjusted according to the will of God. Amen."

Wide-eyed, he stepped back from the altar and looked at Vicky again. She didn't return his look but responded quietly.

"Just the beginning. I'll be here every day. We both have work to do."

Robert stared at the candles for a moment before she extinguished them. In the hall he turned Vicky toward him and pulled her close.

"Sure glad you're feeling better," he said, smiling at the speed of her recovery. "Nothing wrong with you."

"But . . . ?" she added, knowing he had questions.

"One of the things I agreed to in there . . . I don't think is physically possible. The bankers have their Ponzi scheme, which they're holding together, keeping the whole world from flying apart. If we break it by what you're proposing, a lot of people could starve and a lot of people could die in wars. I don't think we're in any position to replace their make-believe money with a gold standard, now or even soon. There can't be any vacuum. We don't have the gold or the assets to make it work. The world banks their virtual money with us. Even if it's pretend money, it still works for now."

"When would the world find it convenient to stop pretending? When these few men decide to break the pretense, on their terms? Then they provide the solution, globally. We procrastinate, they rule indefinitely. We've got precedent, plenty of precedent for an asset-backed economy. Lincoln's greenbacks and Kennedy's United States Notes. Adapt and innovate."

"You can't innovate enough assets to back it. The economy is way bigger, way more complex now. We just physically don't have tangible assets worth what's in circulation. No one does. We'd cause revaluations, global chaos, and that's how wars get started."

"Washington, Franklin, Jefferson, Madison . . . what did they start with? Robert, there is an asset-backed formula waiting for your geniuses to identify. They'll have to run three shifts a day until they come up with a system that you can convince Congress will work. Adapt and innovate."

"And in the meantime . . . ?"

"Meet with the Speaker, the leaders and whips in the Saratoga Room. No watches, no phones. It has to be secure."

"And say what? Those guys are dealers and most of them owe the banks."

"Read this. It's the second dossier from Cord," Vicky said, pressing it into his hand. "It's in two parts. Part one, documented evidence of fraud and conspiracy against the United States. Part two, Congressional debt. I've tagged the pages related to all nine Congressional leaders. Read this and you'll understand why they think they can't move and what you can say to move them. I added a few hints."

"They're compromised into inaction, indefinitely. Whatever I say, they'll leave here saying, 'We'll think about it.' Ten minutes later it's, 'We heard nothing.'"

"They're like nine of the good but indecisive men from the first Congress. They need someone to tell them why they should sign that document."

"And the document is . . . ?"

"Simultaneous bills to rescind the Act. And let the nine know the Attorney General has evidence for felony indictments on a few hundred dominant men for fraud and conspiracy against the United States."

"And while they're in jail they can call a few million dependents."

"They're done, Robert. Cord was here because their time is up and we needed to know it. We trust, like Washington trusted, and we act like Washington acted."

"Vicky, we take their money machine away, they collapse the economy in a couple of days. War comes right after that."

"Which is fraud and conspiracy against the United States."

"If you can catch them in time. They've thought of this. Their lawyers can delay anything forever. You can't tell Congress to rescind the Act if there's any chance of it being delayed. And the nature of Congress *is* to delay."

"So don't allow delay. Everything from now on is derived from that premise. I know you. You're already seeing at least one set of options through this. Take that set where you see it leading. No delays. Take it to the nine leaders. Take this evidence to the Attorney General. Everyone else will catch up with your idea."

"My idea?" Robert said, beginning to pace again. "God help me. Nothing in the governor's office looked like this."

"You're not a governor any more. You are President of the United States. Your country has been taken from you by stealth. No one else knows what to do. George Washington is in the room, Robert! He's standing right here, wanting to know what you're going to do with the office he personified and the evidence in your hand. Tell the President your idea, Robert! He's been where you are now!"

"Okay!" Robert said, thinking aloud and talking to himself as he paced the hall. "I get it! Washington would deal with it. He wouldn't like these bastards any more than I do. But he wouldn't show it. He's career military, so he's going to control what he says. He's going to prosecute them based on the evidence. Simultaneously, we legislate. The key to the Act is Congress, the leaders. That's this dossier. I read the dossier on these nine. What do they owe? Take their debt away and that changes them. So, change them. This whole thing is about speed, coordination, security. It'd have to be . . . a bunch of things happening at the same time. I meet with the nine from the House and Senate, right now, this morning. God, help me say the right thing. The FBI turns up surveillance on the bankers, now, before that meeting. Attorney

General generates documentation and indictments on fraud and conspiracy today. Files on individuals tomorrow or the next day. Time it to the minute with each draft of the legislation. Finance team matches circulation to national asset classes today and tomorrow. I get leaders to push House and Senate Finance Committee chairs to match the same, trade the circulation and asset data with us. No need for them to know any more. Consensus on the national asset value of the dollar tomorrow from Treasury. Secretary of State creates narrative and timeline for instructions to diplomats today. Talk to Russia today, Euro leaders today. And there's more, God, there's so much more. I have to chart critical paths for this on paper. Jon Douglas reviews everything. The minute we get every strand set, we pull all the strings at the same time. Move faster than these bastards think I will. I go to the people with legislation signed. I'll need you there."

"I'll be there."

"Good," he said, breathing heavily. "God help us. I've got to get with Jon Douglas. This has to move way faster than they did in 1913."

An hour later government vehicles brought the nine Congressional leaders through an underground entrance to the White House. The Secret Service ushered the leaders upstairs and into the Saratoga Room, without their phones or watches. Extra leather chairs had been brought in. Subdued light from reading lamps reflected off gold trim on the paneled walls, and the logs in the fireplace glowed and crackled. The Congressional leaders stood or sat, discussing the dangers of Russia's imminent demise. Moments later, the President entered the room and the men turned or rose from their seats.

"Gentlemen," the President said, waving them to their seats, "please, make yourselves comfortable. You've heard the briefings this morning regarding Russia. At my direction the State Department has issued a statement saying we're monitoring the situation. That will buy us time, maybe a day. In the meantime, I've invited you here to talk about you. Each of you."

The President held up a thick FBI dossier and continued.

"Gentlemen, this dossier concerns you, your credit history and your indirect sponsorship by the banking interests that have made your place possible in Congress. I'm not holding it against you. I, too, have a similar history. Chris?"

"Mr. President," Christopher Freney, Speaker of the House interrupted, "We've just come from the joint briefing on Russia. They're on the brink. We can't be here for credit history."

"Chris, Russia's situation may be ours, a year or five years from now. It's a matter of time and will. This meeting is about our will. Some background first, concerning you. A third of Congress has been bankrupt at some point. They're now representatives of the people, sworn to uphold the Constitution. One hundred percent of Congress is dependent on campaign finance directly and indirectly . . . from our sponsors. You hate it, I hate it. For a hundred years we've put up with it. You're in this room because you're good men, but every one of us has been compromised by our sponsors. You know exactly what I mean. We can't control the money supply or our foreign policy. Our sponsors do, and we're conditioned to think there's nothing we can do about it. They have made retaliation an art form. They've warned us and the rest of the world that they're in charge of policy by making an example of Russia."

"Mr. President, with respect, concerning Russia's situation, I'm thinking about their nukes, not about our sponsors, at this point," said Maury Askew, Senate Minority Leader.

"Their nukes are not going anywhere, Maury," the President responded. "What I have to say to you now concerns holding Russia together as well as the United States. Our sponsors provided the catalyst that pushed Russia into crisis. A small cadre of New York bank stakeholders, central bankers and Saudi principals. 'Control your bankers,' our friend in the Kremlin told me. Well, gentlemen, we are going to control our bankers, because it's in our national interest to avoid unnecessary wars."

"So, what do you mean exactly by control, Mr. President?" asked James Sheffield, Senate Minority Whip. "This may not be the right time to piss off our bankers, when they're the only ones standing between us and the Chinese banks."

"The Chinese bankers, James, just laugh at us when we talk about them as the bad guys. The bad guys are on both sides of the ocean. This is the time to stand between the bad guys and the constituents we represent. This is it. Any vulnerability we may have to pressure from Chinese bankers was created by our bankers, for their leverage. If we don't behave, they'll set the Chinese on us."

"But what is the control mechanism?" Sheffield asked again.

"The mechanism is our authority. Let me back up to where I started, which concerns that authority. On paper it's derived from the people. In practice it's derived from an unelected oligarchy. We each swore an oath to uphold the Constitution, to defend the republic against its enemies, within and without. We have compromised. The compromise is that we never effectively challenge the individuals behind the Fed, privately or in public. We are intimidated, so we don't define those charity-supporting pillars of society as enemies within, even though they have usurped our money supply and our foreign policy. Jackson, Lincoln, Kennedy and four other presidents were shot at or poisoned for kicking them out. In our time, we look the other way and hope to be re-elected—with their money.

"But we age, gentlemen, we age. And the day approaches when the verdict will be pronounced on the time and opportunity we were given and the oath we failed. Each of you has a conscience and the understanding of what it takes to lead. Those who led this country to independence from the Bank of England and King George III faced this binary moment. Either you appease them or you take dominion over them. Each choice has consequences.

"Until 1913, most Presidents and most Congresses resisted the usurper in the private central bank. Then the name was changed to Federal Reserve and the Act was passed in the night. Since then we've avoided the subject. Not today! I'm requiring each of you to remember your oath to the Constitution and your constituents and to lead us out of that Act! I'm asking you to rescind the Federal

Reserve Act of 1913, in careful coordination with my finance team and the Attorney General, while the usurpers are distracted, enjoying Russia's torment."

Silence permeated the room.

"My God, Mr. President," House Minority Leader, Harlen Spicher said, almost in a whisper, "you're taking on something that doesn't need to be taken on, and you'll probably be shot at too."

"Does that probability disturb you, Harlen?" the President asked in a loud voice. "Does it disturb you that no President or Congressman is safe from our financiers? Does that mean we are not in control of our own country? Does that mean there's nothing about Russia's breakup that couldn't happen here a few years from now, because you feel it's safer for you to whisper about them? What's going on Harlen? Are you afraid of them?"

"I would say I am, Mr. President."

"What is wrong with that picture? We cower before unelected bankers who send their minions now and then to remind us about our re-election. They let us tinker with laws we think are important, but not with sovereignty. In their minds they are the sovereigns. No! Not on our watch! You are a unique group of people. We haven't had bipartisan Congressional leadership like this since the Founding Fathers. This plan to regain the sovereignty of the United States would not be possible without you, or the people who elected you. I'm going to hand you copies of my draft for simultaneous bills in the House and the Senate. You'll read the draft in this room. No one leaves until we have consensus."

"Mr. President," the Senate Majority Leader, Anthony Burke, said, "I appreciate what you're trying to propose here, but if we take this thing away from them they will come after each and every one of us for the rest of our lives."

"Anthony, the FBI has anticipated that likelihood and has assets in place, as directed by the Attorney General. In effect, we're going to allow ourselves to be bait. Yes, they will be apoplectic. Their fury and their threats will echo around the world. They will foam and fume about retribution, privately to each of us and in the media. They will counterattack, they'll dump the market, sell the dollar, attempt to start war with Iran. Let them roll. Let them threaten. Fraud and conspiracy against the United States carries time in Federal penitentiaries. The Attorney General has been careful and diligent. The surveillance state they funded is now ours. They lunge at us and they're done."

"So the House and Senate Finance Committees become the new Fed?" asked Chris Freney.

"The way it was meant to be," the President answered. "The Fed has always said the money supply is too complicated for Congress and cannot be politicized by Congress. You're going to prove them wrong."

"How do we value the dollar?" Freney asked.

"We bridge the dollar over to Congressional control at the same value and through the same fiat currency for now. We gradually shift toward an asset-backed dollar like China is trying with the yuan."

"I'm seeing foreign Treasuries holders just freaking, en masse," Freney continued. "If they panic and dump Treasuries, we're the ones that are done. And the bankers will say, 'We told you.'"

"How much of our national debt is owed to the Fed and the big banks?" the President asked. "How much of it was created out of thin air? Is twenty trillion in debt, authorized by previous Congresses, enough to paralyze us into thinking this is too big for us? We won't know exactly until you fully audit the Fed and the FBI completes their investigations. But I can tell you the ballpark figure says about half our national debt will go away when the Fed goes away. That and other assurances about honoring obligations by an asset-backed dollar means those foreign Treasuries holders are not going anywhere."

"Where are the assets to match circulation? I don't think we talk much about what's left in Fort Knox. Is that ballpark number in your draft?" Anthony Burke asked.

"It is," the President answered.

"I doubt national assets will match currency circulation, Mr.

President," House Minority Leader, Harlen Spicher, said, "but set that aside for the moment, because they haven't matched for some time now. There's something else we're not addressing. The root of all evil is the love of money. We're pointing the finger at the dominant few behind the banks, behind the Fed, behind the national debt, and I believe you're sincere, Mr. President, in addressing that concern. But are we all failing to imagine how this corruption could reconstitute itself in less than four years? Are we pointing the finger to divert attention away from ourselves and thinking our successors will have no ambition? Are we kidding ourselves and the public that we see our salaries, benefits and pensions as making us very comfortable over our careers here? We are careerists and we and the banks will reconstitute our entitlement as soon as the dust clears from rescinding the Act.

"I challenge every one of you to a test of sincerity. If you mean what I believe I'm hearing here, you will agree to add two crucial amendments to this bill. One, neither the House nor the Senate may vote to increase our own salaries, benefits or pensions. It would have to be approved by the electorate. Two, all soft money campaign contributions are illegal, and campaigns must be funded only by individuals permanently residing in our constituency. Contributions would be public domain and capped at say, $5,000 per individual. That's it, no more money from anyone or anything. Those two amendments would strangle the beast's attempts to reconstitute itself through the next Congress. If you mean what you say, you add them. If you don't, all this is a passing show."

"Gentlemen," the President said, "Harlen is correct. I would add an amendment which includes the same terms for presidential campaigns. We can't merely stab the beast, we have to kill it now. Chris, you're leader in the House, what say you?"

"Harlen's right," Chris Freney said. "I've spoken about our entitlement thing, but no one who wanted to be competitive could afford to hear it. Everyone's thinking re-election is job one. This frees us up from loving and hating the need for infinite, infinite re-election money. Now is the time, when we're all seeing, if we don't stop this it will never be stopped. We're never going to have another moment in history like this. I say we add both amendments and would ask Harlen to draft them."

"Harlen," the President said, "I'm asking you to handwrite the language on a copy of the draft. Anthony and Maury, look over his shoulder and make your comments, like this is 1776 and we're creating a clean, new page. Then I'm asking each of you to read the complete copy of the printed draft addressing the Act, right now. Mark it up, comment and resolve it. Let's get a consensus on this in two to three hours."

"I'm getting the sense here, Mr. President," Chris Freney said, "that this isn't a normal legislative process you're intending, is it?"

"No. If we delay or leak this, or waver now, the way we age would not be good. There would be no peace for us, alive or dead. Maybe this is what the Founding Fathers felt when they realized opposing the King became succeed or die."

"Mr. President, I never thought I'd see this, ever," Burke said. "How did you know one of us wouldn't walk out of this room and take this plan to the Fed?"

"Trust. I trusted the shift in the awareness of the electorate that brought this unintimidated mix into the House and Senate. And I trust we can get a joint bill out of this draft in the next few hours. I need to talk to the Kremlin soon. Timing is everything, gentlemen."

"Before we get started, Mr. President," Burke said, "you took our phones and watches because you're concerned about security here. I understand that, but there's the matter of security for Congress once this hits."

"The FBI and the Secret Service are addressing that as we speak. You will be briefed before you return to the Hill. In the next few hours, though, you will need to accept a reality. You will be accountable to the people for control of the money supply. That's what your re-election chances and your life will ride on. Gentlemen, let's get on with this."

Over the next three hours, the loyalty of Congressional

Majority and Minority Leaders hung in the balance as the President's draft bill was amended point by point. The amendments were detailed and conditioned on the reality mentioned by the President. The men realized the responsibility they were about to take on. The world's most powerful and resilient economy would be in their hands. The world would watch what they did with it. They were sobered by the irony of their willing participation in a lawful coup by a subject government, reclaiming sovereignty from its creditors and minders.

In the White House, Vicky alternated between time with the children, her own staff, Jon Douglas' staff and time alone in the upstairs chapel. There in the candlelight she petitioned by prayer to expand the common wealth, the national assets that did not match the amount of money in circulation. She read lists of names and a summary of the events at hand, asking for the intercession of the will of God, and trusting.

At the other end of the White House, President Gillis' action list grew longer by the hour as he and his team coordinated with the staff of Congressional leaders. As they worked, the Secret Service called in emergency personnel and positioned uniformed and plain clothes agents at entrances and approaches to the White House, the State Department and Capitol Hill.

In the House of Representatives and the Senate, the members were expecting a draft resolution concerning Russia's security situation and were in full attendance. Instead, the leadership in both houses of Congress introduced a joint bill, with bipartisan sponsorship, for the rescinding of the Federal Reserve Act of 1913. The legislative briefing covered continuity of the market value of the existing fiat currency, to be re-issued as United States Treasury Notes, guaranteed by the government of the United States, replacing the fiat currency of the private Federal Reserve. Debate in both the House and Senate was brisk, but limited in duration by the leadership of both parties. The predisposition of a majority of the members of that unintimidated Congress to a distrust of the major banks had been recently reinforced by news of Wall

Street sales of landmark real estate and large blocks of stock to Chinese banks.

Assuming that numerous high-ranking Federal Reserve board members, foreign central bank officials, and board members and stockholders of major banks in New York, London, Basel and around the world were being informed by phone of what amounted to a coup d'etat in the United States, the leadership of both houses agreed to close debate and called for a vote.

In the White House, Vicky stood with the President and his team watching closed circuit coverage of the vote in the House and the Senate. At the moment the Speaker of the House and the Senate Majority Leader announced their identical bills had passed with substantial majorities, President Gillis went to his desk in the Oval Office and signed a prepared version of the joint bill into law. The official White House cameraman recorded the moment with Vicky standing near the President's desk. A second later another photograph showed the President and the First Lady exchanging sober glances, suggesting a guarded victory.

Simultaneously, the Secretary of State issued instructions to foreign ambassadors and diplomats on behalf of the President. Within minutes phone calls began coming in to the White House, to State and to members of Congress from around the world, demanding clarification and confirmation. As calls came in from key Fed officials and foreign central bankers and their minders, those on the President's team who took the calls followed the Attorney General's instructions to accept all questions, disbelief, sarcasm, threats and ultimatums while the FBI documented each conversation for analysis.

At the same time, all available reporters from the White House press corps were invited into the Oval Office by the Press Secretary to witness the President's address to the nation. For expediency, no prior announcement of the address had been given to cable or television news networks. Without apology, the event moved ahead as planned, with or without chief correspondents. A rehearsed White House video team counted down the seconds to air time. The President watched for his cue, looked directly into the camera and began his address.

"My fellow Americans, it is with great pleasure that I address you today to announce that the Congress of the United States has, by a substantial majority, passed legislation that I have signed into law rescinding the Federal Reserve Act of 1913. This law restores Constitutional authority for the valuing and printing of the nation's money to Congress, as intended by the Founding Fathers. The law will have a significant and beneficial impact on every citizen of the United States and on the economies of many nations of the world.

"During a period exceeding the last one hundred years, a gradual usurpation of the monetary and foreign policies of the United States occurred with knowledge of each Congress and each President of that time. It is with great respect that I acknowledge the courage and insight of President Kennedy to attempt to end this subtle and increasing erosion of the sovereignty of your government. That erosion became more blatant and dominating in recent times until recognized by Congress and this White House as a threat to the freedom of the nation and to yourselves.

"To that end, the government has acted to ensure continuity of the value of the dollar, the honoring of Treasury Bond obligations, predictability of the money supply and a commitment to a gradual process of backing the currency with national assets. During this time of valuation of the United States dollar against international currencies, your government will keep authorities of all major economies informed of our intentions. Such intentions have been measured so as to assure as much predictability as possible and a rapid transition to stability in global commodity and currency markets. All Federal government accounts will be maintained with integrity.

"I have instructed members of the Cabinet to make details of the Administration's policies and regulations under the law available to the press. I trust that Congress will also respond to requests for information from the media.

"In conclusion, I invite the people of the United States to examine the history of our money supply, to compare the subtle and blatant erosion of freedom under a century of inflation and expanding national debt with the restoration of sovereignty that has been won this day. I look forward to a continuation of close cooperation with Congressional leaders, who have engaged their Constitutional duty to manage the nation's currency with integrity and fortitude.

"I thank you for your attention and wish you prosperity and a good night."

The President looked around at the thumbs up from his team. The video crew unplugged the microphones and lights and began to move their equipment out of the center of the Oval Office. Vicky was about to lean toward Robert to hug him when she caught sight of Jon Douglas bringing in Press Secretary Evan Baptiste.

"Mr. President," Douglas began in a low voice. "You've fired the first shot, along with Congress. Evan is telling me that tonight begins a contest for control of the media. They're going to try every form of assassination imaginable, beginning with the idea that rescinding the Act is unconstitutional. Evan?"

"Right, Mr. President. They will attempt to assassinate the concept of independence from the Fed, using every credible surrogate on every media outlet they can. We have to anticipate and counter it with our own surrogates. This is an idea list of people we might want to have ready to appear to defend independence. Do I have authorization to vet this list and to prepare additional lists?"

The President scanned the list, nodded and thanked them both. Vicky left the Oval Office with him and wondered how tenuous the victory might be.

"Are you okay?" she asked him as they walked the hall to the residence wing.

"I'm okay. It's the math that's not okay," he said. "The finance team told me before the broadcast we don't have the national assets to make this work. We jumped anyway. We could be on fiat currency for a long time."

"How long?"

"Beyond this term. But it's the next few weeks I'm dreading. I need to give that list of media surrogates some kind of confidence that we've got this."

Proponents of central bank control of the United States money supply appeared on every cable, radio and television network, blogs and newspaper op eds, relegating regular news reports from Russia, Europe and the Middle East to relative obscurity. The disdain and wrath of the proponents was primarily directed at President Gillis for strong-arming Congress into legislative deal-making over a subject they knew little about. Their ability and that of future Congresses to manage the money supply was consequently laughable and disturbing to serious observers. The drumbeat became louder over the next two weeks.

Then the media onslaught of derision for the President and Congress entered its third week with a new angle of attack, the one President Gillis was dreading. News of the attack came on a cold, rainy Monday morning when Jon Douglas and Evan Baptiste entered the Oval Office together. They preferred to stand. The President stood by the window.

"A new situation, Mr. President," Baptiste began. "A consortium of over three hundred economics professors has issued a signed statement saying the plan to back the dollar with national assets is not feasible. They're saying there's no way to match assets against circulation without collateralizing millions of acres of Federal land in the western states. Nixon did just that through the EPA in the seventies, because a lot of gold had left the country. So the parks and forests have been collateralized against the national debt for over forty years under nine presidents and none of these professors have said anything until now. They're saying Nixon came up with just the idea but that you, sir, are the one who will actually implement it. They're implying that if we default in any way the Chinese will own any national park and any military base they want. It's not accurate, Mr. President but they're claiming it on the talk shows."

"Dammit!" the President said. "The Nixon thing is smack but the math is . . . how do we get around it? This is what I didn't want to hear."

"We need to counter it, Mr. President," Baptiste said.

"With what?"

"Release a Fort Knox audit."

"Most of the gold has gone. Ask the Chinese."

"Then we live with fiat currency for a while, Mr. President."

"Great. We overthrow the Federal Reserve and then we operate just like them."

The President thanked Evan Baptiste for his report and sat for a few moments in silence with Jon Douglas before asking him to leave.

That evening Vicky waited for Robert to come to dinner late in the evening. Concerned by his pale, tired expression she drew him close to her.

"What's going on?" she asked.

"We're in trouble. The FBI says the dark side is organized. Goddamn mafia in high towers. We've got fiat currency for a long time. Bastards are calling me the new Nixon. Really?"

"I read that in some blog from the black lagoon this morning," Vicky said, sighing. "Listen . . . related subject. You're the only one I can talk to about this. Another visit from our friend."

"Mr. Cord?"

"He was praying in the chapel this morning. He was on his knees."

"We're in trouble. Did he say anything?"

"Not much. Six words. At first I didn't understand what he meant, so I wrote it down."

Vicky gave him a handwritten note. It read, "Viever's Summit, Cradle of the Hills."

"Where or what is Viever's Summit?" he asked.

"I looked it up. It's wilderness, an old gold district in the Rockies, in western Montana, surrounded by Forest Service land. It's up there, about nine-thousand feet up."

"What does 'Cradle of the Hills' mean?"

"Call the district geologist at USGS in the morning. Forget the bureaucracy here. Call Montana direct in the morning."

"And say what?"

"Tell the man you're the President and you want to know what's going on."

"Right. Cord appears in our chapel and says 'Viever's Summit,' meaning whatever. Secret Service has no clue he's there. Maybe we need to know more about your Mr. Cord."

Vicky checked with Robert the next morning and found he had called a district geologist for USGS in western Montana. Over the course of a twenty minute conversation with the geologist named Brian Lockyer, the President had authorized funding for new surveys of Federal land near old goldfields in Montana and Idaho, then followed up with the Secretary of the Interior.

Three weeks later, three grim weeks of smearing and ridicule in the blogs, the major newspapers and networks, central bank surrogates began a concerted campaign across the media, calling on a popular opposition party candidate to decisively defeat the President in the next election on grounds of hypocrisy, disastrous judgment and economic failure. Vicky was with Robert for a rare lunch together in the residential wing discussing his limited options in response to the challenge, when his phone buzzed and he took a call from Jon Douglas. Vicky watched his expression change from brooding to disbelief. Then he stood up.

"Oh, my God, Mr. Cord," he said, grinning, as he snapped the phone into his pocket. "Going to Montana, right now. Want to go with me?"

"Why? What's going on in Montana?"

"Remember that geologist, Brian Lockyer? He got that USGS funding I had the Secretary move around. Surveyed a bunch of ridges in the high country, Federal land he knew had gold in it."

"And, so?"

"So he called in all the USGS brass in the western states. They verified Lockyer found high-yield lodes on that summit worth two-thirds of the combined gold bullion and gold reserves in the world. That's the largest gold strike, ever! Cord told you, 'Viever's Summit,' right? It's a ten-square-mile plateau surrounded by higher mountains. 'Cradle of the Hills' was Viever's mine. It was abandoned in 1913, just before Congress enacted the Fed. Massive, thick lodes no one knew about for over for a hundred years. Now we have a dollar! This ain't paper!"

As the significance of the USGS discovery sunk in, Vicky was speechless. A miracle like this was what she had prayed for but hadn't imagined the magnitude. Two-thirds of the world's gold on one mountain top on Federal land. It occurred to her that some kind of veil had covered the summit and made the lodes invisible to prospectors for more than a hundred years, revealed only now when the need was acute.

"His timing, how's the timing," Robert mused. "Thank God it was found. But could it have been a tad sooner, a few months ago, so we weren't dying on the vine?"

Vicky had seen the mystery man, Joshua Cord, on his knees in her chapel and knew the timing must have had an urgency, a logic and an undefined price to it.

"A tad sooner?" she answered. "Things that change the world don't work like that. That gold has been there for millions of years. The Providence that's seen the country through until now wasn't going to let it loose if the people hadn't discerned who was robbing them. It was their test. They passed the test of discernment and the invisible becomes visible."

She caught Robert's hand, leaned for a moment against his shoulder, and could tell he was overwhelmed with relief and adrenaline but still wary.

"Thank God," he whispered into her ear. "Thank God they did it, whatever the timing. People have got to hang onto this. Let's be careful now. Let's be careful."

It became necessary to be careful, perhaps more so than for any modern President, and for good reason. Threats of all kinds appeared daily, including subtle observations offered by formerly

337

trusted friends, news of bizarre shooting sprees by anarchists and mysteriously coordinated protest occupations where the urban unemployed danced around burning effigies of Gillis and Nixon in the decaying parts of the major cities.

But a month later, at Vicky's insistence, the White House hosted a formal celebration for specially selected guests, to confirm to the world that the global economy had not disintegrated but in fact showed signs that other nations would peg their fiat currencies against the asset-backed United States' dollar.

Media commentators continued to observe and report on unexpected trends. Russia's government remained obstinate toward the rest of the world and still censored its news and its people, but it had not fallen. Russian agents had been withdrawn from the Baltics and Ukraine. The Chechen terrorists inside Russia were now without funding or direction. Chinese Internet hacking was counter-hacked and their banks' purchases of U.S. Treasury Bonds picked up. France and Spain were receiving credit again. The price of oil matched demand. The U.S. moved toward energy independence, because it could. Civil wars in the Middle East began to take their toll on those who funded them. A Congressional appraisal and FBI investigation of the Federal Reserve system revealed why the bankers had never wanted an audit. The records showed that trillions of dollars had been created from nothing and assigned as public debt owed to the major banks in various forms of interest and tax obligations by the next five hundred years of taxpayers. Three hundred and fifty-three corporate officers, stockholders and consultants of the Fed and of major New York banks and affiliates were under indictment for a wide range of felony charges. The Federal Reserve system and half of the national debt no longer existed. Congress had taken the strain of managing the nation's money supply for the public good. And even more gold reserves had been discovered, this time in Idaho.

In Washington, D.C., the formal event held at the White House was a special evening, an expression of gratitude and relief for the nation, for the invited press, the appreciative guests, the President

338

and the First Lady and even the Secret Service.

At an appropriate time during the evening, President Gillis was introduced to the gathered guests by Chief of Staff Jon Douglas. The President thanked the guests and made a short speech, in which he asked Vicky to step forward. Each of the carefully screened guests and members of the press had at least some understanding of her contribution at a secular level. All gathered closer to offer a standing ovation for the President and Our Lady.

Vicky looked around at a semi-circle of over a hundred and fifty applauding friends. While offering a silent thank-you, she noticed a familiar, serious young man in a three-piece suit and a violet-colored tie standing near the back of the crowd. It was Joshua Cord, evidently not on the guest list again, a slight smile on his face as he applauded with those around him. Vicky turned to nudge Robert, to whisper to him to look at the man near the back of the guest circle, the one with the violet-colored tie, who had somehow bypassed Secret Service protocols one more time. When Vicky turned to point him out to Robert, the man in the violet tie was no longer in the ballroom. It occurred to her that if he appeared with advice only when the nation was in peril, then it might be a good thing not to see him for many years.

"I'll tell you later," Vicky said when Robert asked who she was looking at.

The next morning on a cable news program, a media commentator who had attended the special event at the White House was asked what the celebration signified, a month after Congress had reclaimed control of the currency.

"I looked at the President standing next to Our Lady," he said to a cable audience of millions, "and I thought, if it's true that power is derived from the people and the people get the leaders they deserve, oh, my God, on this old Earth, what a people!"

MANDATE
OF HEAVEN

China, on the edge of self-inflicted
catastrophe, hurls the right to rebellion
against the right to rule. Who would dare
oppose the onslaught, unarmed,
on behalf of the people?

MANDATE OF HEAVEN

A white, unmarked Learjet 40 turned in heat haze at Beijing International, taxied onto a departure runway and paused. Only two passengers were aboard. Both looked out of cabin windows at the cloak of coal smoke and Mongolian dust enveloping Beijing. Moments passed in silence until the hum of the twin jet engines at the rear of the plane changed to a bass rumble of air induction and turbo whine. Wing flaps angled down then up. A soft bell-tone sounded overhead in the cabin and a voice from the cockpit announced flight departure.

"Mr. Liao, Mr. Wen, this is Captain Hou. We are now cleared to proceed. Please fasten your seatbelts, prepare for takeoff."

The jet lurched free of the brakes, full power surged and both passengers were pressed firmly back into their leather seats. Seconds later the jet lifted up into the dirty sky. Each man looked out of his own window at the gray haze and gripped fingers around their armrests.

A flash of sunlight burst into their eyes as the plane cleared the particulate layer, banked and turned to the southwest, toward the Tibetan plateau.

"Mr. Liao, Mr. Wen," Captain Hou's voice said, "we are on schedule and beginning your flight directly to Kangding in Sichuan province. At your request, we will pass over the provincial capital, Chengdu, on our way to Kangding. The weather in Kangding on arrival this afternoon is expected to be clear and windy, with temperatures just above freezing. Your flight time is estimated at approximately three hours. We are expecting flight turbulence between Chengdu and Kangding and will alert you to conditions before they appear. Please feel free to unbuckle your seatbelts and press the pager for assistance or refreshments."

Wen Hua, the younger of the two men, turned to his employer with concern.

"Mr. Liao, are you alright?"

"No. You breathe that poison every day, Hua," Liao Shen stated, releasing his fingers from the armrests.

"Well," Wen Hua shrugged. "Maintenance tells us the air-conditioning filters it. It's Beijing."

Liao Shen nodded in acknowledgment. Wen Hua's salary and bonuses ensured an uncomplaining answer. Then again, Hua had little interest in life outside Beijing. As a wealthy man, Shen had been able to make the choice years ago to escape the city of his birth. Escape had been made possible by the loyalty and fastidious attention to detail of senior managers such as Wen Hua. Foresight, wise investments, diplomacy and tact in relations with the Party had also helped. Over the course of many years and dozens of carefully chosen acquisitions and mergers with other retail banking chains, headquarters managers like Wen Hua had finessed the legal, financial and government aspects of developing one of China's best private banks. In the process, Shen, as majority shareholder, had become a billionaire, rich enough to attract attention from members of the Central Committee.

Though still a Chinese citizen, Shen had been a legal resident of Switzerland for the last ten years. In effect, he telecommuted via encrypted text with his managers in Beijing from the safety of the Swiss shores of Lake Geneva. Shen's home was near a marina for billionaires, where he lived with his socially popular and accomplished wife, Nien. Life was clean and elegant by the lake. Business matters, adjusted for the Swiss time zone, were always displayed on at least one screen in every room of Shen's mansion, even accessible in a waterproof binnacle next to the chromed helm on his twelve-meter yacht.

344

Relationships with members of the Central Committee in Beijing were managed on separate secure phone lines and required a subtle level of dramatic art. Playing a little dumb helped, including the appearance of memory lapses and other signs of aging. A preoccupation with golf also seemed non-threatening. Patriotic concern was always relevant.

The charade was necessary because Shen understood he was dealing with enemies. They were biding their time in envy while he demonstrated the correlation between tangible assets, generous customer service and profitable banking. Those who maintained constant surveillance on Shen's activities from Beijing had bankrupted the four major state banks of China, manipulated the Shanghai stock market and the state media, and robbed investors of trillions of yuan in order to recapitalize their dead banks.

The capital loaned by Shen's bank worked differently. It was loaned at a discount rate to build tangible, middle-class homes and profitable farms and businesses. His bank was perceived positively by the public. Party officials warned him in private that if Mao were still alive all bankers would be hung or driven to suicide. To Shen, the warnings meant the spirit of Mao was still alive within the Party. So it was prudent for Shen to live far away from Beijing to reduce the impression that he and the Bank of the Blue Lotus, with real assets and 580 popular retail branches across China, were a challenge to covetous committee members.

As the Lear passed over the suburbs of the city Shen turned and nodded thoughtfully at Hua's comment on Beijing and decided to express his gratitude for the man's loyalty, as he often did.

"It's Beijing," he agreed. "The most important city in the world. And because of that, I want to reaffirm how grateful I am to you for the expertise you provide."

Hua smiled and bowed slightly. Shen shifted the conversation to the day's objective in Kangding.

"This afternoon," Shen said, "I want you to do most of the talking after our introductions. Take your time. They need us, we need them. What's the gentleman's name again?"

"Zhao Kong," Hua said, "CEO and Chairman of People's Housing Bank of Sichuan. He's a little above your age, Mr. Liao. You'll remember him and his daughter from New Year at the British Embassy in Hong Kong."

"Thank you, Hua . . . my memory, yes. I didn't remember he had a daughter."

"If I may mention it now," Hua said, "Mr. Zhao and company are, in a sense, small fish, only six branches across Sichuan. My concern is, their asset portfolio is weighted toward agricultural loans. I and other managers consider it overvalued. Some of the loans are uninsured."

Shen gently shook his head and pointed upward to the overhead ventilation and paging controls. A mandatory safety inspection had been imposed on Shen's Lear at Beijing International. He indicated that they should assume their conversation was being recorded.

"Yes," Hua said, "now I see. My best guess is, I may have overlooked some regulatory adjustments for their fourth quarter. I should look at them again."

Hua polished his reading glasses, then returned to the keyboard in chastened silence. Remembering a small chore he had been putting off, Shen took his penknife from a holster on his belt and tightened a loose screw on one of the hinges of his briefcase. He folded the tool set into the knife then turned his attention to the window next to him and looked down on northern China. An unbroken layer of airborne soot and dust stretched to the horizon, thousands of meters below them. It entered the lungs and destinies of hundreds of millions of breathing men, women and children, urban and rural, in a pall that epitomized the unending pain and oppression of entrapment beneath the weight of China's long history. For Shen, to be far away and free of the death that fed daily on his people, to leave them at hard labor, resigned to their fate while he flew back and forth from Switzerland, was to be deaf to their cries. A sense of depression and a great sadness seemed to rise up through the imprisoning smog, as if a grieving national soul was aware that someone was listening. To Shen, the soul of the nation could be sensed, pleading in tears for a fair hearing, "When may we leave? Oh, please hear us, when will it end?"

The Lear flew on at cruising altitude over the cities of Hebei province. There was nothing Shen could do but listen. Survival and its alternative were prospects that applied to him too. He leaned over in his seat to try to catch glimpses of the cities, towns and villages they were passing over. Soon, Shen knew, they would all be changed. His intelligence network, inside banking and government, had told him to anticipate that the fatalism stretching across China was scheduled to change. It would grow worse, far worse. Party cadres and undersecretaries for the Ministries of Finance and Agriculture had been unwitting informants regarding the motives behind the Party's national plan for stability and peace. The far-reaching plan would gradually relocate almost thirty percent of China's people from rural villages to new apartment housing in the cities, for their protection from terrorism. The new official mantra was, "China Wants Peace."

To ensure stability and peace, the Party would coerce a population roughly equivalent to that of the United States out of ancient farming villages and into urban high-rises over the next twelve to fifteen years. The Ministry of Finance had warned the Party to anticipate a serious long-term decline in global trade and national economic growth during that period. For reasons of self-preservation, the Party would act to preempt a nationwide rebellion over declining standards of living.

Shen understood who the enemies of stability and peace were. He gazed down on an old, blood-soaked land that had seen prehistoric clans revolve their animosities and rivalries through many subsequent lives, pointlessly lost, life after life, in famines, epidemics and uncounted rebellions against brutal warlords. How many princes of walled city-states had destroyed each other and China's people, armed and unarmed, over mere insults? The cycles of imperial dynasties had risen and fallen on the blood and agony of men, women and children. The repetition of millions of mortal

347

errors over so much time were etched as layers of trauma in China's national subconscious memory.

To hundreds of millions of victims of the Great Leap Forward and the Cultural Revolution the traumas were still vivid, as conscious memory. The nation's collective recollections and fears of terror were the levers behind the appalling logic of the coming Great Relocation. The people wanted to be protected from violent rebel elements. The People's Liberation Army would be assigned to stand guard in the most dangerous provinces. How the Central Committee would pace such a massive rural-urban resettlement and the methods used for coercion were apparently still being planned. If no one outside China were allowed to watch, how would the Party deal with resistance?

A silver-haired reflection in the cabin window stared back at Shen, offering no answers. Age, he thought, surely had compensations. He no longer felt compelled by conscience to take up arms against his enemies. He almost laughed aloud at the thought that any citizen would seriously resist the Party when informed of their vital place in the plan. Shen had already been informed that a place had been found for him and that he was highly valued by the Party. His value would be revealed by undersecretaries from the Ministry of Agriculture during the visit to Kangding, following his acquisition meeting with Zhao Hong. Representatives from the Ministry would arrive at Kangding airport just before him and a photo session was scheduled to be held on the tarmac. The timing and alpine setting at Kangding airport was the Ministry's choice.

The revelation of Shen's value to the Ministry would be nationally publicized. One year earlier, in Geneva, Shen had received diplomatic visitors from Beijing, state agricultural bank officials and Ministerial representatives at his head office. At first he resisted their appeals to his patriotism. But when they grew impatient and the appeals became veiled threats against his growing bank network across China Shen had no choice but to respond with grace and ask how he could assist his country.

The assistance the Party needed had to do with Shen's

extensive holdings in state-of-the-art alpine and sub-alpine beef and dairy companies in Switzerland. It also had to do with his wealth, the popular name-recognition of his bank and the probability that he could be motivated to keep Party secrets. The Party planned to feed its urban population of more than one billion by converting ancient irrigated farmlands and underused subalpine uplands into vast state-controlled agribusiness corporations. Shen would become a propaganda hero and allowed to develop high-tech beef and dairy farms on state land at his own expense. His successful techniques would be copied, his plane would crash one day on its way to Switzerland, and his farms and banks would be nationalized.

While Shen was willing to hear the cries of the hopeless coming from the towns below, there was no one to hear his cries. He was aware he had taken an involuntary one-way ride that by his estimate would end within three years. Soon, he would need to give his wife, Nien, a comfortable new identity and home elsewhere, before the incident. Their married daughter in Monaco would also receive a similar accommodation. Their unmarried daughter, an economics professor in Beijing, would fly out of China on a planned vacation and never come back.

As the Lear flew on, over Shaanxi province now, Shen looked over at Hua and noticed he was asleep, still holding his laptop. As loyal and competent as Hua was, Shen saw no gain in making him aware of matters outside the bank's interests in mergers and acquisitions. Hua would likely be confused and afraid and might find it difficult to remain discrete. China's past, its future and any form of resistance against the Party apparently held no interest for Hua. This was also true for all of Shen's upper management, whom he had recruited for excellence in finance and customer service, not political or personal survival.

The late afternoon meeting in Kangding with Zhao Kong of People's Household Bank would mostly be Hua's show. Terms of the acquisition had already been arranged, with the exception of the matter of rebranding PHB. Hua saw great brand-recognition benefits in investing in a full aesthetics conversion of acquired banks, making them appear as brand new buildings with the Bank of the Blue Lotus' contemporary Scandinavian look, inside and out. However, Hua seemed unaware of the envy held by Party officials toward the bank.

That evening there would be a formal dinner with Mr. Zhao and his management after the meeting. Shen knew the PHB managers' eyes would be on him all night, wondering whether they would keep their jobs. Some would not. Tonight, Shen thought, and in the coming weeks, he would delegate those decisions to Hua.

More pressing was the issue of Shen's mental and emotional preparation for the next day's meeting with the Ministry of Agriculture. Hua would be excluded. At that meeting, state land in upland Sichuan and Yunnan provinces would likely be offered to Shen, with short strings attached. He would receive instructions: Create mass-production beef and dairy farms quickly on under-used hills and mountains in the southwest provinces. The Party would be careful in the way it publicized its preparations for national sufficiency. By Shen's estimate, the minimum time needed to meet these instructions, if no expense were spared, was three years. It meant the Party was just three years away from announcing the patriotic benefits of the Great Relocation. That they would use him to the fullest extent was clear. That his tragic death in a plane crash, just over three years from now, would lead the news was also predictable. There was nothing good he could do in the next year but save his family.

Shen pressed his head against the cabin window and concentrated. Across the aisle Hua remained asleep. Now, during flight time, Shen urged his mind, think through every move the Party can and will make. No vulnerabilities in the Central Committee's planning came to mind. He knew the Party's core goal was to checkmate all future resistance within China. From every angle he looked at it their strategy had no logical flaws. They fully intended to break the cyclical nature of China's history.

Without exception, members of the Central Committee and high-ranking Party officials understood the historical circumstances of the rise of the Nationalists and the Communists a hundred years earlier. Both armed resistance movements were made possible by the decline and weakness of the Qing dynasty, humiliated by foreign invaders. The seeds of both movements came from Marxist socialism and Utopian anarchism. A long tradition of peasant uprisings over the preceding two thousand years allowed abundant precedent for armed dissent. But the naïve idealism of the anarchists and Marxist intellectuals was brutally betrayed and subsumed by the authoritarian Bolsheviks from Russia in the 1920s. Mao's capricious interpretation of Stalin's genocidal rule provided the antidote for China's weakness. Power came out of the barrel of a gun. Nothing less than feudal ruthlessness had sufficed to unify China under Mao.

In discussions with Party officials over the previous ten years Shen had discovered they not only understood the last century but the imperial millennia preceding it. Each imperial dynasty had never been considered to be everlasting but subject to a dread, amorphous concept known as the Mandate of Heaven. The new emperor and his family assumed power by armed conquest of the previous dynasty. Power was retained under the Right to Rule, a mandate for the emperor, believed by the people to be ordained from heaven. The dynasty could continue for hundreds of years under its heavenly mandate. If the emperor erred and allowed invasion, over-taxation, flood, famine or epidemic, the afflicted people took up their equivalent right, the Right to Rebellion. If heaven supported the emperor, the Right to Rebellion would be crushed by the Right to Rule, and the rebels, afflicted or not, would all die. If heaven withdrew the emperor's mandate, he and his family would be slaughtered and the Right to Rebellion would provide one or more candidates for the beginning of a new dynasty, or for a period of civil war. Thus, a merciless, binary dynamism had prevailed in the cycles of China's long history.

Shen had concluded a year earlier that the Party's strategy was to own and control the entire wheel of future history, both halves, the Right to Rule as well as the Right to Rebellion. The first half of the wheel had been firmly established under Mao and the subsequent surveillance state, secured by the Party's power-elite. The second half, the co-opted Right to Rebellion, was already under construction.

Whenever he spent time in China, Shen quietly accumulated intelligence from government, banking and police informants suggesting long-term rural dissent against the Party had aggregated across China into an organized underground movement. The free-wheeling urban groups were mainly comprised of angry, unemployed migrants from rural areas. They were estimated to number in the tens of millions. These were the young peasants who had come to build the government-funded sea of urban high-rises and factories in the cities. Now there was an oversupply of housing, reduced government financing and little new work. Those tens of millions had stopped sending money back to their rural villages. Under the allure of the cities, they no longer wanted to go back to work on their parents' farms. They formed a hidden rural and urban underclass with dangerous revolutionary potential, led by the ultra-left. They were likely to resist the Great Relocation.

The middle class, robbed of their retirement investments by a government-manipulated market, were now also antagonistic to the Party. To many of these hundreds of millions, the Party had forfeited the Right to Rule and the Right to Rebellion would soon be invoked. All it needed was organization, to channel and coordinate the mass anger.

The Party had been willing to assist. Central Committee members knew the profile of the leaders of the ultra-left. Furious young socialists and anarchists had imagined they could debate in secret since the death of Mao. They railed against the theft of power and wealth by the ruling elite. The Party had listened in on their anti-authoritarian speeches, in which the socialists fumed at the governing elites who appropriated state assets for private ownership. The Party's surveillance police had recorded decades of

intellectuals' demands for the state to be democratically accountable to the proletariat. To allow these intellectuals to inflame
tens of millions of discontented and transient men, as the Great
Relocation moved forward, would be to invite the dissolution of
the state and the death of the Communist Party.

A month earlier, Shen had received encrypted accounts from
sources close to the ultra-left. His informant network included
finance undergraduates who had interned with the bank then
infiltrated underground socialist groups. Interns at three university
campuses described muted comments by young radicals in Beijing,
Shanghai and Chengdu about a subversive, dissident leader, a
radical former university professor from democratic Hong Kong.
They called him Professor Yuen Qiang, apparently a compelling
orator who spoke with quiet intensity. Those who had met him
said he was fervently anti-Mao and anti-capitalist. This Yuen
had named Mao and his authoritarian successors as murderers,
thieves and betrayers of the proletariat. He told his listeners not
to repeat his name but to independently form a new Red Guard
in their city, as their part of a hidden national movement. The
movement's name was simply "the revolution," with an agenda for
simultaneous uprisings, targeting military armories in all cities.
The question moving across the underground grapevine was,
"When?" The question for Shen was, "How do unarmed mobs take
locked and guarded armories?"

One of the Bank of the Blue Lotus' branch managers in Hong
Kong had responded to Shen with information regarding a fellow banker, known in Hong Kong as Zhang Jian. Mr. Zhang, it
was suspected, was a Central Committee plant in the Hong Kong
democratic movement and banking profession. Hong Kong bankers had their own counter-espionage apparatus. It was possible, by
inference of timed absences, that the banker Zhang Jian and the
ultra-left radical Yuen Qiang were the same individual.

In the following weeks, rumors of secret meetings between
Yuen Qiang and socialist leaders had surfaced at universities in
dozens of China's largest cities, as well as rural villages in Sichuan,

Hunan and Shaanxi. If it were true, the Party could be setting up the Right to Rebellion, luring tens of millions of intellectuals and the unemployed into a massive purge, in imitation of Mao. Shen could see why the Party would assert its Right to Rule under its own mandate. There could be no place for millions of active young dissenters in the dense, high-security mega-cities of an unending dynasty. It appeared the Party had determined to shape the future of China by voiding the Mandate of Heaven.

As Shen gazed down on rural Sichuan, he reviewed the extent of the Party's control over every institution that could possibly offer rebellion. The Party's dominance seemed complete. There was no effective way to contest control of government, media, finance, agriculture or the military. No foreign power would intervene or even know the extent of the democide to come. And he, Liao Shen, would, for a short while, help facilitate it.

The air turbulence predicted by the plane's captain began as they approached Chengdu, capital of Sichuan. The shaking and jolting woke Hua and he groaned as he looked out the window on his side of the aisle.

"Must be Chengdu," Hua said. "Air looks clearer down there."

Shen took in the vast expanse of metropolitan Chengdu from his side of the plane. He knew the city was ancient, well over two thousand years old, on a fertile plain that had seen Mongol invasions, the rise and fall of dynasties, monstrous warlords, civil wars and horror on a repetitive basis. It had also seen the mundane lives of millions pass through time in their rice fields, shops and simple homes. At the moment, the city and counties around the metro area accounted for over fourteen million men, women and children. But Chengdu would undergo great change soon as the province began the near emptying of the ancient farming villages and their replacement with the systematic installation of high productivity agribusiness.

"Are you ready, Hua?" Shen asked, as he turned and looked at his acquisitions expert.

"Yes, I think so," Hua replied, struggling to sit up straight in his seat. "I don't know why I'm a little nervous. Perhaps because we're so far from Beijing. Might as well be Tibet."

"Who will meet us?"

"Zhao Kong and his board of directors will be introduced on a red carpet on the tarmac, or in a rented hangar if it's raining," Hua said, checking his screen. "Mr. Zhao will provide a limousine for us and we will be escorted to his offices in the banking district in the newer part of the city."

Shen nodded his approval. He had not yet told Hua that official representatives from the Ministry of Agriculture could also be meeting them at the airport. They would probably be aware of Zhao Kong's entourage and may assert pre-eminence. The protocol provided in Ministry emails for the airport photo session had been strangely vague. Mr. Zhao could be placed in the position of having to defer to the Ministry officials. Hua would be informed at that time that other business, not involving him, would be conducted the following day in Kangding.

Uneasy at the Ministry's unusual lapse in etiquette Shen turned back to the window, noting his view of the green, densely populated plain around Chengdu was rapidly being replaced by rocky foothills, followed by the Qionglai Shan, Daxue Shan and Shaluli Shan mountain ranges. The long stark lines of snowcapped ranges ran north-south and marked the beginning of the Tibetan plateau. Kangding could not be far off.

Moments later, the captain's voice warned them to prepare for their descent into Kangding. As Shen buckled his seatbelt, the captain told them it would be cold, clear and windy in the city and that the airport was situated well over four thousand meters above sea level.

The Lear circled over Kangding to align with the assigned runway. Shen saw the city had grown as a ribbon, stretched out along a steep mountain valley, densely packed on both sides of a white-water river. Coming around into the turbulent wind, the Lear swayed left and right, powering down into the bleak mountain valley. Moments later, the wheels touched concrete.

The plane taxied toward a row of closed hangars and stopped on the tarmac. The co-pilot opened the passenger door and Hua stepped out first, into a fierce gust of cold wind. Halfway down the steps, he paused and looked around.

"There's no one here," he called back to Shen, still at the top of the stairway. "No cars, no carpet, no one. Our arrival time and location are correct."

Shen looked at the empty tarmac, closed hangars and the distant terminal for commercial flights. For an airport serving a city of a hundred thousand people, it was quiet. He was about to go back up the steps when Captain Hou appeared in the doorway above them.

"Someone coming," the captain shouted into the wind, pointing toward the commercial terminal.

A man in a flapping black coat was running toward them, all the way from the terminal. As he got closer, Shen could see that he was a younger man and probably not from the Ministry of Agriculture. The black-coated man arrived at the foot of the steps, clearly anxious and out of breath.

"Mr Liao!" he called out. "Mr. Liao. Sir . . . on behalf of the People's Household Bank . . . I have been asked to apologize . . . for the absence of the trustees, shareholders and all who were to be here to welcome you. Mr. Zhao has been arrested."

Shen pushed past Hua and met the young man at the bottom of the steps. He clasped the frightened man's hands and spoke calmly.

"Thank you for informing us. Why was Mr. Zhao arrested?"

"We don't know. We couldn't hear what the police said. Then he was gone."

"How can we assist?" Shen asked. "Is anyone from Mr. Zhao's family here?"

"Yes, sir. Mr. Zhao's daughter and four of the trustees are with airport security inside the terminal."

"Take us to them," Shen said, walking briskly. "Are they under arrest too?"

"No. The security officers don't know why they were told to escort us."

"Are there any government officials in the terminal, from Beijing?"

"I don't know, sir."

Airport security officers waved Shen, Hua and the young man into the terminal building toward a well-dressed group in the corner of a wide lounge area. An elegant lady with large clear eyes strode toward Shen, accompanied by four older men. Wearing high heels, an immaculate white business suit and flawless make-up, the lady had the very proper persona of an unmarried, consummate professional.

"Good afternoon, Mr. Liao," the lady said, standing in front of the dark-suited men. "I am Zhao Mei. My father deeply regrets this unexpected situation. We have no understanding as to why he has been detained. There have been no injunctions issued against People's Household Bank or any of its trustees."

"Thank you for meeting us," Shen said, shaking her hand and wondering if, under all that high couture, she was fifty or thirty. He looked into her eyes as he spoke. "I am sorry that such a concern has fallen on your father. I would imagine, then, that this is a situation best handled by the attorneys. Would you agree?"

"Yes, of course, Mr. Liao. Please call me Mei. I am general manager of the bank and authorized to speak on behalf of the trustees. May we offer you more suitable hospitality than an airport lounge?"

Shen agreed, trying to size her up as an adversarial or conciliatory negotiator. He looked around for any sign of the delegation from Agriculture.

"Ms. Zhao, before we go anywhere, would you excuse me for a moment?"

The head of airport security had not heard of any scheduled visit by officials from Beijing. Shen pondered sending a text to an undersecretary at the Ministry of Agriculture and decided to hold off, on the grounds that they, not he, had embarrassed themselves by their absence.

With apologies for the windy conditions outside the terminal, Zhao Mei had her driver take Shen, Hua and the trustees in convoy to the PHB branch office in the Kangding banking district. The road wound around mountain bends before entering the newer part of the city. As they slowed with city traffic, Shen noted one or two people in line at the sheltered ATMs outside three of the formerly bankrupt state banks, the Agricultural Bank of China, the China Construction Bank and the Postal Savings Bank of China. Hua sat upright and silent in the back seat next to Shen, clearly out of his element. But Shen leaned forward, toward the front seat, wanting to know more about the circumstances leading to the arrest of Mei's father.

"Ms. Zhao, may I ask if your father had the opportunity to say anything to you?"

"All he could say was, 'no reason, just proceed. Please proceed.' And then they took him."

"I'm not sure if we can proceed," Shen said, glancing up at the windswept mountain slopes on either side of the road.

"If that becomes clear," Mei replied, "the least we can do is offer our hospitality. There's been no change in the terms, from our perspective."

Zhao Mei, Shen observed, was being stalwart and gracious, rather than adversarial, considering the implications of what had happened to her father. There was also the probability that if the acquisition of PHB by the Bank of the Blue Lotus did not occur soon, her credit-strapped bank would soon be acquired by one of the Party's state banks, at harsh terms the trustees would wish to avoid. That probability appeared greater if certain Party officials in Beijing had placed surveillance attention on the PHB acquisition meeting. Most Party officials had a history of appropriating assets from the four major state banks. That they would attempt such a blatant act of intimidation after requesting his assistance was so unpalatable to Shen he wanted to dismiss the thought immediately. But it lingered.

When the PHB vehicles pulled into the executive parking lot behind their Kangding branch, Shen noticed Hua sizing it up for renovation. Hua's architectural and branding interest gave Shen hope that at least his acquisitions manager had not given up. He would ask Hua to reread the prearranged terms in conference and to proceed, if possible.

With Zhao Mei leading, they entered the bland, traditional, two-level bank building. Deferring to Hua as they walked, Shen pondered the leverage he may yet have with the Ministry of Agriculture, as the means to prevent the Ministry of Finance from further interference with the Bank of the Blue Lotus. Deep in thought, Shen almost bumped into a slender hostess in a traditional white gown, standing to one side of the lobby. He glanced into her eyes, realizing how absent-minded he had been, stepping so close to the bank's greeter. He knew greeters remained a tradition in rural banks.

"Excuse me, ma'am," he said, noticing her eyes were penetrating but comforting, as if the greeter already knew what had happened at the airport. He paused with a brief smile for her and felt a slight tug on his suit sleeve. It was Zhao Mei.

"Kuan Yin," she said, gesturing to the statue, a wondering look on her face. "A bodhisattva, known for mercy and compassion."

"Yes," Shen answered, embarrassed, as he realized his mistake. "Of course, beautiful."

"Shall we proceed?" Mei asked, courteously. "The stairway for the office level is to the right."

Hua stood to Shen's right as they were positioned around a conference table in the branch's boardroom. Formal introductions were made to the now six trustees. Zhao Mei turned to Shen and invited him to be seated.

"Mr. Liao, in consideration of the unforeseen events of the day, People's Household Bank would understand if you wished to withdraw your terms of acquisition."

"We wish to proceed," Shen answered, "subject to the unforeseen becoming an obstacle to law."

359

But as Shen was speaking, a PHB security officer was ushered into the room by another officer and bent over next to Zhao Mei's ear. She stood up suddenly and began to speak.

"Gentlemen, we . . ."

Her voice was drowned out by a strange rattling of the upper level windows and a shrieking sound in the heater vents. A split second later, a massive explosion several blocks away brought everyone to their feet. The trustees rushed to the windows to see what had happened. Debris smashed through the glass, shattering most of the windows and sending everyone to the floor for cover.

Shen crawled on his knees, close enough to the broken windows to see the scene outside. A pall of black and gray smoke billowed down the street past the rear entrance to the bank. Out of the dark smoke, he saw dozens of young men running down the middle of the street, shouting. In disbelief, he looked down at the running men just long enough to realize that they were armed with semi-automatic rifles. They were not uniformed and probably had something to do with the explosion.

"Out of the bank!" Zhao Mei shouted, from the center of the room. "Ground floor, west door, into the alley, go into the shoemaker's. Quick!"

"Do you have a safe room?" Shen called out to her as they ran to the stairs.

"It wouldn't be safe!" she called back, then turned to the trustees wavering halfway down the stairs. "Go, go!"

From somewhere outside, they heard the cracking of AK-47s over continuous screaming and shouting. Mei pushed some of the slower men down the stairs and toward the west door. Hua was among those who reached the west door, opened it and rushed outside. As he ran, Shen could hear one of the trustees directing the others to the shoemaker's door out in the alley. But the shouting and yelling of young men was suddenly much closer, in the alley itself, followed by volleys of automatic rifle fire. The steel door to the exterior slammed closed with an echoing clang. Shen saw Mei was about to open the steel door again and dragged her

360

backward by her arm.

"Don't go out!" he said. "The roof. How do we get up on the roof?"

Mei turned and ran across the public lobby, past the closed tellers' stalls and into a staff dining area. She pointed to a square access panel up in the ceiling.

"Up there," she said, urgently. "No ladder. Grab the table."

Shen helped her lift a dining table on top of another one, climbed onto it and pushed up on the ceiling panel. It slid away and he hauled himself up into an air-conditioning maintenance cube. He turned round in the tight space and reached down to lift her up. As Mei gripped his hand, she kicked at the top table and knocked it sideways down onto the floor.

"Where now?" Shen asked, as he replaced the ceiling panel over the only available light.

"That way," she said, pointing into the dark behind Shen.

The unlit way to the roof followed a narrow catwalk next to the ducting. Mei picked up an unused padlock from a shelf as Shen opened the door to a flat part of the roof. Shielding his eyes from the sudden glare of daylight, he glanced at the rooftop heating and air-conditioning fixtures while Mei padlocked the door from the outside. A shattering, awful series of gunshots and panicked screaming came up from the street below.

"That won't hold them for more than a minute," Mei said, snapping the padlock. She paused to listen to the horror on the streets below. "Who are they?"

"Stay low," Shen said, pulling her down. "Crawl. Over there. We wait them out."

But seconds later, waiting on the only flat section of the roof was no longer an option. Whiffs of smoke and then clouds of smoke rose up from the gable-roofed south and east sides of the building. Whoever the young men were, they had set the bank building on fire beneath them. Police sirens could be heard now, coming from three directions.

Shen crawled to the flat, west side of the roof and lay prone

361

near the edge, looking down two levels to the alley. He recognized Hua's bloody body immediately, crumpled among six lifeless PHB trustees in the middle of the alley. The impulse to cry out had to be checked. Forehead resting on the rough surface of the roof Shen took several deep breaths, knowing they had to get off the roof, down to where Hua lay, or be burned to death.

The sounds of automatic rifle fire and shouting now came from the blocks to the west, joined by police sirens and rapid exchanges of fire. Another concussion wave, followed immediately by a jarring blast, came from somewhere in the banking district, wherever the terrorists had been screaming at each other. Pieces of concrete and steel shrapnel arced into the clear sky. The roof of the bank and anyone on it was vulnerable.

With nowhere to hide except the lee side of the rooftop air-conditioning units, Shen gestured to Mei to press against the ducting. Hot debris slashed into the thin metal boxes with a staccato din, crushing some sections flat. Larger pieces of debris penetrated the roof itself. Concrete chunks and pieces of metal and glass bounced in all directions in a cloud of dust and smoke. Mei screamed and turned in circles on her knees until Shen dragged her down and placed a hand over her mouth. A moment later, the wind blew the smoke and dust into the next block, and Shen took his hand away.

"Keep low and quiet," he said, looking to see if she had been hit. Smoke poured up through the holes in the roof. "You're okay. Only dust and smoke. We can't stay up here."

He looked around for the rails of a fire escape. There were none. To the northwest, another wide plume of black smoke spread over the outskirts of the city. Whoever the terrorists were, they were organized and were moving according to a plan. He gestured to Mei to stay where she was while he crawled between pieces of debris to the roof's edge. Mei had not seen what was left of her senior management in the alley. She would have to deal with it. There was no other way to the ground.

But seven meters below Shen, as he looked over the edge, he

realized he had no way to avoid the sight of Hua's blank open eyes. How would he lower himself to the ground, then walk past a loyal employee, lying in his own blood, and leave him in an alley so far from Beijing? Keep quiet, he told his aggravated mind. He turned and waved Mei to slide toward him.

Mei crawled in tears to the edge of the roof, squeezing next to Shen. Her crying ceased suddenly as she looked down, gasped and turned away. Shen realized this sight was more than she was capable of handling. He had seen death in army accidents as a young conscript. Mei had apparently groomed herself all her life for the world of high finance, high fashion, aerobics and nothing else. She had no point of reference outside the sheltered life of the new upper class. Her perfect make-up and pure white power suit with its imperial collar were disintegrating by the moment.

"What did we do to deserve this?" she said in a whisper to herself, unconsciously pushing her once-jeweled-up hair away from her face. "Insane, gone all insane."

"Mei, listen. When we get down there, where can we hide?" Shen asked, trying to keep her mind on what had to be done, instead of what could not be undone.

"We can't be seen on the street," she said, her voice cracking as she looked down, gesturing. "I've seen workmen lift the storm sewer lid, behind the truck. But we can't get down."

Shen crawled back to the center of the roof, next to the battered cluster of air-conditioning units. Tucked under one of the units was a dust-covered coil of white electrical wiring. Rolling onto his side he unwound it to check its length. It was too short to tie around the ducts and still reach the ground. As he searched for more wiring, the smoke from the building, now alight under them, curled over the south edge and engulfed him.

Dragging himself away from the smoke to the west edge of the roof, Shen paused and listened to the street fighting below. Instead of more police sirens and more firing, there was less. If it meant what he thought it did, there might be no safe way out of Kangding.

All he could do was pull the coil toward Mei and begin to split the wiring into two strands with his pen knife. He gave one strand to Mei and kept tension on the other as he cut the vinyl coating. Within a minute he had doubled the length of wire, knotted them together and secured one end around a duct unit. The difficult part came in instructing Mei how to wrap the wire around her waist and thighs. She baulked as she looked down.

"I'll fall!" she cried. "How will this hold me up?"

"A few minutes from now, this roof will be too hot to touch," he said. "We won't be able to breathe. Then the roof will collapse underneath us. Slide backward on your tummy to the edge, get your feet out in the air, keep your eyes closed and do what I tell you."

Before she took the tension on the wire, a third large explosion, this time from nearby, hurled fire and fragments into the sky. They felt the concussion, but the mountain wind caught much of the blast and lofted it away from the roof. Lighter debris and dust peppered them. Staying flat, Shen scanned the streets below for gunmen. He tightened the strain on the wiring looped around an air-conditioning unit and his own waist. Mei remained prone in her makeshift harness, her face covered with dust and her feet out over the alley.

"Now, time to go, nice and quiet," he said, and pressing his feet against her padded shoulders gradually shoved her off the edge of the roof.

Out in mid-air, high above the alley, Mei let out a plaintive scream and then another as her bare feet swung into contact with the brick wall on the second level.

"Eyes closed," Shen rasped over the edge. "Now walk backwards down to the ground."

She hesitated, not understanding what he meant.

"Pull tight on the wire, feet on the wall, lean out and walk backwards!" he commanded.

Slower than an infant's first steps, Mei gradually worked her way to street level as Shen played out the wiring. If anyone with an AK came into the alley, they would both die quickly. When Shen saw her bent over on her knees in the alley, facing away from the bodies, he called down to her to untie the knot in the harness. Seconds passed as she hunched over on the dirty asphalt and fumbled with the knot. Behind Shen streaks of fire shot up out the holes in the roof and smoke swirled around him.

The air-conditioning unit was hidden in smoke and hot to touch as Shen held his breath and knotted the wiring around it. It was possible the wiring would melt before he reached the ground. Within seconds he slid over the edge of the roof and strode backward down two levels, letting out the wiring coiled around his waist as fast as he could.

At street level, Shen put his arms around Mei, who was shaking and sobbing, and lifted her to her feet. They were an arm's length from the blood-stained bodies of loyal, decent men who deserved better than death in an alley.

"Don't look, don't look," Shen said, guiding her away. "Nothing we can do except move."

The truck near the sewer vent was pockmarked with debris damage. Its canvas canopy over the rear had collapsed. Shen stood on the rear tires, lifted the canvas and grabbed a short length of rebar from the jumble of equipment inside. At the sewer vent he levered the steel plate up and lowered himself into the dark void. Mei dropped down next to him and the steel plate was dragged back into place. In the dark they could hear each other's loud breathing and the echoing trickle of water beneath their feet. The world of death and explosions outside now seemed surreal. The blackness and the near silence caught up with Mei.

"What happened, what happened?" Mei asked, breathing in sobs and gripping Shen's shoulders. "What are we doing? Why are we here? We were in a conference room."

"We're deciding which way we need to go," Shen answered. "Think of the layout of the streets and point in the direction of the mountains, away from the river."

"That way," she said, still trying to catch her breath.

Shen opened his phone, enabled the flashlight and crouching

down guided her into the sewer water running up to their ankles. After a moment she stopped.

"Mr. Liao, my mind wants to leave my body. I don't think I want to go very far in this. I have to crawl."

Half a kilometer of crouching and crawling in cold, dark water was too much for Mei, and she collapsed on a concrete bench in a wider part of the echoing tunnel. Shen sat next to her and wondered whether they should shelter in place for the night. But he could see she was exhausted, in shock and would not survive for long on cold concrete.

"We have to keep going," he said. "Wait here, catch your breath. There's a way out, somewhere."

"A way out? To what? You saw them. That wasn't a rabble. We're in a revolution, here in Kangding. It's anarchy and murder. Where are the police, the army?"

Shen did not dare say what he suspected, that it was possible this was China-wide, a calibrated setting up of the urban ultra-left and angry rural poor, designed to cull millions of rebels and their leaders before the Great Relocation to the cities. It was anarchy and murder, reinvigorated in Mao's image. Mei reacted to his silence.

"You don't know! How long does a revolution last?" she said, raising her hands. "How long did Mao's last? Decades. Is that what's out there?"

"I'll be back soon," Shen said, tapping her on the shoulder.

But the tunnel stretched on in the dark with no concrete benches for Mei to rest on. Shen used the phone-light sparingly, sloshing along, hearing only the noise of the water and his own heavy breathing. He realized he, too, was close to exhaustion.

When the tunnel came to a Y, Shen found he had taken the wrong fork into a tunnel receiving dozens of lateral feeder pipes from the streets above. He backtracked, took the other fork and kept going until the tunnel ended at a steel grate. A cold wind blew in through the grate. Outside it was dusk, and he could see the shapes of bushes on a steep hillside. The grate was secured by five bolts. If the pliers in his penknife could not loosen the bolts, Mei would probably be unwilling to crawl back to the alley.

Holding the phone-light in his teeth, Shen braced himself against the tunnel wall and patiently wrenched the nuts off the bolts. The grate would not budge until he kicked it hard. It rolled out into an overgrown ditch and clanged against the rocks under the weeds. He paused, waiting to see if anyone was there, then crawled out into the ditch and slowly stood up.

He had crawled a long way. The tunnel exited into a storm-water ditch on the outskirts of the newer part of Kangding. A road under repair ran parallel with the ditch. No one was around, and he could see a construction workers' trailer on a worksite by the road.

Inside the darkened trailer, Shen found a thermos of cold coffee and a box of salt crackers. The trailer was nothing more than a basic work shed on wheels but better shelter than a sewer tunnel.

Fifteen minutes later, he found Mei and offered her the coffee and crackers.

"There's a shed out there that's better than staying here. Eat these and we'll go."

Mei did not protest but moved slowly on her knees through the cold water, meter by meter, until she saw the night sky outside and slid on her side against the tunnel.

"Come on," Shen said. "Give me your hands."

Mei's legs had stiffened and she could barely move. Shen lifted her arm around his shoulder and half-dragged her a hundred meters to the steps of the trailer. Mountain wind tore at Mei's cold, wet business suit with an alpine bite. Her whimpers of pain told Shen she would succumb to exposure during the night if he didn't act quickly.

Inside the dark construction trailer, Mei fell heavily to the mud-tracked floor and stayed where she fell. Above her, Shen found a workman's duffel bag on a shelf and propped it behind her head.

"I'll find dry clothes for you," he said. "You can't sleep like that."

Mei said nothing, barely moving. At the back of the trailer Shen found an assortment of workmen's coveralls and protective gear and offered her several selections in a crate.

"You've got to do this yourself. You can't give up. Sit up now."

Shen changed into a safety-orange winter shirt and coveralls in the office at the back of the trailer and shoved his soaked three-piece suit and tie out of sight under a wooden bench. He was moving forward to see how Mei was faring when he saw headlights reflecting off the white vinyl ceiling. Mei stood up in an oil-stained sweatshirt, grimy, oversize tan coveralls and looked toward the headlights. Shen handed her a workman's used socks and boots as he walked to a window.

"Look at this, at last." he said. "It's the army! That looks like an army truck to me! Maybe it's about time they turned up."

"Wait, wait," Mei said. "Are you sure? Can you see a uniform on that driver? On anyone?"

Shen froze before the window, staring, not breathing.

"Out of here, quick," he said, pulling her toward the door, boots and socks still in her hand.

They staggered down the steps of the trailer and into the cover of tall weeds ten meters away in the storm-water ditch. Voices came from the direction of the army truck. Flashlights scanned the trailer and two more army trucks arrived, bringing more anarchists.

"Go," Shen whispered, pointing Mei away from the trailer, through a construction equipment dump on the sides of the ditch and on, further into the dark.

At the bottom of the ditch, they were below the spread of approaching flashlights but could hear men's shouts coming from the construction site. Shen held onto one of the tall weeds and motioned to Mei not to give their position away. Mei nodded and they crawled out of range of the arcing flashlights. A hundred meters on, around a bend in the drainage ditch, Mei fell into the weeds on the side, breathing heavily.

"Where . . . are they coming after us?" she gasped and then continued, not waiting for Shen's response. "Rest, sleep, freeze here. No more running."

Shen said nothing, realizing he didn't have the strength to carry her. He crawled back to the bend in the ditch and looked through the weeds toward the road. Lights were on in the trailer but no one appeared to be tracking them in the ditch. This was as far as they would go. If he didn't find cover for both of them they would probably freeze to death in the weeds that night.

Clouds scudded across dim starlight as Shen looked at Mei, lying on her side, feet bleeding, her head unmoving when the cold wind tugged at her hair. Some time that afternoon he had left Hua in an alley. In the morning, he might have to leave this fine woman where she lay, curled up in a storm-water drain. It might be that both of them would be unable to get up, frozen to the ground, unnoticed until next summer. The waste, leaving all the good he had built across China and then freezing in an overgrown ditch in Sichuan, while foxes in Beijing laughed at how he had taken the bait, was enough to get Shen to act.

"No more running," he said to Mei. "I'll be back in a few minutes."

Within five minutes, Shen had found the construction dump in the ditch behind the trailer and surveyed the road for movement. The trailer was still lit but the army trucks had gone. It was likely the anarchists would be back that night. In their absence he turned over the junk, masked by the noise of the wind, and pulled out rolls of black plastic road underlayment as well as discarded cardboard boxes. These he dragged, piece by piece, along the ditch and staged in a pile next to Mei. Plastic sheeting went down over the weeds first, followed by three layers of collapsed cardboard boxes and more plastic, even a woolen equipment operator's cap. He lifted her head and drew the cap down over her ears. Next he took the used socks out of the boots Mei still held and pulled them over her bloody toes. She barely budged as he laced the boots on. He checked her pulse and shook her gently.

"Mei," he said, "this will keep you warm. Move over this way. Roll over."

Mei struggled off the ground in a daze and slid onto the plastic sheet. Shen covered her with more plastic and cardboard and tucked her in. The heavy gauge plastic creaked as she moved to look up at him.

"Thank you," she murmured. "If we wake up in the morning, what then? We survive, maybe, but what for?"

"I don't know. No one knows. I wasn't going to let you freeze."

"Back to back," she said, "so you don't freeze too."

Shen sat down on the cold plastic and suddenly felt the weight of the day in every joint. It became an effort to reach for cardboard and black plastic layers that blended into the darkness. The layers cracked and creaked as if to point out the absurdity of surviving under them, in temperatures sure to fall below freezing. Shen pushed against the plastic until his back was against Mei's.

"Mr. Liao," she said in a muffled voice, "I get the feeling you're not surprised by any of this. Am I right?"

"No," he mused. "I thought it would take three years for this to happen. The Party took advantage of my error."

"The Party is done. It's the Mandate of Heaven."

"So, we're on the side of the Right to Rebellion are we?"

"No," Mei began, then hesitated. "They did this. They're as bad as the Party. So who has it? Who has the Mandate?"

"You do," he said, quietly. "It's you."

"Mr. Liao," she said, pausing, "you've been very helpful, but I'd prefer not to be mocked, by anyone. We've had enough of that."

With that Mei pulled the plastic sheet over her face and made it clear she had no further interest in talking.

Shen looked up at the sky. It was clouding over and the wind was diminishing. Fires from all over Kangding reflected as an ominous orange tinge on the underside of the low clouds. It was the calling card of evil, signifying to Shen that the scope of what had happened that day was far greater than he could grasp. Exhausted as his body was, Shen recognized that the Party had hurled

370

intimidation, confusion and death at the people to force them to align either for or against the Party. No other choice would be offered. Surviving one night in the open would only prolong the agony of being alive during another revolution. That it may be a revolution staged by the Party to draw out and then slaughter its internal opponents did not negate the fact that useful-idiot revolutionaries would hunt them the next day and every day until they were found. The Party would allow the anarchists and democratic socialists to do their dirty work, before the ultra-left would be fully exposed as traitors to China and taken down in the millions.

The missing component, Shen reflected, was the military. The People's Liberation Army was supplied and trained to prevent revolution. Instead, they seemed to have opened their armories for anyone to take the trucks, fuel, ammunition, AKs and supplies they wanted. But the ultra-left, in their intense Marxist zeal, failed to recognize that there was only so much ammunition staged for them and that every stolen truck could be tracked by GPS.

Looking up at the orange clouds, Shen began to comprehend the magnitude of his own error. It was worse than overestimating the three-year timing. The Party had never needed his assistance in developing state agribusiness, nor was there ever any time for his daughter's escape from Beijing. When he had heard the phrase "China wants peace" from officials in the Ministry of Finance and when "China wants peace" was also heard from Agriculture, his conclusion was that the Party needed more time to set up and unite the ultra-left, three more years to prepare.

But they had prepared, to their schedule. The Bank of the Blue Lotus, with its asset-backed loans and thousands of customer service specialists, would soon be another secret acquisition for Party officials within the Ministry of Finance. Shen knew each of those officials were already multi-millionaires. None of them needed the money. Only a sophisticated cocktail of envy, greed and competition could have motivated them to take part in so vast a fraud.

No matter how Shen looked at the shameless decadence of

371

their fraud, its execution was complete. The Party had imitated Mao and the Dear Leader of North Korea in establishing a ring of government authority around every possible escape for the people. There was no way out. No high court of last appeal. In the sense of life and death in China, it was checkmate. The Party wanted complete control of an urbanized slave state and they would have it. In the morning he and Mei could take the ditches and backroads to the north, the south, the east or the west and struggle gamely. But death by anarchists or death by the PLA was only a matter of time. If it was so for them, it was so for anyone who would not submit to slavery as the norm for China.

Shen lay shivering under the creaking plastic sheets, dejected at his train of thought. Mei had come to the same conclusion much faster. We survive, maybe, but what for? He had resisted and fought the idea as a man should. He had bristled at the indignity of freezing to death in a ditch, outside a city in which he had landed in his own Learjet. He had come to Kangding because he had been coerced by the Party to assist them and had not complained. Now, the thought of resisting or complaining was as futile as the Party surely intended.

Mei, Shen noticed, was now asleep under plastic and cardboard, apparently warm enough and breathing evenly. Perhaps she was dreaming, he thought, preparing for an early death and receiving the grace to accept it without unseemly pleading. For Shen, there was no easy sleep of bodily exhaustion. As a boy in Beijing, he had lain awake at night planning and speculating how he might follow the amazing example of trees growing from small seeds. If he could earn the seed funds to invest in things that grew because they were useful and beautiful he would follow the trees in their proven formula. He remembered sitting among the bright potted flowers in the still courtyard garden of his parent's home, pondering the growth of the trees that shaded him. The old home and walled courtyard had long since been demolished and replaced by a nondescript office building. But the Bank of the Blue Lotus and all the growth that had come from its asset-backed loans was derived from the imitation of trees, perceived in that courtyard. There were even songs to trees he remembered singing in his boyhood innocence. Now it had come to this, where the important, core things of life were being acknowledged, as if this was his final life review, prior to death by anarchists in a few hours. If it were so and a place had to be found, a kind of home after death, the memory of that quiet courtyard under successful trees in a suburb of Beijing was where he would go.

One by one, Shen pictured in his mind all the Party officials he knew, wondering if any one in particular was the mastermind, the chessmaster behind the checkmate of China. None stood out as the obvious culprit. They blended together as a single class of entitled criminals, their strange black eyes dead to any kindness. They were the epitome of group evil, the cunning, selfish mindset he expected.

But something happened at that moment in the darkness that Shen did not expect. It was as if a pressure stronger than his own power of recollection began to offer a contrast to the study of soulless Party officials. Without knowing why, Shen's memory recalled the embarrassing encounter with the statue in the lobby of Mei's bank. Perhaps he really was beginning to age if he had returned the greeting of a marble statue. Mei had covered for him and the entourage had continued on toward the stairway. But neither Mei, nor anyone else present could have known that for Shen, in that one moment, there was a person of kindness radiating from within the statue, making direct contact between her eyes and his. Something unspoken and dear had been conveyed to him by that contact. It was the only moment in the day that Shen could not rationalize. Every malevolent betrayal of the people by the Party could be understood by worldly logic, but that one moment in the presence of the exquisite, silent exchange in the lobby could not.

The mystery of that exchange was Shen's last conscious thought under the plastic and cardboard. Exhausted by trial, rest was now the assignment of his body, feelings and mind. But always awake, in a hidden spiritual estate within his lower body, Shen's soul's attention was on the peace of the private courtyard of boyhood memory, far away in Beijing.

Unhindered by political reasoning, the arguments of his ego or the heaviness of flesh and bone, Shen's intangible body rose above the darkened ditch and in an instant was in a bright sky, perceiving a far horizon. Its luster drew him on, knowing its brilliance would change him if he went to it.

Even as a long-time student of the Creator, Shen's soul was not all-knowing. As a work in progress, he always had the choice to either lean into each challenge and mature by yet another increment of attainment, or shy away, as not yet ready. At that moment, high over a pristine land, uncertain whether this soul journey was about a home after death, he leaned into it.

In his approach there was time to notice the crystal clarity of the air. Fields, farms and streams as well as the colors of the countryside formed intricate geometric patterns of satisfying harmony. With a surge of joy he realized he was seeing China perfected, unfolding beneath him with a beauty unending. Here, there was no reason to avert his eyes from the grim particulate layer over the Party's China, the filthy buildings, the poisoned streams and the depressed people. He was gliding over a paradise that was certainly China, but not the China his physical body lived in. Every erg of energy within him tingled with an ecstatic bubbling of exuberance. If this was China as it should be, there was no reason to ever want to go back.

Beneath him the quilt-work of farms, towns and forests were spread out over a green and fertile terrain. The land and people seemed to be at one in an arrangement that exuded peace. Ahead of him, a terraced temple complex appeared in the light on the horizon. At the distant center of tiered gardens a bright, golden pagoda rose nine floors above lesser buildings. An array of fountains appeared around the pagoda in the upper gardens. The effect of the whole was of such stateliness, symmetry and grandeur that any thoughts of settling for a lost courtyard in the lower world were forgotten.

There was so much to see. Questions of how and why he was there needed to be asked. He circled toward the terraced gardens near the great pagoda, hoping someone would be there to explain how this perfect version of China could exist.

He found himself on a trimmed lawn, partly enclosed by trees and flower gardens and immediately began to explore. A path under trees led him to a wooden bridge arching over a clear pond. Benches were set into floral nooks and alcoves around the pond. The path followed a brook to a small, trickling fountain at the edge of an orange orchard. He looked around and saw no one.

On the other side of the orchard, an open area of lawns separated long, parallel rose trellises. He looked between the climbing roses to discern the source of a glowing light moving on the other side of the trellis. When he moved, the light moved. He parted the roses and found himself looking into the beautiful eyes of a lady in a white gown, matching steps with him on the other side. She was the source of the light. He stopped in amazement and stared at her, unable to speak. She smiled and acknowledged him.

"I thank you for your greeting," she said, between the roses. "Most people avoid seeing me in bank lobbies. You were kind enough to notice."

The same eyes that had conveyed kindness in a bank lobby in Kangding now looked at him with warmth and amusement.

"You are most welcome, here in my gardens," the lady continued. "I invited you here to walk with me and to converse, if you would like to. I am Kuan Yin."

"Thank you," Shen began, wondering if he should even acknowledge so mundane a place as Kangding. "I do remember you . . . You're very gracious. May I ask, where are we?"

"This is the Temple of Mercy and we are in Beijing."

"This is so clean, so beautiful and clear," he said, looking around. "Beijing is not like this."

"Beijing will be like this," she responded, "for those who choose it."

Wanting to see her more clearly, Shen stepped to the end of

the trellis. Kuan Yin was waiting for him on the lawn in a glowing white ovoid, radiating soft pink light in all directions. In her hands she held an oval mirror. Shen bowed and looked into her eyes.

"For those who choose it?" he asked. "Everyone would choose it."

"For aeons I have observed the choices people make."

"But if they knew, if they saw this," he said, "they would have an informed choice."

"That is why you are here. To make an informed choice. For now, you are filled with light and feel sure you will remember all you see and hear."

"I will. How could I ever forget this?" he said, marveling at the beauty in the gardens and the colorful birds around him, seeing no urgency to go back to the abyss of the revolution.

"You are not yet the master of your conscious mind, your memory or your feelings in the lower world," Kuan Yin said. "Your body carries you in near-constant fatigue and pain. You are life, separating from a death civilization that wants to take you with it. It is possible you will forget this meeting. Survival will demand most of your attention."

"We repeat our history," Shen said, lowering his voice. "Will I survive the Mandate of Heaven?"

"I am aware of all energy that has passed through China's history. I am aware of the journey of your soul through the antiquity of China and other civilizations."

"Then you know I have committed to China."

"Walk with me," Kuan Yin said, gesturing toward the gardens. "I am your mother in God, and you have known me as a friend for longer than you realize. That is why you recognized me in the marble. I invited you here to explain something of the Mandate of Heaven to you. It is important that you remember what I am about to tell you."

"I would welcome that," Shen said. "The Mandate, I'm sure, has been usurped. The Right to Rule and the Right to Rebellion are now controlled by the same entity."

"Neither concept is of heaven. They are the interpretations of men. The Mandate of Heaven is mercy."

"The powers don't see it that way," Shen said. "They are 'authority.'"

"The quality of mercy," Kuan Yin said, "has allowed mankind to play out the free will of each individual over the course of time. The mountain of error accrued by each has been withheld, set aside for resolution at a time and place of greater attainment. If all error were to be returned in one day, there would be no life."

"Some," Shen said, "have no intention of resolving their errors with anyone."

Their stroll through the gardens had brought them to the wide, rounded flight of stairs leading to the first level of the pagoda. Kuan Yin extended a hand, inviting Shen to ascend the stairs with her.

"So, we shall speak of them," Kuan Yin said. "We begin a broader understanding of the Mandate of Heaven. There are indeed those who have no intention of ever making things right, in this or future lives. The law would return their error instantly. Mercy mitigates, buys time and teaches wisdom. Is it mercy to extend infinite opportunity to the shameless?"

"I couldn't say."

"The Father of all life," Kuan Yin responded, "extends renewed opportunity and mercy to his creation, to those who squander their lives through ignorance. He is imprisoned within them. He pities his own and is generous and patient. But there are those who persecute the ignorant, who knowingly invert the gifts of the Father for motives of revenge. I speak of those who fell from heaven. They have received renewed opportunity. As cycles supersede cycles, there come those moments that are for the judging of a certain portion of life, of attainment."

Shen climbed the stairs side by side with Kuan Yin and paused when she paused at each landing, to look out at the view over Beijing. He understood her but did not say anything.

"One cycle of creation comes to an end, another begins," Kuan Yin continued. "We are at that moment. Mercy now enters the arena of the unmerciful."

"How?"

"The children of our Father have the authority to invoke the intercession of heaven on Earth. By law, we of heaven may not intercede in his name without your request. You are free to request assistance or remain silent. You are responsible for your world."

"The Party does not teach that."

"Then you, for one, will know it," Kuan Yin said, pausing to turn to him, lifting the mirror. "Cry out to me, whisper to me, speak to me, command me by the authority of the presence of the Father of all life within you and me, and I will hold up my mercy mirror in front of each of the unmerciful and return their non-mercy to them, tenfold. And in His name, I will place my mercy mirror in front of those who need mercy and will bless them with healing, peace, comfort, protection, understanding, forgiveness, opportunity and victory. Speak this with faith and with your God-given authority. Then seal your command, that it be adjusted according to the will of God. Do you understand?"

"I do, but how could mercy turn around a revolution already underway? They have planned and positioned for years. It's already checkmate."

"By grace, each of the saints and buddhas hold the Earth and everyone on it within our awareness. Each of us may state, I AM one with the Father. I AM the Father's presence, within the spaces between the electrons and their nuclei in every atom of this planet. I AM all matter. I hear every thought, I feel every pain. Yet by law, heaven may not extend mercy at the personal or planetary level unless you request it, congruent with the will of God."

"But mercy is forgiving and yielding and gentle. The revolution has already started. It was hatched by people so unforgiving and unyielding they laugh as they crush people."

"Mercy judges anything unlike itself."

"They would laugh at that, too."

"Until the landslide. As this cycle ends, those who are the unforgiving and unyielding and ungentle receive the full return of their own miscreation. That is, if you decree it, according to God's will."

"The full return?"

"Consider what non-mercy is."

"Cruelty, envy, anger, murder. They would destroy everything in their fury."

"Command me, in God's name, to hold this mirror in front of the souls of the unmerciful, at least once every twenty-four hours and mercy will act gently to secure the Earth, without global war, economic debacle or cataclysm. The full return will be tempered over time, for life's sake. Your children, grandchildren and all who follow you will benefit from your faith and duty to them."

"That would be merciful. I would ask this for them, for the nation."

"By this faith," Kuan Yin said, "the candle that glows in your heart can be increased, sufficient to light all universes."

"If I live."

"In time you will find your way to Switzerland."

"But others won't. I'm still responsible for thousands of employees across China."

"Then you are responsible for commanding all of heaven to secure their safety and that of their families."

"And the bank? They will confiscate it. I'm responsible for people's money."

"Continue the activities of your bank and see that your loans are backed by tangible assets. Continue your investments in farming and distribution, for the time will come when it is you and those like you who are responsible for the helping the people feed themselves."

"Are you saying the Party will not be capable?"

"There are those within their disintegration cycle, for whom the judgment is final. Others will be constrained. They will live out their natural lives. In future lives, they will be confined to other systems of worlds more suited to their state of evolution."

"But in China, this day, I've seen the domination, the

callousness and cruelty of Mao living through the Party. The people accept it as "authority," whether it's capitalist or socialist. If they accept that authority as patriotic and normal, will their attention draw that one back into another life in China?"

"The soul you speak of has passed through a final judgment and the second death. Many from a supportive class of fallen ones, having similar vibration, did follow him."

"The second death?"

"The end of the identity of that soul and the recycling of the accumulated misqualified energy. The energy is returned to the sacred fire of creation. God takes no pleasure in the death of the wicked. That soul was once a perfect concept. The gift of free will was given and accepted."

"Free will can be a dangerous thing," Shen observed. "I've wondered why so many people in China defer responsibility to someone else to make their decisions."

"Do you accept the responsibility of acting on what you have understood here?"

"I understand the responsibility now, while I'm here. But in living through a revolution I could forget this. There are distractions, like survival."

"You are the master of your conscious mind, or should be. Should you ever forget, I promise I will remind you, gently."

"When I speak to you every day, you'll hear my thoughts, even if things are not going well?"

"Our communication will flow both ways. It comes from a sustained and tender regard, which is mutual within our hearts. The daily imprint of mercy will gradually and gently change you and your world. Think of me in your prayers before sleep, even in Switzerland. Now that we are almost at the top floor, there is someone I would like you to meet."

At the center of the wide open ninth floor of the pagoda stood another great lady of light. A soft, shimmering ovoid of turquoise blue and green glowed around her. She wore a white cape over her wavy, golden hair and a robe of turquoise green. Beyond the soft turquoise aura, dazzling rays of violet light shone in every direction. Shen stood still at the top of the stairs in silence. He knew her instantly of old as Mother Mary, but didn't know what he should say.

"My beloved one, I greet you once again," the lady said, apparently glad to see him. "You remember me as Mary, mother of Jesus, our Lord. You were there for us in France, in England and in Portugal so long ago. It was I who introduced you into the service of Kuan Yin. Her mercy for the people of China may flow through you, if you will it. I am here to add to your understanding."

Shen nodded, acknowledging his recollection and his awe. She beckoned him to come closer.

"Be not afraid. The command you are asked to make daily, for Kuan Yin's mercy to selectively judge the unmerciful, by their own works, is not only for China. The mercy mirror is placed before all nations, all peoples. Further, you are not the only token of mercy in the world. Others will make the same command, by their free will."

"I understand," Shen said, bowing his head. "May I ask, when will it start?"

Mother Mary glanced at Kuan Yin who turned to address Shen.

"Within minutes," Kuan Yin replied.

"May I return here, with your permission? I may have many questions." Shen asked, looking at both of them.

"We expect it," Kuan Yin said. "The doors of the Temple of Mercy are open to you."

"And the doors of our retreat in the Pure Land over Fatima in Portugal are open to you as well," Mary said, her hands extended to Shen. "You have shown balance and discipline in your business. Now those qualities must be applied through the mirror of mercy, once a day or better."

"I will remember," Shen said.

As he tried to focus on the radiance expanding around Mary he noticed the same light around Kuan Yin. It was more than his eyes could cope with. A tapping sound and the sensation of cold

381

rain on his face woke him to a dark, overcast night. He listened to the rain becoming louder on the plastic sheets covering him and realized he was in a storm-water ditch in the mountains of Sichuan. In the east, a dim, gray dawn was beginning.

Reluctant to move at all in the cold air, Shen glanced at Mei and noted her plastic covers moving slightly as she breathed. She was still asleep. Then images from a dream flooded his mind with light too bright to bear, emanating from a lady who expected him to do something that day. What was it he could possibly do on a freezing morning in an open ditch when he was too cold to move? He sat up, remembering, threw off the plastic and got to his feet.

Mei was still sleeping as Shen draped plastic around his shoulders and climbed out of the ditch. A scrub-covered knoll on the side of the mountain stood out in the drizzle. It faced north, overlooking a broad valley, far enough away from the construction site around the bend. Shen stood among low bushes at the top of the knoll and realized he was looking toward Beijing. He took a deep breath, and thinking of the light from the lady, began to speak.

"Kuan Yin! Kuan Yin! In the name of God, place your mercy mirror in front of the unmerciful and return their non-mercy to them, multiplied by ten! And place your mercy mirror in front of those who need mercy and fill them with comfort, protection, healing, peace, understanding, forgiveness, opportunity and victory! Let this be adjusted and done now, according to the will of God! It is done."

Shen stood for a moment and wiped the rain from his eyes. A rustling sound behind him made him turn suddenly. It was Mei. She climbed a few steps up the knoll and stood near him, rain dripping off the plastic sheet around her.

"I heard," she said, looking at him for a moment. "I owe you an apology. I thought you were ignorant when you bumped into her yesterday. I have asked her to be present each day in our branches. You were the only one who saw her."

Standing in the rain, on the side of a mountain, Shen had no response but Mei wanted to know more.

382

"What made you ask for these things, as if you could issue a decree to the Mother of Mercy?"

"It's about trust," Shen said, looking into the sheets of rain falling over the valley.

"How did you manage to gain her trust?" Mei said, "You seem to be so comfortable with the world."

"Anything but. We have to leave this place. They'll be looking for us."

"Leave? For where?"

"We'll go up higher into the mountains, look for a village, stay off the roads."

But before either could leave the knoll, they heard the beating sound of helicopter blades somewhere in the rain. Shen motioned to Mei to move quickly under the branches of a taller bush. Then, to the east, they saw dark shapes in the air.

"This could be the army," Mei said. "It has to be the army."

"Do not wave or go toward them," Shen warned.

"Why not? They're here to restore order, to rescue the city. You thought so last night."

"The rebels will see us before they do. There are only two troop carriers. Where are the gunships? Where is the support?"

"It's a reconnaissance," Mei said, wanting to stand up. "There will be more."

"I don't think so. I think what's happening is China-wide. The PLA is spread too thin. The revolution was planned to pin them down in every city. Right now they're probably trying to save Chengdu."

"Then how do we get to the helicopters they have sent?"

"We don't. The Party planned the revolution. The PLA opened the armories. The rebels we saw last night, well, they're going to kill all of them. Across China, they're drawing out the ultra-left. They would be trouble for the Party in the new cities."

"How do you know these things?" Mei insisted. "That's terrible! That's like Mao, all over again. No! We're long past that! You can't spread such a horrible rumor."

"How did those young thugs come through Kangding yesterday in such numbers, killing police and everyone they could, with automatic weapons? Where did they get them? What happens to those young thugs when they run out of ammunition?"

Mei crouched against the bush in silence and disbelief until the sound of automatic fire could be heard coming from the older precincts of Kangding. The PLA helicopters were taking fire from buildings in the city as they attempted to land. She stood up to look.

"Nothing we can do," Shen said, as they watched the helicopters circle. Lines of tracers hit buildings. Smoke poured out of a stricken helicopter.

"When we head higher into the mountains, this rain will become snow," he said.

"Where will we go?"

"I don't know," Shen said. "You may want to stay away from your head office in Chengdu. Find a mountain village, change your name. Say you're a refugee from Kangding. The Party thinks you're dead. You burned to death in your branch in Kangding."

"You're saying the Party did it? Is it that bad, for all of us?"

"There will be no more private banks. Only Party owned banks."

"And you?" Mei asked. "What will you do?"

"Until they find my body, they'll assume I'm still alive. I'm a problem for them. I have to get out of China."

"How? If this is China-wide, the Party will close the borders."

"Over the mountains, into Burma. First, I have to get from here to the south of Yunnan."

"I can't leave yet. My people are still in the alley," Mei said, hesitating to move.

"They left with Kuan Yin last night. Only their bodies are there. The city will bury them, along with the police and everyone else. Mei, I'm sorry, but we have to go now, while we can."

Mei stayed where she was until she got used to the idea of walking away from tragedy. At first, they stayed out of sight of the road and climbed through snowy terrain that became increasingly difficult for both of them. Traffic on the road was sporadic, either revolutionaries at high speed in stolen trucks or ethnic Tibetans in slow farm vehicles. No government or military vehicles appeared. By mid-morning Shen saw that Mei was exhausted.

"Take a rest here," he said, gasping. "We're a thousand meters above the tree-line, there's not as much oxygen. We need food. Closer to the road we can get a ride on a farm truck."

"To where?" she asked. "These mountains are the Dauxe Shan. On the other side you can see Tibet."

"How do we get to Yunnan?"

"If you want to get to Burma from here you have to go through part of Tibet and then Yunnan."

"Are you coming with me?"

"I don't know," she said, trying to catch her breath. "Climb the Hengduan Shan and down into Burma? The tribes there don't speak Mandarin. Not in the slightest. Maybe I'll go on to Kunming."

"Will a Tibetan speak to us, on this road?"

"I speak Tibetan. We have Tibetan clients in Kangding."

"Alright," Shen said, noticing a blanket of low clouds now sweeping in over barren rocky hills, obscuring the mountains. "If anyone asks, we're highway inspectors from Yunnan. We lost everything in Kangding."

"That might not work in Batang. We cross into Tibet there. It's a national highway. The military will inspect every vehicle."

"We go around them," Shen said. "We get another ride south into Yunnan."

Around a bend they found a stretch of road straight enough to observe the speed and type of approaching vehicles from behind cover. After a few last-second decisions to avoid suspect vehicles Mei grew nervous.

"I can't stand this," she said, falling on her knees in the snow behind a roadside bush. "Anyone can see us. We hide all night and now we're willing to trust whoever comes along?"

"Who would you trust?" Shen asked, sitting beside her, watching traffic. "What would they look like? What would they be driving?"

"I ask one question, you ask me three. I need to rest for a while."

"How about this one?" Shen called out as he got up quickly and walked onto the road. "This is what we need."

"No," Mei said, "stay under cover!"

"Come on," Shen yelled, waving to her, "translate!"

Shen had flagged down an old Tibetan herder woman, driving alone in an ancient, faded blue truck. Half her teeth were missing and her face was wrinkled, but her steady eyes didn't seem to miss a thing. Whatever her first words were from behind the wheel Shen perceived she was skeptical, even sassy. He waved again to Mei. But when the old woman saw Mei struggling up through the snow to the road she started laughing and slapped her knee.

"I think she likes you," Shen said to Mei near the driver's door.

Shen could not understand the dialogue between Mei and the old woman, but after a brisk exchange they climbed into the truck. The truck may have been fifty years old, but the cab heater worked, and the old woman seemed to think Shen was hilarious. Mei sat next to the old woman and turned to Shen.

"She's in a good mood, she says. Just sold fifteen yak in Kangding. She's heading for Markam in Tibet, where we want to go."

"Tell her we're grateful," Shen said.

"She knows we are. She said, 'highway inspectors, my ass.' She thinks we're eloping."

"We're not exactly eighteen any more," Shen said, surprised. "Look at me."

"She told me, 'I always know when people have been sleeping together. Hell of a time to elope during a revolution.' She thinks we're the worst highway inspectors she's ever seen."

"Nice."

Shen heard the old herder woman mention the name Batang, and Mei told him the military were ordering people out of their vehicles at the Tibetan line.

"Her family calls her Du," Mei said. "She doesn't like the PLA, so she'll let us out before the line and wait for us on the other side of Batang."

"Tell her she's a sweetheart," Shen said.

The banter in Tibetan went on for about a minute.

"She's offering us a room in Markam," Mei said, smirking. "Her family runs a hostel. She says we should get married at their shrine and spend our money there."

"Do the smart thing," Shen said, returning the smirk. "Don't turn her down. We could use some help."

The old herder woman, Du, kept her word at Batang, letting Shen and Mei out in pedestrian traffic on the Sichuan side. It took only fifteen minutes to thread their way through littered, narrow alleys to evade the PLA roadblock. Tibet itself was on the other side of the bridge across the ice-cold Jinsha Jiang. Du was waiting for them in a crowded part of the city near the bridge. Before they got in Mei told Shen she had asked Du if there was a second roadblock on the Tibetan side of the river. Du had already driven across the bridge and found no PLA inspectors.

"Ask her if she's heard of Kuan Yin," Shen said, as he pulled the door closed on the third try.

"She says, 'How did we think I sold fifteen yak in Kangding and got out without being shot?'"

Shen exchanged a glance with Mei and stayed out of the ensuing conversation in Tibetan. On either side of the highway, multi-colored Tibetan prayer flags fluttered on long poles in the snow, at roadside shrines and at higher elevations in the treeless, misty hills.

Du was again good to her word at her family hostel in Markam. When they arrived late at night, she offered Shen and Mei a room that passed as the bridal suite and gestured for him to carry Mei over the recently swept threshold.

"Keep her on our good side," Shen said to Mei, pulling cash out of his wallet, hidden in the coveralls, "and tell her we'll pay her very well for the room. This is for the ride."

When Du laughed in glee at her matchmaking and began to call her family together to celebrate, Mei spoke softly to her, then tugged Shen off the porch and into the room.

"I reminded her," Mei said, as she locked the door, "that we were eloping and wanted to avoid attracting any undue attention from the authorities. She thinks we're wonderful. You will sleep by the door and I will sleep over there."

The next morning, Du arranged a long ride south into the lowlands of Yunnan with one of her sons, who was delivering sheep to Xiaguan. The son, Dalan, who was quieter and more wary than Du, spent most of the journey watching his rearview mirrors and talking on his two-way radio in Tibetan.

"There's chaos in Kunming," Mei said to Shen as they rode, well above the speed limit. "You were right. The revolution is under way there too. He said, 'Tens of thousands of protesters in the center of Kunming yesterday. Then the shooting started.'"

"He's nervous," Shen said. "But I have to know about Burma. If he had to find a way, how would he get over the mountains undetected?"

The son, Dalan, laughed and responded in broken Mandarin.

"Nervous for good reasons. Revolutionaries have roadblocks. PLA have roadblocks. These sheep will get a high price if I live. If I hear something and have to turn off the road, you pay me a good price to tell you how to get into Burma, very quiet."

But the reports over the two-way radio indicated no hazards before Xiaguan. Existing roadblocks and reports of firefights halting traffic were between Xiaguan and the provincial capital of Kunming, on the national highway running east. Still, Dalan seemed anxious as they approached Xiaguan.

"Girl I know in Xiaguan has family who help you to stay. You pay," Dalan said to Mei. "Not very safe in Kunming for many days."

"Thank you, I appreciate that," Mei said.

"Very special business," Dalan said, glancing at Shen, "to sell sheep in Xiaguan, very quiet. High price, but not too high. Buyer, he is nervous. If I live, I take you to Tengchong. Walk into mountains from Tengchong. Burma other side. You pay for danger."

Shen nodded in acknowledgment and wondered how much money the danger would require. He had given generously to Du and normally carried credit cards rather than cash.

"I've got this," Mei said to Shen, as if reading his mind.

Dalan let them out by a tea stand at a fuel station on the rough outskirts of Xiaguan, promising to return. He then drove off in his truck taking his sheep to an uncertain negotiation with a nervous buyer. For Shen, the scarcity of traffic around the fuel stop created an eerie quiet.

"Don't go to Kunming," the girl at the tea stand told Shen. "Trouble there."

When Dalan returned with an empty truck, he seemed anxious to move on.

"Good price, very quiet," he said, waving his hand toward the east, "but not good for anyone in Kunming."

At the home of Darlan's girlfriend, on the better side of Xiaguan, Shen got out of the cab with Mei to say goodbye.

"To better days for China," Mei said, hugging Shen. "Thank you for making me live."

"We had some help."

"Keep saying your prayer," Mei said to him, clasping his hands.

"You too," Shen said. "I don't know what happens from here. There may be a different kind of China we don't recognize. But if you ever decide to leave China and I'm able to introduce you to my wife, please don't tell her I slept with you. In that ditch."

"Very quiet," Mei said, touching her forehead to his shoulder.

The last Shen saw of Zhang Mei, she was holding her hand up high, outside that home in Xiaguan. She had lost her father, his banks, his trustees, her home and freedom, and possibly her nation.

Dalan wasted no time heading west on the highway and then taking lesser roads to the agricultural valley around Tengchong. He pulled over on the shoulder of a gravel road outside the city and pointed to the mountains.

389

"Two days, Burma," Dalan said, holding a finger to his lips, before waving goodbye. "Very quiet. Lady pay already."

Dalan turned out to be correct. Shen made it over the mountain border and into Burma without being noticed in just two days. By the third day, he was on a bus to Mandalay, where he bought clothing and a disposable cell phone and called his wife in Switzerland on an encrypted business line.

Shen's wife, Nien, was relieved to hear his voice, but unaware of what was occurring in China. All she had heard was there were contradictions in the news and foreigners, including journalists, were being forced to leave. Even as Shen explained his situation, she began email contact with a travel agency and arranged a business-class evening flight for Shen's alternate business identity to New Delhi and on to Geneva.

A day later, Shen flew into Geneva on a commercial flight, without luggage, passport, his plane or his pilots. At the international terminal, Swiss Customs accepted his alternate identity and ushered him through a secure debarkation procedure away from potentially curious press. Nien was waiting for him in a private lounge. She held him tightly, then looked at him, apparently grieving at what had occurred to China and to his hopes.

In the car on the way home, Shen fielded Nien's many questions, appearing calm, but his mind was restless.

"What's going on?" Nien asked, as she drove. "What's on your mind?"

"I need your help," he said. "I need designers, artists, sculptors. You're in touch with those kinds of people. I'll show you what I mean at home. It's important."

That evening Shen laid out an idea for designing and commissioning bids for a statue of Kuan Yin holding up an oval mirror. The design template would need to be scaled to offer sizes ranging from miniature to life-size. Inside the base of each statue would be a ribbon-tied parchment scroll with the simple prayer for mercy. Nien liked the idea immediately, as well as Shen's new interest in the things that interested her.

390

Each day by Lake Geneva, while Shen tried to put together scattered fragments of encrypted intelligence from his besieged informants across China, he offered the mercy prayer to the breeze, morning, noon and night. Nien locked into the Kuan Yin project with her panoply of contacts and reported new results daily. It was a gratifying compensation but Shen found himself thinking about the dream and the conversation in the pagoda so often he began wondering which world was most real to him.

For Shen there was no safe return to the bank's offices in Geneva while the Communist Party of China remained capable of surveillance, even in Switzerland. The bank's managers were told that he was missing and they should regain contact with branch managers in China and record their coded recommendations. They were to do all they could to morally support thousands of staff and managers in China, most of whom were sheltering at home without income.

Within a week after commissioning the statues, dozens of designs began coming in to Nien's website. The top five were so refined and beautiful that Shen couldn't choose between them. Nien suggested producing all five in a range of sizes and materials and letting customers choose. It was Shen's hope to make the whole range available worldwide at an accessible price, so Nien signed contracts with statuary factories and distributors in Italy, Egypt, Taiwan, Chile, the U.S. and Australia. It was expensive and risky and outside Shen's area of expertise, but Nien was delighted and said it was the right use of their wealth.

The encrypted intelligence from managers and contacts in China though was sobering. There was no apparent wave of miracles across the nation. The chaos was increasing. After two weeks of confusion in the news, it began to become obvious to Shen that the Party had lost control of the counter-revolution they had set in motion. What the foxes had created as a carefully calibrated entrapment plan for the ultra-left, confident they could turn a rheostat dial on or off, low or high, had now engulfed all of China in murderous disorder.

Key components among Shen's informant network were first-hand and secondhand contacts with foreign reporters who had gone underground and refused to leave China. All channels of the state media were in various forms of paralysis. It was a theme the foreign reporters began to notice at all levels of the state. Chaotic infighting was reportedly occurring at the highest levels of the Party. Power factions had formed to initiate purges of officials deemed responsible for allowing the counter-revolution to get out of hand. The initiating factions were violently opposed by the accused who instead blamed them for incompetence. The state media reported nothing, certainly not a fist-fight between six elderly members of the Central Committee which ended in murder and summary executions. Armed PLA officers had been seen entering government buildings. Shots had been fired inside the Central Committee chambers and armored tanks from two PLA factions had taken up positions facing each other across an empty Tienanmen Square.

The anarchic ultra-left opposing the authoritarian Communists were faring no better. The radical Hong Kong Professor Yuen Qiang had been found dead in a field in Shaanxi province. Without the mastermind who had incited, united and betrayed them the anarchists reopened their century-old intellectual arguments with the socialists over who would control the state. The anarchists insisted there be no state. The socialists argued only the proletariat was democratically justified in running the state. Each faction accused the other of being secretly bourgeois and responsible for sabotaging the revolution.

The printed reports piled up, day after day, and Shen found himself pacing the upper floor of his mansion. Now and then he would stop walking and reading and look out at the lake, as if somewhere out there peace and comfort for China could be plucked out of the breeze. He would make yet another call for mercy and then try to understand why there was no miracle, no mitigation for 1.3 billion people in pain. Were his pleas not being heard?

To calm himself, Shen began taking Nien and two trusted

winchmen out on the lake in *Trust*, his twelve-meter racing yacht, needing to do something active, other than pacing. There was plenty of exertion in the stiff breezes on the lake, but eventually Nien had other commitments to attend to, including Kuan Yin statuary sales conferences. Shen would go out each day, sometimes all day, with just the two winchmen. But as much as he wanted to talk about the course of mercy, he could not confide in paid athletes, former yachting Olympians, with no interest in the agony of the devolution of China into warring states.

On the lake each day, Shen would keep one hand on the helm and one hand scrolling the electronic screen mounted in the waterproof binnacle directly in front of him. The gravity and consequence of the disintegration of the Party and the absence of a viable alternative for the people preoccupied him. The reports on the screen showed a thoroughly corrupt state devolving into a dysfunctional and chaotic state, on its way to becoming a failed state. There was no end to it and no miracles, no mercy.

But one beautiful day, when *Trust* was close to the wind off the mansioned French shores of Lake Geneva, under a blue sky too bright for the eye to endure, an icon on the screen in front of Shen began to flash. The incoming message was from one of his bank managers in hiding, somewhere near Chengdu. Shen shaded the screen with his hand and reread the text.

The message read, in part, "Sichuan Province now acting autonomously, in absence of national Ministry officials in Chengdu. They have fled. No recent instructions from Beijing. No funds likely from Beijing. Former mayor of Chengdu (not Party member) appointed by city officers to replace absent Provincial Secretary. Cholera cases rising, some hospitals abandoned. Starvation numbers increasing in Chengdu. Province proposing outright land sales in fee simple as incentive to livestock growers. Your name mentioned. Blue Lotus has undamaged liquid assets in multiple cities. Would you consider negotiations with Sichuan Province?"

Shen held his knee against the helm and typed with both hands, "On my way."

He sent the message, grabbed the helm and called out to both his winchmen.

"Ready about!"

Trust came about, winches whirring, sails snapping taut, turning ninety degrees in seconds, heading with a following wind to the Swiss side.

EPILOGUE

In the years and generations following Liao Shen's return to China, the Bank of the Blue Lotus became a standard bearer for the competition within China between an asset-backed free-enterprise economy and the advocates of a state-owned economy. Under the law of free will, the citizens of China needed time to experiment with personal responsibility for profit and loss, opportunity and freedom.

Although the asset-backed economies of the United States and India led the world and helped pull Europe out of self-inflicted poverty, a providential series of sages emerged from China to lead the world in wisdom. These gained enough safety and freedom to distill the lessons of the intricate history of China. By their works the wisdom of mercy became revered knowledge around the world.

The works of Liao Nien took on a magical life of their own. The initial five designs of Kuan Yin statuary, each holding up a version of the mercy mirror, as well as the printed salutation to Kuan Yin on the ribbon-tied scroll, were creatively adapted worldwide into appeals to the holy ones of all major religions. Appeals to the mercy mirror of Sarasvati became commonplace in India, to Jesus and Mother Mary among Christians, Shekhinah among Jews and Gautama, and Maitreya among Buddhists. As the holy ones of heaven are and have always been all one in the mind of the Father of all life, Kuan Yin, walking among them, observed the planetary flow of mercy and was greatly pleased.

394